Cover
the Butter

Cover the Butter

Carrie Kabak

PIATKUS

All the characters in this book are fictitious and any resemblance to real persons, living or dead, is entirely coincidental.

Copyright © 2005 by Carrie Kabak

First published in Great Britain in 2006 by
Piatkus Books Ltd.,
5 Windmill Street, London W1T 2JA
email: info@piatkus.co.uk

This edition published 2006

First published in the United States in 2005 by
Dutton
A Division of Penguin Group (USA) Inc.

The moral right of the author has been asserted

A catalogue record for this book is available from the British Library

ISBN 0 7499 0781 9

Set in Berkeley Book by
Phoenix Photosetting, Chatham, Kent

Printed and bound in Great Britain by
MPG Books, Bodmin, Cornwall

For Mark,
with all my love

The rabbit-hole went straight on like a tunnel for some way, and then dipped suddenly down, so suddenly that Alice had not a moment to think about stopping herself before she found herself falling down a very deep well.

Either the well was very deep, or she fell very slowly, for she had plenty of time as she went down to look about her and to wonder what was going to happen next.

—ALICE IN WONDERLAND,
Lewis Carroll

PART ONE

♦

THE SIXTIES

CHAPTER 1

◆

1965

Saturday, April 17
33 Cherry Blossom Road, Dorton,
United Kingdom, Europe, Planet Earth

I bite my lip. "Can I have a suspender belt instead?"

My mother, Biddy, runs her nail along the top of a packet to split open the cellophane. "You need a girdle for support," she says, pulling out a corset the color of salmon-paste. "And take that look off your face. It's a beautiful foundation garment." She pats her fresh hairdo, a lacquered helmet, before opening a second packet.

Spirals of stitching, three sets of hooks, powernet panels, and longline, too. It's one hell of a bra.

"Try it on," she says.

I fasten it at the front, swivel it around, and pull the wide straps over my shoulders.

My first bra, and I loathe it.

"Mum, I really don't think I have enough to fill these cones yet."

"They're called cups, Kate, and sure, the size is only a small thirty-two A."

"The other girls have trainer bras."

"Fine. And in two months they'll all need a good brassiere like yours."

Snatching Biddy's shopping bag from the floor to see what else she bought, all I find are a couple of pastel twinsets, a pair of brown stirrup pants, and what's this? Drop earrings. All for her, nothing cool for me. A cheap shift dress would have been okay, one of those polka-dot ones with a Peter Pan collar.

Or a trainer bra.

"Kate, stop poking inside my bag."

I pull out a leaflet before I stop poking. It shows a busty blonde skipping around Piccadilly Circus wearing nothing but my salmon-paste set. *"With the firmest control,"* she says, eyebrows arched, teeth flashing, *"my Cross Your Heart bra shapes and my girdle flattens."*

"Hey, Mum, did you see this? 'Shapes and flattens with the firmest control.'"

"I read it in the shop," she mutters.

"Don't I have enough control already? Forget the girdle. You're doing a great job."

"What a smart aleck you are, Kate. Pity you're not as quick at school." Biddy claps her hands over her ears. "Would you turn down the music? That Mick Jagger eejit gets on my nerves."

Holding the girdle by its suspenders, I dance toward the radio.

Biddy's lips are all pinched and tight. "Stop jigging about half-naked," she says. "And put the girdle in your underwear drawer. Look after it nicely."

Turning the radio down, just a touch, I hear the soft thud of footsteps.

"Your father's coming upstairs—quick, cover yourself, Kate. He shouldn't be seeing you like this."

"Like what?"

She points at my chest and moves her finger in circles.

"You mean Dad mustn't know I've grown breasts?"

Biddy picks up her shopping bag. "Don't be disgusting. You know what I mean."

Well, I suppose I do know what she means. Dad did look a bit upset last week when Aunt Shauna said, "Tom, will you just look at Kate, sure hasn't she got the loveliest little figure, and won't she be turning boys' heads soon?"

CHAPTER 2

◆

Friday, September 17

Five months later, and my Cross Your Heart bra still doesn't have enough to lift or separate. And the girdle kills, especially now, chafing the tops of my thighs as I climb up Bryre Hill Lane.

Me and Moira had to stay for detention after school because Father Flanna-gan caught us eating communion wafers during altar-cleaning duty. Moira didn't know what the fuss was about. Nothing had been consecrated. "It wasn't as if we were snacking on the Body of Christ, miss," she told the headmistress.

For that remark, we were awarded an extra hour.

Still, being late home has its advantages, because Barry Finch was on the same bus and he's walking up the lane right behind me as I speak. The *fab* Barry Finch, I should add. What are the odds Moira will phone as soon as I get home, dying to know if he spoke to me?

But damn, fat chance of that when I'm wearing a green blazer, pleated skirt, and tie.

Totally *uncool.*

"Hey, nice uniform," he drawls.

"Huh," I reply, finding it difficult to remain aloof when I can feel my stocking tops approaching my knees. I told Biddy the girdle was too long. I'm the third shortest girl in my year, for God's sake.

"Hoighty-toighty, aren't we?"

He's walking alongside me now. Heat creeps up my neck, and, oh shit, I'm turning red. Keeping my head down, I study the scuff marks on my Mary Janes so he can't tell.

"What's life like at Snobhurst Girl's School?" he asks.

He wears drainpipe jeans, a leather jacket, walks with his hands in his pockets.

"Very funny," I say. "Shawhurst Roman Catholic School, actually."

"For girls." He winks a green eye.

Green eyes, black hair. Thick eyebrows, dark skin. A Romeo, a Montague. No, on second thought—like Tony in *West Side Story*.

My tummy does a somersault.

"Your hair would look better loose," he says. He smells of cigarette smoke and Aramis aftershave. A little parenthesis appears on one side of his mouth when he smiles. Must remember every detail for Moira.

"I always wear my hair like this," I reply. We're nearly at the top of the hill and I know he lives in the fourth brick house on the right, the one with the little iron gate. As I'm swinging my long braid to the left, to the right, because he might think it's cute, my beret flies off, and he swoops to pick it up and reads the name tag inside. His ears stick out a bit. Short fingernails. Tight purple shirt. A peep of chest hair.

"Kate Cadogan, LV2."

"Lower fifth, class two."

"You're only fourteen, then."

"So?"

I won't be fourteen till October the seventh, actually, but he doesn't have to know that.

"I was seventeen last week," he tells me.

Wow! A whole seventeen! Birth sign, Virgo.

"See you on Monday," he says, opening his gate.

See you on Monday. I do a who-cares shrug, take my beret back, flatten it onto my head, and turn away without a second look. I try to saunter off, but I can't because the girdle has slipped way down now, so I end up walking like a goose instead. I hope to hell he's not watching.

❖

I turn the key in the latch of number 33 Cherry Blossom Road. No sign of Biddy, but I do hear a rattle of cutlery in the kitchen, so she is home.

The TV is on in the living room, and the Rolling Stones are on *Top of the Pops*, singing about telephones.

Ha! And *our* phone rings. I join in with Mick Jagger and sing down the receiver, because it just *has* to be Moira.

"Cute."

Breathe slowly, Kate. It's Barry. Don't pass out now.

"I found your number in the directory, Kate Cadogan."

"So you did, Barry Finch."

"How do you know my name?" he asks.

The whole of LV2 knows his name.

"Sheila Colby told me. You're friends with her brother, aren't you?" And Sheila Colby fancies him like nothing else, but he phoned *me*! And he's *seventeen.*

Hearing the soft pad of footsteps on the carpet, I swing around to see Biddy walking toward me. Her arms are folded.

"Got to go," I tell Barry. I put the receiver down, praying he won't think I hung up on him, praying Biddy won't ask who I was talking to.

Biddy says there'll be plenty of time for boys when I go to college, when I'm eighteen. Girls grow up too soon these days, she says, wearing short skirts and showing their knickers. No wonder they end up in trouble.

My mother taps her foot. "Who were you speaking to, Kate?"

"Moira," I say, fidgeting with a strand of hair.

I see Biddy has new shoes, burgundy, with sharp stiletto heels. They look kind of funny with her green hospital dress and starched apron. She must have been trying them on. That's another pair to add to the hundred and twenty-five she already has.

"Make sure you get your homework done tonight. Don't leave it till last minute on Sunday," she says. "You were talking to a boy, weren't you?"

Inside, I'm saying, *Yes, I was talking to a boy, and so what, and do you have a problem with that?* But I wouldn't dream of saying any of those things. Not to Biddy.

"Who is he?" she asks.

"He?"

She turns on her new pointed toes and makes her way to the kitchen. "Dinner will be ready in half an hour. Daddy's coming home early tonight. I wasn't born yesterday, Kate. I know it was a boy you were talking to. I can tell."

Something tells *me* I haven't heard the end of this.

◆

The *boy* isn't mentioned during the Irish stew with dumplings, thank the Lord. We gather around the Formica kitchen table, where my dad always sits to the left and Biddy to the right. My place is in the middle, facing the twirling teapot wallpaper.

Biddy starts the conversation rolling by describing an outpatient's genitalia and how embarrassing it was for her having to shave the bank manager "down there" today. And Mrs. Bootsby-Smythe, who does she think she is, with all her airs and pompous graces? Well, she was brought down a peg or two when she had to wait for Dr. Morrison, her legs in stirrups, her privates looking like a cockerel's comb.

I stifle a giggle, at the same time hoping I look okay "down there." Please, God, may I never have to go to the village hospital when my mother is the nurse on duty.

"Kate, now don't you let this get any further than the kitchen table, but Sophie Greengough is pregnant, and only sixteen years old."

Sophie is in the pudding club? She's going to have a *baby*? But I've never seen her with a boy, she's an A student, forever winning awards at school. She's brilliant at tennis and hockey and everything.

"God help her poor mother," says Biddy. "There was Mrs. Greengough, weeping in the waiting room while Sophie attended the antenatal clinic."

I try and imagine what it would be like doing *it*. Letting a boy touch you, and . . . God, I wouldn't even let Barry Finch do it. Moira has explained everything to me in great detail—her married sister, Fiona, told her all *she* wanted to know.

"Kate, what are you thinking about?" asks Biddy. "Tom, please cover the butter."

The meal is over, and as per ritual, my parents light up their cigarettes. Dad must put the lid on the butter dish in case the smoke taints it, and I must remain seated. It wouldn't be polite to leave the table just yet.

"What's on your mind, Kate?" asks Dad, echoing Biddy. A wisp of smoke escapes from his nostrils, curls into his eyes. His hair is Brylcreem-shiny, black, combed flat, like one of those film stars in old movies.

"Nothing. Can I phone Moira?"

I want to tell her about Sophie Greengough.

"Sure. Didn't you talk with her as soon as you came home?" Biddy clicks her fingernails on the Formica. "I'm not stupid, my girl—far from it." She takes a long drag from her cigarette. "It wasn't Moira Murphy making your face beet red."

Dad makes a halfhearted move to stack plates. He always looks for something to do when he senses conflict. And as usual, Biddy tells him to sit down.

"You'll tell Dad he never lifts a finger to help next," I say.

"We will not allow you to meet with boys, will we, Tom?"

"You're still a child, Katie," says Dad.

I count the worry lines on his forehead, one, two, and three, and so I lie. "I don't meet with boys," I say, then I ask if I can please have another fruit scone.

Monday, September 20

It's been a miserable day. My period started and I didn't have anything with me, so Moira told me to go to the school nurse and I ended up with pads the size of a nappy.

"Do you have a sanitary belt?" asked Nurse. "No? Then here we are, dear."

Padded, belted, girdled, strapped, I could barely walk. Was I glad when the last bell rang.

Moira spent most of the bus journey home teasing the braid out of my hair while I peered in a mirror, trying to cover a pimple with concealer.

She was really decent lending me her peach lipstick and kohl liner.

You see, I'm hoping to bump into Barry Finch.

Almost at the top of Bryre Hill Lane now, but still no sign of Barry, and I've got *killer* cramps.

But when I get to Cherry Blossom Road, I see a younger version of him riding a bike in circles, in front of number 33 Cherry Blossom Road.

"You live here?" he asks me.

I nod.

"Kate Cadogan?"

I nod again.

"Barry says I'm to give you this."

"Are you his brother?" I ask, taking a folded piece of paper.

"Yeah, and I read the note," he smirks. "You his girlfriend?"

Am I? I don't know. "Could be," I say.

He cycles off down the road yelling: "Woooeeeeee." God, am I glad I don't have a brother. *But I do have a note!* I feel prickly all over and my heart thumps. Am I the luckiest girl in the world, or what? I stuff the note up my sleeve and search for my key.

Biddy opens the door.

"Hi, Mum."

We kiss and she asks why I always pick at my pimples, and why is my hair loose and why am I wearing makeup?

"Just trying stuff out," I reply.

"Sure, and you look as pale as paper. What's wrong?"

"Period."

Biddy takes my duffel coat, tells me to lie on the sofa while she fetches a blanket, a hot water bottle, and aspirins. And she will make me a hot mug of tea and she thinks she might have a couple of ginger biscuits somewhere.

My mother loves being the nurse at home.

She switches on the TV, and I relax, relishing every bit of her care and concern, because it doesn't really happen that often.

And the note in the sleeve of my sweater still waits to be read.

❖

By six o'clock, we've eaten the pork chops, the baked potatoes, and the apple sauce. The butter is covered, the cigarettes are lit, and Biddy inhales deeply and says, "Kate, I looked through the bedroom window and saw a young boy hand you a note."

"A note?"

She never misses a trick, ever.

"What did it say, Kate?"

I look at my Dad. *Do I really have to tell her?* He tap-taps his cigarette over the ashtray and avoids my eyes. I've never known him to challenge Biddy.

"I don't know what it says," I mumble.

Which is true.

"Then read it now. It's inside your sleeve."

Dad, please say something. He's watching her, reading her, and he'll side with her. As he always does.

"Show me the note," says Biddy.

I slide it out, scrunch it up, then hold it in my clenched fist.

"Show me."

I look at Dad. He puts on a stern face and nods at me, meaning, *Go on, show her, do as she says.* I look straight ahead at the wallpaper and focus on a twirling teapot. A blue one.

"No, Mum."

And she has my fist and she's trying to pry open my fingers, and her nails dig, and she's saying through clenched teeth: "You will let me read this note. I am your mother. Tom, tell her."

"What are you trying to hide?" he asks, looking sidelong at Biddy.

I jump up and the chair topples over and I snatch my hand away. And I'm running, and my damned stockings are falling down, and this *bloody* stupid girdle won't let me scale the stairs two at a time. Biddy is in hot pursuit and Dad is yelling, "Do as your mother says! Do you hear?"

I'm in the bathroom, and I catch a glimpse of Biddy's face before I slam the door shut.

Her eyes were angry, but her mouth laughed.

"Open this door *NOW*!"

Bang, bang, bang!

I open the note, a page torn from an exercise book, and my heart leaps.

> *I'll wait for you at the bus stop on Tuesday, Kate Cadogan. For one kiss, I'll buy you coffee in Dorton. For two, I'll take you for a ride on my bike.*
>
> Barry

But Biddy mustn't see this. I shove the note inside my bra.

BANG. Her voice deepens. "Open. This. Door. Now."

"In a minute."

Silence.

I flush the toilet, wait a bit, and let Biddy in. "I flushed it down the toilet," I tell her.

She's breathing hard, like she's out of breath. "I don't believe you," she says.

Grabbing my wrist, she tunnels her fingers up my sleeve. She lifts up my sweater and I try to pull it from her grasp.

"Don't you dare stretch this good sweater," she warns.

I let my arms fall limp, because I don't know what else to do. I'm backed into the corner of the bathroom and tears burn hot on my cheeks as her hands travel to my breasts, feeling, ferreting for the note. My mouth opens and shuts. I want to yell, I want to tell her to get off me, but I can't. It feels like a dream when you scream, but no sound comes out.

Then she opens the note, and reads it silently, her lips moving like they do when she's praying with rosary beads.

CHAPTER 3

◆

Friday, November 5
Shawhurst High School, Brayminster

"Remember, remember the fifth of November
Gunpowder, treason, and plot.
I see no reason why gunpowder treason
Should ever be forgot.
Guy Fawkes, Guy Fawkes
'Twas his intent
To blow up the King and the Parliament. . . ."

Our History teacher, Mrs. Noonan, finishes reading the poem and asks what year the Gunpowder Plot occurred. Yes, quite right, Amanda, in 1605, good girl, she says, and who was the king at the time? No, Kate, it wasn't Charles the Second. Yes, Martha, it was James the First of England, who was also James the Sixth of Scotland. And why did Guy Fawkes wish to blow up Parliament? Do we remember?

"Remember, remember, the fifth of November," says Moira, tapping her foot, snapping her fingers. *"Burn him in a tub of tar, burn him like a blazing star, burn his body from his head, burn him till he's good and dead. . . ."*

"Moira Murphy, I can both see and hear you clearly. Quite the little comedienne, aren't we? Brenda, would you like to stand up and jog our memories?"

"James the First was not very tolerant of the Catholic religion, Mrs. Noonan."

I yawn, and my mind wanders, and I see Barry Finch flipping his hair from his eyes with one movement of his head.

"Alas, the king was not tolerant, and this angered a number of young men, please wake up, Kate Cadogan, and pay attention. Go on, Brenda."

"Guy Fawkes and a group of conspirators decided the thing to do was blow up the Houses of Parliament."

"And who would be killed in the process?"

I gaze out of the window and see a crow striding across the hockey field. He looks just like Mr. Scargill, the Maths teacher.

"Kate Cadogan?"

"The king!" I blurt. "He wanted to kill the king."

"Yes, along with the Prince of Wales and members of parliament. But Guy Fawkes was caught in the act, and subsequently tortured and executed."

I nudge Moira. "Shit! Bloody barbarians, all of them."

She looks at me cross-eyed.

Sometimes, Barry Finch does that to make me laugh.

"GIRLS!" Mrs. Noonan claps plump hands. "Let's get on with our projects, shall we? No more talking, Murphy, Cadogan, please."

Moi and me tape six sheets of paper together to lay on the floor, and we start drawing the Houses of Parliament. We do an amazing job, considering we have to use sign language.

We call our project "Guy Fawkes's Dream," and I reckon it's brilliant. A few more explosions, a bit of billowing smoke, and we're done.

"Moira—you're dripping paint all over Big Ben."

"Those are sparks," she explains, flicking on a few more. "Hey, do you think Dawn Massey and Mary Dunn are disturbed? Their collage shows Guy Fawkes with his guts spewing out."

"Yeah, pretty sick, aren't they?"

We shake in a silent fit of giggles, and God it hurts, and then Moira goes and lets out a loud splutter.

"Quiet over there." Mrs. Noonan peers over her glasses. "Twenty-five minutes left, girls."

I dab on a bit more smoke with a sponge.

"What time are we meeting Barry and Geoff?" asks Moira under her breath.

"Seven."

Moira's coming home with me tonight. She's staying over. Leaning closer, she whispers in my ear. "I have this fab new lipstick. It goes on transparent, and—"

"Right, Murphy and Cadogan, you've gone too far. See me after last bell."

"Pray she'll be gentle," I murmur. "Say a prayer to your guardian angel."

"My patience is wearing thin," sings Mrs. Noonan.

"Angel of God, my guardian dear, to whom God's love commits thee here," I whisper.

"Shut *up*," urges Moira.

"MURPHY!"

Mrs. Noonan's face is mauve. If she disqualifies our project, I've had it. My grades will take a nosedive.

Well, the bell goes, and Nazi Noonan gives us a detention—which I can cope with. "Notice will be sent to your parents," she reminds us.

Me and Moira tear downstairs to the cloakroom, shove our feet into outdoor shoes, throw on our duffel coats, slap on our berets. We manage to wave the school bus down before it zooms away without us.

"So here's the plan," says Moira, breathless. "We say we're going to Saint Francis's Youth Club, and everything is fine, because Father Tierney will be there."

"But instead, we're going to see the firework display at Brayminster College."

"Yes, with *them*." Moira rolls her eyes and pretends to swoon.

"With *them*," I say. "We're meeting Barry and Geoff at the bridge, right?"

"Yeah."

A couple of weekends ago, we bumped into Geoff outside Woolworth. He said he was a friend of Barry's, they were doing the same course at school. Said he'd seen Barry and me together. Anyway, to cut a long story short, Moira and Geoff have been hanging out ever since.

Moira says her mum and dad are okay about it—I wish my parents weren't so weird about boys.

I look out of the bus window, at the rolling hills dotted with sheep. Then we pass through Brayminster, with its crooked houses, little shop fronts, and ancient pubs. It isn't all that different from Llandafan, the little Welsh town where my gran lives. I stayed with her and Griff, my step granddad, over half-term. I told Mamgu—she likes me using the Welsh name for gran—that I'd like a trainer bra for my birthday. Here, *bach,* she said, which means "little one," and she pressed pound notes into my hand, and what else would I like? I said some bottle green tights for school, please, which meant I could ditch the girdle. She gave me a fiver and promised another ten shillings if I'd wipe the blue paint off my eyes. *Achyfi,* she said, you'll end up blinded. But I told her I wanted to look like Twiggy, and she laughed and said I was a *twpsen.* (A nice way of telling me I was stupid.) Here, said Griff, take the ten shillings, buy some purple as well, let's make your Biddy really mad.

"Come on, Katie." Moira's tugging at my sleeve. "Let's get off the bus. We're in Dorton."

"Shit. Already? Hey, pass my satchel."

We climb Bryre Hill Lane and it reminds me of all the little asphalt roads I walked along with my grandparents. Griff pointed out the baby adders in the hedgerows, so I'd know not to touch them, because they'll give me a nasty nip, *bach,* he said.

When I got back from Llandafan, Biddy asked me what gave Mamgu the right to decide what her daughter wore. Oh, so she knows what bra I need, does she? She couldn't even dress her own son properly, knitting him sweaters with wool she found in the sales. And what kind of nourishment was there in a plate of salt fish and broad beans? And poor Tom had to eat that sitting at a table covered with bleached flour sacks. And he stood on carpets made of rags when he was but a wee infant with no shoes. And didn't she give birth to my father when she was but a child herself. Good job Griff came along to marry her.

Gosh, I thought, just like the Virgin Mary and Joseph.

Anyway, I bought this groovy bra covered with Mary Quant daisies, and a pair of cream lace tights as well as the ones for school.

The salmon-paste girdle and brassiere are in Biddy's chest of drawers now. She was mad at first, but she told me the girdle fits her nicely, and what do I think of a mother who can fit into her daughter's clothes? And did I realize she's still as slim as she was when she married Daddy at twenty-four?

Moira said I should never, *ever* forgive Biddy for what she did in the bathroom.

I don't know what happened to my note. I searched all over the house, but couldn't find it. I did find a couple of Dad's books, though, on top of his wardrobe. Edna O'Brien wrote them, and they're fantastic. Dad hasn't noticed they're missing yet. Biddy thinks books look untidy in the house. The only ones I thought they had were a few nursing manuals, and the odd metallurgy book Dad sometimes brings back from the lab where he works.

Anyway, in these Edna O'Brien books, there are some great naughty bits to show Moira tonight. One of the books is about these two friends who get expelled from the convent for writing, *Father John stuck his long in Sister Mary's hairies,* or something like that, on the back of a Mass card.

"Hey, KATIE, wake up! What are you smiling at? I've been talking to myself all the way up Bryre Hill Lane. You're *always* going off into trances." Moira jabs me in the ribs. "Look, we're passing Barry Finch's house." And she grins. "Tell me something. When he kisses you, does he put his tongue inside your mouth?"

I nod. "Does Geoff do it?"

She nods too, and we collapse with laughter, hanging on to each other, and then we walk the rest of the way with linked arms.

"How are you going to wear your hair tonight?" she asks.

"Loose."

"Hmm."

I just love Moira's new hairdo. It's totally short and blond and it really suits her. She's built like a stick insect, the lucky thing. She says I eat too much, and I look great now, but if I'm not careful, I'll soon be as bouncy as Mrs. Noonan.

Biddy is raking leaves in the front garden when we arrive at 33 Cherry Blossom Road. She's always working, never stops, she has the most amazing amount of energy. She knocked down a wall in the kitchen all by herself to get rid of the pantry. Just got up and did it before Dad came home. And two days later, she had everything papered with twirling teapots. Sanderson wallpaper, she said, very exclusive, and wait till Aunt Shauna sees it, so *now* who has the biggest kitchen?

"Hello, Mrs. Cadogan, thank you for letting me stay tonight," says Moira.

"You're welcome, Moira." Biddy puts on her posh telephone voice. "I hear you came first in Chemistry and Physics this year."

"And Katie did great with Domestic Science," says my best friend ever. "Got an A-plus."

"And where will that lead her? I'm frying cod for supper, Moira." (She calls dinner supper when we have visitors.)

We help Biddy put the garden tools away and remember to take off our shoes before we step inside.

Moira takes her stuff upstairs and Biddy starts peeling potatoes at the sink. She's worked all day at the hospital, raked leaves, and now she's cooking dinner for my friend.

I kiss her cheek. "Thanks, Mum." I get a smile and a kiss back and I'm told to set the table. I pull the table away from the wall, and I set down four of our second best plates.

Biddy apologized for what happened in the bathroom two days afterward, but explained it was her duty to keep watch over her daughter and keep her safe. When I wouldn't show the note, she had no choice but to use force, did I understand? And Daddy forbids me to go *near* that boy again, do I hear?

Biddy always pretends my dad is in charge, but I know he's not.

Guilt mixes with the thrill I feel when I think about seeing Barry tonight. He's been meeting me at the bus stop for five—or is it six—weeks now. Sometimes I ride on the back of his bike, holding on to him, pressing my cheek against his leather jacket as he freewheels down Bryre Hill Lane.

I have a boyfriend. And he's seventeen.

I think disobeying parents is a venial sin. I wonder if French kissing is a mortal. There's no way I'd confess that one to Father Flannagan. Moira says Ingrid Beddoes looked through the confessional grille last Thursday and saw Father playing with himself.

French kissing. I get shivers when Barry does it, but I sort of get frightened, too. I can tell he wants to go further, but I'll never, ever let him. I don't want to end up pregnant like Sophie Greengough. I saw her last week. She left school and has a job now. She was wearing a tent dress, and her tummy was enormous.

◆

Biddy makes the best chips. Moira gives me a look when I take a second helping, so I tip them onto Dad's plate instead when he gets up to fetch the teapot. We rush through dinner and excuse ourselves from the table as soon as Biddy says, "Tom, cover the butter, please."

Moira loves the fawn corduroy dress I made myself. It took ages because I had to make buttonholes, sew on a collar, and everything. I shortened it another inch last night.

"Now let's cut your hair," says Moira.

"*What?*"

"Let me cut you a fringe."

"Are you kidding? Biddy will flip her lid."

"Come on, Katie, a fringe would look cute."

I fetch the sewing shears, Moira points to the bathroom, and I'm told to sit on the toilet as she goes to work. Snip, snip, snip. She measures with a ruler to make sure everything's dead even.

She steps back and frowns.

"Katie, your hair is so long, it reaches your arse."

"Okay, cut."

Snip, snip, snip.

We dump all the hair clippings inside a plastic bag. "*Christ*, Moira, you've taken off a shit load."

We can't find any shampoo, so Moira sneaks down to the kitchen for dishwasher detergent and vinegar.

"It'll be okay. The vinegar will bring out the red tones in your hair. Honest."

She half-drowns me in the sink, takes an age drying and brushing, and after what seems like forever, she says, "Finished. Now stand up straight. Oh God, I'm serious, you're gonna love it. Turn around."

Moira's absolutely right. Dead on. I love it, love it, love it. The fringe reaches my eyebrows and my hair is a velvet curtain, lying heavy over my shoulders. Like Cher's. I stare at the mirror, and I'm choked. "You're brilliant, Moi," I whisper. "I don't look like me anymore."

"Come on, do my makeup," she says.

I give her enormous cat-eyes with black liner.

"Brill, Kate. Okay, pass me my lipstick. Look, it goes on transparent, and '*the color will develop in fifteen minutes to a perfect shade of dusky rose.*' "

She smears on a second coat when no color appears.

Pulling on a red and brown striped top, she squirms into a white miniskirt and then pushes her feet into a pair of PVC boots. Groovy. She looks so like Mia Farrow, it's incredible.

She applies more lipstick. "What's wrong with this stuff?" she asks.

We run downstairs and grab our duffel coats, scarves, and mittens. We keep the lights off in case Biddy and Dad come out to the hall and see how much makeup we've plastered on.

"Bye, Mum, Dad," I shout.

Here comes Biddy, clip-clopping in her heels.

"Bye, Mr. and Mrs. Cadogan." Moira grabs my arm. "Let's scoot." And we make it out of the door just in time.

Our breath puffs into the frosted air. The sky is splashed with fireworks, sprayed with sparks. Whine, crack, zip, whoosh—rockets splinter into thousands of stars.

Moira turns to me, smiling. "Are we going to have a great night, or what?"

She stares at my face and her eyes open like saucers. "What? Why are you gaping at me like a goldfish?"

"Oh dear God, Moi, your mouth is crimson! You look like you've been sucking blood."

CHAPTER 4

◆

We gallop down Bryre Hill Lane to get to Dorton, and our first stop is at the public conveniences, so Moira can wipe her mouth.

"Hurry up, will you?" I hiss. "Perverts hang around here."

So Moira screams like an idiot and laughs like a hyena.

Funny.

"Come, on, Moi," I say, pulling at her coat. "This place stinks."

We turn right and run down toward the river—and there he is. There's my Barry, leaning against the wall with his hands in his pockets. Deep in conversation with Geoff.

I catch my breath when he sees me.

"Babe." He lifts handfuls of my hair. "Whoa." And he kisses my lips and I can taste toothpaste.

"I love the hair," he says.

I think I love *him*.

We all get into Geoff's Triumph, and I feel like I'm twenty years old. Barry slings his arm around my shoulders and offers me the last drag of his cigarette, but I shake my head because Dad and Biddy have put me off cigarettes for life.

He throws the butt out of the window and turns to plant his lips on mine again. His tongue probes, hard, and it feels different, not as gentle. I hear the screech of fireworks, smell sulphur in the air, and Moira and Geoff are talking, ooh-ahhing, saying wow, did you see that one?

Barry keeps on kissing. His face is like sandpaper against my cheek. I really want to look out at the fireworks, look for the glow of bonfires as we drive by, and listen to kids laughing and screaming. But I circle my tongue around his instead, to show him I know what to do. He's stroking, pressing. I weave my fingers through his hair like I've seen in films—and then his hand is on my knee, rubbing, rubbing, fingers spreading. His thumb works on the inside of my thigh, and that is when I pull away.

Touching my nose with the tip of a finger, he says, "Little babe."

He lights up another cigarette and lies back to blow a stream of smoke at the roof of Geoff's Triumph.

And the little parenthesis appears on one side of his mouth.

◆

Geoff drives through the entrance of Brayminster College and onto the playing field. "There's no fucking place to park," he says, smacking his hands on the steering wheel.

We all search for a space among row upon row of cars.

"Back up, oh, no good, a motorbike got there first."

"Look, see? Two cars down."

"No, behind us."

"Try the third row!"

"Okay, turn the wheel hard to the right and I'll guide you in," says Barry.

We're parked at last, and Barry helps me out of the car. "C'mon, cutie," he says, grabbing my hand.

Moira and Geoff say, "Let's get hot dogs," and, "How about a burger and Coke?"

"Or beer." Barry kisses the top of my head. "Shall I buy you a beer, Katie?"

I shrug. A shrug can mean yes or no or whatever.

◆

The bonfire is gigantic. Huge flames leap, grab at a purple sky, and spill orange sparks all around. Barry's arm circles my waist, and I smell leather and sweat.

Beer. I'll drink my beer. I look over at Moira to see if there's some cool way of drinking it. She's waving her bottle around, using it to talk with.

"Isn't the bonfire fantastic?" I ask Barry.

The beer tastes okay. Flat, kind of moldy, smelling of hop fields.

"Stop waving it around, babe. You'll spill it. Geoff, we're off to buy a hot dog. See ya later."

I look back to see Moira giving me the thumbs-up.

Girls keep looking at Barry, which isn't surprising, because he's a hunk, and who's his girlfriend? Me. And guess what—I see a bunch of girls standing around the barbecue, and they're from Shawhurst High School. Ingrid Beddoes, Sheila Colby, Sue McCooke, Dawn Massey, Dottie O'Shea, and Val Hickey.

And Sophie Greengough, whose arms rest on her big tummy like it's a shelf.

"Ingrid, Dottie—" When I reach up to wave, Barry grabs hold of my arm, swings me around, and marches me toward the school buildings.

"We'll get a burger instead. Or a potato—fancy a baked potato?"

"Barry?"

"Come here." He opens his leather jacket, pulls me to him, wraps me inside, and kisses me. A soft kiss. "I just want to be alone with you, babe."

I've done my research, I know he's dated a stack of girls before me, but I just *know* I'm different. I'm special. He's been out with me the longest. Ingrid says so.

Barry sits me on his lap on a low brick wall and we share the burger. I bite where his mouth has been. He's drinking his third beer, I'm on my second.

"You're hot," he says. "Did you know that?"

Tonight, I feel I am, with my new hair and dress and all. I look like one of the models in *Jackie* magazine, Moira said.

"Want to see the technical drawing room?"

Barry's learning to be an architect.

"Okay."

He leads me through the foyer, up some winding stairs with iron handrails, opens a door, number 113A. He shows me his work. Complicated lines, measurements, angles, and grids.

"Moi and me painted the Houses of Parliament for an exam," I tell him.

"You did?" He lifts my hair to stroke the back of my neck.

"If I don't get an A, I'll be in trouble."

"You know what turns me on?" His eyes are steady, his breathing fast. "You in that little pleated skirt. Your uniform. Drives me crazy." Tongue again, his hands on my bottom, pulling me to him. I can feel his thing against my tummy.

He leads me to a sort of stockroom. *But it's okay,* I tell myself. *He knows I'm fourteen, doesn't he?* He slips the buttons of my dress through the button-holes I sewed myself. And his hands are inside my Mary Quant bra that's covered with daisies and his fingers feel for my breasts. I'm backed into the corner of the stockroom and my dress is up, and his nails scratch as he works his way down between tights and skin.

Barry's fingers are touching me *there.*

"Come on, Katie." He nuzzles my shoulder.

"I love you, Barry."

The door is ajar. I have a thin vertical view of the windows and I can see the fireworks and the sky. Why aren't we out there? I want my friends to see me with Barry Finch.

Green sparks, red flares, gold spears, we're missing it all. Barry moves against my leg.

"Come on, Katie."

"Do you love me, Barry?"

A fountain of stars, plummeting teardrops, scattered lights. So this is what it should feel like, a flutter, a tingle. And his fingers keep moving.

"Do you love me, Barry?"

"Yeah." He pulls his hand away and pushes into the pocket of his jeans. He takes out a little foil packet and starts to fumble with his zipper.

"No."

No, no, not that.

"No?" He hangs his head and his hair flops forward and he curses, sighs, hits the wall with the flat of his hand.

Then below the crack-crack-crack of jumping jacks and the shriek of Catherine wheels, I hear him whisper, "Damn—you're a good girl."

"I'm sorry," I say.

Please don't hate me now.

Barry buttons up my dress, closes my duffel coat. "No big deal," he says. Even though his face didn't mean it.

❖

He doesn't put his arm around me in the car. He smokes and stares out of the window instead.

And when I say it's best if me and Moira are dropped off by the bridge, in case my mum and dad see us getting out of the car, he says, "Christ."

❖

My dad lets us in at number 33 Cherry Blossom Road, and when I take off my duffel coat, he tells me my dress is too short.

"What have you done to your hair?" asks Biddy. "It hangs like rats' tails."

"But Mrs. Cadogan, she looks so pretty." Moira makes me sit down and she bunches my hair high on my head. "Imagine a ponytail, Mrs. Cadogan. Isn't she cute?"

"Kate, come with me," says Biddy. "You'll need an extra pillow for your friend." And when we're upstairs by the linen cupboard, she asks, "Why did you let that little madam cut your hair?"

I sigh.

"Did I hear you sigh?"

"No, Mum."

I just want to go to bed.

"Moira," I shout, "come upstairs."

❖

Me and Moira lie side by side in bed, staring at the ceiling. "Katie, you did the right thing, saying no."

"God, Moi, it wasn't like I wanted him to and stopped because I shouldn't. I stopped because I *didn't* want him to. Do you get what I'm saying?"

"Messing around is okay, but going all the way is different."

"Have you ever . . ."

"No."

We lie in silence for a while, then Moira whispers, "Hey, Katie, switch on the lamp—let's have a look at the rude bits in your dad's books."

I fish under the bed. "Here."

"Let me read," says Moira. *"I remembered the funny hang of the pouch be-tween his hairy thighs and how I had been afraid."*

" 'It won't bite you,' he said, and to the touch it grew miraculously like a flower between the clasp of my fingers."

"Girls, go to sleep, please," shouts Biddy. "It's one o'clock in the morning."

"Sorry, Mrs. Cadogan, we were reading the catechism," Moira replies.

We shake in a silent fit of giggles, and it hurts like hell and then I go and burst into tears.

I was scared stiff in the stockroom. Do I have to go *all the way* to keep him?

"Oh God, Moi—"

"What's the matter, Katie?"

"Barry will never want to see me again now, will he?"

CHAPTER 5

◆

Thursday, November 11

I haven't seen Barry since Guy Fawkes Night. Not for six days. Moira says play it cool, play hard to get, don't phone or anything.

But I couldn't wait, so after school today, I hung around Dorton for a while, bought the latest copy of the *Jackie* mag, drank a Coke. And now I'm hoping that if I wait outside Barry's house long enough, he'll turn up.

I had my school report today, and it stinks:

English Language
C+. *Kate has a feeling for the subject and has produced some outstanding essays, but her work is rarely consistent. She spends most of her time in class daydreaming.*

English Literature
C++. *Term work excellent, exam result disappointing.*

Mathematics
D+. *Weak. Daydreams. Shows no effort.*

Chemistry and Physics
E. *Not Kate's forte.*

Biology
C--. *Shows promise when she's awake.*

Latin
B+. *What happened? I'm amazed.*

Geography

D++. *Would like to arrange meeting with parents.*

History

C. *Satisfactory, but her incessant chatting with Moira Murphy is unacceptable.*

Art

A-. *Very creative, but Kate is on another planet most of the time.*

Domestic Science

A+. *Excellent. A pleasure to teach. Shows much interest.*

Parent's signature: ——————————— Date: —————————

I lean the report on Barry's gate and sign Biddy's name carefully, remembering to make the B and C curly, just like she does. *Bridget Cadogan.* I only ever show her the end of year reports—that's all she thinks we get.

"Kate."

I swing around. It takes a while to realize Barry is standing in front of me. "Hi," I say in a whisper, with a cough.

I swallow, then roll my report up, feeling stupid.

"What are you doing here?" He avoids my face, looks up the hill, at his feet, down the hill. Hands in pockets as usual.

"Moi said you only wanted one thing," I blurt out. "Is she right?"

I can't believe I just said that.

He does a "no" shake with his head, but I can't work out what his smile means.

He walks past, saying, "I'm sorry, but you're too young, doll." He unlatches the gate, walks up the path a short way, stops, and turns. "Listen, you're too good for me. Does that make you feel better?"

"Barry, don't go. I love you, really I do."

He kicks at loose stones. "Look, Kate, get the hell out of my life, okay?"

I can't move, my legs are jelly.

He glares at me. "Got the message yet?"

Stuffing the report into my satchel, I run, I run like I've never run before. When I stop, I have to hold my breath or I'll be sick. Clouds gang up and darken the sky, dropping needles of rain, and then I sob, I sob my heart out, because no one will notice the tears now, will they?

◆

When I reach Cherry Blossom Road, I know I must stop crying because I don't want Biddy asking questions. Yellow light is warm in the windows of number 33 and I see her drawing the apricot curtains that match the vinyl sofa and Axminster carpet.

"Take off your shoes and come in. Why didn't you wear a raincoat this morning?" she asks, dropping a kiss on my wet cheek. "Did I not give you a rain hat to carry in your satchel? By the way, your aunt Shauna and uncle Frank are coming over for supper."

Oh, no. Josie, too, I'll bet.

"Would you set six places in the dining room?"

Yep. Six places—Josie, too. Damn. That's all I need. My cousin.

"Yeah."

"Kate, the word is *yes*. Go and wash your hair. Push back the fringe. Please God it will grow out soon. Put on a dress, but don't wear that corduroy thing you made. It's far too short and the buttonholes are all wrong."

As I climb the stairs, Barry's words buzz in my head.

Listen, you're too good for me. Does that make you feel better?

Peeling off my damp uniform, I look for comfort clothes. Jeans, a thick black pullover, warm socks. I pull my hair into a ponytail—I don't feel like washing it—then I look at myself in the mirror.

I'm sorry, but you're too young, doll. Got the message yet?

Ding-dong. Dad is here. Biddy will want the linen tablecloth spread on the dining table, set with the Royal Doulton plates and the silver-plated cutlery. I'd better see to it.

Dad hands me a bar of Fry's dark chocolate, the one filled with peppermint cream. "For my baby daughter," he says.

Tears pain my eyes.

"Tom, thank goodness you're home." Biddy runs from the kitchen, wiping her hands in a dishcloth. "Would you go and buy another Bristol Cream? We only have a quarter of a bottle left. Kate, you're wearing a pair of *jeans*. Didn't I tell you to wear a dress?"

Look, Kate, get the hell out of my life, okay?

"Tom, did you see the way Kate ignored me?"

Yes Biddy, no Biddy, of course Biddy. I run back upstairs to phone Moira before Dad has a chance to say I must do as my mother says, do I hear?

And Moira is saying, weird, Katie, weird. Barry said *that*? But it doesn't make any sense, so what did you say then, and what did *he* say? How did he say it? Okay, start from the very beginning. What exactly happened that night in the stockroom?

So I give her details, and when I say, there, I've told you everything, I hear a *click* and then Moira's voice is clearer, louder. And that's when I realize Biddy's been listening to the whole conversation on the other line.

Well, shit, shit, shit.

The smell of braised steak rising to meet me on the stairs does nothing to dilute my pain—or dread. I'm really in for it now. Biddy heard everything, I feel dirty and I shall surely burn in hell.

"Kate, do you not hear the bell? Answer the door please."

Biddy's order is clipped and precise, and her icy glare confirms my worst fears. Oh, yes, she heard everything all right. The Stockroom. The Beer. His Tongue. His Fingers. Oh, shit, shit, shit.

I open the door to Aunt Shauna's kind face, Uncle Frank's comical grin, and Josie's overbite.

"Come and give your aunt a big hug, my darling." Aunt Shauna wraps me in her arms and I want to stay cushioned in her embrace forever. "Oh, will you look at that fringe," she says, smoothing it down onto my forehead. "Doesn't Kate look grand, Josie?"

"Yeah." Josie flips her hand at me and gives me a quick "hi" before shouting, "Aunt Biddy, where are you?"

"In the kitchen, sweetheart."

Frank beams, hugs me, and claps me on the back. "Now, don't you look well, Katie?" He smells of Guinness and pickled onions. "And what have we for dinner? Well, hello, Tom, aren't you looking great?" And he makes his way to the kitchen to tell Biddy how good she looks, too.

I follow him to find Biddy pulling at Josie's frizzed curls. "Doesn't she look stylish, Kate?"

"Thank you, Aunt Biddy," says Josie, keeping one eye on me. "Actually, it's a perm. I had it done at Vidal Sassoon's."

God, she's a liar.

"You did not," Aunt Shauna shouts from the hall. "Our neighbor Caitlin did it. What do you think, Biddy?"

"Beautiful."

Josie wears a lilac turtleneck with a black skirt. Her thighs pudge out, pale inside net stockings. "Can I help, Aunt Biddy?" she wheezes.

Josie has asthma. She can trigger an attack if she pants hard enough in a locked bathroom—and then she can't possibly travel back home, can she? Not when she's ill. So can she stay? Aunt Biddy will look after her.

Truth is, Biddy spoils her like crazy. God only knows why.

"Yes, you can help, Josie. Here, put out the napkins. Oh dear, are you wheezing? Did you bring your inhaler?"

"I forgot it, Aunt Biddy."

Of course she did.

"Then sit down in front of the fire. Help yourself to a nice glass of lemonade. Kate, I want a word."

I take steps toward the cooker where Biddy is hammering the potatoes to make mash.

"Kate, would you go and change your clothes, please?"

Josie clumps out in her high-heeled lace-ups.

"Mum," I say, "my jeans and sweater are comfy." I pull her to me, but she stiffens.

"Ah, do what you like," she says, shrugging me off. "Tom, help me carry the vegetables. Put them down, Kate. Didn't you hear me ask your father?"

◆

And the meal is all, but aren't you bright, Josie? Why, thank you, Aunt Biddy, I came second in class. How are you doing, Kate? What books are you reading in English Lit? Ah now, Josie, the only book Kate ever reads is *Alice in Wonderland*. Oh, and boys are her big speciality, too.

Aunt Shauna winks at me.

Biddy starts again. And what will you do when you leave school, Josie? You'll study law? Well, isn't that fine. What lovely nails you have. Kate, take your fingers from your mouth.

When the apple pie is on the table and the conversation switches to decorating, Josie's wheeze turns into a whistling rasp. When Aunt Shauna and Uncle Frank are discussing a career for me in domestic science, and let's see, what else could I do, there are so many things, Josie's rasp turns into a rattle.

And when Dad pours the glasses of sherry, and Aunt Shauna won't allow Biddy to let Josie have just one sip, one tiny sip, to help her breathe, the rattle turns into a harsh gasp.

Uncle Frank leaves to collect the asthma pills and inhaler, because after all, sure, don't they only live three miles away, says Biddy, poor Josie, and she trots upstairs to change the sheets on my bed.

Josie is to sleep in my room.

I'm kind of glad this time, because I'm dreading the showdown. The confrontation. I can't imagine Biddy wanting to bring up *the phone call* while Josie's here.

◆

Uncle Frank is soon back with the prescription. "Thanks, Biddy and Tom. Are you sure this isn't too much trouble? Kate, you're a good girl giving up your room."

"See you again on Sunday," says Aunt Shauna, holding my face in her hands.

Josie managed to wangle two days off school and a two-day stay here.

I count the hours I'll be safe from Biddy's wrath.

◆

We're in a line. Dad in front of me, Biddy behind, and we wave from the pavement as Aunt Shauna and Uncle Frank zoom away. The frost bites my fingers and makes my nose run—I think I'm getting a cold.

Following Dad back to number 33, I say, yes, Dad, it is freezing, did he look at all the stars in the sky? Did he see the big red one? I'm not kidding, it really *was* red, bright red, and the next thing, I'm shoved sideways against the doorframe as Biddy squeezes past, and she turns and blocks my way.

Her hand rises.

And my eyes snap shut as I feel the sharp burn of a slap across my face. And then another, and the third one is so hard, snot flies out of my nose.

When Josie peers down from the stairs, I see the flash of her buckteeth when she smiles behind her fingers.

Dad stares at me, at Biddy, back at me. "What did you do, Kate?" he asks, with eyes popping.

"Nothing. Bloody nothing." The palm of my hand is cold against my cheek as I wipe at tears. "NOTHING," I gasp, using my sleeve to wipe my nose.

Josie is sitting on the third from top step now, enjoying the show. She has her fat nose shoved through the railings.

"What the fuck are you looking at?" I ask her.

"Did you say . . . did you say . . ." Biddy can hardly talk.

"Did you say *fuck*?" asks my dad. And he nods, as if to say, there, Biddy, I said it for you.

Then he takes two steps toward me and raises his hand too, and I try to find his eyes through the blurred vision of my tears. I wait, wondering if he will smack the same cheek. *Go ahead,* I'm thinking. *Why not?* But his hand falls to his side and he says, "Go to your room."

"I can't," I whisper. "I'm to sleep on the sofa."

Does he even *know* why she hit me yet?

Putting my hand into my jeans pocket, I pull out the bar of Fry's dark chocolate, the one filled with peppermint cream, the one Dad brought home for me.

His baby daughter gives the chocolate back to him.

And it's soft now, and the peppermint oozes from the split wrapper.

CHAPTER 6

◆

Friday, November 12
Shawhurst High School, Brayminster

"How long is the little bitch staying?" Moira has to raise her voice above the clamor of the lesson-change bell.

"Josie? She'll stay as long as she can keep wheezing."

Although, I'm doing a fair bit of wheezing myself today. I'm full of a bloody cold and I've gone through half a box of tissues already.

As per school rules, we keep to the left as we walk along the corridors. We yak about the fab Beatles, the Stones, Gerry and the Pacemakers—and of course, Barry, analyzing what he said, how he said it, what he did, and how he did it.

Why he decided to break my heart.

I got up from the sofa this morning to find Biddy in the kitchen, peeling off rubber gloves. There's your breakfast, she said, jabbing a finger at a bowl of cereal. She stirred instant coffee with boiling water, *clink, clink, clink.* Do I want milk? Do I want milk? How many times does she have to repeat it?

And Dad? He spooned cornflakes into his mouth, not saying a word.

Last night, I wanted to leave home. This morning, I woke heavy with guilt because I'd made real plans to catch a train to Llandafan. I was desperate to talk with Mamgu and Griff, but hell, what was I to tell them?

Tell them what happened with Barry, tell them what Biddy heard on the phone? Tell them I said *fuck?* Let's face it, I lie, I cheat, I swear. No wonder my mother hates me. What was I thinking? Am I a slut? Biddy says I am.

Shit, Katie, said Moira, *your mum shouldn't have hit you.*

Perhaps I deserved it, I said.

But Moira shook her head.

I'd go to confession, but Ingrid still swears Father Flannagan plays with himself behind the grille.

"Wake up, Katie, you keep bumping into everyone," says Moira. "What a Daydream Doris you are. And wipe your nose."

I can just about smell the musk of incense as we pass the open doors to the church. It's actually part of the school, and Moi and me often take a peek inside to see if there's a funeral going on.

"Oh dear God, Katie," says Moira now. "There's an open coffin by the altar, and I'm not joking."

I nudge my body next to Moira's and look in. The coffin looks like a piece of antique furniture with brass handles and hinges and nuts and bolts. Tall candles and trumpetlike flowers are cool and cream and peaceful all around it.

"I know how to cheer you up, Katie." Moira's grin is devilish. "We'll take a look at the dead body after English Lit."

Something cold slithers down my spine. "You're nuts, Moira Bernadette Murphy."

"I dare ya, Kate Marie Cadogan."

"Let's run, Moi, we're late. Another detention is the last thing we need."

Moira and me have the one from Nazi Noonan to do this evening.

"Who'll be on detention duty?"

"Miss Everett."

"Pushover."

❖

Sister Philomena doesn't see us sneak into the classroom, slide onto seats, slip out our copies of *Romeo and Juliet.* We choose desks near Ingrid Beddoes, because she's a hoot.

"Her vestal livery is but sick and green." Sister Philomena has a lisp, so it comes out as, *Her vethtal livery ith but thick and green.*

Ingrid pretends to pick her nose, then she examines her finger. "Thick and green," she whispers, looking disgusted.

"Ingrid, would you like to take the part of Romeo?" asks Sister Philomena.

"*O, wilt thou leave me so unsatisfied?*" Ingrid casts a glance at us and raises her eyebrows.

I nudge Moira. "Look at the next line."

"*Hitht! Romeo, hitht!*"

"I'll pee my knickers, soon, I swear," whispers Moira.

Trying not to laugh is sheer agony. Sneezes take over, thank God.

"Bleth you, Kate. Well, LV2, I have a treat for you. Betty Barlowe, would you like to tell the class about it?"

"I brought in *West Side Story,* Sister Philomena, which is based on *Romeo and Juliet.*"

Sister skips over to the record player singing a high-pitched "I Feel Pretty," and a snigger ripples through the class.

"Behave like ladieth, or I'll change my mind," warns Sister, wagging a finger.

I pray she will. Barry the Jet—my Tony.

Moira pats my arm and gives me a *don't worry it will be okay* smile as Tony and Maria sing their hearts out. Why is life so painful?

Am I glad when the bell goes. Everybody stands to face the statue of the Virgin Mary for prayers. Moira speeds through the sign of the cross and says: "Come on, Katie, let's go and look at the body."

"Aw, shit, Moi, I'm not in the mood."

"After detention, then. I dare you to go in by yourself."

"And if I do?"

"You can come home with me, and I'll ask my mum to phone yours and say you're staying over." Moira's eyes dance.

"I don't want to commit a sin."

"What's with you all of a sudden? Gone all religious? What's wrong with looking at a dead body? Aren't you curious?"

"Haven't I enough sins already? I bet my soul is blacker than soot."

"*Christ,* Katie."

"Okay, okay."

◆

In detention class, Sheila Colby and Sue McCooke look over at me and start whispering again. What the heck's wrong with them? *Pss, psss-pssss, psss.* They've been at it all week. I keep asking Moira, Are my teeth yellow?

Is there wax in my ears? Am I wearing my sweater inside out? What? What?

Moira sticks her tongue out at them. "They've been acting weird ever since they discovered you and Barry were an item," she says.

Were is right. Past tense.

Then Dottie O'Shea arrives, breathless. "Thank God Everett isn't here yet." She hops onto the teacher's desk. (She has tons of awards for gymnastics.) "Hand me a chair, Ingrid." And she stands on it, reaches up to the wall clock, and moves the minute hand forward by fifteen minutes.

"Hey, Dottie, has Sophie Greengough had her baby yet?" asks one of the seniors.

"Yes, a baby girl—talk about *gorgeous.*"

Pss, psss-pssss, psss. Sheila Colby and Sue McCooke start whispering again.

Here's Miss Everett.

She strides into the classroom, stares at the wall clock, and sits behind the desk with a puzzled look on her face, but I think she's fallen for it.

Moira and me are at the front. I didn't realize how thick Miss Everett's moustache was, or how proud the wart on her chin was, or that it had three long hairs curling from it.

One of the second years is asked to hand out sheets of lined paper, ten sheets each.

Bad sign.

"Girls, you are to write the Act of Contrition fifty times," says Miss Everett.

"Oh, my God," sighs Moira.

Oh, my God, I write, *because You are so good, I am very sorry that I have sinned against Thee, but with the help of Thy grace, I will not sin again.*

I'm on my eleventh *Oh, my God,* when I feel Ingrid tapping my shoulder from behind. She passes me a note, and jerks her head over at Sheila Colby meaning, *It's from her.*

"Ahem," says Miss Everett. "Hand me that note, please—yes, you—what's your name?"

She's looking at me, of course.

"Kate Cadogan, miss."

Ha. Sheila Colby's in deep trouble now.

Miss Everett turns a warm shade of crimson. "The content of this note is somewhat *disturbing*," she says

Wow. What did it say? Moira looks at me with moon-eyes.

"Carry on, girls. And unless the young lady who altered the clock owns up within the next five minutes, I shall ask for a further *ten* Acts of Contrition from each one of you."

"Please, miss! Dorothy O'Shea did it," whines Sheila Colby.

◆

Moira closes the doors behind me, and I'm alone in the dim church, with the tall candles and the masses of trumpetlike flowers that look cool and cream and peaceful. I take quiet steps toward the coffin that looks like a piece of antique furniture with brass handles and hinges and nuts and bolts. It's on a platform covered with folds of black cloth.

Curved hornlike shadows play on the altar floor. Devils? Kate, you stupid twit, I tell myself, demons wouldn't hang out in a church. It's the flickering candlelight playing tricks, that's all. Don't be such an idiot. Keep going, show Moira you can do it.

Ha! And then it's her turn.

When I look inside the coffin, I expect to see someone really old, but she's about the same age as Biddy. Biddy's black hair, Biddy's round face. Made of wax, not skin, like a figure from Madame Tussaud's.

So this is what happens when your soul sets off for heaven. Or hell.

There's peach lipstick on the mouth, a shadow of blue on the closed lids. Orange powder hasn't been blended in properly, so it's all chalky around the ears. The fingers are woven together, all dry and shrunk up at the ends.

I should never have wished my mum dead last night, after she'd hit me. The last thing I want is for Biddy to be a corpse lying inside a satin-lined casket.

Jesus, forgive me.

I charge toward the closed doors.

And Christ—*let me out of here.*

CHAPTER 7

❖

Sunday, November 14

When I got back from Moira's house yesterday, Biddy seemed less icy. She'd bought fabric remnants from the sales to make little *outfits* for herself and a pair of kitten heels. Just look at the quality of the leather, Kate, she said, she's always lucky, finding bargains like this, on account of her small feet.

We took Josie back to Aunt Shauna and Uncle Frank's this morning, and by the time we were ready for eleven o'clock mass, Biddy had defrosted completely.

And my cold was gone, too.

And everything was great until the headmistress, Miss Kendrick, stopped my parents in the church car park to say, sorry to have to ask now, Mr. and Mrs. Cadogan, on the Sabbath, but it's about *that note* written by Sheila Colby. Would it be possible to arrange an appointment next Wednesday? Yes, it is a grave matter, and it does involve Kate.

Me?

Yes, ten-thirty would be perfect. Father Flannagan will be present, and she does understand why Mr. Cadogan can't be there, but she thinks he might like a word with his daughter later.

Notes, notes, notes. They'll be the death of me. What the heck did Sheila Colby write?

❖

"Well, Kate, I never thought you'd be this hard to rear." Biddy sighs in the front seat of our Morris Oxford on the way back to Cherry Blossom Road. "You used to be such a sweet little girl. What next, Kate, what next?"

She puts her missal and gloves into her handbag and takes out her rosary beads, and her lips move as she prays silently.

For my soul, probably. Dad says nothing, but when he's upset, he sucks in his bottom lip, and a collection of dimples appear on his chin. And I can see them there now.

Wednesday, November 17

I'm missing Domestic Science, and it was bread-making today. I wanted to learn about yeast and flours and baguettes and stuff. Mrs. Washington said we'd make a cottage loaf.

It's almost ten-thirty, and I'm waiting in reception for Biddy to arrive. The most reverend member of the Inquisition, Father Flannagan, sits opposite, fast asleep. He has a red bulb of a nose, a halo of gray hair, and his head is cushioned in rolls of double chin.

His dog collar is a touch grubby. I wonder who washes his clothes. Nuns probably.

Clip-clop. I recognize Biddy's high-heeled steps approaching. Her sharp rap on the door stirs Father Flannagan, and he shakes himself awake.

"Good Morning, Father," she says.

She takes his hand and I pray she's not thinking of kissing his ring.

Phew, she doesn't.

Father Flannagan pats her fingers. I bet his hands were around his willy half an hour ago.

Funny, I thought he was God Himself when I was three years old, when I saw him dressed in his golden robes for Benediction, speaking the language of angels in clouds of incense.

Adoremus, in aeternum, sacratissimum, sacramentum.

"Kate?"

"Hello, Mum."

Biddy props herself beside me.

Miss Everett strides out of the headmistress's office in thick tweed and brogues, and nods a greeting to Biddy, who's in teal Crimplene.

"Good morning, Father, please go ahead. This way, Mrs. Cadogan, Kate," she says, with a sweep of her arm.

Here we go.

Miss Kendrick says, "Sit down, please."

Please do this, please do that.

Moira says the headmistress looks like a bulldog because her jaw juts past her upper lip. She has one hell of a pair of shoulders.

"How shall we start?" she asks. Her right eye keeps flicking about—it never stops.

Amazing.

"Permit me to read the note passed to young Kate during detention," says Miss Everett. *"I hope Barry Finch wears a rubber when he does it to you. Sophie Greengough's baby is called Tracy. Guess who's a daddy now?"*

"We've already had a quiet word with Sheila Colby," adds Miss Kendrick.

Holy shit.

Rubber. Pregnant. Daddy. Baby. I let the words sink in. Guess who's a daddy now? My heart hammers. *I'm sorry, but you're too young, doll. Got the message yet?*

Father Flannagan makes a sign of the cross. Biddy blushes pink and her mouth tightens into a thin line.

Miss Kendrick studies the ceiling. Well, with one eye she does, the other is totally out of control now.

Biddy darts me a look. "Holy Mother of God," she whispers, and to Father Flannagan, "Forgive her, Father."

Forgive who? Me?

"Kate, did you have sexual intercourse with this young man?" asks Miss Everett.

Talk about straight to the point. What I say comes out like a burble. "We just, we, I, but, then . . ."

"Did the young man use contraceptives?" Miss Everett snaps her fingers. "Come on, Kate."

She's getting off on this, I know it.

And I can't answer. I try, but only manage a stupid squeak.

"Mrs. Cadogan"—(Miss Kendrick's turn now)—"we can recommend an excellent school doctor."

"A Catholic home for unmarried mothers," says Father Flannagan, patting my knee, "would look after poor Kate well."

"The school and church will help in every way they can," adds Miss Everett.

And Biddy? She sinks into her chair and weeps quietly.

When she's done, when she's finished blotting her eyes with a hanky, they all turn to face me. The priest and his chins, the headmistress and her one eye, the science teacher and her hairy wart.

Biddy's face is swollen with misery. I stand up and put my hand on her shoulder. "Mum," I say, "I'm not pregnant." A tear drips from her chin, and I just have to hold her. "Mum"—I pull her head against my chest and pat her hair—"I didn't let him do anything." She whispers into my sweater, and I have to bend down because I can't hear what she's saying.

"Enough now, sit down. You're spoiling my hair."

So, Father Flannagan blesses me, asks the Lord to protect me, bids farewell to all, and hurries away muttering something about having twenty-five confessions to get through before he can eat lunch.

Miss Kendrick pulls the phone toward her, sweeps up the receiver, and dials. "Mrs. Healy?" (She's the school secretary.) "Do you have a copy of Kate Cadogan's punishment report?"

What's this for? To make Biddy's visit worthwhile? Awww. Jesus Christ.

Two lists arrive on the desk and Miss Kendrick prods at them. "Not good enough, Mrs. Cadogan."

I read my own copy:

DETENTIONS

1. *Consumed communion wafers.*
2. *Talked in history class.*
3. *Forged signature on report.* **How could they tell?**
4. *Intrusion of privacy.(Explanation of "just paying final respects, sir," not acceptable.)*

Oh yes. I forgot. Moira ran into Old Crow Scargill. Nearly winded him. He already had me by the scruff of the neck, there was no way I could warn her. She came tearing out of the church after looking inside the coffin, gabbling, *Totally gross, scary, jeez, yuck, never again.*

But fair dues to Biddy, who must be delighted I'm not pregnant, wonders, Miss Kendrick, if the school might concentrate on the issue of Kate's low grades, and please excuse her, she has to ask this, but how are the staff helping Kate academically?

❖

Of course, as soon as we leave Miss Kendrick's office, I still get it in the ear for forging the report—but wow, she stuck up for me!

I kiss her good-bye. "Thanks, Mum."

"Kate, do NOT go anywhere near that Barry Finch again, do you hear?"

I nod.

Because I hate him.

"We'll talk with Daddy." And she tugs at her costume jacket, straightens her hair, then clip-clops out through the school doors into what's left of the November morning.

❖

After the butter is covered, after the cigarettes are lit, and as I stare at the twirling teapot wallpaper, I take part in a *serious discussion.*

I must pull my socks up and improve my grades, and Kate—

"What I heard on the phone was disgusting." Biddy wrinkles her nose. "You and Moira act like two little tarts. What if you *had* got pregnant? What then?"

I remember the little foil packet Barry had in his pocket. Dear God, he came all prepared, didn't he?

Biddy slaps the Formica table. "I think you should drop Moira Murphy. She's a bad influence, Kate, and her parents have no control over her at all."

No, no, no. Never. Moi's my best friend.

"I don't want anything to happen to my little girl," says Dad. "If any boy touches you again, I'll . . ."

He doesn't finish. He sucks in his bottom lip, and a collection of dimples appears on his chin.

Friday, December 17

I went shopping in Brayminster, to spend the money mailed to me inside Christmas cards. Five and ten pound notes from Mamgu, Griff, and my Irish grandmother.

And Oona.

Who's Oona? I asked Biddy.

Uncle Barney's wife, of course.

She can hardly blame me for forgetting. My mother rarely mentions her sister-in-law—who's a pure leech, apparently.

I bought a yellow dress with a mandarin collar for me, a night-dress case for Mamgu, socks for Griff, posh writing paper for Biddy, ginger chocolates for Dad. And for Moira, I bought a Beatles diary. There's no way I'm dropping my best friend.

The bus is packed downstairs, so I have to climb to the top deck, where the cigarette smoke is thick.

The bus chugs on the spot, waiting for the traffic lights to change from red to green. I look down at people bustling along the pavements, carrying parcels, bags, and dead turkeys. The street is lit up with the sparkle of Christmas lights, and mistletoe is bundled with holly and strung to lamp-posts.

And there's Sophie Greengough, pushing a navy pram, weaving it in and out through droves of shoppers. All I can see of the baby is fighting little fists and the tiniest head inside a pink hat.

And there's *Barry* trudging behind, walking along the curb, wearing an overcoat, and looking so different. He stops to kick at lumps of snow, skidding them into the road.

Sixteen and seventeen years old, and married.

How do people know you're watching them? How do they sense it?

Barry looks straight up at me, and I see an older face than I remember. The bus rumbles forward, and I twist around to catch a glimpse of those green eyes. I have to hold on to my parcels as the bus gathers speed—and then he's gone.

I wonder if the little parenthesis still appears on one side of his mouth when he smiles.

Dad and Biddy aren't home yet, they're both still at work, so I phone Moira to tell her I saw Barry and Sheila and the baby.

"Hi, Mrs. Murphy."

"Hello, sweetie. Poor Moira's very upset. Let me fetch her for you."

What now?

I hear footsteps, then—

"Oh God, Katie, you won't believe this, but Dad's been transferred to Cardiff."

Cardiff?

"We're moving," whispers Moira. "Mum's started packing already. They're buying this massive house, 'cause Dad's had a raise, but oh . . ."

She lets out a sob.

"I'll miss you so much, Katie."

My best, my special, my closest friend—she's *leaving* me?

What made Biddy move the phone from the living room to the hall, with its white walls and gray floors, where it feels hollow, where it's so bloody empty and cold?

"*Oh God, Moi.*"

My voice echoes, and suddenly, I'm so very, very alone.

Chapter 8

1968

Monday, May 20
33 Cherry Blossom Road, Dorton

My mother hates working at Dorton Cottage Hospital.

"I'm exhausted, Kate." A cigarette wags between her lips. "I've been a nurse for too long."

I cover the butter and hand Biddy her lighter. "I have an exam this morning, Mum—I must dash."

"Don't you have five minutes to spare your own mother?"

There's no time to answer and I need a safety pin. I had trouble pulling the waistband of my skirt together this morning and the button popped off. I search through the drawer where odd coins, string, and seed packets are thrown, the kind of drawer that holds all the rubbish when there's no better place to put it.

"Kate, your skirt is riding your backside. Have you put on weight?"

"A bit."

"Do up your cardigan. You look slovenly."

"I like it open."

To tell the truth, I can't get the damned thing to meet across my bosoms, and oh God it's eight-thirty, and I haven't got all the stuff together yet for Domestic Science.

"Mum, can I take these eggs? This bacon? Lard, do we have any lard?"

Biddy yawns. "I should leave nursing altogether," she says. "I'm worn out, so I am."

I ram ingredients for Quiche Lorraine into my basket and tuck them in with a gingham cloth. "Wish me luck," I say as I shrug on my school blazer.

"What kind of luck do you need for *Domestic Science*?"

I blow a kiss and remember to close the front door with a click, because if I slam it, the hinges will fly off.

Apparently.

It's a fantastic May morning. The sun drops watery light onto the rooftops and trees, and for once in my life, I look forward to going to school. By that, I mean I look forward to the lessons, not meeting up with the other girls.

But that's another story.

Things have changed at school. I'm in the sixth form now, a senior, no less. My grades have gone up to As and Bs for good work, Kate, interest shown, Kate, top marks, Kate, well done, keep it up, Kate.

"Letter for you, pet," says Bill Bailey the postman. He winks. I wouldn't trust him in a dark alley if you paid me.

"Thanks." I don't encourage him, one or two words are enough.

He clucks his tongue. "Is it a love letter?"

"Doubt it," I say, marching off, shoving the letter into my satchel.

Hoping my skirt isn't riding my backside.

◆

On the bus, Moira's familiar scrawl makes me smile. We've been writing ever since she left Dorton.

Thursday Night 10pm

Hiya, Katie.

Did I tell you what God-awful teachers I have? Yes, I know, I tell you every time I write. Talk about old cows! And I thought it was bad at Shawhurst! Still, at least it's a mixed state school, so we don't have to say 50 Hail Marys a day or go to confession.

So when are you coming to visit your bestest friend EVER??!!
We haven't seen each other for three whole years. I don't think your Biddy likes me anymore, or I'd be back in Dorton like a shot.

I think I'm in love. (Again.) His name's Aled Rhydderch. (Try getting your mouth around THAT one.) HA! Do I have a dirty mind, or what?!

Phone me from Ingrid's and I'll tell you all about it.

We've got to start thinking about college, baby. I'm thinking about applying to U.W.I.S.T.*—Hey, Kateeeee, move to Cardiff! There are a TON of colleges here. We could share a bedsit or a flat or something. Wouldn't that be a total gas?

Luv Moi

XXXXXX

P.S. *University of Wales Institute of Science and Technology, you moron.

A thrill nips me in the stomach. That's what I'll do! I'll work my brains out to get good grades and I'll go to catering college in Cardiff and I'll share a flat with Moira and—and wouldn't that be the most fabulous thing to do in the world?

◆

The Domestic Science exam didn't go too badly. Mrs. Washington said my quiche had "good color," and the texture of the crust was spot-on. Mushrooms would have been a nice addition, Kate dear, but well done all the same. Mmmm tasty. Excellent choice of cheese. Are we thinking of a career in the Domestic Sciences?

We could well be, but Biddy would go crazy, because when she's asked, "How's young Kate doing at school?" her answer is, "Oh, very well indeed. My daughter plans to study languages at university."

Nudge, nudge. "Mum," I remind her, "I'm best at Domestic Science—you know, Home Economics."

And when we get back home, she asks, "Do you *have* to show me up like that, Kate? Will you stop talking about *Domestic Science* like a dumb-cluck?"

God. Biddy thinks catering is some low-life job. I have more choices than she ever had, she says. She was never given the opportunity to attend university. Oh no, Shauna was the apple of *her* mother's eye, the only one funded for college, the favorite daughter.

"You'll attend a university and study languages," says Biddy.

"Just because I got a B+ for Latin? Doesn't mean I like it."

Who's singing my name?

"Kat-ie, Kat-ie, Kat-ie."

"Katie, come back to earth, dear."

It's Mrs. Washington.

"Girls, you all did a fine job. Your quiches were wonderful. Now let's make our tables super-tidy and spick and span. You have fifteen minutes to clear up before the lunch bell."

"Sit by me at lunch?" asks Ingrid Beddoes.

"Course," say I.

The school canteen smells of boiled cabbage, as always. We sit at a table with Jenny Doyle, Veronica Scott, Jill Mowbry—and Val Hickey, who starts whispering in Ingrid's ear behind a cupped hand.

"So will you come?" she asks, sitting up, helping herself to a spoonful of peas.

Ingrid puts an arm around my neck. "Only if Kate is invited, too."

I don't know why, but the other girls started getting really mean when I put on a few pounds.

In Netball they call me *thunder-thighs.* In History they offer to get me another chair for the second cheek of my bottom. When Sister Philomena asks who'll be the Wife of Bath with *a foot-mantel aboute hir hipes large—joly as a pye,* miss, miss, they say, Kate will!

Since Moira left, Ingrid is the only real friend I have at school.

Val wrinkles her nose and looks me up and down.

I make circles in a scatter of salt with my finger.

"Okay," she sighs. "The party starts at seven o'clock this Friday, at my house. The old folks will be gone till midnight."

I have nothing to wear.

"I've asked a crowd of boys from Brayminster High to come."

Nothing to wear at all. I'm serious. I could have worn a nylon sweater, a powder-blue one, but when I pressed it last week, I melted a hole in the middle. I had to scrape hard stuff off the iron with a bread knife.

Biddy cut off the sleeves, made short ones, and used the leftover bits to patch the front. It will do to wear with my jeans, she said, because no, they can't buy me a new sweater. Daddy and she have enough to fork out already. A new uniform costs a hundred pounds every six months. *A hundred pounds, Kate.*

Ingrid bodges me with her elbow. "Eat your Spotted Dick, Katers. I want to smoke a quick fag behind the bike sheds."

Picking up my spoon, I delve into the raisin-infested sponge.

And I eat the whole lot.

CHAPTER 9

Wednesday, May 22

The Hit or Miss TV show is over and the panel voted the new record
"Judy in Disguise (With Glasses)" a miss. Well, I think it's great. I can't get it
out of my head.

So I'm singing away when I decide I'd better say good night to Biddy and
Dad before I go to bed.

"We're thinking of buying a shop, Kate."

What?

"A shop? What kind of shop?"

My parents have a spread of newspapers on the table. Biddy prods at a
tiny ad. "A baker's shop," she says.

Dad circles it carefully with his pen.

"Selling biscuits and buns and things?" I ask.

Funny. Biddy doesn't want me to do catering, but *she* wants to run a
bread shop.

I don't get it.

But it would be great practice for me. Hey—I could make stuff to sell!

"Your mum could stop nursing." Dad hands me a bar of Fry's dark
chocolate.

"Thanks, Dad. Hey, Mum, I could make cakes! Suppose I made jam? Or
chutney. Can you imagine shelves full of jars and—"

"You'll have your schoolwork to concentrate on, my girl. I've been in the
medical profession for too long, and now I need a change. I deserve this,
don't I, Tom?"

"Yes, Biddy."

"You can work in the shop at weekends for pocket money," says Biddy. "But the shop will be *my* little project."

"It will be her little project," says Dad.

"Tom, I'll look at the shop tomorrow. I have two days leave from the hospital."

Oh heck, and in two days' time, it's the party.

"Mum, all the seniors are going to Val Hickey's house on Friday. Can I go?"

"Are boys invited?"

I've asked a crowd of boys from Brayminster High to come.

I shake my head. No.

"I don't see why not," says Dad.

Biddy folds up the newspapers and she looks at me, just like Val Hickey did. "Your hair is like two old curtains hanging each side of your face," she says. "Why don't you have it cropped short? And a perm would dry up some of that grease."

"Okay."

I'll try anything.

"I'll make an appointment at my hairdressers for Friday."

"Okay."

"*Yes, Mammy,* would sound so much better than 'okay,' Kate."

"Mum, I don't have anything to wear at Val Hickey's."

Biddy has on this new sweater that's cream at the top and black at the bottom with three-quarter sleeves. She can't lend me anything, she says, because she's two sizes smaller than me. She stops to smooth her hand over her waist. But she does have a length of Crimplene upstairs. She was going to make herself a little skirt and jacket, but she could make me a dress instead.

Biddy can run dresses up in five minutes. She's pretty clever like that. I hope it's the coffee-colored fabric I saw, not the orange.

No, of *course* she means the coffee.

"Can you do three-quarter sleeves? Will you make it short?"

"I'll try my best."

"Thanks, Mum." I break my bar of Fry's dark chocolate in half to share with her, but she shakes her head and tells me I ought to be in bed.

I bound up the stairs. A haircut! A new dress! It's gonna be great! I wish my bosoms wouldn't bounce. They hurt like hell.

Friday, May 24

Biddy hasn't shown me the dress yet, it's to be a surprise, but now I'm about to meet her at *Posh Perms* hair salon in Dorton.

The pong of ammonia greets me when I open the door. A girl behind the counter stops writing in a ledger and lifts her head.

"Name please."

I tell her, and she uses her pen to point over at Biddy, who sits in the corner wearing a plastic cap full of holes. Wisps of hair have been pulled through, and they're tinted yellow.

I wave, and she curls a finger at me.

I'm introduced to Sadie in pink overalls, who'll be doing the cut and perm, dear, and who's the lucky one being treated to a brand new hairdo by their mum today? And won't we soon look lovely?

I drop my satchel, shed my blazer, cardigan, and tie, and turn in my shirt collar. I'm wrapped in a cape and told to sit in the chair by the window. I ask Sadie, who's already poised with the scissors, if I could please have one of those trendy styles with long bits left at the back and little sideburn-things cut at an angle?

"Sadie, don't you let her have any tendrils." Biddy is bent over a sink having her hair shampooed—how the heck can she hear what I'm saying?

"Mums always know best, don't they?"

Sadie's a bit of a twit, if you ask me.

I watch as my hair falls to the ground. Masses of it. Oh God, oh God, oh God. It's not looking good, it's not looking good.

Calm down, Kate, she hasn't finished yet.

Clip, clip, clip, the scissors and Sadie's fingers work fast.

Hold still, she says, close your eyes, look up, look down, bend your head.

Then there's a buzz of razor. A razor?

And it's over. The deed is done.

"Shows your jawline," quips Sadie.

What jawline?

I swallow away panic and tears. She's given me a *fucking* man's haircut.

"Now for a nice soft perm." And because Biddy is deaf and hotly crimson under a dryer, she yells, "What do we think, Mum?"

I want to die.

Biddy's eyebrows shoot up to her forehead, her eyes widen, and her smile is crazy. "Nice," she mouths.

Who's she trying to kid? God Almighty.

My hair is tugged and wound and wrenched around a million curlers, and then a perm solution stinking to high heaven is dabbed all over.

A pile of *Woman's Own* magazines is plonked onto my lap. "Tea or coffee, miss?" asks the Ledger Girl with the pen.

◆

Half an hour later, Sadie asks, "Are we cooked yet?" We must be, because she douses me with neutralizer. Then I'm put under a dryer as Biddy is led from hers. Her new bleached bits look fabulous.

And me? I hold on to a twinge of hope that the perm will save my day. Well, it bloody didn't.

◆

Biddy is mad because I won't talk as we climb up Bryre Hill Lane. I can't talk. I'm in shock.

Thank God Barry Finch doesn't live in the fourth house to the right, the one with the iron gate, anymore. He'd die if he saw me now. He'd die laughing.

He took handfuls of my hair and said, babe.

Unreal.

Clip-clop. Biddy's smart heels are as sharp as her mood. "There's no need to hang a puss," she says. "Stop pouting, would you? It doesn't suit you one bit."

It's the haircut that doesn't suit me. Let's be bloody honest here.

As soon as Biddy opens the door, I head for the phone. I have to call Ingrid—there's no way I'm going to that party tonight. I'm about to lift the receiver when Biddy says, "You've hardly spoken a word to me, and now you'll expect to see the dress I spent hours thumbing together, won't you?"

I bite my lip. I could wear the coffee-colored dress with a pair of cream tights and the brown suede boots Aunt Shauna gave me, the ones Josie couldn't get her feet into anymore.

And after this, after this—

After this day, I will grow my hair long again, and starve myself.

I follow Biddy up to the spare bedroom where she keeps her sewing machine. "Here's your dress," she says.

Not only is it a *fluorescent* orange, it has a sort of bubbly texture to it, like unburst blisters.

Clearing my throat, I say, "Mum, I thought it would be a brown dress."

I point to the coffee material draped over an armchair.

"That's my fabric," says Biddy.

That's her fabric. The blistered orange is mine.

"Try it on," she says.

I take it to the bathroom.

"I made it a decent just-below-knee length," shouts Biddy. "Daddy's home, I'm going to make a cup of tea. I didn't hear any thank-yous, Kate."

I can't bear to pull the thing over my head.

◆

When Dad sees my hair, he says, "Never mind, Katie, you could wear a little hat," and I burst out crying.

When Biddy arrives with a tray of tea, she says, "Will you just look, Kate's weeping again. The tear is very near her eye, isn't it? What's the matter now?"

Pulling at the scouring pad I have on my head, I blame *her* for letting *Posh Perms* do this to me.

"She's so ungrateful, Tom, and what do you do about it? Nothing."

"Dad, the dress is horrible. I'm not kidding." I hold it up by the shoulders for him to see.

I catch a one-second flash of sympathy in Dad's face before Biddy darts a "You ungrateful little bitch" at me. She slams the tray down onto the ottoman, and Dad leaps over to tip the slopped tea back into the cups.

"Working all night, not sleeping a wink, sewing her a dress with top-stitching and finished princess seams, and did you hear what she said, Tom?"

The dimples appear on Dad's chin and he tells me to: "Wear the dress, Kate. It's a very pretty color."

And when I say I'd rather die, Biddy screams, "Get out of my sight."

And then they're both shouting at me. All I see are snapping mouths, wagging tongues, and clenched teeth.

Any minute now, I'll be sent to my room.

You would never think I was seventeen.

"How dare you speak to us like that—we're your *parents,*" yells Dad. "Get upstairs, NOW."

◆

It always happens this way. I tear up to my room after a row, and I vow I'll stay there forever. I'll hear them downstairs going through the scene over and over. I'll hear Biddy saying, then she said this, then she said that, and so I said to her—. And after a while, Biddy will sob and run into the hall, and Dad will tear after her saying, Biddy, Biddy, don't torment yourself, she's not worth it.

And Biddy will cry out to Mary, dear Mother of God, Sister of the Angels.

And I will creep downstairs, where I know I will find my mother back in the kitchen, weeping over the sink with a soggy tea towel clutched in her hands. And Dad will have an ashtray on the Formica table with three stubs in it. He'll be onto his fourth cigarette, and I will see his worry lines, one, two, and three, but the dimples on his chin will fade when he sees me, because he knows I've come down to say sorry.

"I'm sorry, Mum."

I am very sorry to have sinned against thee, and with the help of thy grace, I will not sin again.

And we hug and we both cry and Dad says, Kate, go and wash your face, wear the dress your mother made for you. Go to the party and enjoy yourself. You'll have fun with all the girls.

Don't ever think we don't love you.

Dad drops me off at Ingrid's farm, and I walk over the dry cow muck and knock on the kitchen door.

"Don't say a word," I say when Ingrid opens the door.

She grabs me by the hand and runs me up the stairs. I tell her everything, and she starts laughing. She collapses flat on her bed, and her bobbed hair falls like the Virgin Mary's halo around her head.

"Oh, poor, poor Katers."

Well, I'm standing there in my raincoat, and when I loosen the belt, she screams.

"Good Lord, Kate, where did you get that bloody awful dress?" And she screams some more. "Everyone will think you're a Belisha beacon."

"Yeah, a flippin' flashing orange light."

Ingrid pulls at my hair, and I tell her to cut it out because she can't stretch it, for God's sake.

We search through Ingrid's closet, but nothing will fit me. So she sneaks into her mother's room and comes back with this neat cheesecloth smock and a pair of jeans. My tummy bulges over the waistband a bit, but the smock is long enough to cover everything. I smear on Candle Glow makeup and do a major job on my eyes. Then Ingrid has a brainwave, and she runs out of the bedroom and comes skipping back with a cream scarf. We wrap it around my head gypsy-style, and pull out a few fuzzy curls around my ears.

Okay, I say, I'll brave the party.

Ingrid is absolutely fabulous-looking, of course, with her soot-black hair, little green blouse, and black miniskirt.

"Let's hurry," she says. "A bus is due in ten minutes."

◆

It could be worse. The other girls are too busy chatting up the boys to say much about my Romany getup. Of course, all the boys ignore me, but I can hardly blame them.

But I watch, and smile when I should, and laugh when I should, and drink cider, and I hide in a corner until Ingrid forces me to dance with her.

I've never danced before. I try to copy Ingrid, but my knees won't bend when I want them to and my feet won't shuffle through the shag pile like hers do.

"Loosen up, Katie!"

So I try stomping to the Beatles as they sing "Chains," the sort you can't see.

◈

CHAPTER 10

Sunday, July 28

THE BREAD SHOP
UNDER NEW MANAGEMENT

Wide variety of breads: white, brown, wholemeal, granary, batch, cottage, French, tin, milk, malt, rye, currant, caraway, farmhouse, and butter-rich brioche.

Sponge cakes for special occasions: chocolate, vanilla, orange, or lemon, covered with a soft icing. Choose your own fillings: fruit, double cream, or butter cream. Or how about a seasonal fruitcake made with real brandy (optional), covered with marzipan (optional), and royal icing?

Please allow ten working days from order to delivery date.

I'm reading Biddy's advertisement in the *Dorton News*, the local rag. I wish it also said, *Taste our jams. Apricot and almond, blackberry and apple, or how about a pear and ginger, or potted raspberry?*

I have a huge scrapbook full of recipes for preserves. I cut them from the magazines Biddy brought back from the hospital when she resigned. But I'm still not allowed to make anything for the shop.

All the bread and cakes and stuff are bought ready-made from a bakery and grocery warehouse.

I work here at weekends. I still can't believe Biddy trusts me to look after the shop all by myself on Sundays, but she does. The shop is painted the same green as a Laura Ashley store with green-striped awning, and the counters and shelves are made of pine, and there are baskets everywhere.

When customers come in and exclaim, why, hello, Nurse Cadogan, so she's working here instead of the cottage hospital now? Good morning, Mrs. Bootsby-Smythe, says Biddy, well actually, she resigned from the medical profession to *purchase* this business.

Biddy has started confiding in me when we're alone in the shop. She's forever moaning about Dad. She looks around first, makes sure no one's listening, then she's off. Daddy has never earned enough to support a family, she tells me, never earned much of a salary. Think he'd make some sort of effort, but no, he watches everyone else get promoted right in front of his nose, and what does he do about it? Nothing. All her married life, she's had to work her fingers to the bare bone.

Oh, yes, Kate, she goes on, a week after they married, he took her to Llandafan to meet Mamgu and Griff for the first time, and her heart fell into her shoes when she saw where he came from. A tiny house, Kate, joined in a row with others. No front yard, and a dirt garden. And where had Biddy come from? A farmhouse in Cloondray in Ireland, with a hundred and fifty acres of pastureland and wheat fields, seventy head of cattle, and a bull. Over two hundred sheep and three rams.

And eight fat sows.

No boar? Poor sows, I said, and boy did I get a dirty look.

"Miss, miss. Yoo-hoo!"

A customer bangs coins on the glass display case. I toss the *Dorton News* under the counter and say in my shop voice, "Good afternoon, may I help you?"

"Six bath buns, please. Big ones."

Of course, I'm having a devil of a job resisting the Eccles cakes, the garibaldis, the jam donuts, and the custard slices. Oh, and would I die for a lump of lardy cake with a cup of tea right at this very minute.

But I'm on a diet. And this is what forced me to take action:

For one thing, since Barry Finch, no boy has looked at me twice. Which is probably why Dad approves of me being plump. Not to worry, he says. I'm still his little girl.

"Oi, miss, I want to order a birthday cake. I want something real special for my grandson's third birthday."

"We have a brochure. Let me fetch it for you."

What *really* forced me to go on a diet was when Gabby Coles sang, "Kate Cadogan has blubber and zits, frizzy hair and big tits," in the school library. Yeah, not nice.

I asked Biddy if I was as pretty as her before I got fat. She fluttered her eyelids and smiled, showing the gap in the middle of her two front teeth. Kate, she said, you take after your father's side.

Whatever that means.

Still, I've lost eight pounds so far. I'm preparing for Cardiff, for catering school. And won't a bomb drop when Biddy finds out.

"Miss, I don't like any of these cakes, here." My customer slops her head to one side and twists her mouth. "I wanted something real special."

"Your grandson is three? How about this one?"

Nope, her head keeps shaking. "Like I said, I want something real special."

"What does he like? Cars? Rockets?"

"He loves sausages, he does. With fries and baked beans."

My customer beams at me, showing pink gums, no teeth. "You'll know what to do, love. Make me a nice cake. Go and get your order book. My name's Beatrice McGee."

And she spells out her name and says she'll be back on Wednesday, the seventh of August, and she'd like the chocolate sponge cake with orange butter-cream filling.

"He loves sausages," she reminds me as she backs out of the shop clutching her bag of bath buns.

It's been a hot, hot morning, and it's two o'clock, thank God, and time to shut shop. I bundle the takings into a cloth bag to shove in the safe. Licking two stamps, I press them onto two envelopes, one a letter for Moira, the other an application to the Cardiff College of Food and Technology.

I'll post them tomorrow.

After I've boxed the unsold cakes and bread, I do a quick check in the mirror before I lock up. My hair has grown an inch, and the perm frizz has calmed down. Oh, how I would love one of those pageboy styles.

I can but dream.

Another ten pounds to lose, another six inches of hair to grow.

◆

"You've completed an application for *where*? Tom, did you hear what Kate said? Tom, didn't I ask you to take out the rubbish?"

Dad walks in a small circle, not knowing what to do first.

"You'll do languages, Kate. I'm not paying fees for you to learn how to stir a sauce for three years. Tom, put your good jacket away. Isn't it still hanging across the back of the chair since we got back from Mass this morning?"

Biddy says Cordon Bleu is nothing more than a fancy sauce dribbled over a piece of meat the size of a half-crown.

"I might get a scholarship, Mum."

"Oh, will you now? We'll see."

"Katie, where is this college?" asks Dad.

"Cardiff."

"What's wrong with Brayminster College?"

"She wants to be with that Moira Murphy, Tom."

Dimples pepper Dad's chin. "You're still young, Katie. You might like to live at home."

"Cardiff has the best courses, Dad," I lie.

To change the subject, I show Biddy the Celebration Cake order book. Look, eight orders, I say. Good for a Sunday.

What's this penciled in at the back here, says Biddy. Why is it crossed out? Oh, Beatrice McGee? She changed her mind, I say.

You'll know what to do, love, said Beatrice McGee. *Make me a lovely cake.*

And I will. I'll show Biddy what I can do.

Wednesday, August 7

I've lost another two pounds already, I swear. "The hair" doesn't look half as bad sitting on a thinner face. My thighs don't look like porridge, and life would be absolutely, fabulously wonderful if—

—if *only* I'd got higher grades for maths and physics. Any hope of a scholarship has piddled down the drain.

Which means I have to convince Biddy I'm worth paying for. And how will I do that?

Well, I took two more secret orders. I went to the baker's myself and bought chocolate, lemon, and vanilla sponge cakes with soft icings, and I bought a wad of fondant, some marzipan, and a few little vials of color.

I told Dad a girl needs her privacy, so could I please have a lock on my bedroom door? I was lucky—he actually obliged, despite Biddy fretting about him spoiling the good door.

Anyway, I worked on the cakes in my bedroom for three nights, kept everything clean with white sheets. For Beatrice McGee, I turned the top of her cake into a plate, with a tiny checkered border. I added marzipan sausages, fondant fries, orange jellybeans. I made a crown with Rowntree's fruit gum jewels for Mrs. Rainbow, who said her daughter was a "proper little princess," and the third cake was a fondant lady sitting in a bubble bath, naked. I had to go to a toy shop for the Cindy tub. That cake was for a secretary's roommate, a Miss Jones, who worked in the insurance offices opposite the Bread Shop.

Ingrid will turn up any minute now to help me carry my boxed cakes to Dorton. I can't wait to see Biddy's face.

A horn *beep-beeps* outside. Ingrid passed her driving test and she's allowed to borrow her mum's black Mini. And the three cakes fit perfectly in a row along the back seat.

"Katers, I landed the place at Cardiff Uni. Do you realize what this means?"

"Holy cow! You, me, Moira—together again?"

"Right on!"

We sing "Mrs. Robinson" like idiots the rest of the way to Dorton village.

And when we arrive, there is Beatrice McGee squatting on the stone step outside the Bread Shop, waiting. I give her a wave, and she comes waddling over, not taking much heed of the traffic.

"Afraid I couldn't wait, dear," she says, breathless. "I'm dying to see Billy's cake."

I lift the box lid and her face shines, and she claps her hands. Rifling through her purse, she tells me I deserve a little extra, love, for all my hard work. Here, here, take it, she says, shoving notes down the neck of my school shirt.

"Thank you so much, Mrs. McGee." I grin like a Cheshire cat. "I must give you a receipt. Shall we go back across the road?"

I see Biddy holding her hands to her eyes like they were binoculars. She disappears into the shop as soon as we reach the pavement.

"Hello, Mrs. Cadogan."

"Hello, Ingrid."

Ingrid places my other two cakes on the counter.

"Are you Kate's Mum?" asks Beatrice McGee. "Did you see what your daughter made for my Billy?"

"Very nice."

I look up from the receipt book, anxious to read Biddy's face, but her eyes tell me nothing.

I hand the receipt to Beatrice McGee, and she shuffles out with her cake. Silence.

Finally, Biddy speaks.

"I don't know about sausages. They looked more like two poops in a pot," she says, eyes angry, mouth smiling. "When did I give you permission to fill cake orders yourself, Kate? And what else do we have here?"

"Oh, they're just great, Mrs. Cadogan," says Ingrid, blushing bright red on my behalf.

And of course, the first box Ingrid just *has* to open is the naked lady sitting in a bubble bath with one leg up showing daintily painted toenails. Daintily painted nipples, too.

"Jesus, Mary, and Joseph."

I take it she doesn't like this one much, either, and my stomach churns.

"I'm ashamed to think a daughter of mine would produce something like this." She slaps back the lid, picks up my cake, and marches through the beaded curtains. I hear the clip-clop of her heels on the paved courtyard at the back, followed by the tinny clang of the dustbin.

Scrawling the word *princess* on a square of paper, I tape it to the remaining cake and head for the door. "Drive me somewhere, Ingrid, please. Anywhere."

And I'm glad my friend doesn't put her arm around me, because the tear is so very near my eye.

PART TWO

◆

THE SEVENTIES

CHAPTER 11

◆

1970

Friday, April 10
315 Corbydd Road, Broath, Cardiff, South Wales

A jumble of words bounces in my head, refusing to travel down my arm, through my pen, and onto paper. Here I am, trying to pull an essay together on the *id, ego, super-ego,* and all things phallic, when I have to pause and wonder: Why did I let Biddy push me into teaching?

I examine my chewed nails and the mangled end of my pen.

Kate, be a teacher, said Biddy, *not a skivvy-in-the-kitchen. Forget Cardiff College of Food, go to the University instead.* She whispered the word *university* with such reverence, you'd think she was referring to the Vatican.

Yes, Mrs. Bootsby-Smythe, Kate studies the sociology, physiology, and psychology of child development and education, no less.

And so, Moira's training to be a pharmacist, Ingrid a journalist, and me? A first and middle grade Domestic Science teacher, may the Lord help me. And the little kids drive me nuts. Apart from adding sweater fluff, grime, and snot to everything they make, I turn away for one second and they've plugged each other's ears with dough, stuck raisins up their noses, powdered their faces with flour, and—

—and my heart just isn't in this game and my grades are abysmal.

Trying to fathom out whether id goes with the anal phase or the genital, and when does life become oral? I watch patchouli fumes writhe around the living room of our flat.

"Moi," I yell, "if you don't get rid of this joss stick, I'll throw up, I swear!"

Moira comes flapping in like a bird to display her new poet's blouse. The winged sleeves are pretty generous.

"How do I look?"

"Wonderful," I say.

"What about the hair?"

The new shag cut really suits her. She's wearing purple flares with a huge belt resting on her hipbones.

"You look great, Moi."

"Come with us tonight, Katie. We'll have a fantastic time."

"Aw, shit, I can't. My essay is already three days late."

Ingrid clatters through the door carrying the ironing board. "Oh, sod your essay," she says. "Slade are playing at the Students' Union. You'd be crazy to miss them."

"Slade?"

"Yep, you know, that group from Birmingham with Noddy Holder."

Moira sits down in front of my armchair and rests her chin on my knees. "Tons of medical students will be there."

She knows about my present penchant for trainee doctors.

The iron hisses. "Bugger, it spat again!" says Ingrid. "Come on, Katie, I'll press your jeans for you."

Ingrid is one neat freak. She's the only one I know who presses jeans.

I snap my folder shut.

I give up trying to determine the similarities between a tube of toothpaste and a penis. What the heck has all this to do with the development of children anyway? I have all weekend to finish the essay.

In the kitchen, I fold bread over a slice of Caerphilly cheese and proceed to the bathroom to sort through my collection of hair tints. Tonight I'll wear my bleached jeans, the ones I split to sew in flowery inserts. The bells are *seriously* wide now.

"Moi," I yell, "will you trim my hair after I've washed it? I have a stack of split ends."

I have this great pageboy now, and it slants all the way down to the middle of my back. I raid the bathroom cabinet for all the stuff I'll need to look my best: baby lotion, razors, shadows, lipsticks, loose powder, and Aqua Manda perfume.

◆

At seven o'clock, we clatter out into the wet April evening on platform heels and skid over patches of oil that fan into rainbows.

Ah, this is Cardiff! With its smell of roasted hops, exhaust fumes, seaweed, and Indian curry—I love the place.

When I can, I take the train to visit Mamgu and Griff in Llandafan. I return to Dorton when Biddy says they haven't seen my face for *four* weeks, Kate, *four* weeks. When the phone in the kiosk dies, begging for more coins, I hear Dad in the background saying wait, don't go yet, he misses his little girl.

"Come on, Katers," says Ingrid, shaking her umbrella. "Are you with us? Returned from Wonderland yet?"

The double-decker pulls up with a whoosh of brakes. We toss coins into the mouth of the *Please Proffer the Exact Fare* box, and squash together on one seat because we have so much to say, so much to look forward to, and too much to laugh about.

This, I call freedom.

My parents: out of sight.

How I wish I could say: out of mind.

◆

When we enter Cardiff Students' Union, we're greeted with a crashing beat of drums. Our hands are rubber-stamped with the words *Piss Out,* so we can make visits to the bathroom.

Male students huddle together in corners, in frayed jeans and sleeveless vests. Thin and bearded, their hair straggles down their backs. A gathering of Jesuses.

"Let's grab a drink," says Moira.

"Wonder who'll be the first to get off with a bloke tonight." Ingrid is already surveying the goods.

I don't see many student teachers here.

And I've had my share of *those.* They don't tend to hang around for long. You see—I won't let them inside my pants. *What do you want, a fucking wedding ring?*

"What do you want, Kate?"

"Kat-ee, what do you *want?*"

"Yikes, sorry Moi, Ingrid. I was miles away."

We order cider because it's cheap and served in a tall glass.

What I want—is a soul mate. Forever and ever love.

"Hi, what's your name?"

What I want—is passion.

"HI THERE! What's your name?"

"Hey, Kate!" Moira flaps her hand in my face and whispers, "The rather gorgeous man standing to your left is dying to know your name."

My eyes meet his sleepy ones. Such pale eyes. He has a short, fine nose and his hair is a blond floss, parted in the middle. Tidy beard, maroon shirt, new jeans.

"I'm Kate."

"Jack," he says, taking my hand and touching it with a kiss.

Slipping my fingers away, I curl them into a fist, then I cover my mouth and cough, hoping it looks natural, not wanting to offend.

"Let's go, then," I say to Ingrid and Moira. "We're missing Slade."

I hear them trotting behind me asking, didn't she like him? Why not? Looked okay to me.

"Come on, you two. He's not my type, that's all!"

The floorboards are bouncing when we arrive. Wearing top hats and stacked heels, Slade are going at it full gusto, devouring the microphones, filling the hall with a pulsating beat. We finish our ciders, then throw our handbags to the floor and start gyrating with the crowd. We dance alongside one another, never together, bobbing on the spot, and with a swerve of hip, we swing to reach a new space, fill a gap, becoming part of an ever-shifting mass.

Through the strobe light I see the flickering image of Ingrid lighting a cigarette in slow motion, I see Moira's hair spread and fall, her beads loop and float, and I sweep my hand up, down, watching my fingers multiply—and suddenly they are locked, clasped—

By Jack.

He drops my hand and short-steps in circles, it's called the Turkey, he says, and I think, *What a prize idiot,* and then I laugh, because it's the funniest thing I've seen for ages. The more I laugh, the crazier he becomes. He strides a tango with an imaginary partner, and his finale is a spinning pirouette.

And Slade sing, "Cum On, Feel the Noize."

CHAPTER 12

◆

Saturday, July 11
Penbarth Beach

"How long?"

"Three months and one day exactly." Jack turns over onto his stomach and I smell peaches and pears on his breath as he kisses me.

"So we're going steady?" I ask.

He smiles and answers with another kiss.

Ash and charcoal lie inside a circle of stones where we burned a fire. We toasted marshmallows skewered with driftwood sticks, bit into fruit, pulled at the crust of French bread.

The sea breathes in, then out, as the tide takes it away, and I let my head sink onto a soft cushion of sand. I play with razor sharp grass, letting it rasp through my fingers. I close my eyes and feel the sun baking my bare skin.

"When will you let me?" Jack traces a finger down the length of my nose, over my mouth, under my chin, along my neck, down, down, between my breasts. He sits up to walk two fingers over my stomach and his hand flattens to nudge its way further, further.

The tingle turns to a burn to a sweep of pleasure, to a surge of panic and I jump to my feet, and I brush the sand off my body, my movements frantic.

"Kate?" Jack pulls me back down and takes my face in his hands. "What's the matter?"

"I want it to be special."

"What could be more special than this?"

"I need time, Jack, I'm nineteen, you're twenty-seven, I've never—"

"I love you."

"I love you, too."

"When?"

I've got to do it sometime, haven't I?

Taking a deep breath, I say, "The weekend after next. When Moira and Ingrid are away visiting parents."

And I squeeze Biddy's face out of my mind.

Tuesday, July 14

Why do I bother taking notes? It's all gobbledygook as far as I'm concerned. Learning Piaget's theory will be a great bonus, I'm sure, if I survive this course and end up teaching kids how to boil eggs. I'm sitting by the window in the lecture room, studying the sky and wondering how many blues there are in a paint box. Prussian, indigo, cobalt . . .

"The concrete operational stage is the third stage in Jean Piaget's theory, a stage typically occurring between the ages of seven and twelve years old. During this stage, the child begins to reason logically, even organize his or her thoughts coherently. However—Miss Cadogan? Are you with us? Do you think you could organize *your* thoughts, and let me believe I'm not wasting my time? Thank you so much." Cough. "This stage is also characterized by a loss of egocentric thinking. During this stage, the child has the ability to master most types of conservation experiments and begins to understand reversibility."

Ho hum.

Of paramount significance to me at the moment is that I'm about to lose my virginity. The weekend after next, to be precise.

Barley and vegetable casserole. That's what I'll make, because Jack's a vegetarian. Candles. I'll turn the lights low, play James Taylor. I'll wear the burgundy mididress I made last year. White tights? Black patent shoes. Soft pillows on the floor to remind me of that dreamy day in the sand dunes.

Must buy more Aqua Manda.

"The concrete operational stage is also characterized by the child's ability to coordinate two dimensions of an object simultaneously, arrange structures in sequence and perhaps Miss Cadogan would like to complete my lecture for me?"

God, so what's the difference between school and college? Teachers, professors, they're all the bloody same. All eyes are on me and I feel an utter fool. I chew on my pencil and my eyes dart over the textbook, trying to find where Prof. Owen left off. Oh, help me, please, Virgin Mary, Mother of God— although, why should she? I won't be a member of her club for much longer.

Found it! I clear my throat. "—arrange structures in sequence, and transpose differences between items in a series."

Phew.

The bell drones and it's time for lunch. Chairs scrape, and the silence is broken with the singsong of Welsh accents from the valleys, from the North, the odd twang of Cardiff itself, and a few broad English. Yorkshire, Newcastle, Bristol.

Dai Morgan catches up with me—*God,* he looks just like Cat Stevens.

"Going to the Union tonight?" he asks.

"I can't," I say. "Prof. Owen told me to rework my Freud essay. He wants it finished by tomorrow."

"Just say everything in society is designed to look like a prick."

He's thrilling, sort of dangerous almost.

But I love Jack.

"I'll help you with your essay," says Dai.

"Another time, maybe?"

I *do* love Jack. Safe, comfortable, funny Jack. Dependable, twenty-seven-year-old Jack, a mature student, who will be a fully-fledged *doctor* in two years' time.

Dai shrugs, and I'm left watching his long legs stride into the college canteen.

Nah. With him, I'd be no more than a one-night stand.

And I need much more than that.

Saturday, July 18

At nine o'clock, Jack's at the door, wearing shorts and a striped T-shirt. I'm all dressed up in a skirt and blouse. I thought this was a special day. I hide my disappointment and gabble on about breakfast, has he eaten yet? Well, does he want coffee or toast? Eggs—we have eggs. Ingrid's mum sent eggs from the farm.

"Shh." He pecks at my lips and tells me not to be nervous.

Nervous?

"I'm just getting a prescription, that's all," I reply.

For The Pill.

"You'll be examined first, but it won't hurt."

He's almost a doctor, silly, I tell myself. Of course he'd know.

He winks. "Wish I could do it myself."

"Let's go," he says.

"Bye Ingrid, bye Moira, I'll be back in an hour or so."

"Have fun," they shout.

I haven't told them where we're going.

Jack links my arm and takes me to his car. "In you hop," he says.

Someone has written *Clean Me* on his windscreen.

The wipers flick left then right, making two clean semicircles for us to look through. We pull out, and the gears whine as we gather speed to turn onto the main North Road.

After five silent miles, we arrive at the hospital. Jack doesn't stop to read the signs, he knows where to go, he says. And I'm thinking, well, if I'm to be examined, then it's a good job I decided to wear a skirt because I won't have to take much off. We swerve into a driveway that leads to a flat building and he nods at the double doors meaning, *off you go*. But he's coming with me, isn't he, I ask, and he says no, I'll be fine, he has some errands to do, he'll be back in exactly sixty minutes, waiting in this very spot.

He pinches my nose, and tells me he'll bring back a surprise, just a little one, because he has something far more important to give me next weekend.

I wanted us to do this together, but I smile and nod anyway.

◆

"Name?"

"Kate Cadogan."

"Middle initial?"

"M."

"Date of birth?"

"October the seventh. 1951."

"How's your menstrual cycle?"

"Fine, thank you."

She looks up and clicks her pen against her bottom teeth.

I get a cynical smile. "Regular, irregular, when was your last period?"

"Regular, um, just finished."

"A date would be good."

"Fourteenth of July."

"Take a seat. Your name will be called."

My form is slapped on top of others in a wire tray. "Next!"

I recognize many faces from college. We acknowledge each other with half-smiles and averted eyes.

I'm hating this.

Twenty minutes have passed, and I'd get A-plus if I were tested on the various forms of contraception available—and their dependability. I've read the damned booklet five times now. I start again from the beginning.

- *Abstinence*
- *Cap*
- *Condoms*
- *Diaphragm*
- *IUDs*
- *Natural*
- *The Pill*

"Kate Cadogan?"

- *Sterilization.*

At last.

A nurse with big white legs says, "Follow me," and I'm to strip off behind the curtain over there, then pop this gown over my head and make sure the ties are at the front.

I make three perfect bows, but as soon as I "Hop onto the examining table, luvvie" she pulls them open. "I hear Doctor Duffy coming," she says, cocking her head.

Thank God it's a she who bursts through the door and announces: "We'll check *up top* first, dear."

I guess *down below* comes later. She reminds me of Miss Kendrick, my old school headmistress. She has that same sort of bulldog-look, the same blond hair on her arms.

"Do you have a boyfriend?" asks Dr. Duffy as she kneads my breasts.

"Yes."

"Have you had sexual intercourse with this young man?"

Kate, did you have sexual intercourse with this young man? asked Miss Everett.

"We just, we, I, but, then . . ." What I say comes out like a burble.

"Did the young man use contraceptives?" Dr. Duffy snaps on gloves and her eyes examine the ceiling as her fingers examine me.

Miss Everett snapped her fingers. Did the young man use contraceptives?

"Small speculum, please, nurse."

Holy Mother of God, whispered Biddy. Please forgive her, Father Flannagan.

The doctor's fingers leave me. I am so glad.

Mum, I didn't let him do anything.

"Intercourse has not taken place," I mumble.

Is that how I'm supposed to say it?

"Would you like to speak with our counselor, dear? You seem uncertain, undecided. Are you ready for a sexual relationship?"

I can't answer. I try, but only manage a squeak, so I shake my head, then nod. No and yes.

"But we don't want to get pregnant, do we? Not at nineteen. Flop your legs open, that's the girl."

What Dr. Duffy holds now looks like pair of curling tongs.

"You'll feel a little discomfort and—"

—and it hurts like hell when she cranks it open.

"There we are, all done." The metal slides out. "Well, you appear to be nice and healthy. Were you thinking of The Pill?"

I was thinking, let me get out of this place, but I say yes, I was thinking of The Pill, and I'm certain there's no history of thrombosis in the family.

◆

Outside the clinic, I wait for Jack, who's late. I'm clutching a paper bag full of leaflets, a prescription, and a packet of condoms, which must be worn by the young gentleman, dear, for one month until it is safe enough to rely on The Pill alone.

And finally, Jack shows up, waving something at me through the car window.

He lays a box of After Eight dinner mints in my hand, those wafer thin chocolates filled with peppermint cream. And I wonder, am I truly ready to be another man's little girl?

CHAPTER 13

◆

Saturday, July 25

Damn, Ingrid took her James Taylor LP with her. I scatter the records over the carpet in the living room and kneel over them looking for something else.

Apprehension clutches at my stomach, the same sort of feeling I get before exams. The clinic experience last Saturday threw me. All of us sitting there, waiting to be fixed up. This is the seventies, baby. Free love, equality for women, it's not just the men who get to sow the wild oats anymore.

Ugh.

But, I want forever and ever love.

I know which record I'll play. "Baby I'm-a Want You."

The voice of Bread's lead singer soothes.

The barley and vegetable casserole is in the oven and the supermarket plonk cools in a bowl of water. I wish we had a fridge. I bought a massive bunch of flowers; they cost me forty-five pence because they were past the sell-by date. I snipped all the slimy bits off the stems and stuck them in an enamel jug. I just hope it doesn't leak over the table I shone with spray polish—it's so glossy, you can see the reflection of the yellow and orange chrysanthemums in it.

I ought to run my bath.

Mark my words. If a boy wants to do it before marriage, it means he has no respect for you. And you'll never see him again after he's had his way. Am I right, Tom?

You're right, Biddy.

I pour a stream of sandalwood oil in the tub and scented steam puffs into my face.

◆

After my bath, I wrap myself in a towel and wander into the kitchen to gulp the last drop of red wine Ingrid left behind on the counter. The barley's cooked, the vegetables are tender, and everything is ready too damned soon. And Jack won't be here for another hour. I shake vinegar and cooking oil together in a jam jar for salad dressing. That's all we can afford in this joint—

Joint.

We keep the stash hidden on top of Ingrid's wardrobe, in a cough drop tin.

In the kitchen, I tap the shrivelled weed onto a plate, and with finger and thumb, I pick out the seeds. With finger and thumb, I roll the paper. With finger and thumb, I put the joint between my lips and pull in deep, and hold, until the smoke wisps from my nose and into my eyes.

The oral phase begins at birth and lasts eight months, characterized by the infant's concern for her mouth and the gratification she feels from oral stimuli. Sucking, biting, swallowing.

Eating.

I shovel spoonfuls of Shreddies into my mouth, then check the time.

Apprehension continues to grip my stomach.

So I roll another joint.

I move to the living room to change the record, to hear Free sing "All Right Now."

Tightening the knot on my towel, I dance to the steady beat of guitar and drums, and my arms are reaching up, reaching up. That ivy on the wallpaper, it twists and twirls. So intricate, so detailed. Those berries, so real, I could pick them off, one by one.

A female undergoes a complex wherein she desires her father and rivals with her mother for her father's affections. Eventually, however, she will pass through the various complexes and begin to identify with the mother. This marks the end of the phallic phase. The genital phase follows the latent phase, which is similar to the anal phase, and Freud believed—

The doorbell rings. I pinch the end of the roach and leave it in Ingrid's ashtray. Peeping through the net curtains, I see Jack standing in the front yard. He's early and I'm not dressed. My burgundy outfit still lies waiting on the bed.

Matches nip, burning my fingers as I light the candles, and the doorbell rings again. Never mind, I can get dressed while Jack sips wine, relaxes, and listens to music.

And then we'll eat at the table that's so shiny, you can see the reflection of the yellow and orange chrysanthemums in it.

Our night will be perfect.

There are thirteen steps on this stairway before you reach the hall. I just counted them. God, that's so funny. Thirteen!

"Katie, look at you, you gorgeous creature." Jack buries his face in my hair and I giggle, because did he know that the genital phase is the longest of five stages of a child's development, according to Sigmund Freud?

"What have you been doing, you naughty girl?" He shakes his head as if to say, don't tell him, he knows already. He wants me to stop, curb the habit, because yes, smoking weed *is* as bad as smoking cigarettes.

No, he doesn't want me to recite the Act of Contrition in Latin. He'd like to go upstairs.

He leads me to the living room, and my towel is pulled off and then Jack sits cross-legged on the floor. His pale eyes drink me in before he pulls me down, then we're rolling, rolling, over the carpet that's covered with cabbage roses. He's on top of me, still in his jacket, still wearing his trousers.

"Katie, you smell delicious," he murmurs. The music stops. "Katie, Katie." His tongue crawls behind my ears, under my neck. His hands prowl, his fingers slither.

Jack pulls his hand away and reaches into the pocket of his cords. He takes out a little packet, the one I got from the clinic. And as I stare at the wallpaper, I hear the rustle of foil. And I feel pushing now, and a dull, then sharp pain, but it's soon over and I turn my head as Jack moves on me. Water is leaking from the jug and onto the table, and I count the drips of water as they plop onto the cabbage rose carpet.

We were to eat barley and vegetable casserole before this—happened. I would have worn my burgundy dress, and candlelight would have danced on our faces, and above soft music, I would have whispered, *Jack, I love you.*

"God! Katie!"

And with a groan, Jack rolls onto his back.

And the water still drips, and I weep with it, and then I shake with silent laughter.

Jack laughs too, says he won't allow me to smoke that stuff ever again, not now I'm *his* to look after and care for. From his jacket pocket, he takes out a tiny velvet box. He springs back the lid and inside I see a glint of diamonds surrounding a ruby. A ruby the same red as the spot of blood that stains the white towel I lie on.

Jack pinches my nose. "Here's the surprise I promised," he says.

"Are we engaged?"

"We're engaged."

And now—

Now I'm another man's little girl.

CHAPTER 14

◆

1972

Saturday, October 7
Room 2B, 350 Albion Road, Cynboyd, Cardiff

What should we buy for Katie's twenty-first? Kinky underwear of course, Moira and Ingrid told everyone they'd invited to the party.

I shall surely kill them.

God. Sometimes, I really miss living with my friends. I miss all the fun.

Our laughing brimmed over to hysteria as the Asti Spumante frothed and spilled down our arms. We were beautifully drunk by the time the first guests trickled in. The atmosphere buzzed as the rooms filled with more and more people, all carrying a plate of sausage rolls, sandwiches, or quiche.

And then the dancing began, and the music roared, and everything burst into a party.

A *real* party.

I heave a sigh.

Ah well, I'd better sort these gifts out. Separating the beautiful from the gaudy, I lay the lingerie in two drawers. I hope there aren't any moths in this crummy old chest. Jack insisted on furnishing the one room we share with "bargain antiques." I can't imagine where half the stuff came from. The road-side, most likely.

He's crazy like that.

I look over at the table and smile, because there's one last parcel sitting there, waiting.

Inside folds of tissue lies a long scarf with tassels, a sage paisley design on one side, lilac spots on the other. Cashmere and silk! So fine, it slithers through my fingers. God, I *love* it. Moira and Ingrid are the best—it must have cost heaps. And there's more. A pair of cotton panties, embroidered with a line of pastel-colored bumps.

What on earth?

I open the card to read Moira's handwriting.

> *We wanted to embroider*
> *Some panties just for Kate.*
> *We thought the words:*
> *DO NOT TOUCH*
> *Were most appropriate.*
>
> *Using threads of pink and blue,*
> *We knew we could not fail*
> *To make the panties pretty*
> *As we stitched away in BRAILLE.*

Priceless.

Bugger—I'm late! Snatching a glimpse at my watch, I grab my *Cosmopolitan* magazine. I rap my keys on the fish tank to say good-bye to Abbott and Costello, who pop their eyes and gobble frantically and damn, Jack keeps telling me I mustn't do that. He says our goldfish will die with fright one day. I slam the door to our room, *our home* until Jack qualifies as a doctor and I qualify as a bloody teacher.

❖

Sun bronzes the few leaves left clinging to the trees in Albion Road, and I crunch those that lie in the path of my boots. A very satisfying thing to do. *Crackle, scrunch, smash.* I'm twenty-one today! And thrilled to be spending my birthday weekend with my grandparents in Llandafan.

Jack had to leave for a course in London. He was so sorry he'd miss my twenty-first party, be away on my special day. I'm his sweetheart. He'll make up for it, he said, handing me a big fat tome on the history of Cardiff.

A book! I said. Your present, he smiled, and he blew a kiss in the air, and he'd better hurry. He'd see me on Monday.

The distant trill of a guard's whistle tells me I'd better sprint—I have two escalators to run down and ten minutes left to reach platform 9A.

But I make it.

I love the distant rumble of a train, and the warm breath of it against your legs as it wooshes along the platform. I love the sound it makes as it whines to a stop. I love the slam of doors, the clatter of feet on concrete. I love the way the train snakes along dark tracks until it bursts out into the light again. And you blink from the suddenness of it all, until your eyes become accustomed to the October skies. You sit there, on the dusty moquette and study the passengers that surround you. The businessmen, the mothers, the babies, the shop assistants, the teenagers, the pensioners.

You see the blank faces of those performing their honorable duty: leaving the city to spend the weekend with parents.

Which is what I must do next weekend.

I open my *Cosmopolitan*. There's a feature on the compatibility of birth signs. Let's see how Jack, Aries, and me, Libra, fare.

This combination is not a great one, since there's no room for such opposing temperaments in one household.

I must admit, living together in one room with a double bed, a rusty stove, a wardrobe, two chests, a table, and four chairs hasn't been easy. Pretending we're *not* living together hasn't been easy, either. Dad and Biddy would die if they knew. Thank goodness they've never taken it upon themselves to visit. Can't possibly leave the Bread Shop, says Biddy, not to those *amadáns*, those half-wits who claim to be shop assistants. God didn't grant them two brain cells to share.

The Aries love of leadership can intimidate the Libra and this may lead to some problems. Therefore, even if a relationship is possible, it probably won't last long.

Yikes. Who really believes in this stuff?

I read on.

Madame Zena Zodiac says Libra is the most sexual sign of the zodiac.

Sex. The first time was awful, but once I got used to it, I did learn to sort of like the closeness of it. I toss the magazine to one side.

No, everything is fine.

Two more stops to go and I'll be in Llandafan.

Talking of intimacy, when Jack and me visit Dorton, I tell him not to kiss me too often, because it makes Dad's worry lines appear on his forehead, and the dimples appear on his chin. Jack says my dad's just plain weird, but I say, not really. He'll get used to you, just give him time.

One more tunnel after this one. A rattle, a clatter, and again the train shoots out into the sharp light.

As for Biddy, well, she's enjoying herself. Not sure how much she likes Jack, hard to tell, but she tells all the Bread Shop customers that her daughter is engaged to a *doctor.* Yes, Mrs. Biddle, Mrs. Houghton-Davis, a doctor!

Even though he's still a medical student.

God! The passenger I'm sitting next to is driving me nuts, grinding her teeth on mints, one after the other. Here, my love, she says, please take one. Well, I do, not wanting to hurt her feelings. Am I crazy? Take two, she insists. Then gazing out of the window, she says, it's a pity winter is catching up on us, isn't it? Yes, I reply, it really is a pity.

Hmmm.

Biddy said it's a pity about Jack's looks. "Wouldn't you think he'd get a decent haircut? His hair is like floss so it is, standing an inch away from his head."

"He can't help that, Mum. His hair is fine. Anyway, he's a dish. Don't you think the new goatee suits him?"

"A lump of red meat would do him good," says Biddy.

"He's a vegetarian, remember?"

"What good is a handful of seeds and a few beans to a man? He should know better, being in the medical profession. He's anemic, so he is, and half-asleep from lack of iron. See this wooden spoon?" Biddy stopped stirring the gravy to hold it up for me to see. "He's thinner than this."

"Jack's watching his weight."

"Sure, and what's he left with? A woman's waist, that's what." Biddy grabbed the egg timer as a second visual aid.

One more stop to go before we reach Llandafan.

Visual aids. They're all the rage in schools now. Show the kids an object, a film, a 3-D graph. Forget numbers. Give them blocks and cubes and sticks instead. Think in pictures. W? What's a W? Why, it's the Wicked Watery Witch!

Witch.

Well, she can be. But I'm used to Biddy, I suppose. Smiles follow sneers, gentleness follows gibes—you know I love you, Kate. Spontaneous hugs follow spite. Arms will squeeze, then tug like a reprimand, insisting I squeeze back.

The engine whistles. Brakes hiss and the train pulls into Llandafan Station.

And there they are, waiting on the platform.

My grandparents.

Mamgu and Griff.

CHAPTER 15

◆

Llandafan, South Wales

There's Mamgu, her hair a rinsed lilac, her ample frame soft and round inside a gray coat and a dress sprigged with violets. I fall into the softness of her embrace, and I'm wrapped in her familiar scent of Imperial Leather soap and pear drops. "*Shwmae?*" she asks.

"I'm fine, Mamgu. How are you?"

"*Iawn.* Happy birthday, girl! By the way, your mam addressed her card to Llandafan. It's her writing on the envelope, anyhow."

"Welcome, *cariad.*"

Griff's false teeth click as he kisses me on the cheek, and I hug his bones. He's been stick-thin for as long as I can remember. He presses a brown paper bag into my hands, wishes me a happy birthday, and tells me he's bought me a pair of slippers.

But when I peer inside, I'm met with an oily fish smell.

"They're kippers, Griff, not slippers."

He laughs.

"Oh, you!" I say, swiping at him.

"*Twp,*" says Mamgu, scowling. "Stupid, that's what you are, Griff. He thinks he's a comedian. I bought the smoked herring for our supper tonight, Katie. I thought you'd like them."

Her accent rises and falls as she tells Griff to take my case. He points to a red telephone kiosk by the ticket office. "Mildreth, will you call Biddy to say Kate arrived safely?"

She shakes her head and reverts to Welsh as we leave the station. "*Cês i bryd o dafod mawr. Dw i erioed wedi cael pryd o dafod fel 'na o'r blaen.*"

Of course, I don't understand a word of it. The sum of my Welsh vocabulary amounts to fewer than thirty words. Griff limps over to my side as we walk along the first winding road that leads to their little terraced house. "Mamgu got a big telling-off from your mam."

"I'm finished with that woman," says Mamgu, raising her hands in the air. "All I said to her was, pity you and Tom can't join us for Kate's twenty-first birthday."

My parents don't fuss about birthdays. We exchange gifts and cards, but I can't remember any parties or anything. Well, not since I was five. I've never really thought much about it.

"Well, *bach,* I mean, it's a special birthday, your twenty-first."

"Being here in Llandafan is special," I say, squeezing Mamgu's hand.

"You know what your mam said? Who do you think *you* are, Mildreth, telling us what we should and shouldn't do?"

We're on the dirt track leading to a row of houses that nestle at the base of slate rock. Mamgu and Griff live in the fourth whitewashed house to the right, the one called *Ty Wen.*

Griff creaks open the brown front door and asks, "*Tisho panad?*"

Now, I do know what that means. "*Plîs,*" I say. Please.

Because there's nothing I'd like better than a cup of strong tea.

"No, Griff, I'll make the tea," says Mamgu. "You hang Kate's coat up, then take her case upstairs."

"Suit yourself," he says, pulling a face at me and winking.

"Come by the fire, Kate." Mamgu disappears into the pantry with the bag of kippers and comes back with a biscuit tin. "I made a batch of Welsh-cakes. Now if you reach for three plates, we'll sit and plan our day."

Two envelopes lie on the dresser, one big, one small. "These my cards?" I ask.

"*Ie.*"

I tear open Dad and Biddy's first. A loopy *With God's Wishes Too* trails across a sky above a thatched cottage. Biddy bought a box of these at the Immaculate Conception Bazaar last Christmas. Among the hollyhocks inside, she's written, *Love galore, Daddy and Mammy. Gift next weekend.*

The next card is covered with paintings of shells. Clustered together, they look so real, I have to touch them.

"I love it," I say.

"Griff's choice," says Mamgu. "She won't want shells, I told him. But he said, yes she will, Mildreth."

He knows I love everything about the beach, the sea, and the sand. As usual, there are pound notes tucked inside the card. A wad of them.

"This is too much, Mamgu."

"Quiet now. Pass me the cups and saucers."

I set the china down on the tablecloth that was made with bleached flour sacks. I see Mamgu has finished the edges with tiny cross-stitches since I was last here.

"This cloth looks really pretty now."

"I've just finished another big one. It's a late engagement gift for you and that boy."

My arms only reach halfway around her waist as I hug her.

Griff clunks down the last step of the stairway. "So, Jack will be a doctor, eh? Now there's posh for you."

"Thanks for the money," I tell him, smiling. "*Diolch yn fawr.*"

"See, Mildreth? A proper little Welsh princess, she is." He looks into my eyes. "Are you happy, *bach*?"

I think I'm happy, so my answer is yes.

"What did she say?" asks Mamgu above the whistle of the kettle.

"She said, *ydw*, Mildreth."

Yes.

"Sit down, you two," says Mamgu."How about we go to the beach and search for winkles after we've finished our tea? Do you have strong shoes to wear, *bach*? I'll lend you some crepe-soled boots. The soles of yours look like horse's hooves."

"Platform boots, they're called," says Griff. "Don't you know anything, Mildreth? I have a better idea. Let's visit Hendron Castle and climb the spiral steps to the very top of the tower."

"What—with your leg?" laughs Mamgu. "Now, that I can't wait to see."

"*Mildreth, mae'r te ma'n ofnadwy,*" says Griff, screwing up his nose and reaching for the biscuit tin.

Mamgu pulls the tin from within his reach. "Telling me my tea is awful, and you expect me to share my Welshcakes?" She gets up and heads for the pantry.

I bite through a layer of butter as I watch Griff stride after her. "Behave yourself, now, Griff," she warns, laughing.

When the dry crumbs of my Welshcake melt inside my mouth, I'm left with tiny raisins to squash between my teeth.

And I think—*I'm home.*

◆

Puffing away, Mamgu takes one narrow step at a time, refusing to take a break. We climb the Norman tower at Hendron Castle, gripping hold of every jutting stone to keep our balance.

Griff manages to drag his bad leg all the way to the top, for soon we hear, "Mildreth, you lost your bet—pay up." His voice echoes, spiraling down to meet us.

"*Ach,* proper clever clogs, you are," she shouts back.

We finally manage to join him. As we marvel at the river squirming at the base of hills, as we drink in the vast plateau of fields and forests below, Griff asks me again, "Are you happy, *bach?*" His blue eyes look concerned.

"I'm happy."

Then his arm shoots to the sky, and when I follow his pointed finger, I see a hawk. Dipping, dropping, flying, floating.

Free.

"Time for the beach," says Mamgu, breaking the silence.

◆

We often go to the beach to search for winkles. In the spring, Mamgu shows me where to find spears of dandelion for salads. She tells me to nip the leaves from nettles to add to a broth called *cawl.* She teaches me how to rub dock leaves over the stings afterward. In late summer, we walk along heather-bearded hills, or we get up at five in the morning to search the sheep field for flat mushrooms.

And now, we take the sloping road down to Morfa Bychan to see a spread of sand corrugated by the tide. Seagulls squabble over jellyfish that are woven with seaweed, rotting rope, strands of plastic. All twists together along a line of silt and other washed-up debris.

I slip, snagging my ankles on the teeth of rocks, not as experienced as my grandparents, who know exactly where to place their feet.

As well as handfuls of winkles, I find a few shrimps lying still and transparent in pools. I snatch at them before they flit away. Holding up my polythene bags, I admire my harvest, and I feel the tingle of a breeze on my face. It's getting late. The sea and sky are both steel gray, and I realize I've wandered far from Mamgu and Griff.

Licking the salt from my lips, I call to them.

"Is it time to go home?"

◆

Back at Ty Wen, I help with the vegetables. I push beans out of velvet-lined pods and slice potatoes to fry in butter. As the kippers sizzle in an iron pan, Mamgu plunges the shrimps and winkles into boiling water. Then she holds a loaf of bread against her waist to first butter, then cut, paper-thin slices. We clink glasses together, full of ginger beer to toast my birthday.

After Mamgu smothers the seafood with vinegar and pepper, we peel the shrimp and use pins to pull each winkle from its shell. I savor each tangy, briny mouthful. And my tummy aches as I laugh at Griff, who must wear reading glasses to pick out the bones from his kippers.

"Just swallow them, Griff," says Mamgu, shaking her head. "They're finer than the hair on your head, you great *twp.*"

I'm wondering what hair, where, for Griff only has a border of down left.

"I swear your mamgu wants me to choke and die, Katie."

I laugh again, and to push away the thought of anything happening to either of them, I reassure myself that Griff's a mere sixty-six. Mamgu, just sixty-one.

She was only sixteen when she had Dad.

She gave birth to your father when she was but a child herself, you know. Good job Griff came along to marry her.

And when the night wraps Ty Wen, Griff holds a taper to the oil lamps until they begin to hiss and scatter orange light. The fire crackles, sparks play, and Mamgu sets a fruitcake dribbled with sugar icing on the table.

More flames, more light, more magic. I count twenty-one candles.

"You have to blow them all out at once for your wish to come true," says Griff.

So I wish, but the two candles nearest to me are stubborn.

I feel the puff of Mamgu's breath, and she says, "Happy birthday, *cariad*. You got *every one* of them!"

But I know I didn't.

CHAPTER 16

◆

1973

Monday, September 10
Eglwys First and Middle School, Cardiff

Her hair is a mass of coiled springs. She wrinkles her nose. "We're getting *her*?" The emphasis on the *her* reveals a gummy gap between the little girl's teeth.

"Seems like it," an imp of a boy hisses back, peering at me through a brown fringe.

"I wanted the tall one with the pretty dress."

"Me too."

Well, this is a great way to start my first day at Eglwys First and Middle School. Dressed head to toe in varying shades of drab, I'm wearing a pair of suede flats and a twinset I gleaned from Biddy to match my serge skirt. My hair is twisted into a topknot, and my new class hates me. I thought they'd appreciate a motherly school-marm approach.

I'm a dwarf standing next to the Pretty Tall One, whose black hair flows, whose Greek-island tan simmers under the palest of yellow dresses. Who wears strappy sandals with impossible heels.

My final teaching practice was Domestic Science with sixteen-year-olds, in one of the worst areas in Cardiff. The girls sneered. They ain't cooking no fuckin' beef casserole for anybody. The boys leered. Getting any, lady? If not, they'd do me.

Which is why I opted for a class of angelic seven-year-olds.

"She's horrible, she is," a red-haired mouse whispers.

I grab the mouse's paw—she and I will lead the rest of the crew to my classroom.

My classroom.

"Keep in a straight line," I sing, just like a professional.

"Oooh. Is it your birthday, Miss Cadogan?" The sweetest boy under a mop of blond hair points at my good-luck cards with a fat finger. I have a stack of them displayed on my desk.

My very own desk.

Cards from Mamgu and Griff, Aunt Shauna, and Jack.

And Oona in Ireland.

Cards from Moira and Ingrid. They couldn't find decent jobs in Cardiff, ended up in London instead.

And so did Jack.

I secured a teaching post here, he applied for a position at the Cardiff Royal Infirmary. He was damned sure he'd get the job, Katie, the interviews were plain sailing.

He received the *regret to have to inform you* letter just four weeks before I was sent notice of term dates.

I chalk my name on the blackboard.

My very own blackboard.

So I am to stay in Cynboyd, in our tiny bedsit with the goldfish—but not for too long. Jack will work twelve months in London, no more, he said. We don't really want to live in the big city, do we, pet? We'll move to the Welsh countryside just as soon as we can.

"Miss C-A-D-O-G-A-N," chants my class.

I'll be Mrs. Thorpe next May! Let's keep our wedding date, said Jack. No need to change anything. It'll all work out.

I hear whispers behind me and smile. *"What's her first name? I don't know. You ask her."*

God, Kate, said Jack on the phone. Working at St. Bartholomew's is challenging, and totally dynamic! Armed with such experience, he's bound to land a fantastic position in, say, St. David's Hospital next year. It's not far from Cardiff. Would I like to live in Cowbridge, sweetness? We'll buy a home of our own. We'll have money saved and everything.

Jack keeps spare clothes and stuff at our bedsit. I've yet to see where *he* lives, but it's early days yet. He shares with two blokes in Islington. It's a pretty cool house, he says.

I turn to face my class. *My very own class!*

"Choose a seat anywhere for now, boys and girls. I'll sort you into groups later."

"Can I stay with Danielle?"

"Peter Palmer smells like poo, miss. Nobody wants to sit by him."

Twenty-six round faces look at me.

Help.

"Okay. Right."

"I need a wee, Miss Cadogan."

Let's see. The register. I'll do the register.

"Marina Davis?"

"Here, miss."

"I'm here, too," shouts Matthew Gruen.

"Barbara Holt?"

"I need the bathroom. Honest I do, miss."

"Mark Kurth?"

"Here, miss. Are you our teacher forever?" His bottom lip quivers.

"David Llewelyn?"

"Here, miss. Martin really needs to go."

"Karen Morrow?"

"Here, miss. The other teacher has long pink nails."

"Yvonne O'Connor?"

"I'm here."

"Yvonne, take your finger from your nose, there's a good girl." I pause and wait for the class to recover. When the giggling fades to the odd titter, I cough.

Ahh—a cough means *let's proceed.*

Or shut the hell up. "Elizabeth Ogle, Janet Philips?"

"Martin's wet his trousers now, miss. He does it every day."

Stay cool, finish the register, Kate. Deal with it later.

"Nicola Richards, Ben Riggle, Becky Stroud?"

"Ugh, miss, it's all over the floor."

I'll finish this register if it kills me. A smiling little beaver with pendu-

lous breasts walks in, says, Good morning everyone, she's the school secretary, oh dear, do we have a little accident already? Shall she fetch the
mop and bucket? They keep spare underpants in the locker by the office,
Miss Cadogan, and of course she would watch the class while I fetch dry
garments.

By now, *every* child is in danger of wetting themselves after hearing the
word *underpants*.

"QUIET, all of you." Clap, clap, clap.

Good Lord, it worked.

"I'll be straight back, Mrs.—?" I wait for the little beaver's answer.

"Miss Broomhead."

Broomhead? Of course, now we don't have laughter, we have shrieks.
Clap, clap, clap—and silence. Miss Broomhead resumes register-taking,
and I tell Martin-wet-pants to follow me.

How will I manage a whole year of this?

"I like you, Miss Cadogan." Martin grins at me. Enormous eyes, a button
of a nose.

I'll soon get used to this teaching lark.

◆

I peek into the staff room.

"You new here?" asks a lanky specimen with flaxen hair and ripe acne.
"Can I get you a cup a tea?"

"Yes, please."

"I'm Rowland Picken."

"Kate Cadogan." I shake his hand and ask what class he teaches.

"The thirteens. Doesn't it hurt with your hair scraped back like that?
Take sugar?"

"No sugar, thanks."

The milk is sterilized, heavy and thick. "Where do you live, Rowland?"

He smirks. "Why do you want to know?"

"Just curious." *Trying to be friendly, you dope.*

"Digs in Dewey Road," he says. "What about you?"

"Albion Road."

I flash my engagement ring, but Rowland's eyes jump in the direction of the door. "Miss Angela Braithewaters," he says, "you gorgeous creature. I missed you, honeybunch."

I'm abandoned for the Tall Pretty One. She stands by the tea urn and Rowland Picken offers to carry the heavy cup and saucer for her.

"How about fetching me a couple of fig rolls instead?" She swishes her hair over one shoulder and looks down at me, squatting on the lowest armchair. "Awful staff room, isn't it? Hi, I'm Angie."

"I'm Kate—hi!"

She descends like a swan onto the seat next to me. "Rowland thinks with his dick," she whispers. "Here, have a fig roll. Addictive, aren't they?"

She's been teaching at Eglwys School for three years, has a boyfriend, oops, correction, she *had* a boyfriend, dumped him halfway through their holiday in Corsica. Has a new guy now, nothing serious, he lives in Holland Park.

"Holland Park?"

Yes, she says. What? You have friends, and *a fiancé*, no less, in London? Superb. Let me see your ring. Gorgeous! Do you drive? No? Then how about a lift, the last weekend of half term break?

"Angie, that would be wonderful. Thank you."

She stretches her arms, points painted toes, clenches a fist to cover a delicate yawn, and reaches for her tea. "Thank you, sweetie," she says to Rowland. She nods and smiles as each member of staff files in. I'm introduced, but I'm hopeless with names, and I tell her so.

She blinks smoky eyes. "You haven't forgotten mine, have you?"

Come closer, she says. "Let me give you the rundown on this lot. Picken, you've met, who at this very minute is willing you to open your legs a little more so he can see the color of your knickers."

I slam my knees together.

"Then there's Miss Broomhead, school secretary, always the busy little . . ."

"Beaver?"

"Yes." Angie smiles, revealing perfect teeth. Ted Ashcroft, the one shaped like a Buddha, yes him, the one with the red beard and comb-over, he teaches history and woodwork. Brian Wharton, class teacher for the twelves, gentle, great shoulder to lean on. Hattie Harris, the one with candy floss for hair, is a total hippie. Wears caftans and Jesus sandals most days.

She's the art teacher. The dark-haired lady over in the corner is Evie Cudrow. She's always knitting sweaters. Never stops.

And I learn about the deputy head, a bundle of joy, a roly-poly of a man. As for the year three teacher, Jane Paltrow, I won't hear much from her, keeps to herself, a mysterious little spinster. Then there's Eunice Banks, who has five children and a househusband.

Angie has to stop at this point, because Basil Kirby, the head teacher, sweeps in. Oh God, yes, I remember him now. Mr. B. J. Kirby Ph.D. The worst on the interview panel. I can't believe he offered me the job. Red-faced, his shock of silver hair matches his silk suit. He glares, his chin juts, his hands shoot to his hips. "Members of staff, it is five minutes before eleven. Shouldn't you be in your rooms ready to meet the children?"

I'm studying his profile when he swivels to face me. He crouches. His eyes are one inch from mine. Mauve spider veins creep over fleshy cheeks. "Miss Cadogan, this is your first day." Beads of perspiration dot his upper lip, and gosh, he has no eyelashes. "You of all people should be in your room now. And I mean now. Do you have your lessons prepared?"

I give him an enthusiastic nod. I still have tea in my mouth and I dare not swallow it.

He storms out.

Angie holds a middle finger up at the slammed door.

She's a goddess.

"Didn't get any last night, that's his problem," says Rowland Picken.

"You do know the dirty bugger has a preference for little boys, don't you?" says Ted Ashcroft, smoothing strands of hair across his scalp.

"Now, don't you get upset," croons Eunice Banks, pinching my chin. "His bark is worse than his bite."

"Half a sleeve to go, and I've finished," says Evie. "Kate, do you knit?"

"Sometimes."

"I'll lend you some patterns."

"Thanks—that would be great."

Rowland Picken takes my empty cup and saucer, and winks. "Fancy a drink tonight?"

"Gosh, I'm sorry. I'm busy. Another time?"

Brian Wharton offers Angie and me his arms. "Shall we go, ladies?"

"Katie, fancy a drink at the Queen's Head tonight?" asks Angie.

I nod. And when out of Rowland's earshot, I whisper, "Seven o'clock?"

Before we go, I take one last look at the staff room, my future refuge from kids, lessons, chalk, ink, paint—and of course, flour, rolling pins, and mixing bowls. I'm the school Domestic Science instructor as well as class teacher. I catch a glimpse of Hippie Hattie dropping handfuls of fig rolls into her crocheted bag.

Stealing them.

Ha! Oh, yes. I think I'll enjoy the Eglwys School staff.

Not counting Basil Kirby, that is.

CHAPTER 17

◆

Wednesday, October 24
33 Cherry Blossom Road, Dorton

The cream satin is backed with curtain lining, and I'm not talking about curtains here, I'm referring to my wedding dress.

"It's far more substantial than dress lining," says Biddy, scraping my scalp with hairgrips as she secures my veil.

To be fair, she's done a beautiful job. The body is sleek, the sleeves puff over the tops of my arms. From the knees, the dress flounces out in three tiers. "Come here," I say, nuzzling my cheek against hers. "Thank you, Mum."

"The guests will think I paid over three hundred pounds for this. Step onto the chair while I pin the hem."

I hope Jack will like the dress. He grabbed the early train back to London this morning. He had to be at St. Bartholomew's by ten.

I was to enjoy my few days off in Dorton, give his regards to Biddy and Tom, he'd see me on Saturday as planned, sweetness. I'll see the house he shares in Islington at last!

He lay in bed watching me make cocoa last night. *Tra-la-la*, I sang, I'm having a wedding dress fitting tomorrow.

By the time I slipped into bed, Jack was asleep. I couldn't rouse him to share wedding chatter, so I cuddled into his back instead.

"Kate, did you hear what I said?" Biddy talks through a row of pins clamped between her lips. "Turn around, let me check the back."

"Mum, how about we go to the stationer's to choose the invitations this afternoon?"

"I can't do anything with you jigging about, hold still. And sure, haven't I already got the invitations."

"You've got them?"

"I have them in the bureau downstairs. Three packs of fifty. Now, let me see if I have everything even."

"*Three packs of fifty?* How many guests are coming?"

"I have a list of one hundred and eighty so far."

"Who the hell—"

Biddy asks who taught me to speak like that, was it Jack? She works all day at the Bread Shop, comes home each night to labor over my dress after cooking Daddy's dinner, and she thinks she's entitled to invite a few nurses and customers along with the family to her own daughter's wedding. Wouldn't I agree?

Of course, I reply, but won't the reception cost a fortune at this rate?

Daddy will take out a loan, she says, and I'm to keep that to myself, Kate. She doesn't want the whole of Dorton or Jack Thorpe's family thinking we're poorer than church mice.

"Now, get down off the chair, remove the veil, and slip the dress over your head."

"Ow." I lick my arm when a pin stings me. "Let's go to Brayminster for tea and a sandwich or something. I'll pay."

"As long as we get back in time to take the roast out of the oven. Kate, what size bra are you wearing?"

I turn away and push my arms into the sleeves of my green top, pull it over my head, and step into denim dungarees. "Thirty-four D, why do you ask?"

Biddy works a hanger through the neck of the wedding dress and says, no reason, shall we go?

I developed Dolly Parton breasts when the doctor changed my prescription to The Mini Pill two months ago. I pray Biddy doesn't put two and two together. I fold my arms, higher up than usual, and tell her I'm ready.

"But you look like a tinker, in that outfit. Don't you have a nice pleated skirt to wear?"

I tell Biddy the only outfit I have is the one I traveled in, and I promise to shroud myself in a big black coat, and if I'm asked, I won't let on I'm a Cadogan.

I pull on the leather gloves my parents bought for my twenty-first. "Shall we see how Dad's getting on at the Bread Shop?"

"Ah, no, now. If he sees me, he'll expect me to take over. It won't kill him to run the shop for one day. Betty and the new assistant Carole are there to help."

◆

At Brayminster, we cover a round of shoe shops, and Biddy buys a couple of pairs of flats because she deserves them, having to stand in the shop all day. Did I know my father wouldn't lift a finger unless she practically begged him to pick up a towel and dry a few dishes at night? And he's still in that same old job at the lab, watching everyone get promoted in front of him, too meek to ask for a raise. Not so meek when he's at home, though, oh no, he's defied her a few times recently, Kate.

I lead her toward Farthing Lane to avoid the discount shoe shops ahead. Actually, it's hardly a lane, more like a cobbled alley. Tudor buildings stack together along each side, complete with wooden beams and latticed windows. The café we're heading for is called Ye Olde Tea Shoppe. There must be one in every single town in England.

Inside, it's all gingham, dried flowers, and brown teapots with knitted cosies.

"Very nice," says Biddy as we sit at a corner table. "Very pleasant," she tells the waitress.

She orders tea, and please don't give us teabags, we want good, strong tea *leaves* please, and we'll pour the milk into our own cups, thank you, dear.

The waitress rolls her eyes to the ceiling before scribbling on a pad. "A pot of tea for two. Anything else?"

I ask for a tuna and cucumber roll, please.

"Chicken sandwich for me." Biddy turns the menu card over. "No mayonnaise." She runs a finger down the list of cakes and desserts.

"Mum, let's stick to sandwiches."

"And two toasted tea cakes. Do you serve real butter? Don't bring margarine."

When the waitress leaves, I say, "Let's talk about what colors the bridesmaids should wear."

The tea arrives.

"What about pale blue?" suggests Biddy. "By the way, I asked your cousin Josie to be a bridesmaid."

Wheezy buck-toothed Josie.

"*You* asked?"

"I'm entitled to ask. Who's paying for the wedding?"

"SHITE! For God's sake, no. Not Josie."

"Shite? Who taught you to say shite?"

Biddy taught me to say shite.

Plates are set on the table, and we eat in silence. Biddy's chicken sandwich passes the test, but as I feared, the tea cakes fail miserably.

"Kate, the ones we sell in the Bread Shop would beat these hollow."

Well, I knew that.

She waves to the waitress. "Excuse me? Would you take the butter away? We've finished with it now." She lights a cigarette and pulls the ashtray toward her.

"Mum, I want Moira and Ingrid only," I say. "Just two bridesmaids."

She sits back in her chair and has a silent conversation with herself, lips working, fingers tapping. I catch the tail end of a sentence: *those trollops.*

"Trollops?"

"Yes, trollops," she hisses. "Listen, Kate, ever since Moira Murphy was thirteen years old, she's been hanging onto a boy's arm. One boy after another. Can't keep her legs together. And that Ingrid Beddoes, well, fine family *she* comes from. They're a bad influence, Kate."

My hand goes to the scarf around my neck, the one with the tassels, a sage paisley design on one side, lilac spots on the other. Cashmere and silk, so fine, it slithers through my fingers.

Biddy's face changes, her voice lowers. "You wouldn't be taking The Pill by any chance?"

I chop out a "Ha!" and swirl the spoon in my tea. *I wouldn't be taking The Pill by any chance?* Just like that, out of the blue. Biddy always waits for the right bloody moment.

"How about spring flowers instead of roses for the bouquet?" I wonder out loud. "I mean, considering it'll be May and all. Here, do you want the rest of my tea cake?"

"Are you letting Jack take advantage of you?"

My face prickles with heat. What the shit or shite do I say?

"No."

When Biddy snaps open the clasp of her handbag, I remind her I'm paying; it's my treat.

"What are these then?" My mother slaps a blister pack on the table, displaying a spiral of contraceptive pills.

"Sex before marriage?" Her lip curls. "What kind of Catholic girl *are* you?"

"When did you go through my bag?" I ask.

"After I saw the size of your chest. I've been in the medical profession for too long to be fooled."

She stands to button her coat that's navy, quilted, too big for her small frame. She pockets my pills, picks up her shoeboxes, and looks down at me. "You *stupid* little bitch," she hisses. "You think you'll get a man to stay with you this way?"

I catch the waitress's eye and mouth the words, *Bill, please.*

◈

I follow Biddy to Brayminster bus station, but I wait at bay number nine, not three. And when the coach arrives, when the driver changes the sign on the front to "Cynboyd," I climb aboard.

For this coach will take me straight back to Cardiff.

And on that coach, I imagine Biddy in Dorton, hacking at the joint of beef, saying, Kate's nothing more than a slut, Tom. She doesn't have an ounce of sense.

And I see Dad watching, listening, nodding. In his eyes, I'm the deflowered child.

The Pill, Tom, she's on *The Pill.* Does he hear what she's saying?

What does he think of his precious little daughter now, eh?

CHAPTER 18

◆

Friday, October 26
Room 2B, 350 Albion Road, Cynboyd, Cardiff

A rumble of engine, a squeak of brakes, and a car horn honks.

It's Angie!

I grab a prescription from behind the clock—I need more pills, I have no spare. Biddy kept the last packet I had. I'll get more in London, that's what I'll do. I've only missed a couple of days. No harm.

After sprinkling fish food in the tank for Abbott and Costello, I swing my case through the door, and I step into an October night.

Angie waves a head scarf at me. "You'll need this, Katie," she sings. "Pop your case in the trunk."

I jump into the MGB Midget, and with a roar, we're off.

Angie tells me to find something on the radio to put us in the mood.

"Let's join in," she shouts, pressing a pointed boot on the accelerator.

Trees are ribbons of color, street lamps streak into neon light as we pick up speed and sing "Born to Be Wild."

I lean back to look at an early moon in a sky blotted with clouds. Tonight, I'll be with Moira and Ingrid.

And tomorrow, Jack. But not, worse luck, until he's had a chance to sleep after working all night in intensive care.

"London, here we come," yells Angie.

67 Solborne Road, Notting Hill, London

"So you'll come to Josh's birthday party?"

"Yes, Angie, fantastic. And thanks for the lift, too."

"The fun will start around eight." She pecks me on the cheek. "Can't wait to meet Jack. Remember, a little mews house, iron railings, number twenty-five, okay?"

"See you tomorrow!"

As I climb out of the car, a clatter of footsteps drowns the purr of the engine. With outstretched arms, I brace myself. Wham! Moira and Ingrid throw themselves at me. God, your hair! Look at your hair! Absolutely fab shoes, Katie.

Oh my God, Moi, those earrings are *gorgeous*. Ingrid—you're wearing a *wig*? No, seriously, it looks lovely. No, I'm not kidding, it does. Shit, it's so great to see you both again!

I lift my case from the trunk of Angie's car.

"Must fly, girls," she shouts. And she dabs on lipstick, smacks her lips, closes her compact with a snap. "*Ciao.*"

And she's gone.

"Gee bloody whiz," says Ingrid, "when did she fall off the catwalk?"

"Yeah, I know," I say. "So, how are the jobs going?"

Moira laughs. "At the pharmacy?"

Pharmacy. Prescription. Must remember to get more pills.

"Oh, selling remedies for hemorrhoids, loose stools, and intimate itching," she says, "—is great fun."

"Don't ask," says Ingrid. "If I don't snag a decent story for the *Bugle* pretty soon, Dykie Dora will give me the sack. No kidding."

"Dykie Dora?"

"The editor. She wears men's suits and shaves her chin."

I follow Moira and Ingrid down to their basement flat, and natter on about my class, my bundle of seven-year-olds.

The kiddies sound adorable, how sweet, how funny. Awww. Rowland Picken said *what*? God, what a creep, Katie. Okay, here's our den, come on in.

"Damn, this place is fabulous!"

"Decorated it ourselves." Moira beams.

Ingrid strokes the side panel of a bookcase. "We found this b
ticoat Lane."

"Cost us a whole month's wages," says Moira.

The bookcase is pine, as warm as honey. Yes, they stripped it o   ...ie
backyard. It took five gallons of caustic.

I run my fingers along the books and LPs that stand to attention in rows.

The wallpaper is William Morris. Curling ferns and fat flowers in shades
of turquoise and taupe. A black-and-white TV in the corner. A patterned
rug, muted and weary, lies under three floor cushions, one round, one
square, one a triangle.

Look, look, says Moira, lifting a corner of mustard fabric to reveal two
tea chests—this is their coffee table.

"I love this room," I say.

Ingrid flips through the LPs. "What shall we play, Moi?"

"This one."

As soon as I hear the first line, I know what it is. Alice Cooper's *School's Out*.

I cover my ears and pretend to scream. "Agghh, no, please no—"

"You can't fool us, Katie love, we can tell you adore being the teacher. Tea
or wine?" asks Moira.

I think—yes, I adore the kids, but I'm already hating the *control*. School,
college, school again. Forever bound and gagged by rules.

"Wine, please." I grin at my friends. "A decent red would hit the spot
nicely."

"French table for you, Angie Braithewaters. God, I'd sell my soul for
cheekbones like hers."

"Oh, guess what?" I say. "Angie invited us all to a party. Tomorrow night,
in Holland Park."

"Should be good." Ingrid passes three glasses to Moira. "I'm famished, do
you wanna eat?"

"Somewhere in Covent Garden?" suggests Moira.

❖

It's rush hour, which means we must stand. We hang onto one another as the
underground train wheezes out of Notting Hill Gate to Queensway. It sways
into Lancaster Gate, then whines like a siren all the way to Marble Arch.

After Bond Street we find seats, but are separated by stone-faced businessmen, blank-faced secretaries, sallow-faced tourists. No one speaks, yet bodies are intimate, too close, rocking in unison to the beat of the train. *Clink-clunk, clink-clunk.* Oxford Circus, Tottenham Court Road—we peer out of dust-smudged windows, waiting for the first glimpse of a sign saying Holborn.

Jump up, jump out, jump to the side. Look for a space to join the horde and bulldoze your way in silence. Tag onto the snake of people on the escalator. March, keep to the left, keep the motion going, advance to the turnstiles—quick, there's a train waiting—

Clink-clunk, clink-clunk. "Ugh. London. Don't you just love it?" asks Moira.

I do.

Jump up, jump out, where's the lift?

Our ears pop when it comes to a shuddering halt.

And here we are. Covent Garden. It's jesters, clowns, and acrobats. It's Irish jigs scraped on fiddles, protest songs strummed on guitar strings, jazz coaxed from saxophones. It's the beat, the rhythm, the noise. It's the heat of London hammered on drums.

London.

Yes, I love it. God, I could live here. I really could. I'll talk with Jack.

"How about the Punch and Judy?" Ingrid leads the way to a courtyard past the street entertainers, and we enter the happy, busy atmosphere of a cellar bar.

"Whoa, look at the menu." I savor the list of comfort food, kicking my legs against the bar stool like a child. "Bangers and mash, steak and kidney pie, toad in the hole." It doesn't take me long to decide. "I'll have pie."

"Me, too," says Ingrid.

"I'm having roast beef with Yorkshire pudding, so there," says Moira. "And let's be utter pigs, shall we? Let's have a Guinness each, yes?"

Yes, and yes.

I'm loving this.

And there's a party tomorrow, to boot.

And I'll be with Jack.

My Jack.

❖

CHAPTER 19

Saturday, October 27

"Let's whiz around the capital, then go clothes shopping," says Moira. "What say you, Kate?"

I say yes.

The smell of coffee is blissful, my friends aren't working this weekend, and life is wonderful, isn't it? Outside, sparrows chatter, bottles clink, the milkman whistles.

"Here," says Moira, handing me a fat mug of coffee. "I'll take Ingrid hers. Eat your breakfast."

I bite into toast, sip coffee, eat forkfuls of egg.

And I plan on buying something very special to wear tonight.

❖

By ten o' clock, we're dressed and ready to hit the sights.

Ingrid pulls her beret to one side. "Do I look like a French mademoiselle?" she asks.

Down to the Underground we go, down steps grimy with dust, sticky with gum. We tag onto the queue for all-day tickets, push through turnstiles, push past tourists, cameras, zoom lenses, and backpacks.

Onto the tube.

Up we jump, out we go—we're taking a bus tour of London.

"Let's run."

We climb to the top of the double-decker and grab front seats.

The commentary is recorded and in three languages. What did he say?

It's a static crackle. What was that? It's a nasal buzz. Shit, I don't understand a word.

"If you shut up for five minutes, Katie, you might," says Moira.

I dig her in the ribs.

Porticoes, pilasters, and balustrades. Arches, domes, and dentils.

The buildings crowd, lean, crouch, and reach for the sky.

We pass Guardsmen outside Buckingham Palace. We see chasing, flashing lights in Soho. *Strip Tease, Naughty Nudes, Wine and Wenches.* Pigeons mill, peck, and poop in Trafalgar Square. West End billboards shout: *The Rocky Horror Show! Jesus Christ Superstar!*

Tower Bridge, St. Paul's Cathedral, Piccadilly Circus, Waterloo Bridge. The recorded commentary says look left, look right, look up, look down, and, "Behind Parliament Square is the magnificent Westminster Abbey, Big Ben, and—"

"Hey, Kate—look, the Houses of Parliament. Do you remember that mural we made at Shawhurst School?" Moira hoots with laughter.

I join in with a shriek. "Oh God, yes, and we got a bloody detention for talking!"

"Those were the days," says Ingrid.

Yes, those were the days. Have I grown up yet? It doesn't seem so.

As soon as the bus chugs to a halt, we tear down the steps, jump off the platform, run to the Underground, head for Oxford Street.

We buy records, strings of beads, and cheap earrings. We see SALE slashed across windows. *Magic!* I find a hot-pant suit, khaki-colored, with bronze buttons.

"Go on, Katers—get it."

"Wear it with the brown boots you have on now."

"Wear it tonight."

"Okay," I say, hugging it to my body.

Would Biddy like it?

No. Would *Jack* like it?

I haven't heard from my mother, and I'm not likely to for a while.

◆

Back in Notting Hill, we grab hot dogs from a street vendor, then pop into the off-license. We club together to buy a Cabernet to hand over to

Angie at the party, and a bottle of cheap white to give us courage before we go.

I take Moira's arm. "And now, show me where you work," I say. "I need to fill a prescription."

And back at the flat—

"Katie? Did you have a good time with the girls?"

"Jack!" I nestle the receiver between my shoulder and ear as I reach down to peel off my boots.

"Don't be upset with me, sweetness, but I have to do a few hours at the hospital again tonight. Cancellations, reschedules, you know how it goes."

I'm so disappointed, I can't talk.

"Katie?"

"Yeah?"

"Ingrid, pour some wine," I hear Moira say.

"Okay, look," says Jack, lowering his voice. "I could meet you at the party, say, around midnight. It won't be a total all-nighter at Bartholomew's."

Yes, he knows exactly where Peignton Mews is. And afterwards, darling, guess what? We'll have the place in Islington to ourselves. The other blokes won't be back for a week or so. They've gone to Ibiza. Lucky for some, eh? Wait till I see the house, I'll love it.

Ingrid puts on her new Stones LP, *Exile on Main Street.*

"Would midnight be too late, pet?" asks Jack. "Think the party will still be going strong by then?"

"I suppose so."

"I'm missing you, sweetie," he says.

"I miss you, too, Jack."

Midnight? I suppose it's better than nothing.

CHAPTER 20

◆

25 Peignton Mews, Holland Park

Peignton Mews is tucked away in a quiet cobbled street.

"*Très* posh," says Moira, pressing the bell.

"Gorgeous," I say.

All neat brick and black paint-work, with a wrought-iron fence.

"Kate, your mouth's open," says Ingrid.

I count three stories of windows. It's like a doll's house.

"Damn, no one can hear us," says Moira.

Not above the chimes of Mike Oldfield's "Tubular Bells," they can't. Ingrid bangs the door with the brass knocker and a curtain shifts. Then, "Christ, how many more guests did you ask, Angie?" and, "Get the bloody door, someone." The letterbox flaps open and a pair of eyes peer through the slit. "Seems we have three fillies standing outside."

"Oh, good Lord, Giles—I'd better let them in."

The door opens.

"Hello, girlies." Angie's boyfriend wears a brocade waistcoat and he has cold fingers. "I'm Josh," he says. "Pleased to meet you."

We wish him a happy birthday.

The one called Giles leans oh-so-casually against a doorframe and displays a lopsided grin.

Angie gushes toward me wearing a little black dress with spaghetti straps. "Katie, I just adore those hot pants!" She pecks me twice on each cheek. "Ingrid, Moira, you're both welcome." Swerving on delicate heels, she says, "Follow me."

We clunk behind in our round-toed platforms. And oh shit, the women are all in cocktail dresses. Satin and crepe and gathered tulle. My wooden beads are blocks of oak compared to the strings of pearls and diamanté chokers.

We're led to an elegant living room. Yellow and gray, with touches of rose offered by the odd cushion, lampshade, or dangling tassel.

"Kate, you didn't say"—Moira talks through the corner of her mouth, stops to nod at the other guests as we're introduced—"it would be like this!"

"Sorry," I mumble. Smile, smile, pleased to meet you, yes, I do work with Angie, oh, yes, it *is* wonderful in Cardiff. I agree, the castle is gorgeous.

"Coats upstairs, did you say, Angie?" asks Moira. Then to me she hisses, "Why are you sorry?" She grabs my arm, then Ingrid's. "Come on, this is gonna be fun!"

She winks at Giles as he saunters by.

The bedroom is powder blue, gold, and white. A tapestry stretches across one wall, displaying a dying stag with an arrow stuck through its neck. We add our coats to the pile on the counterpane.

"Did you give the Cabernet to Josh the Posh?" asks Ingrid.

"Yep. Hell, he's not much of a looker, is he?" says Moira.

"The image of my cousin Josie," I say.

Moira grins. "Yeah, what a pile of teeth."

"So now what?" I ask.

"We get drunk, that's what." Ingrid's eyes widen. "And hey—did you see the spread?"

"Prawns, pâté, fondue, and caviar," I say.

"Caviar? Are you fucking kidding?" Moira leads the way. "Let's go, my fillies."

But, oh, do I feel a frump. The Mirandas, Audreys, Deirdres, and Penelopes stare as they comb every inch of my body.

I make a mental note to buy a little black number and a pair of heels with my next salary check.

Angie sweeps to my side with a tray crowded with schooners of sherry. "Have a drinkie," she says. "Don't be shy. Why not circulate like your friends?"

Yes, my friends are definitely circulating. Moira's fascinated with Giles. *Oh really? You are clever. Do tell me more. Now is that a fact?*

Giles isn't bad looking, but hell, he must be at least thirty-five. His eyes slope down at the corners—they are the clearest blue, and his hair is coarse, thick, and black. Square hands. Not very tall. Velvet jacket.

Ingrid has managed to cadge a smoke from some portly sort in a psychedelic shirt. *Mais non! Quel horreur. C'est pas possible!*

Oh, dear God, she's a French mademoiselle again.

I chase after Angie for more sherry, then head for the buffet to fill a plate with a helping of salmon mousse, a few triangles of Melba toast, four fat prawns, and—yes! Oysters. Wow. This is the life. I try a blob of caviar, the tiniest forkful, and pop the eggs between my teeth.

Josh waves a bottle at me. "We can't have you wandering around without a drink in your hand. Try a little Chablis."

I try a little Chablis.

Jesus Christ Superstar? Who's in charge of the music? I smile over at Moira, who tries her best to jive to "Hosanna." Dancers clap their hands. Sanna-senno-Soho, they sing. Or something like that.

A willowy blonde leans against the wall. "He's a member of the cast," she tells me, waving a tumbler of wine at the dancers.

"Who?"

"Zak Neeley. Here, have some of this wine, you've finished yours." She misses my glass and it dribbles down my hand. "Zak is a disciple at the West End," she says.

Wow—an actor? This is the life!

"That's him over there, with the trailing beard." She looks at me and smiles. "He's an utter bastard, you know."

"Oh?"

"He's my fucking fiancé, and he's playing with some French tart. Do you see?"

I do see. The French tart is Ingrid. "Please excuse me," I say.

"Ingo." I tap her on the shoulder. "Follow me." I zigzag toward the buffet table. Moira joins us, and I explain why Zak Neeley is a bastard.

So Ingrid announces she'll seduce Oscar with the National Health glasses instead.

Moira's in love. Doesn't Giles have the dreamiest eyes? His voice is smoother than golden syrup. He's hers, okay? I try to clink my second glass of Chablis with Moira's martini glass. "He's yours," I say, trying to focus on her face.

I check my watch. Nine-thirty.

My friends step off in rhythm to "Stir It Up." That's more like it. Lights are dimmed, candles are lit. I take a clean goblet to fill with our Cabernet.

I twirl into a space behind the sofa to dance by myself. A James joins me. He's a producer, he says, shaking his dreadlocks to the beat. Documentaries, darling.

Wow—a producer? This is the life!

I do antiques, says Rupert. (Seventeenth century.)

Wow—an antique dealer? This is the life!

Eleven o' clock.

Should I be dancing with these men? Why not? Just harmless fun, but I still keep an eye on the door. I wouldn't want to upset Jack. Am I drunk already?

Estate agents, physicians, consultants, my dance partners come and go. The music is soft when Roberta Flack sings "Killing Me Softly With His Song." The music is loud when the Stones sing "Brown Sugar." Boom, boom, boom.

One o' clock in the morning.

My head swims and my glass is empty. I head for the kitchen in search of alcohol. There's a ton of caviar left, so I eat two heaped spoons of it.

The fingers on my shoulders make me jump, but when I hear a voice smoother than golden syrup, I know who it is.

I turn around and Giles pulls me to him. "Where's Moira?" I ask.

"Who's Moira?"

Where's Jack?

Giles strokes my hair. "Gorgeous thing," he whispers. "Jailbait."

Lordy.

The velvet of his jacket caresses my arms.

I look into his face and hiccup. "What time is it?" I ask.

He throws back his head and laughs.

I'm grabbed by the hand, pulled toward the door, through the hall, up the stairs. I trot along like a drunken lamb. When I look down from the landing into Moira's upturned face, I read a mixture of surprise, confusion, and hurt.

"Moi, I—"

Giles pushes me in the direction of the bathroom.

Once inside, he closes the door, picks up a hand mirror, and holds it to my face. Smile, he says. And I do, and my teeth look like they're pitted with cavities.

Damn the caviar!

He grins. I fill a tumbler with water to swish in my mouth. I'm an idiot, a child.

"You're jailbait," repeats Giles.

"Nights in White Satin" plays downstairs. I love this song. Where, oh where, is Jack?

"Let's dance," says Giles.

"I'm waiting for my fiancé," I say.

"So where is he?"

Not bloody here yet.

We walk along the hallway, and I think, *Oh God, what about Moira?* I don't see her anywhere. The front door is open, the night outside is cloaked in black. I follow Giles to the living room.

I wonder what he does. "What do you do?" I ask as the Moody Blues sing about red being gray and yellow, white.

Giles's breath is hot in my ear. "Stock Exchange."

"In London?"

"Yes, and in Buckinghamshire. I live in the mews house two doors down, when I'm here on business, that is."

He kisses my earlobe. "Have coffee with me, Kate." When I look into his face, he nods in the direction of his house.

People pass by in coats, they say, *ciao,* wonderful party, Josh, super. Happy birthday, old boy. Angie pads around barefoot, collecting discarded napkins and empty plates.

"I can't have coffee with you," I tell Giles.

Because Jack has just walked in.

I shrink from Giles's arms, and run to meet my fiancé.

"Jack, it's nearly two o'clock," I say, pressing my lips against his. His tongue dips into my mouth, and when his arms tighten around my body, I melt into him, so grateful to see him at last.

"Sorry, sweetness. Had to deal with an emergency."

When introductions with Angie and Josh are over, we find Ingrid sitting on the stairs with Oscar, sharing a plate of sachertorte. "The party isn't over yet," she grins. "I'm staying a bit longer. Hi, Jack."

"Where's Moira?" I ask.

"She had a headache, went home early. No big deal."

Ingrid follows my eyes to the front door where Jack waits with my coat.

"Was she upset?" I ask.

"Don't think so. Why, should she be?"

"I danced with Giles."

"I'll say," quips Oscar.

"Moira wouldn't care," says Ingrid with a shrug.

I wish I could be so sure.

CHAPTER 21

◆

Sunday, October 28
218 Brewery Place, Islington

It's a breath of wind that wakes me. Jack must have opened the window while I slept. I lie still, watching the curtains ripple as I count the chime of church bells in the distance. They stop at eleven.

And now he stands in the doorway, watching me.

Last night, his fingers coaxed, his body persisted, his words caressed until I ached for him. It's never been like this before.

"Sweetheart, I made breakfast. Sit up."

The tray is laden with toast, marmalade, and two cups of the blackest coffee. He kisses me, smiles, untangles my hair with his fingers, apologizes for messing it up. Everything is renewed, repaired, different, somehow.

He climbs into bed. I want to stay with him forever in this house with its white walls, dark furniture, and plants as big as trees growing in clay pots.

"Seems the separation is doing us good, Jack."

He grins.

"But I'd *love* to live in London."

He smiles.

"I'm serious, Jack."

"Property's just too expensive here, pet."

"We could rent an apartment, even buy one, we don't need a whole house yet, I'll look for teaching posts in the *Educational Times*."

He pushes my cup toward my lips. "Drink," he says, "while it's hot."

"Or, what if I search for a different job altogether? Something in catering. Let's face it, Jack, a teacher's salary is abysmal."

I tell him as much as I love children, I don't want the rest of my life controlled by lesson bells. He slips the last bite of toast into my mouth, then lays the tray on the floor. He rolls over, teases my legs open with his, and it's easy. His movements are smooth, his tongue sweet. Such a change, what a contrast, since we were last together. Pleasure spreads through me in long, lazy waves. I whisper that I love him, let's live in London, not Cowbridge. Look what happens in London, see how we are?

He replies with a short gasp, a holding of breath, and a final sigh. Warm whispers follow, comforting words, gentle persuasion. Reassurances that we're doing the right thing, our house in Cowbridge will be surrounded by fields and trees and rivers. Let's stick to our original plans, Katie.

"Take a bath with me," he says.

I slide from under black sheets, and he leads me to the bathroom.

He shampoos my hair, slides soap over my arms, my legs, my back. I pray the day will never end. And when I'm wrapped in the thickest towel, I open the cabinet to look for Jack's deodorant, because it's been rolled over his skin. My man's skin. I sort through ladies' razors and orchid body spray.

Realization stings.

Channel No. 5 perfume. Tears spring to my eyes.

Max Factor lipsticks. My head spins. *Jack?*

"SHIT!"

"Jack?"

His face darkens when he sees me clutching a packet of tampons. "Sweetie, I can explain. No, don't cry, don't get mad."

"Explain?" I hurl the box at him. "Forgot to check the bathroom cabinet, did you?"

"Katie, don't go, please, *come back.*"

I run downstairs, and I just stand there, dazed, in the middle of the living room with its aubergine curtains and matching Persian carpet.

"Kate, wait, listen." I hear Jack panting, and he grabs me by the shoulders and gives me a shake. "Bloody hell, look at me, would you?"

He's naked, dripping, with suds sliding down his legs.

"Okay. Explain."

"My housemate—well, she's a woman."

My face creases up. "What about the two blokes?"

"There are no blokes. No, no, you must listen, Kate! I mean, just look around you, would you have turned this down?"

Dear God.

"Aw, c'mon, Katie, you wouldn't have understood."

They live like two strangers, sweetheart, be reasonable. Hardly know each other. Separate bedrooms, Katie, separate lives. Did he say anything about finding me in the arms of some Hooray Henry at the party last night? No, he didn't, because he trusts me, he knew it meant nothing. Think about it, Kate, come on. For God's sake, isn't it obvious how much he loves me?

"Oh, really?"

"Shit, yes."

I sit on the sofa to gather my thoughts. Apricot walls. Did she choose the color? Did she buy these green velvet cushions?

"Is this her house?"

"Yes."

"Does she know about me?"

"Of course! Katie, it's all right, everything's fine."

He promises with all his heart.

I shiver, damp inside the towel. "Hold me, Jack."

I want to believe him.

He sits down and pulls me to him, drops kisses on my cheeks. "Is she pretty?" I ask as he works the towel loose.

"Ha! Are you kidding? Felicity could be a sumo wrestler." He buries his face in my lap. "Come back upstairs, Katie."

"I want to move to London."

"Come on, Katie." His breath quickens. "Let me prove how much I love you."

◆

When I'm dressed at last, I carry the breakfast tray down to the kitchen, add the plates and cups to the pile already in the sink.

I must phone Moira.

There's a phone in the hallway, shouts Jack, use that one.

I pick up the receiver and dial the number.

"Hello."

"Moi?"

"Oh, it's you."

"Are you okay?"

"Wonderful. You knew I fancied Giles. Wasn't it obvious enough? Shit, Kate, you've got a nerve. Thanks very much, friend."

"What? But—"

"Ingrid will be here all day if you want to collect your suitcase."

Bang.

The line dies.

Blinking away tears, I look down at a note on the desk in front of me. And when the words stop swimming, I read them.

JACK!

Fancy seducing me shamelessly and making me miss my plane, you naughty boy. But what an evening for a girl to remember. Three times in a row—mm—mmm.

Thank God you managed to secure a seat for me on the next flight!

Hope you enjoyed the party—did you behave yourself?

Will call from Ibiza. See you in seven days, studmuffin.

Felicity X

I count seven days in my head, and I reach Saturday.

"Sweetness?"

Jack comes thundering down the stairs.

"Sweetness?" he calls again. "Why don't I call that ogre of a headmaster tomorrow and say you're sick?"

I turn away when his footsteps echo, when he reaches the mosaic tiles of the hall.

White dots spark behind my closed eyelids.

Jack presses his body into the curve of my back, his lips brush my neck, his breath is warm in my ear when he whispers, "Spend a few more days with me, Katie."

"Until Saturday?" I ask.

"Best you catch the train back to Cardiff on Friday, pet, when I can see you off. Shall we go to the West End tonight?" He circles his arms around my waist. "*Grease* is showing at the New London Theatre. I've heard it's terrific."

"Who told you it was terrific, Jack?"

"Felicity."

Of course she did. A splintering pain grips my stomach.

Jack's body sways, he hums a tune, starts singing about me being the one he wants, oh, ooh, honey. He's got chills that are multiplying. . . .

My fingers work on the note. I squeeze it, roll it, tighter, tighter, until it's as hard as a marble. Pulling from Jack's embrace, I swing around, and my face burns as accusations spill from my mouth. He's a cheat, he's a fraud, a low-life. There's a blank expression on his face, and when I detect stupid confusion, my "how-could-yous" degenerate to screams of, "You're such a fucking, *lying* bastard, aren't you, Jack?"

Does he think I'm a half-wit? I slam the balled-up note into the palm of his hand and wrap his fingers around it. "Here, I think this is for you."

I watch him pick at it, and when it's still a half-opened, crumpled mess, I know he's read enough, because he backs against the wall, and slaps his forehead.

Then for the second time today, he's saying, no, no, you must listen, Kate.

"You're, you're . . . *pathetic*." And I sob with frustration, because pathetic is too feeble a word, and I need to hurt, insult, cause him pain, too. "It's over." My heart hammers, my head throbs, there's no going back. "We're finished. How could I ever marry a . . ."

A what?

"You're a disgusting worm, Jack. A loathsome creep."

I'm filled with rage, so shocked, my legs are weak.

He's a stranger now, he's dirt, and I'm wanting to know where he put my coat, and when he reaches out, the bastard had better not touch me, does he hear?

I push past him to phone Angie.

I don't tell her what happened, I ask her if she would mind picking me up from Notting Hill, after I've collected my case.

"Oh, damn, has Jack been summoned to St. Barts?" she asks.

"Yes," I lie.

Then I leave 218 Brewery Place, closing the door behind me without another word. Walking along a lonely pavement toward the tube station, I wonder how long Jack's pitiable, sorry expression will live with me.

Oh, dear, dear God.

CHAPTER 22

◆

350 Albion Road, Cynboyd, Cardiff

As soon as I step out of Angie's MGB, I smell the fog. Along Albion Road, a gray veil blurs the outlines of hedges and street lamps. It's strange how fog softens footsteps, fades traffic, mutes voices. Depresses. I let myself into the main entrance of number 350 and unlock the door to the bedsit.

The goldfish gulp, the alarm clock ticks, water fizzes in pipes.

Black. Everything's black.

Curling my arm around the door frame, I feel for the light switch.

The solitary bulb reveals a stark tidiness. No abandoned clothes, no scattered LPs, no dragging bedsheets, no stacked plates. No humming radio left on to welcome me back. Jack's personality disappeared from our bedsit when he left for London. Today, he slipped out of my life, too.

I switch the radio on and hear Gilbert O'Sullivan wailing about being alone again.

Naturally.

My God, Jack, Felicity taught you a few tricks, didn't she? And in such a short time! Did you enjoy your practice session with me? Was I good, studmuffin? I fumble my way to the sink, hold on to the taps, and wait for the nausea to pass. I'm wearing your ring, Jack, I sob, and there's a wedding dress in Dorton, with puffed sleeves and three tiers to the skirt, and Biddy bought invitations, three packs of fifty.

This is the seventies, baby. Free love.

A dull thud pounds between my ears. Damn, was he planning to use Felicity for a year's entertainment before settling down with me in fucking Cowbridge?

My handbag slips from my shoulder and onto the floor and lies there looking stupid, so I snatch it up and hurl it against the wall. Lipsticks, combs, keys, receipts, ticket stubs, a blister pack with a spiral of pills. They scatter, roll, skip, and spread.

I sink into an armchair, pluck at its loose threads, then twist the engagement ring I've worn for three years around my finger. Underneath, a red welt itches. Does he want his ring back? I toss it to the floor with the rest of the debris. Standing up, clumsy, frantic, I grapple with buttons, try to kick off my boots at the same time. My hands don't feel like they belong to me. I don't know why I'm doing this. Then naked, shivering, I look around at the few things left in the room that could be called *ours*. Our goldfish, our posters, our packets of rice and tins of soup, our curtains, the ones I made with the blue fabric I found in the market.

I look at what was once our bed.

Slipping between the sheets, I clutch at them, smell them, search for the scent of Jack's body. And then I sob, hard, not caring if my throat hurts, or if my eyes burn.

You stupid little bitch. You think you'll get a man to stay with you this way?

The goldfish gulp, the alarm clock ticks, water fizzes in pipes. I lie facedown on a wet pillow that smells of mold. I turn onto my back and cry out. Once. Twice. Not caring if the other tenants hear me, fuck them.

Fuck them.

Monday, October 29

I sank into an hour's sleep this morning, that's all I could manage. Scraping a comb through my hair, I rub crusts from my eyes and pull on yesterday's clothes. We never did manage to afford a phone, Jack and me. I never felt desperately in need of one until now.

I will my legs to walk out of room 2B, open the main door, drag myself to the end of Albion Road to the kiosk and pull open the heavy iron door. The smell of pee and disinfectant assaults my nose. Picking up the receiver, I push coins in the slot, dial numbers, and listen to the dial tone buzzing in twos. It goes on and on. Neither Moira nor Ingrid answer.

I phone Basil Kirby and tell him I can't teach today, I have a streptococci infection.

Now what? *Fanny Smith loves Phil Hywel. Bryn Jones has a massive cock.* I read the messages scrawled over the glass panes, then catch the straggly reflection of my hair in a square of chrome.

Your hair is like two old curtains hanging each side of your face.

Biddy. Dad. I dial their number. They won't have left for the shop or work yet.

"Mum?"

A sharp sigh is followed by a snapped, "What do you want?"

I close my eyes to squeeze tears away.

"You left me stranded in Brayminster," says Biddy. "Fine thing for a daughter to do to her mother."

A sob escapes from the pit of my stomach.

"What is it? What happened?"

There are whispers, hollow clunks, and I sense the phone changing hands.

"Katie—it's your dad."

"There'll be no wedding, Dad."

In out, in out, I listen to him breathing, taking it all in. But his sigh carries a trace of excitement. "We're driving down."

"No—"

God, no. My mind spins. They'll find out I've been living with Jack.

Dad's voice is muffled, but I still hear, "Biddy, the assistants can look after the shop. No, you don't have to phone my boss. I'm capable of doing that myself." Then a clearer, "Katie, we'll be with you in a couple of hours."

I blot my nose with a tissue.

"Katie?"

"All right, Dad."

◆

Did Jack leave a toothbrush or his razor behind? Evidence? No. The drawers in his old chest contain two dried moths and a hairgrip.

I splash my face with icy water, then rub foundation onto my face, try to conceal the shadows, mask the rawness. I pat blusher onto my cheeks, slick on pink lipstick, tie my hair into a tight knot. I find a pleated skirt, one I use for teaching, thick tights, brown sweater. I fill the kettle, reach for the coffee, and search for a mug. After spreading two slices of toast with butter, I remember to cover the dish because there are mice. I wouldn't let Jack set traps.

I should get a kitten. My own kitten.

The kettle whistles. I leap over to the cooker to turn the gas off because I really need to hear every word of Jimmy Cliff singing "I Can See Clearly Now" on the radio.

I indulge in a deep sigh and a gulp of coffee. Oh damn, damn, the carpet is filthy. I bash it with the Bex Bissell, the bloody useless excuse for a vacuum. Dear God, this place is a mess. What will I do? I dust, polish, scrub, then shine the windows. Change the bedsheets. Throw Jack's smell into the wash basket.

When I hear a loud knock on the main door, I yell, "It's for me," into the communal hallway.

And there she is.

"Mum."

I'm held, rocked, then Biddy takes my face in her hands and plants rapid kisses on my forehead. "You're better off without him," she says, picking up a strand of my hair, tucking it behind my ear.

When Dad wraps his arms around me, my whole body convulses.

I rub at my nose with his hanky—damn, and I was doing so well. I was going to name the kitten Dinah and everything.

"So this is where you've been living, Kate," says my mother, working the toe of her fur-cuffed boot over a stain on the hall carpet.

"Come on, Biddy, let's go inside." Dad ushers her into room 2B. "Or people will hear us."

I dart my eyes to the left, to the right. Did I leave any other traces of Jack lying around? God, I didn't check under the bed, behind the wardrobe, or—

"So this is your room," says Biddy, laying her coat on the armchair. "Oh, Kate, was this the best you could do? Tom, didn't I say we should visit?" Biddy straightens the counterpane, walks over to my blue curtains, checks the hem. "Always allow at least four inches for turning up, Kate." Then, "Did you borrow a sewing machine?"

When I tell her I stitched them by hand, she says, "You poor creature."

And she sits at the table and weeps into the palms of her hands. "You must come back and live with us," she says.

I lean against the closed door.

Dad walks over, bends his head to meet my eyes. "I never did like Jack," he says. "Why don't you come and live with us?"

Oh.

"Kate?" The question remains in Dad's face. He takes my hand in his. "Don't make yourself all upset. He's not worth it."

"I can't leave Cardiff just yet," I say. "It's best I finish my probationary year at Eglwys School first."

"Afterwards, then." My mother claps her hands. "Only nine months to go. Sure, and doesn't time pass quickly? We'll look forward to it, won't we, Tom?"

"I'll think about it, Mum."

Dad's gray-blue eyes are bright, his grin wide. He suggests I spend weekends in Dorton until then. Would I like that?

I say I would. The thought of returning home is strangely comforting. Not *quite* sure about moving back lock, stock, and barrel, though.

"Now, how about a cup of tea?" asks Dad. "Do you have any chocolate biscuits?"

"Get some mugs, Dad. They're in that wall cupboard."

"You don't have a china cup and saucer?" asks Biddy. Then, "It's cold in here, Kate. Do you have a warm cardigan I could borrow?"

Pushing hangers along the rail, I search the wardrobe. And there's Jack's old coat. Shit! I skim it along, but I'm too late. Biddy has her chin resting on my shoulder.

"Is that Jack's? What's it doing here?" She pushes me to one side with her hip.

Dad sorts through my knives, forks, and spoons. "Katie, where do you keep the matches?" he asks.

Biddy shoves her hands into the pockets of Jack's coat, throwing cough drops, coins, and bus tickets onto the bed. Then she pulls out his old student ID.

Dad spits into the sink. "Is this milk fresh? Ugh, Katie, it's rancid."

Then Biddy spits too, at Jack's photo, before marching to Dad's side to show him what she found.

His lips tighten. "You bastard," he tells the photo.

"You weren't living with Jack before he went to London, were you?" asks Biddy.

Oh, what the hell does it matter now.

"Yes."

And my pathetic self sinks into a pit of misery and guilt.

Let a man have his way before marriage, and you'll never see him again. Am I right?

Seems you are, Biddy.

We sit at the table sipping tea with powdered milk. Not a word is spoken.

The goldfish gulp, the alarm clock ticks.

Water fizzes in the pipes.

CHAPTER 23

◆

Friday, November 16
Eglwys First and Middle School, Cardiff

"A Doctor Jack Thorpe called, says he received your message, and suggests you get in touch with him at lunchtime."

"Thank you."

I watch the secretary weave through the tables of the Domestic Sciences room.

"Paul," I say, "hold the door open for Miss Broomhead."

My attention reverts back to the gingerbread men. Perfect. Browned to a crisp, and now cool enough to wrap. The class made three each, and it didn't go too badly. Only a couple of the boys chose to add willies along with a row of buttons, two eyes, a nose, and a mouth.

"Sam, Myfawny, and Sara, wipe the tables please. Here are the cloths."

"I like your cardigan, miss. It's lovely."

"Thank you, Myfawny. Gather the crumbs in your hand, Sam, don't swish them onto the floor. Yes, Sara, I did see David Llewelyn pull your hair, but he won't do it again, will you David?"

Like a mad thing, I scoot around with a brush. Everything has to be ready for the thirteen-year-olds' theory lesson this afternoon. I check my notes. *Vitamins, minerals, carbohydrates, diet, and deficiencies.*

The lunchtime bell screams in my ear and my heart leaps.

Twenty days have passed since my trip to London, and I have to phone Jack, tell him what's on my mind. What I fear.

"Stand by your desks, everyone. Don't forget to collect your gingerbread men after school, now will you?"

They shake their little heads in unison.

"You all did a wonderful job. Good afternoon, children."

"Good afternoon, Miss Cadogan," sings the class, and they straggle out, holding on to each other, as seven-year-olds do.

Rowland Picken clucks his tongue at me as I pass him in the corridor. "Drinks tonight at eight?"

"Sorry—can't," I say, not stopping, keeping my head down, determined to reach the phone in the office before anyone else does.

A few yards later, Angie holds her arm out to stop me. "What's the hurry, Katie? Did you ever hear from Moira?"

Sorry, Katie, says Ingrid, always the one to answer the phone, Moira says she's too busy to talk right now.

"No, not yet."

Angie puts on a pout, says what a dreadful shame.

I take faster steps, hoping not to bump into anyone else on the way. I reach the office at last, open the door, peek inside, and find the coast clear.

I dial the number for St. Bartholomew's, and then the extension.

"Doctor Thorpe. Can I help you?"

"Jack?" I swallow. Words are jumbled in my head, and I can't put them in order.

"Kate, darling, at last . . ." His words come out in a rush. "It was just sex, sweetness, nothing more, I swear, I don't *love* her. Listen, I'll move out of that house, okay?"

I look at the ceiling and scrunch my eyes tight.

"Look, Katie, nothing like this will ever happen again, I promise. Huge mistake. Wasn't thinking. I've been under a lot of pressure, you see, and . . ." His voice trails off.

What an evening for a girl to remember. Three times in a row.

My body turns cold.

"Jack, do you think I'm a complete fool?" I ask. "Want to know why I called? Listen here, you moron, you use me, then—" I take deep breaths to stop my heart from bouncing. "And now—"

I lay the receiver on the desk and listen to him bleating my name, and I leave it there until the line purrs.

I couldn't tell him. I couldn't bloody tell him.

I find Angie in the staff room shaking her newly painted nails dry. She takes one look at me and says, "Let's go grab some lunch."

And as we pull out of the school drive, she says, "You should learn to drive, Katie. Just think of the freedom you'd have."

I tell her she's right, I should, and I will.

She cuts in front of another driver, and gives him an *up yours* sign at the crossroads, and I have to shout above the blaring of horns to tell her I just phoned Jack.

"Oh, Lord, Katie. What happened, love? Tell me everything."

We order a spinach and carrot salad at the Wholefood Café, and Angie sympathizes, she really does care, Katie darling, and we wallow in misery together. But I can't bring myself to tell her *everything*.

Oh, Moi, I think to myself. *I really miss you.*

Ingrid? Oh God, call me sometime, would you?

◆

When we return to the staff room after lunch, we admire the pullover Evie made for her husband.

"It's really beautiful," I say.

And it is, a textured patchwork of trellises, bumps, and ropes. It's the warmest brown shade imaginable, with flecks of blue. I think how perfect it would be against Jack's skin.

Damn!

I'll make something for Griff.

"I'd like to borrow one of your patterns, Evie," I say.

After all, I'll have plenty of time to knit now, won't I?

The lesson bell rings.

Rowland bursts in, grabs papers from a chair, and says, "I forgot these." Then, "Angie, Kate, which one of you lovely ladies can I take out tonight?"

"I'm free," I tell him.

Angie's eyes open wider than Rowland's. "Not him," she mouths behind his back.

Well, heck, she did tell me I should start dating again. I mean, Rowland's harmless, all talk, no action. Just a quick drink, that's all, to stop her pestering me. Might as well start somewhere, dammit. We can all play this game.

I scribble my address on a piece of paper.

"Eightish?" he asks.

I nod, and he follows Angie out of the door with a skip.

❖

I find the headmaster, Basil Kirby, in the Domestic Science Room, sitting at the desk with a Bible in his hand.

The children are silent, their heads still. Only their eyes move, darting from me, to him, back to me. The hairs on the back of my neck rise as I approach the predator.

"Good afternoon, Mr. Kirby."

I clench my fists, but it's no good, my legs are the ectoplasm of an amoeba.

"Miss Cadogan." Basil Kirby stands, creeps toward me and circles. "I checked your classroom. You don't have a Bible in your drawer."

"Why would I need one, Mr. Kirby?"

After all, I'm beyond redemption now.

His face changes from white to red to purple. "Every house, every hotel room, every teacher's desk-drawer in the whole of the *United Kingdom* should contain a copy of God's Book."

With the Bible resting in his upturned palms, he offers it to heaven. Well, actually, to the classroom ceiling.

"Mr. Kirby, why don't you give me the one you have?"

He rams God's Book under his arm and leaves with a toss of his silver hair.

He's a lunatic.

Stark raving mad.

I smile and sigh at the class of thirteen-year-olds. "And there we are," I say, shrugging. "So let's discuss *vitamins, minerals, carbohydrates, diet, and deficiencies,* shall we?"

"He's crazy, Miss Cadogan," says Dimitri Kasoulos.

Now, as a teacher, I'm supposed to support the powers-that-be, and *never become over-familiar with the pupil,* say the teaching manuals. But fuck it.

"You can say that again, Dimitri."

I open the register and count again how many weeks have passed since the party at Holland Park.

Please say I'm wrong, that it's not possible.

Albion Road, Cynboyd, Cardiff

Inside the telephone kiosk in Albion Road, I explain why I can't travel to Dorton till tomorrow.

"What's the occasion?" asks Biddy.

"I'm meeting one of the teachers for a drink."

"Not that Angie, I hope."

"Rowland."

"Go on."

"White hair, tall and thin. Lots of pimples."

"Has he tried a prescription of Megortizone?"

"God, Mum, I don't know."

"Should you be going out with a man you hardly know?"

"He's okay."

Forget and move on, suggested Angie. Play the field.

"He might be after only one thing," warns Biddy.

I wait for more.

"Sure, Kate, and how well did you know Jack Thorpe? Didn't you learn your lesson?"

"I'll see you tomorrow, Mum."

There's a possibility I'll be learning a lesson for the rest of my life.

◆

I climb into the passenger seat of Rowland's Vauxhall. A plastic troll with fuschia hair dangles from the rearview mirror, and, God help me, a stash of *Playboy* magazines are strewn across the back seat. Cloth interior, black dashboard, a radio tuned to BBC Radio 1, and I'm sitting next to a sex maniac.

"Where are we going?" I ask.

"To the Dirty Duck in Pontycullin, and may I say you are one sexy woman, Kate Cadogan."

"Take your hand off my thigh, Rowland."

The Dirty Duck is a crooked pile of seventeenth-century beauty. All oak beams, low ceilings, and wattle and daub. I ask Rowland for a lady's glass of pale ale, please, and then I aim for the fireplace, because it's cold, and there's nowhere to sit. The pub is full of farm workers. Herds of them.

I watch flames curl over logs, and wonder whatever possessed me to go out with Rowland. Some sort of retaliation? Like Jack would care.

When my date returns, he tells me I owe him seventy-five pence. Oh, right, I say, darting for my purse, thinking, that's good, we're going Dutch, which means he got the message.

"It's a busy pub, isn't it?" I say. "See any empty seats yet?"

"Nope."

I try to get the conversation rolling. "It used to be called the Black Swan, you know."

"I know."

"Where did you go to college?"

"Bath."

"Do you like teaching?"

"Yeah."

Hum.

Rowland takes a gulp of beer, then grabs my free hand. Quick, he says, before someone else nabs it. We push through bodies, and head for a wooden settle. And Rowland sits, pulls me off balance, and wham! I land on his lap. My drink slops down my sleeve and I say, *"Rowland!"*

"That's better," he replies.

At least he's talking now. We discuss Basil Kirby, who's deranged, a raving psychotic, says Rowland. We touch on my broken engagement, and I move quickly on to what we'd do instead of teaching. I'd start a catering business, I say. Do paid dinner parties, create gourmet sandwiches for offices. Open a restaurant. Yes, Rowland, it's true, I'd really like to open up my own restaurant.

Well, *he* would start a taxi business, pick up rich birds, or maybe provide limousines for weddings, and he'd get to drive the bridesmaids.

Oh, do I yearn to escape Rowland's clutch and leap from his lap. He's all bone, and his knees are poking into my left thigh. But I don't want to offend.

But when my *right* thigh feels the poke of something else inside those maroon flares, I soon spring to my feet and offer to fetch more drinks.

I wait at the bar wondering how long I must endure this date-from-hell. I consider ordering a cognac, but think better of it.

"Are you next, love?" asks the bartender.

"A pint of Brains and an orange juice, please."

And back at the settle, I say, "Here's your beer, Rowland." When he drags his fingers across my palm, I shake my head and tell him to pay up.

He reaches into his pocket, pulls out change, and says, "Let's go to the pictures."

"Okay."

Why not? What the heck?

"What's on at the Odeon?" I ask.

"The Exorcist."

Oh dear Lord.

"Fine," I say.

◆

There's quite a queue for tickets. I gaze at the posters showing a wasted child with yellow goat-eyes, and I'm debating whether to ask Rowland if he could please take me back home now. We shuffle forward, ten couples away from *"The movie that will open the door to my deepest fears."* Do I really want to see this? Yes, *"because somewhere between science and superstition, there is another world."*

We each pay for our own ticket and in we go. The theater is dark, the atmosphere electric. We settle in our plush seats, and boom, the film starts rolling.

The bellow and rasp of the music springs my nerves into tight-wires. And when the she-devil-child cackles and retches, I'm a lump of shivering jelly. Rowland's fingernails bite into my knee with a passion.

When the movie is over, we walk out in silence. That was one hell of a film.

"I suppose I'd better take you home, Kate."

"Thanks, Rowland."

He opens the door to his Vauxhall and I climb in. He has to turn the ignition key three times before the engine chugs to life. He slams his foot on the accelerator and says, "Fucking car."

And when the fucking car comes to a spluttering halt outside 350 Albion

Road, Rowland lunges at me. His tongue rolls into my mouth, and his hand clutches at my breast, and he snorts like the she-devil-child, and the damned gear stick jabs into my hip. I pummel his chest with my fists, but it makes no difference, so I grab handfuls of his hair to wrench his head away.

"Get off me, you—you pervert!" I swat his mouth away from my lips. "Damn you!"

Rowland collapses against the steering wheel and covers his face with his hands, laughing. "I'm sorry," he says.

"What's so bloody funny?"

"Aw, c'mon Katie, what's wrong with a bit of fooling around?"

I flatten my hair down each side, pull my jacket together, and with one foot out of the car for a quick getaway, I say, "Good night, Rowland."

What's wrong with a bit of fooling around?

Are they all the bloody same?

CHAPTER 24

◆

Sunday, November 18
33 Cherry Blossom Road, Dorton

Nothing much going on in Cardiff, so I gave in to Dad's "Come home for the weekend, Katie, why don't you? It must be really cold in that bedsit of yours."

Which it is. Bloody freezing, in fact.

Of course, Biddy likes me to go to church when I'm in Dorton. But it's almost eleven o'clock now, and she didn't wake me. Even though we're probably too late, I tiptoe down the stairs in my Sunday best, with missal and rosary beads in hand.

"Poor, poor Mammy."

"Oh dear God, the poor creature."

"Poor Granny."

What's going on?

In the hallway, Biddy and Aunt Shauna are joined together, quietly weeping. Dad hovers behind them saying oh dear, oh dear, oh dear, and Josie stands to the side holding a lump of tissue under her nose.

"Granny in Ireland had a heart attack," says Josie. "Have you been in bed all this time?"

My mother and aunt ask the Virgin Mary to guide their Mammy to God's side in Heaven.

I wrap my arms around them both, and say sorry, I'm so sorry, when did it happen, where was she?

"In Cloondray, in her rocking chair," says Dad. "The doctor said she died in her sleep."

I hardly knew my Gran. I'd only seen her four times. Three times in Ireland when I was a child, then after her one visit to England ten years ago, something happened. An argument of some sort. As Biddy watched my grandmother sail back to Ireland on a ferry called *St. Patrick,* her lips and hands moved as she conducted a silent, sighing conversation with herself.

Then in the car, on the way back to Dorton, it all came out. Mammy wouldn't admit Barney and Shauna were her favorites, Tom, or that Biddy might as well rot in hell.

My mother's sob brings me back to the present. "Sure, and Barney, that great brother of mine, now isn't he all set up with the farm willed over to him?"

"Poor Mammy was only seventy-seven years old," says Aunt Shauna, pulling away to blow her nose. "You'd think the Lord would have granted her a little longer. He took Daddy away soon enough."

I still have one arm around Biddy, with my rosary beads dangling over her shoulder. She taps my hand, then shrugs me off.

"Shall I make a cup of tea?" I ask.

"I'll make it, Aunt Biddy," says Josie, marching off with her arms folded.

Well, I'll get the damned biscuits, then. I drop my missal and beads on the stairs and follow her into the kitchen and shout, "Mum, Dad, Aunt Shauna, you go and sit down."

"What an awful shame about Gran," I say to Josie, as I reach for the gingerbread snaps.

"Yeah. I'll ask Colin to come with me to the funeral," she says, fanning her fingers under my nose.

"What a beautiful ring," I say.

"Sorry about you and Jack," she replies.

Her fiancé is a fellow cashier at Barclay's Bank. Josie hasn't landed a job with a law firm yet, says Biddy, but isn't she the bright one, ending up with a law degree?

I carry the tray into the living room, leaving Josie to follow with the teapot.

She lays it on the coffee table, then takes an inhaler from her pocket before sitting next to my mother. Yes, she's fine, Aunt Biddy, or she will be, as soon as she's had a couple of puffs.

I sit at my dad's feet.

"Who will have laid Mammy's body out?" asks Shauna.

"Ah, the neighbors no doubt. Not Barney's wife. Oona hasn't an ounce of sense." Biddy pours the tea. "Kate, you forgot my saccharine. You know I won't touch sugar. Oh, thank you, Josie, aren't you the great girl? They're in the kitchen, third cupboard along."

"Well!" says Shauna. "We had better take a boat over to Dun Laoghaire. Will we go on Wednesday, come back Sunday?"

I sip my tea. "Will I go, too?"

"Kate, do you have a black skirt?" asks Biddy. "I'll lend you a decent coat and hat."

I'd better break the news to Basil Kirby tomorrow.

"We'll take money with us," says Aunt Shauna. "For the food."

"We'll take bread and a couple of fruit cakes from the shop, Shauna, and no more. Barney and Oona are well able to afford a good spread for the wake."

"Music. What will we do for music?"

The discussion goes on. What type of coffin? Oh, says Biddy, Mrs. Dunstable, a good customer at the Bread Shop, said she ordered a lovely one for her mother. Oak veneer, lined in white, with a ruffle and side sheets. Fitted with shiny brass furniture, and complete with an engraved nameplate.

Well, says Aunt Shauna, she has the number of a funeral parlor in Cloondray itself, that Frank's friend gave her last year. Now, *Shamus* buried his wife in a deluxe Buckingham casket.

I inhale biscuit crumbs and cough.

"Pure oak with a raised lid," continues Aunt Shauna. "Are you all right, Katie? Take a drink of tea. Superior quality linings, die-cast brassed furniture, and a hand-painted nameplate."

"We must have the best for poor Mammy," says Biddy. "And make it evident to all in Cloondray that you and I bought the coffin and stone and, what's more, are well able to afford the best." She pauses, then adds, "Despite not inheriting even a china vase, let alone a square inch of the farm." She pours more tea. "Oh, Shauna, I'll need new shoes. I saw a black pair with suede buttons only last week. They would be grand."

CHAPTER 25

◆

Wednesday, November 21
Holyhead Docks

Aunt Shauna heaves at the thought of being out at sea, and we haven't even left Holyhead Docks yet. I sit next to her on a bench, and the day is as miserable as my mood. The sky is a pewter gray. The sea churns. The waves chop. We're going to have a rough journey, and oh dear God, I'm thirteen days late now.

No monthly visitor.

A squad of noisy children pass by. Five of them, toddling, laughing, skipping. Running circles around a mother heavily pregnant with her sixth.

"Ah, now, wouldn't you want to pity a woman in a situation like that," says Aunt Shauna. "Forget what the old Pope says, you'd think her husband would use something and give his wife a rest."

Oh God.

The cars sit as a stationary block, each row waiting for permission to move. Josie and her fiancé are sleeping in the back seat of Uncle Frank's car while he snoozes in the front. My parents are filling their car with smoke to pass the time away.

I had to get out to escape the "what's wrongs," "I haven't much to says," and "would I please have the decency to answer my father?"

Fine company I am.

Oh, Jack.

Aunt Shauna gives me a nudge. "The cars are moving onto the boat, in the name of the Father, and of the Son, and of the Holy Ghost. Let's go, Katie."

I drag my feet after her. We got up at four this morning. I step back into the smoke capsule and Dad edges his way toward the boat. I close my eyes and listen to the yells. Whoa, whoa! Left, hard right, one inch, come on, come on, forward, *bang*! Right, switch off your engine, sir.

Then there's a clang of chains, a honk of horn, and a smell of gas and oil and frying bacon. They've already started cooking the Irish breakfast in the canteen.

"Tom, lock the car. Have you checked all the doors? Did you remember your coat? You forgot my pillow. I need my pillow." Biddy pats at her hair in the wing mirror, asks me if it's lying flat at the back.

And we're ready, the Cadogan and the Boyle party, to face the crossing over the Irish Sea to Dun Laoghaire.

I aim for the lounge. The rest of the party head for the black pudding, the gelatinous eggs, the sausages, the fried bread, and boy, will Aunt Shauna need a brown paper bag after that little lot. And so will I if I keep thinking about it.

"*Cead mile failte*," says a freckled-faced steward. "Welcome."

The boat lists a little to one side, then I feel the dip and roll of it moving with the waves.

I feel terribly, terribly sick.

CHAPTER 26

❖

Thursday, November 22
Longshank Farm, Cloondray

Well, I'm here, at Longshank Farm in Cloondray, Eire. We arrived at six o' clock yesterday evening.

Uncle Barney welcomed us with a warmth I didn't expect, and I met his wife Oona—at last. She fed us soup and soda bread, and had beds made ready with fresh linen. I collapsed into this one at ten, and soon drowned in sleep.

And now I'm awake, following the route of plaster cracks in the ceiling, and thinking about my grandmother, who lies in the next bedroom surrounded by candles. I gazed at her body last night, it was an empty shell, stiff inside a frilled habit, and I saw both Biddy's face and mine in hers. Her name was Theresa Geraghty, née Connolly.

Shit, it's only five-thirty, but I'd better get up. I'm doing far too much thinking for my own good, and I doubt I'll catch any more sleep with Josie snoring next to me.

I swing my feet out of the feather bed. The floor feels cool and I think of Biddy as a child running over these stone flags. To think she was pushing her way into the world in this very room, while Theresa Geraghty screamed out, asking God to end it all, her wrists tied to the bedposts with torn sheets. Aunt Shauna said she witnessed the births of both her brother and sister, fetched the hot water, the soap—even the bowls for the afterbirth.

I wrap myself in a long cardigan and push my feet into clogs. These will take me over the grass, the gravel, and through the mud to the shed outside.

And the morning is damp, the sun is pale, and the colors of hedges and trees are vivid shades of mustard and green. I knock on the shed door and look back at the stone body and thatched roof of Longshank, the picture-postcard house my mother grew up in.

Well, it seems the outside WC is vacant, so I step in. I brace myself before I lift up the toilet seat. I don't know what it is about that turquoise chemical inside there, but it has a sickly sweetness that makes me retch.

Okay, that's it. I leave the shed, climb over a gate, and find my own private place to squat in the field.

It's a relief to walk back into the warmth of the house. As I make my way toward the kitchen, a sweet aroma like pipe tobacco fills me with a sentiment I can't define. This is the smell that welcomed Biddy every morning. It's the smell of burning turf—and there's Oona, pushing compressed bricks of it into the range. An Aga.

"Good morning, Katie. Aren't you the early bird? Did you sleep well? Will I fetch you some breakfast?"

"That would be great. Thanks, Oona."

She wipes her hands on a checkered apron and holds out her arms, so I respond by taking two steps closer.

"You're very welcome," she says, hugging me. "It's grand meeting you at last, Katie. Pity it has to be at such a sad time. Last night it was too dark to see, but it's clear you're Theresa Geraghty's grandchild."

I slide onto a long bench and rest my elbows on the table, my head in my hands. And that's when I see a neat pile of kittens sleeping in a cardboard box. "Where's their mother?" I ask.

"Prudence will be after a drink in the parlor. She's always there at milking time."

I watch Oona slicing bread and putting eggs to boil. "I plan to get a cat," I tell her. "I'll probably call her Dinah."

Oona bends down to lift one of the kittens. She spreads a tiny paw between her finger and thumb. "Will you look at this?"

"Wow, six toes!"

Oona kisses the squirming bundle before placing it in my lap. "Only one girl in this litter, and she's for you. Take her home."

I gather the tiny limbs and body in my hands and ask Oona if she's sure.

"A gift from me," she says.

"Thank you!"

"I'll get Barney to find a wooden box for your Dinah. Sure, it'll be no trouble taking her back to England."

She pushes a strand of damp hair from her forehead, and I see the shine of perspiration above her green eyes. "Well, Katie, I've cooked two roasts and a leg of ham, and I have a churn of fresh butter ready. With all the bread and cakes and beer, let's hope we have enough for the visitors and mourners." She wipes a tear from her cheek with the back of a hand. "God rest your grandmother's soul."

Oona's a lump of a woman, as lazy as they come, and didn't she always have her eye on every penny of Mammy's money, let alone the land?

"Oh, here are the cows now," she says. "The milking is done. Now Barney will want *his* breakfast." She works flour and cold potatoes together in a bowl to form a dough.

"Potato cakes?" I ask.

"Will you try some?"

I put Dinah back with her brothers and smile a yes, and Oona waddles to the sink to swill her hands. Then I hear a shuffle, a clatter, a squelch, and Barney's *yip-yip*. Black-and-white cows sway past the open door, lowing softly. There's a pungent odour of milk and hay, and a few of the cows step out of line to gaze into the kitchen. They flare pink nostrils, roll their eyes, and swish their tails before they're moved on with more *yip-yips*.

"Now, aren't they nosy?" says Oona, setting my breakfast down.

I watch the procession until Barney slaps the last cow on the rump to send her through the gate to the field.

I love it here.

"How did you get on with my grandmother?" I ask Oona.

"Well now, Kate, I'll tell you the truth. Theresa had a vicious tongue, and she controlled with an iron fist. So strange. The sour would follow the sweet. She'd love me one minute, despise me the next."

So like Biddy.

Oona laughs, but it's a sad laugh. "Your mam doesn't like me much, either."

She freezes.

"Oh, Katie, I'm sorry. I shouldn't have said that."

Covering her mouth with a plump hand, she sits at the table. I dip a spoonful of egg into the tiny heap of salt on my plate, then eat it with a bite of toast.

Here goes.

"I don't think my mother likes *me* much, either. But why, Oona?"

"Where exactly is your father's heart?" whispers Oona. "It's obvious he's obsessed with you, Katie."

Our eyes meet. Biddy's jealous?

But no more can be said, because Josie walks in. Oona squeezes my arm and nods, then strokes the back of my head.

A sinister wail intrudes into our silence.

"What the hell was that?" asks Josie.

Oona scrapes her chair on the stone floor as she jumps to put the kettle on. "Take no heed. That will be old Mrs. Rooney."

Mrs. Rooney started keening after poor Theresa was laid out on Monday, says Oona, as she rolls out the potato dough, then cuts circles with an old jam jar. Keening's not done much around these parts anymore, but the old lady insisted. She's been at Theresa's side all night. She must have had a little sleep in the armchair and just woken up to start her wailing again. Oona had better take her a cup of tea and a slice of something as soon as she's browned these potato cakes on the griddle.

She leaves the kitchen. Her skirt is a mass of gathers, and her brown hair, a haphazard mess, is strung together with a ribbon. How in the world could anyone dislike her?

Josie has her backside to me, warming her hands over the Aga. "Aunt Biddy says Barney and Oona could give me a few items of furniture, at least. After all, Colin and me *are* getting married soon," she says.

I ignore the silly bitch and when I finish eating, I leave to get dressed. I'll help Oona get things ready for the funeral. I don't think she slept at all last night.

I meet her in the hallway. "Old Mrs. Rooney will start the lamentation again soon, so don't be alarmed," she whispers. "Will you help me feed the chickens and calves when you're dressed?"

As I'm saying, "I'd love to," Biddy appears, fully dressed.

"Morning, Kate," she says, offering me a brief smile.

"Morning, Oona," she says, not offering her a glance.

◆

We feed the calves from buckets, and I help Oona mix a meal-mash for the hens. And it's above the clucking as they feed that she tells me Biddy can be a cruel woman. How many a time she would watch Oona cry when she made it obvious she didn't want her a member of the Geraghty family, when she and Barney were engaged. Go home, she said, to your seventeen brothers and sisters, do you think Mammy can help you support squads of children when you give birth to them?

"Well, Oona, Biddy only had me," I say. "What do you think she did? Abstain? She's a staunch Roman Catholic."

"Ah, no, didn't Biddy tell me in no uncertain way how Barney must pull out in time—if we ever did get married." Oona nudges me. "Can you imagine anyone giving you that kind of advice?"

I can imagine my mother giving all manner of advice.

"Here's the sad thing, though," says Oona, scraping out the last of the mash to the floor. "I can't have children. God didn't even grant me one wee baby of my own."

Poor Oona. And dear God, I hope I haven't been granted one.

That would be so unfair.

◆

At twelve o'clock, the visitors and mourners file into the dark bedroom to pay their last respects. Biddy is there, stroking the solid oak casket with its superior quality linings, raised lid, and fitted die-cast brassed furniture complete with hand-painted nameplate. Yes, it is a lovely casket, she says. She and Shauna decided only the best was good enough for Mammy, who would have chosen the very same one herself.

I go to the kitchen to help pass out rolls filled with slices of beef and ham. Josie's fiancé, Colin, is having a hard time pouring the drinks. His face is a flushed tomato as he tries to keep up the pace.

"A whiskey, sir? Right away."

"Ah now, will you give us a decent measure?" asks a toothless character, nudging the neck of the bottle with his glass.

"Keep your ice," says a massive bear stuffed in a black suit. "Are you trying to spoil a good drink?"

"A large Guinness will do nicely," whispers the frail Mrs. Rooney.

"Sweet sherry here."

"A drop of Scotch."

"One red, three white wines."

"Another Guinness over here. Do we need a new bartender, boys? Sure, aren't we standing in line dying of thirst?"

Poor Colin.

When I say I'm family, sympathy is expressed, condolences are offered, and I'm left with words that build a picture, teach me a little more about my grandmother. She had the thickest hair, the rosiest of cheeks, the deepest eyes for miles around. She cooked a fine roast, could dig a field of potatoes in one day. Could raise turf in the bog along with the most burly of workers, help bale hay, man a tractor. A strong soul, a tough soul—no one would dare cross her, may she rest in peace.

Cheers, Kate, and don't you have your grandmother's eyes? She does, doesn't she, Oona? Will you just look?

Longshank House is soon milling with people celebrating the full and fiery life Theresa Geraghty enjoyed on this earth.

When Father Rafferty arrives, each decade of the rosary is recited en masse, ending with *et lux perpetua luceat ei. Requiescat in pace. Amen.*

Amen.

My grandmother is carried to the sterility of a hearse. And that's when I cry.

Biddy adjusts my black hat, a little pillbox with a feather, and steps back.

"Pull your skirt down. It's rising up at the back. Do you have a spot of red lipstick? You look as pale as paper. Let me see now. Good. Pull your shoulders back. Shauna, will you bring a box of tissues for the church?"

Dad is all starched and upright. His hair is neatly plastered, and he sports a new side parting. Biddy licks her finger and rubs at something on his collar, then says, "Tom, lead me out."

Uncle Frank and Aunt Shauna follow, then Josie and Colin, and when I look around, there's Barney with his hands on his hips. "Take my arms, girls," he tells me and Oona. "It's time to say good-bye to Mammy."

We pass the musicians on our way out, who sit on a stone bench in the yard, drinking stout. "We'll put on a good show," they assure Barney, raising their tankards.

"Mammy always loved a decent jig," says Barney.

◆

After the service, when we stand in the graveyard for the burial, I take Biddy's gloved hand.

"Kate," she whispers, "you must let go. I need both my hands to pray."

I watch as she fingers her rosary beads with a quiet ferocity, mouthing a silent prayer.

The authority, the discipline. I cling to the belief that this translates to love and her need to protect. Whatever it is, there's an odd security about it all.

Especially now.

"O God, by Your mercy rest is given to the souls of the faithful," says the priest. "Please bless this grave. Appoint Your holy angels to guard it and set free from all the chains of sin the soul of Theresa Geraghty whose body is buried here, so that with all Thy saints she may rejoice in Thee forever. *Per Christum Dominum nostrum.*"

Sunday, November 18

Oona asks Dad if he has any space left in the trunk of his Saab. When he says yes, she scuttles into the dining room and reappears with a parcel marked KATE/FRAGILE.

"Tom, it needs careful packing," she says, giving me a wink. "I'd hate any of it to break."

And when we are hugging and saying our good-byes, Oona says, "It's your grandmother's glassware. I wanted you to have it."

A smile dimples her cheeks. "Barney, did you put plenty of newspaper in that wooden box?"

"I did indeed. Here we are, Katie."

When I see Dinah's round eyes peeping back at me, my thanks come out in whispers.

"Now don't stand here wasting time thanking us," says Oona, with tears in her eyes, "or you'll miss the boat, and then you'll be in trouble with your mam." She lowers her voice. "Katie, concentrate on Biddy's good points. Those odd loving times. That's I how I tolerated Theresa. God rest her feisty soul. Now, be off with you, and don't forget to write a postcard or two."

CHAPTER 27

◆

Saturday, December 1
33 Cherry Blossom Road, Dorton

It's the weekend. So I'm in Dorton again, sitting cross-legged on my old bed. Pulling at a strand of wool, I watch the loops dance as I unravel my knitting row by row. But when I reach the cuff of the sleeve, the yarn snaps.

Broken yarn. Broken heart.

I grab the wriggled pile of wool and bury my head in it. Will I ever master this sodding Aran pattern? Will I ever finish this sweater for Griff in time for Christmas?

And I'm whispering, Jack, Jack, Jack.

I think I still love you, Jack.

I allow tears to fall, hot and heavy.

Separate bedrooms, Kate, separate lives.

His words caressed, his fingers coaxed, his body persisted until I ached for him.

Do you love me?

Let me show you how much, Katie.

Damn, damn, damn.

Dinah interrupts my misery with a chirrup. She bounces on the bed, circles, then collapses into instant kitten-sleep. I stroke her tiny body.

The front door slams, and I listen to the rise and fall of a heated conversation. Biddy and Dad are having another row, but my mother will win. She always does.

Easing off the bed, I creep to the door, open it a crack, and listen.

"When did you last take me on holiday, Tom? Just tell me that."

"What are you talking about, Biddy? Every summer, I drive the caravan wherever you choose."

"And I do most of the work. I pack it, clean it, cook in it. Most wives are taken to a hotel, but not me."

"Where are we supposed to find the money for hotels?"

I know what's coming next. She thinks he'd make some sort of effort. But no, he watches everyone else get promoted right in front of his nose, and what does he do about it? Nothing. Throughout their married life, she's had to work her fingers to the bare bone, because he's never earned enough to support them.

"I'm sick of hearing this, Biddy. Sick. You never give up, do you?"

I close my door and lock it. She does work hard—with an obsession—no one could deny that.

I listen to a mumbled, "I try my best, Biddy."

Poor Dad.

What a worthless evening. I look through the window to see rain fall in billowing sheets. Again, the front door slams. I can just about see Biddy's frame standing in the driveway, with the red spot of a cigarette between her fingers. A car swishes by, and its headlights reveal her face. She looks up at me, her features puckered with anger.

I tug at the curtains to close them and her voice rings clear. "Don't you dare tear those good curtains."

Yes, this is Biddy. This is my mother. Still carrying the scars, bearing the grudges of childhood. Or was she born this way? Is this her, how she is, never to change?

As it was in the beginning, is now, and ever shall be, world without end.

Perhaps I should spend my weekends in Cardiff from now on. Oh hell, what do I really want to do? What *shall* I do? When will I make a decision and stick to it for once in my life?

I switch off the light and lay next to Dinah.

Sleep will help. It always has in the past.

I cradle my stomach and close my eyes.

◆

Dinah wakes me up, mewling. She wants the litter tray. What time is it? Light flickers through the curtains and a rumble follows. And with a thunder-crack comes a hard knock on my door.

I grab hold of the clock. It tells me it's one in the morning.

"Mum?" I wrench myself from the bed, turn the lock, and Dinah scoots out between Biddy's legs.

"Your meal is waiting on the table downstairs, cold."

Dad is hovering behind her. "Why didn't you come down?"

"Because you were having a row," I say. I put my hand to my knotted hair, try to comb it with my fingers.

"Will I throw the plate in the bin or will you eat your dinner?"

Frustration simmers inside me. I need to snarl, snap, retaliate, but I'm too weary. What's the bloody use, anyway?

"I'll eat it. Thank you."

❖

After Biddy has warmed up the fried fish, I try to push mouthfuls past the lump in my throat. Were there any phone calls for me, Dad? No. Why am I sleeping so much lately? I don't know.

They sit on either side of the kitchen table, watching me play with the food. Thunder continues to roll and roar.

"Listen," says Biddy. Her hair is still damp. "Daddy is treating me at Christmas. We're going to the Isle of Wight."

"Staying in a hotel for a week," says Dad, looking all pleased and proud.

"The staff will cope with the Bread Shop," says Biddy. "Where will you go, Kate?"

"Llandafan," I reply, without a second thought. "I'll spend Christmas in Wales."

"That'll be nice for you," says Dad, smiling.

I push my plate away and stare at the newly painted kitchen walls. Seagull gray. I swallow that lump in my throat and I want to heave. Am I pregnant?

"Look at her," says Biddy. "She resents the fact we're going away."

"No, I don't." I keep my voice low, desperate to avoid conflict. I don't need this now.

Biddy picks up my dinner and drops the whole lot, plate and all, into the bin. "Let's go upstairs to bed, Tom. I'm tired."

One, two, three, four . . . I silently count to ten.

"I'll be up in a second, Biddy," says Dad.

"Come on, Tom."

He looks at my face, then turns away, rescues the plate from the bin, puts it in the sink, and walks out.

Dinah slinks around my legs. I pick her up and tuck her head under my chin. She can sleep in my room tonight. I need the company.

As I pass my parents' bedroom, I hear, "Tom, I am *not* being ridiculous. You've always thought more of Kate than me."

"For God's sake, Biddy. What are you saying?"

"I mean it, Tom."

CHAPTER 28

❖

> 67 Solborne Road,
> Notting Hill, London.
> 5th December '73

Katie,

You can't believe how happy I was that you wrote to me. But love, it's ME who should have said sorry. Will you ever forgive me for being such a vile and horrible bitch? I don't know what came over me, sulking because some bloke fancied you instead.

We've been best friends forever, and I nearly ruined it. Angie phoned, told me about Jack. Look, I'm about due to give my folks a visit. Shall we get together? I'll cadge a few days leave. It would mean I'd have to work over Christmas, but I wouldn't care. I'm here for you, as always.

Are you okay? God, I've missed you. I'm sorry, sorry, sorry.

> With tons of love,
> Moira X X X X X

CHAPTER 29

◆

Christmas Day
Ty Wen, Llandafan

I scrape frost from the window with my thumbnail to watch snowflakes fall in busy swirls. And in the distance, I see a blur of pheasant feathers: scarlet, emerald, and rust—it's a lone male.

Sinking back on my pillow, I relish the comfort of the bed here in the attic of Ty Wen.

Mamgu will mix the onions with sage and breadcrumbs to stuff the turkey. And she might husk the cobnuts she saved from the hedges and crush them with a rolling pin and add them, too, along with the eggs.

I'll get up in a minute and help. I'll drizzle the Christmas pudding I made in Dorton with a little more brandy before wrapping it in muslin. Then I'll leave it to steam for hours over simmering water. It's full of sultanas, orange rind, prunes, walnuts, black treacle . . .

My stomach rumbles. My round stomach. My hand moves to my breasts and their tenderness dismays me. Thank God Biddy hasn't noticed. Yet. And I shall keep my baby, no matter what, but I mustn't think about it now. Not today. Not on Christmas Day.

I think of cribs and shepherds and wise men and gifts. I finished the scarf, as light as a cobweb, for Biddy, and when I cast off the last row of Dad's waistcoat, I labored over that Aran sweater again for Griff's small frame. I got it right this time. I hid parcels in my parents' cases before they set off for the Isle of Wight. They were wrapped in paper covered with holly.

When I hear the muffled chime of bells from Llandafan Chapel, my mind drifts back to that Sunday in Holland Park, to that morning when I lay in Jack's bed watching the curtains ripple at the window.

I know I should phone him. Moira said I must. In fact, she threatened to do it for me if I left it any longer. WHAT? You're pregnant? That fucking bastard, Kate. Of course she and Ingrid will keep it a secret. When will I tell Biddy? Do I want them with me when I do?

Oh God.

I must get up.

◆

Mamgu and Griff don't go to the chapel. They had enough with Sunday school when they were young, they say, when religion was poured down their throats. I shudder, cold, as I pull on thick socks, shove my legs into cords, and struggle into a Fair Isle pullover. I run downstairs, and the aroma of herbs and spice, the glow of a coal fire, and the lilt of a Welsh choir warm my heart and mood. This is just the place to be.

I turn the radio up higher.

"*Nadolig Llawen.*" I kiss and hug my grandparents in turn. "Happy Christmas."

Mamgu has strung star-shaped biscuits around a little spruce tree by the back door and a jumble of gifts leans against the bucket it sits in.

"I'll get breakfast!" I say before I close the bathroom door.

The water is warm—the gas boiler did its job. I lather my hands and face with Imperial Leather soap, and as I pat my face dry, I determine to enjoy Christmas day, 1973, in Llandafan.

Boxing Day, December 26

The clock ticks away the hours. It's four in the morning, and I can't sleep. Why did I eat so much? Now I have a stomachache. Was it the food, or did I give myself a chill?

Griff insisted we throw snowballs yesterday after dinner. The tip of his nose glowed red as he limped after me.

"*Twpsen,*" shouted Mamgu with her hands resting on the ridge of her hips. "You'll kill yourself, Griff." He hurled a snowball at her plump rear as she stalked back to the house.

"Fool!" she yelled.

Griff laughed so much, his top teeth fell onto his tongue, and it was my turn to crease with laughter, and I collapsed, backward, onto a blanket of snow. And I lay there, fanning my arms to make a snow angel.

Or perhaps I need the bathroom. I light the candle and slip my finger into its holder, and I try my best to tread on each step in a different place to avoid the creaks. I know this stairway by heart. I've been climbing it since I was a toddler in pigtails.

Damn. I should have dressed first, it's bloody freezing—but there's Griff's new sweater draped over a clotheshorse. I squeeze a handful of the wool. He must have left it here ready for the morning.

I'll wear it. Already, it smells like Griff, of tobacco and soap.

And there are Mamgu's slippers by the hearth, the tartan ones with the pom-poms.

Perfect.

I slop my way to the bathroom.

But now, back in the kitchen, the pain is a vise, clamping down, releasing, clamping. I put the kettle on to boil and pace the floor, and as soon as I hear the first bubbles, I snatch the kettle from the fire. I fill a hot-water bottle, and then the teapot in the light of the gas flame.

I curl up in an armchair. The tea is a comfort as I grasp hold of the cup and sip. The warmth from the hot-water bottle penetrates and spreads, dulling the stabs and cramps.

Yes, they're cramps. Oh God.

I'm losing my baby.

My baby.

Pulling myself up, I sway back to the bathroom, grabbing onto furniture, leaning against walls, trying to keep the candle steady until I reach the toilet.

A crimson bloom tells me there's no need to call Jack now. It's all over.

I place the candle on the edge of the bath and drop my head forward. Isn't that what you're supposed to do, when everything turns black and spots of light flit before your eyes? My hair falls between my legs and I grasp hold of my knees and rock forward and backward, willing the pain away.

"Katie?" Mamgu's call is soft.

I can't answer her. Blood is sliding, slipping from me.

The bathroom is washed with light from a paraffin lamp. *"Beth sy'n bod?"*

I should have locked the door. I look up at Mamgu's face, and I'm trembling. I can't move, dare not move. She asks me the question again in English. "What's the matter?"

"Dim byd."

Nothing. Why I am I saying *nothing*?

Mamgu places a cool hand on my forehead and then on my cheek. "Your face is damp, *bach*. You have a cold sweat. Can you stand?"

She places the lamp on the floor and bends for me to plait my fingers behind her neck. Her hair is wound in plastic curlers.

Blood dribbles down to my ankle and when Mamgu helps me to a stool and stands back, she sees it, and she looks into the toilet and says, "Oh, *bach*. How many weeks?"

She knows.

"Two months. Three months. I'm not sure how I'm supposed to count."

As the pain eases, tears stream and a shuddering sob brings Mamgu to my side. The fleece of her gown is soft against my face as she cradles my head.

"Shh. No need to tell your mam."

Griff calls out from their bedroom next door. "Mildreth, *beth sy'n digwydd?*"

"Nothing's the matter. Go back to sleep." Mamgu locks the door and turns the switch high on the gas boiler, then twists on the taps. The bathroom is filled with steam. "Lift your arms," she says, easing Griff's sweater over my head. The bloodstained nightie is slipped off and deftly rolled up. "Are you well enough to take a warm bath?"

I nod.

Jack held out his hand. "Let's take a bath," he said.

He shampooed my hair, slid soap over my arms, my legs, my back. I prayed the day would never end.

Mamgu helps me step in. She dips a washcloth into the water. "Here. You'll soon feel better, *cariad*."

She turns to flush the toilet. "I'll be straight back," she says.

My baby has gone. Did it have little arms and legs?

Clouds of blood still escape from me, but the warmth of the water melts the last of the pain away. Mamgu returns with one of her nighties tucked under an arm and starts tearing up a sheet of gauze. "We'll soon have you fixed up."

◆

When I'm clean and dry, she helps me to the attic. She spreads the comfort of a second quilt to the bed, and climbs in next to me. Snow pitter-pats against the window, and when a barn owl squeaks, another responds with a mournful wail.

I turn onto my side. "Mamgu, did you ever lose a baby?"

"Yes, *bach*. After five months. We buried the little mite in the orchard, when the trees were full with blossom. We thought he'd like it there."

She circles her arm around my waist, and in the drift of sleep, I catch a whisper.

"We called him Jack."

CHAPTER 30

◆

1974

Friday, November 29
33 Cherry Blossom Road, Dorton

The atmosphere is cool, the conversation crisp, in the kitchen at 33 Cherry Blossom Road.

"Tom, butter your bread on the plate, not on the palm of your hand."

"What? What now? Oh."

"Thank you."

The meal goes on. My parents gulp their tea, slice their ham, chew, swallow, spit out a comment—

"I'll live in the caravan. Keep the bloody house, Biddy."

"I paid for that caravan. There's no way you'll get it."

"Take everything, why don't you?"

"Oh, I will. The Bread Shop, too. It was me who earned a decent wage to afford it in the first place."

"Ah yes. If it wasn't for you, we'd have nothing, would we?"

"Tom, why don't you SHUT UP?!" screams Biddy.

"Shut up? Shut up?!" Dad bangs a fist on the table and stalks out of the kitchen.

Of course, they don't really plan to split up. This is how most of their arguments end. Things have got pretty lively since I left Cardiff.

Gathering the salt, sauce, and sugar together, I plan on creeping back to my bedroom because I have some knitting to do. Evie gave me a bundle of patterns before I left Eglwys School. Try this one, Katie, she said, pointing at a picture of a jacket. Now there's a challenge. Master that one, love!

"KATE!"

I grab hold of the sink. Dear God, my mind is a knot of rope, blackberry, and moss stitches.

"Sit down," says Biddy. "I'm still eating, can't you see?"

Pouring myself a cup of tea, I obey, and use the time to think about the Home Economic lessons I ought to prepare for Heybridge High next week. Talking of challenges, teaching sixteen-to-eighteen-year-old girls is a task in itself. Most of them are a foot taller than me.

Biddy rattles her fingernails on the Formica table.

"Your father's fuse is very short these days," she says. "Have you noticed?"

I'd noticed sparks flying and *both* fuses short.

"Mmm," I say.

Why did I move back to Dorton? I list the reasons, the circumstances, in my head.

Number one: Life was lonely in Cardiff. Angie married Josh, so bang, there went my only friend in the city. Number two: I'd finished my probationary year and couldn't wait to get shot of Basil Kirby. Number three: I failed three interviews in London, so my dreams of moving in with Moira and Ingrid were dashed. Number four: My parents decorated my room at 33 Cherry Blossom Road, and bought me a furniture set in white. Queen Anne style, said Biddy. And look, said Dad, he'd built a shelf to hold a TV and my record player beside it.

How could I say no?

And in Llandafan I lost something precious that would have offered unconditional love. My baby. From then on, I was a muddle, a complete mess. I sought order in my life, and who better to provide that than Biddy?

So here I am. Back at the Formica table, where my dad always sits to the left and Biddy to the right.

It's not just the rows, it's the "when did I come homes," the "where did I goes," "who was I withs?" Dad worries, that's all. Who did I talk to?

Biddy knows how much I earn. She'll do my accounts, she says. I wouldn't know where to start. I don't have a clue. How did I afford that new skirt? There's nothing left in the bank.

I certainly have order now.

They *can't* be period pains, Kate. Not possible. How does she know? She has my dates marked on a calendar. Why? So she knows when to pick up a packet of tampons from the pharmacy, that's all. And she squeezes my hand.

Biddy knows the very timetable of my body. She's familiar with every root of hair on my head, every toenail, every eyelash, every mole and freckle. The invasion is both comfortable and disconcerting at the same time.

It's my secrets that save me from total control.

Like the miscarriage.

"Kate, what are you thinking about?" she asks.

"Knitting patterns."

At least my thoughts are my own.

Click-flick goes Biddy's lighter.

Shall I scream when she asks me to cover the butter?

She inhales deeply. "Your father treats me like a piece of dirt, so he does. I won't stand for it. Put the lid on the butter dish, Kate. Are you listening to me?"

"Yes."

Agghh.

Moira said that if I had my own way, I'd stay in every single night. But I need to hibernate for a while, I replied. You know, after Jack and everything. And anyway, I love knitting.

Oh, c'mon Katie, you're over Jack, she said. That was a long time ago now. How many sweaters have you made? she asked.

Ummm. Eight.

And a half.

Call that hibernation? It's depression, she said. Listen to her, Katie, she's deadly serious. Put everything in the past. Start over. She'll look in the paper, in the employment section, under education, see what else turns up.

"TOM!" yells Biddy.

I jump, then carefully lift the saucer to pour the tea back into the cup.

Biddy cocks her head toward the living room door. "Do you plan to sit in front of the TV all night, Tom? Or would you think of helping us in here?"

And so we clear, wipe, wash, stack, and dry in silence, until:

"Shall I make another pot of tea?" asks Dad.

"No, thank you, Tom." Biddy's voice is the clip of a scissors.

But he makes one anyway, and presents a china cup and a slice of cake on a plate. And Biddy melts, because after all, Dad did make the first move, and that's all that counts.

And *he* melts, because he'd never survive without her.

He has this desperate dependency thing going on. I'm also left wondering if he could survive without *me*.

He taught me to drive last month. He enjoyed our nights out, he said. His face would light up, his mood dance, his step quicken as we left the house arm in arm. We had fun, he taught me well, I passed the first time. I ran out of the test center, waved the magic slip of paper, said, *Freedom, at last, Dad!* I hugged him, kissed his cheek, and said, shouldn't I have done this years ago?

When I stood back, a tight smile sat in his gray face.

Poor Dad.

And now, it's a Friday night. I have my Fiat 127 sitting out there, costing me a fortune in so-called easy payments. I ought to go out, somewhere, anywhere, but what's the point?

"I'm off to do some knitting," I say.

"Sit down with us in the living room, why don't you?" asks Biddy. "*General Hospital* will be on soon."

The phone rings, and Dad runs to the hall to answer it.

"It's for you, Kate," he calls. "It's Moira."

"What does *she* want?" asks Biddy.

Dad pats my shoulder and hands me the receiver.

"Hi, Moi."

"Hi, Katers. I'll be in Dorton tomorrow to visit the folks, and then you and me are going out—okay?"

"Where?"

"To a dance at Brayminster Town Hall. It'll be a blast."

"Oh, Moi, I don't know . . ."

"Come."

"What sort of dance?"

"The Young Conservative's Ball."

"Oh, good God."

"*Come.*"

I answer with a sigh. "Okay."

"Wonderful. We'll meet at the Plough around seven. Drinkies first, as usual."

I say my good-byes, then poke my head into the living room. "I'm going to a dance at the Town Hall tomorrow night."

"With that *Moira*?" enquires Biddy.

"Oh, for God's sake, what do you want me to do? Stay in, sip tea, sit in a cloud of cigarette smoke for the rest of my life?"

Her face pinches.

Dad's crumples. "How dare you speak to your mother like that," he says, folding his arms, nodding at Biddy.

"I'm TWENTY-BLOODY-THREE, for *Christ's* sake!"

Dear God. I'm actually screaming.

I storm out.

"If you've broken the hinges, you'll pay for the repair!" yells Biddy. "You bad-tempered little madam!"

I lean against the door, put my ear to it.

Five minutes pass and I hear nothing. But then—

"Ah well. She might meet a decent man."

"He'd better be decent," says Dad.

"I sometimes wonder if you want her married at all, Tom."

"Don't start that again, Biddy—*please?*"

CHAPTER 31

◆

Saturday, November 30
Brayminster Town Hall

"Listen to this," says Moira. "*Built in 1906, Brayminster Town Hall is one of the finest venues for banqueting and balls within the area. Richly colored carpets, decorative plasterwork and a magnificent vaulted ceiling. Exquisite detail to reflect the importance of any occasion. Such an elegant interior and tranquil setting belies its convenient location.*"

Moira folds the invitations her sister got for us and shoves them into her pocket. "So there we are, Katers."

She grabs my arm.

"Very impressive, Moi," I say, holding on to her for support, "but the location of the flipping car park isn't so convenient, is it?"

I'm cold, I'm damp, and the hem of my dress trails through mud and grime. We've had three days of rain.

"Bloody puddles," I say as water squelches between my toes.

When we reach the building, I usher Moira inside, telling her to hurry up, I need the loo.

"We'll dry our feet with a couple of paper towels," she says. "Just take that miserable look off your face, Kate Cadogan. We're here to enjoy ourselves."

After layering on a second coat of makeup, I make a futile attempt to turn my hair under with a brush. "Oh bugger it, Moi. You wouldn't believe how often I feel like cropping this mane. You always look so neat."

She grins like an elf when I take off my coat.

I take a sidelong look in the mirror. "Whatever possessed me to buy this dress, Moi?"

Yellow fabric springs from a smocked bodice, and the sleeves are like Bo Peep's. I tell Moira to stop with the sniggering, okay? But that makes her laugh even more.

She finally catches her breath. "Oh, Katie, we're going to do some serious shopping when you're next in London."

We deposit our coats at the cloakroom, hand over our invitations, and enter a ballroom, where it's too dark to appreciate the exquisite detail and the richly colored carpets. It's packed with dancing, prancing Young Conservatives.

So what now? We head for the bar, of course. It's conveniently located along the wall to our left, very fancy, created in a style that reflects the importance of this occasion.

"Cheer up," warns Moira.

"Gin and tonic?" I offer.

We sit in a corner and I think back to our early days. Shawhurst High, detentions, school dinners, benediction on Fridays. Father Flannagan, Miss Noonan, Guy Fawkes, firework displays.

Barry Finch.

I scan the crowd like an idiot. *Like he'd be here, stupid,* I tell myself. I bet he and Sophie Greengough left town years ago.

After two more gin and tonics, we're ready to hit the dance floor. A strobe light sparks things up a bit, and the exquisite plasterwork shimmers.

Moira shouts above the pounding of ABBA's "Waterloo." "Hey, Kate, I forgot to tell you—I met this fabulous guy in Euston Station yesterday. Oh, I love this song!"

We dance, and I wait for her to finish singing along with ABBA, oh yeah, about history books on shelves, they're always repeating themselves.

"Anyway, he asked me if the train was late, and then we got talking."

Moira swings her arms above her head, and oh, she couldn't escape if she wanted to, she's finally facing her Waterloo—

"Moi, get on with it."

"His name's Gus, he wore a trench coat, and he took my phone number, woah, woah, woah, woah, Waterloo."

The strobe dissolves, and we pause for breath. Where does Gus work? In publishing. Wow, I say. Brown hair, blue eyes, drop dead gorgeous. Dreamy voice.

Paul McCartney and Wings launch into song, and we're off again. As we dance, I notice two figures standing by the bar. One short, one tall.

The tall one smirks at me. He cradles a pint of beer against his chest like it's a precious child. There's a lot of pointing going on, and nodding of heads, and what's the betting they'll be asking us to dance? Any time now, I tell Moira, does she see them?

She says she doesn't think much of mine. Which one, I ask. The short one with eyebrows like hairy caterpillars, she says.

But she has it all wrong. The caterpillar's hers, I reply.

So we bounce to the music, keeping wary eyes to the left, and it's during the last throes of "Band on the Run" when fingers tap our shoulders.

"Having fun?" asks the tall one.

"Yes," I say, listening for the next record.

The disc jockey purrs into the microphone. "Folks, let me now play for you, the Hollies singing 'Air That I Breathe.' Grab your partners for a bit of ro-mance. Totally groo-vay."

Moira's eyes widen in mock horror before she's swept away by the cater-pillar.

The tall one holds me in place with a firm hand, flat on the back of my smocked bodice. I'm Kate, I say, as we circle the dance floor.

Pleased to meet you, is the response. His name's Rodney. Am I from around here?

"Dorton."

"I'm from Oakley Green," says Rodney. "Played hockey in Brayminster today, a chap from the opposing team invited us here tonight. Nice place."

"Built in 1906, and recently renovated," I say. "Such an elegant interior and tranquil setting belies its convenient location."

Har.

"I tend to agree."

I'm on a level with his paisley cravat. He smells of musty tweed and deodorant. His chest is solid, his arms are long. I look up and see high cheekbones set above a square jaw. A straw-colored moustache lies under his nose, and his eyes are huge behind thick glasses. I try to determine if he's good-looking. The word presentable comes to mind. Biddy would like him.

"My grandfather was a very important person," he announces.

"Oh?"

"He was the Lord Mayor of Tinchley."

Ah yes, Biddy would like him.

Rodney's a partner in the family business, has two sisters. Shares a house with his friend, Bob.

I'm guessing Bob is the caterpillar.

What do I do?

"I'm a Home Economics teacher," I reply.

"Interesting. Know how to cook then, eh?"

His frame is wider than Jack's. He speaks like a BBC newsreader. Mature. Solid. Safe.

"I went to King's in Worcester," he says. "Did you board, Kate?"

Ha! Did I board. "I went to the local Catholic school," I say, feeling small and unworthy in my Bo Peep dress.

Oh Lord, I am not worthy to receive You, but only say the word and I shall be healed.

The Hollies repeat several times that all they need is the air that they breathe, but finally, the song, and the dance, comes to an end.

Then suddenly, Moira appears, with our coats draped over one arm. She tugs at my puffed sleeve. "We must go," she hisses. Then in my ear, "Quick, before Caterpillar Bob comes looking for me. He's in the gents'."

I smile at Rodney. "I'm sorry, but we must dash."

I'll kill Moira later.

"May I have your telephone number?" he asks.

Moira hands me my bag. "Here, Kate," she says. "I hope we haven't missed our bus."

Bus?

I write my parents' number on the back of a receipt and hand it over.

As we scoot toward the exit, Moira says she's sorry, Kate, but Bob gave her the creeps. A caterpillar in every sense of the word, his hands were crawling everywhere. Did I mind leaving early? Looks like I was doing okay with the tall bloke, did she spoil anything?

"Let's get something to eat," I laugh. "I'm bloody famished."

◆

At the Hanged Man, halfway through our chicken-in-a-basket with chips and peas, we speculate as to whether Gus—or Rodney—will phone next week.

CHAPTER 32

❖

1975

Saturday, April 5
The Bread Shop, Dorton

"**Will I make duck with** orange sauce?" asks Biddy. "Or lobster thermidor?"

"Why not beef and Yorkshire pudding? That's what we always have on a Sunday."

"I'm well able to roast a duck or boil a lobster, Kate."

When Mrs. Bootsby-Smythe enters the Bread Shop, Biddy says good morning, please do look at the hot cross buns, aren't they wonderful? Fresh and spicy. She won't be long, just a few more items to add to the shopping list for Kate, her daughter.

". . . and two plucked mallards. There. I think that's everything. Now, how can I help you, Mrs. Bootsby-Smythe? I'm planning a dinner for Kate's new boyfriend tomorrow. He's the Mayor of Tinchley's grandson."

I grab a couple of baskets and set off for the Fresh Game Store.

Rodney's parents certainly have a grand lifestyle. Nancy serves tea using the finest porcelain: Royal Doulton, Worcester, and Wedgewood. Rodney Senior drinks the rarest of brandies, smokes the richest-smelling cigars. The Fanshaws lounge in vast leather sofas. Their oak table is a monster on clawed feet. Curtains are lavish, in Italian brocade and the thickest of velvets.

But, oh boy, if only Biddy knew. Money they may have, but dust, grime, and a lingering stench lie thick and still.

It's a touch mucky, chez les Fanshaws.

But I like Rodney. Sensible, down-to-earth Rodney. Dependable and trustworthy, a Jack Thorpe or a Rowland Picken he is not. No groping, no mauling, no expectations.

Well, he's coming for dinner tomorrow evening, and I'm praying Biddy will take to him. Her comments following brief glimpses and polite exchanges at the door or in the hallway have been favorable, and she likes all she's heard so far. A partner in his father's business? Now if that doesn't impress Aunt Shauna, nothing will.

Sunday, April 6
33 Cherry Blossom Road, Dorton

"Kate, change the tablecloth. The Irish linen I said, not that old dish rag. Where's the brass candelabra? Sure and won't Rodney Fanshaw be here any minute?" asks Biddy. "Am I the only one with their eye on the clock? Tom, light the candles, take off your slippers, why aren't you wearing your good shirt?"

She tears off to the kitchen asking why I didn't check the ducks. I poise with a fistful of silverware, wondering if I'm to set places, do a second run with the vacuum cleaner, or tidy my hair. I can't remember the sequence of orders.

Ding-dong.

"I'll answer it," I shout.

Rodney wears a navy jacket, striped tie, and gray flannels. We exchange kisses, he squeezes my arm, strides into the living room, and calls, "Where's the lady of the house?"

"Here," sings Biddy, smiling. "Hiding in the kitchen."

With a flourish, Rodney presents her with a bunch of freesias.

She pats her hair. "Why, don't they smell lovely! Kate, fetch the Waterford vase."

When I return, Rodney and Dad are engaged in an enthusiastic handshake, while Biddy takes the opportunity to inspect. Her eyes are quick, her look is one of approval.

"Put the flowers on the sideboard, Kate, and let's leave the men to talk. Proceed to the dining room, please, Tom, while we see to the dinner."

Good job Dad knows a bit about hockey and cricket, but he stutters, stalls, totally in awe.

As I lay the steamed asparagus in a dish, Biddy tells me I did well finding such a fine man. But dear God, what kind of ducks did I buy? There isn't an ounce of meat on them, they're all bone. Should we fry up a few sausages? Doesn't Rodney speak well? A lot more cultured than that Jack.

Then my mother puts down the carving knife, kisses me on each cheek, and because she approves of Rodney, I'm elated. I've done something right at last.

But oh, I'm so ready to leave home, because she drives me insane.

"Kate, will you wake up?" she asks. "Stir the sauce. No, not with a wooden spoon—here, use this one. Take hold of the saucepan handle or you'll tip the whole lot onto my good kitchen floor. Now what are you doing?"

"Stirring in a figure of eight."

She nudges me out of the way. "Well, isn't this great, will you look at the lumps? Hand me a whisk."

"That's orange peel, not lumps."

"Get the sausages in the pan. Oh, Kate, for crying out loud, prick the skins with a fork first, or the meat will burst out."

After beating the sauce to a foam, she turns up the heat, and when I suggest there's a danger the whole lot will end up as caramel, she tells me I'm not keeping my eye on the potatoes, and sure don't we have soup now, because they've boiled into the water? Would I think of putting the duck and asparagus into the oven to keep warm? No, don't bother, Kate, she'll see to everything, as per usual. Open the wine, would I? Because my father will have forgotten about it. Oh, and the starters. Get those out of the fridge.

I balance the Riesling and the starters on a tray and carry all to the dining room.

When Dad takes his place at the table, he stares with horror at the wriggle of pink I set before him.

"It's prawn cocktail," I explain.

He swallows hard. Cockles, winkles, or whelks he can handle, but he loathes prawns.

Too bad, said Biddy, when I reminded her. Like them or not, they were to remain on the menu for the Mayor of Tinchley's grandson.

Rodney asks if I'd like him to pour the wine, then, "What have we here?" he asks, dipping a finger into his cocktail sauce.

"Just mayonnaise mixed with ketchup," I reply.

"Mmm," he says. "Rather a delicious dressing."

In comes Biddy. "Please, Rodney, do help yourself to brown bread. Sit down, Kate."

Dad curls his lip when a prawn slithers from his spoon, back into its bed of lettuce.

"Tom, don't forget your serviette," says Biddy, shooting him a narrow-eyed warning.

I smile at Rodney, to save Dad, to divert attention.

"Gosh, you must be starving, Rod," I say, watching him pop two triangles of bread into his mouth at once.

And so we proceed, and the conversation rolls along. Yes, Rodney, Biddy was indeed born in a farmhouse in Ireland. It sits in the hundred and fifty acres of land her grandfather Bernard Connolly once owned. And yes, Rodney, he's quite correct in thinking she must come from a family of landowners. Oh, Tom, she's sure Rodney has no idea where the Welsh miners' cottages are in Ffynnon Beuno.

"Isn't that where Griff was born?" I ask.

"Kate," she snaps, "help clear the table ready for the main course, please."

I whisk away Dad's untouched starter, wondering how he'll deal with the *canard à l'orange* when it lands in front of him.

Back in the kitchen, I'm to add a generous portion of butter to the potatoes, be careful with Biddy's new oven-to-table Evesham dinnerware, please. Don't chip the eighteen-carat gold rim. Did I hear the Fanshaws own a holiday home on top of everything else? Did I hear that?

Yes, I know, Mum, I reply, in Crickmouth Bay, on the sea front.

Now don't go telling Rodney that my parents have to make do with a caravan, says Biddy. Doesn't Rodney look smart?

I'm to tug my skirt down at the front, lay my collar flat, pull my shoulders back, are the carrots overdone? Put the cherry pie in the oven to warm, whisk the cream, then set out the stilton and port, nicely now, for later.

Stilton and port?

"Kate, did I tell you to make gravy?" asks Biddy.

"It's for Dad. He won't like the orange sauce."

She asks me to hand her the saucepan, then she slams the gravy onto the draining board, and I'm to take that look off my face, right now, or it will be the last time she'll do anything for me, do I hear?

I apologize, not wishing to endure the embarrassment of repercussions at the dinner table. The short answers, the cold shoulder, the unfortunate remarks. Dear God, how much longer am I to live here? Try as I might, I still haven't managed to find a teaching job in London.

Rodney makes appreciative noises as he chews through sausages, bites into roasted potatoes, and licks Biddy's orange sauce from his knife. And the cherry pie is delicious, oh yes, rather, he'd like a third helping, and lashings more custard and cream, please.

He politely declines the Cockburn's port, because he must see which team he's been picked for next weekend, and when he rubs my knee, says he'd like to take Katers along to the clubhouse for a drink—

I see him as my savior.

Then my all-merciful advocate pleads my cause, hearkens to my cries, and through his infinite merits, intercedes. Because he tells my parents I'm invited to spend a few days with his family in Crickmouth Bay this summer.

Alleluia.

CHAPTER 33

◆

1976

Friday, July 9
Cliff House, Crickmouth Bay, Farmouth

"Rod, I'm trying to remember what you wore the night we met." I smile at his profile. I see a strong nose, I suppose it's big, and a jutting chin. The moon is reflected in the lenses of his glasses.

He turns to face me. "I wore a tweed jacket and a cravat," he says, then looks back at the sea. "Kate, I've been doing some thinking."

A train chugs by in the distance, and waves lap under the wooden pier, making slopping sounds.

"What have you been thinking?" I ask.

I sit down on the boards and dangle my feet over the edge. Bells ding and dong on anchored boats and their sails shiver in the breeze.

It's a beautiful night, and a beautiful place. I look back at the ribbon of houses that run along the base of the cliffs. The pink one called Cliff House belongs to the Fanshaws.

"I was wondering if—"

"Oh Lord, Rod, just look!"

His mother's body is pressed against a window and she's stark naked, showing a dark triangle and two balloon breasts for all to see.

"I'd better tell Mother to keep the bedroom lights off at night," he says.

"Or remind her to draw the curtains," I suggest, covering my mouth.

"Yes, yes," he says, flapping a hand toward Cliff House. "Kate, I have something to ask you."

"Okay."

Hmm. The knees of my jeans are wearing out. Must patch them.

"We've known each other for over twenty months." Rodney raises his face to a navy sky. "Would you consider marriage? There's a decent house for sale in Oakley Green."

I'd been hoping for this.

Kisses, a link of arm, a touch of hand, a little more when we're alone, but he'd held back.

Not that I minded—

If a boy wants to do it before marriage, said Biddy, it means he has no respect.

—but I was left to wonder if Rodney found me physically attractive. But he must do, because I've just had a proposal. *Weyhey!*

Rodney makes life bearable. He takes me away from 33 Cherry Blossom Road most weekends, to watch him play cricket, hockey, or billiards.

Moira and Ingrid asked if that's all we do, but I explained that after the games, we socialize, drink, sit around clubhouses. Sometimes go for a meal afterward.

And he found a house, he's asking me to leave Dorton. And oh God, this means I'd be leaving Biddy, too.

"Well, Kate?" Rodney sits down and takes my hand.

"Rod, do you love me?"

"I believe I do. Very much."

"I'll marry you," I whisper.

When he places his mouth over my closed lips, his moustache tickles my nose.

Saturday, July 10

"Here you are, Kate. You can borrow these jodhpurs."

Gaynor, Rodney's sister, tosses the trousers into my arms.

"Do I need these?"

"Up to you," she says, flouncing out with a flick of her black hair.

I smooth the jodhpurs onto the bed. They're sort of tulip-shaped at the top and the inner thighs are lined with leather. I'll look ducky in these. I pull a brown T-shirt from my suitcase and proceed to get all geared-up for the pony-trek. Betsy, the younger sister, says I'll need boots or shoes with a sturdy heel.

Tap-tap. "Rodney here. All ready, Kate?"

"Almost."

"Jolly good." He opens the door a crack and sticks his hand through. "Here's a riding hat."

I find Gaynor standing next to him in the hall, sleek in a pair of tight trousers. Betsy, healthy and plenteous, fills a pair of tracksuit bottoms.

The girls snigger as I flap out in my jodhpurs.

"Rod, wait, I'll change," I say, laughing, showing I have a sense of humor.

Bitches.

"Too late, you look fine, let's go."

"We'll meet you there," says Gaynor, jingling her car keys.

◆

When we arrive at the stables, five fat ponies stand tethered in a row along a fence. They're motionless.

"Ah, the Fanshaw party. Hello there, my name's Joe Nagel." He waves and reaches for the widest pony's bridle when Betsy waddles across the yard. "This one's for you, miss," he says.

I watch the family trio mount with ease. Betsy's poor pony takes a few staggering steps sideways and flattens its ears. Joe Nagel sees me cowering behind Rodney's car and calls me over. "Nice outfit," he says, winking. "Okay, approach Webster on her near side."

"Pardon me?" I say, dithering.

Joel Nagel chews on a matchstick, pushes back his flat cap, then slaps Webster on her left side. "Here," he says, "stand next to me. Listen carefully, and watch. Are you ready?"

I nod.

"Facing the pony, the reins are held in the left hand, and that left hand is placed on the pommel of the saddle. Got that?"

Okay. Pommel.

"The reins should be held tight enough to prevent Webster from wandering off when you try to mount, see? Now, turning to face the pony's rear, take the stirrup in your right hand, turn it clockwise like this, to allow you to place your left foot in, so the ball of your foot rests on the bottom of your stirrup. Am I clear so far?"

As mud.

"With your left foot in the stirrup, the right hand should be placed over the cantle. Then, with a small spring, jump up, straightening the left leg as you swing the right leg over, remembering to move your right hand forward as you do so, and then you gently sit in the saddle. Got it?"

My lower lip trembles. I'm so inadequate. Gaynor and Betsy are firmly planted on their ponies, yawning with the tedium of it all. I want to impress Rodney.

"What's your name?" asks Joe Nagel.

I tell him.

"Kate, face Webster's rump, left foot in the stirrup."

He whacks me hard on *my* rump.

"*Hup!* Over, turn, and SIT."

Rodney trots over. "You'll soon pick it up." He takes a deep breath. "Smell that mountain air. Give your pony a kick, Kate. Let's go."

I obey, and so does Webster, and the saddle creaks, and this is great.

Joe Nagel takes the lead, I'm to follow, and Webster's body sways into motion, her shoes clopping along the road. When we reach a steep track, she loses her footing and she shudders, puffs, takes more determined steps.

"Grip with your knees, Kate!" shouts Rodney. "Hold onto the saddle."

Up, up we go, climbing, climbing, until we reach a plateau. I pat Webster on her chestnut neck, run a handful of her mane through my fingers. I pull her reins and she stops. I loosen my grip and her head drops to graze.

Rodney pulls up alongside me, and without a word, we take in the scene. The land tumbles down to a lake that's bearded with heather, and in the far distance, there's a spread of sand and a strip of sea.

When I look at Rodney, the word stability sits in my mind, and it's underlined.

"Rod! Fancy a gallop?" yells Gaynor, circling her pony.

"Go ahead," shouts Joe Nagel, "but not Kate."

No fear of that.

Betsy nudges her pony toward me. "I canter, but I don't gallop," she explains.

She has the same sand-colored hair as Rodney. Same style, too, cut short, and in tufts. Her cheeks are pink, and the strap of her riding hat cuts deep into the flesh of her chin. "Rodney's a great horseman," she says.

His pony's legs curl into a trot, then with a lunge, he's off and gathering speed. He leans forward as he and his sister gallop neck and neck.

I slide off Webster, pull the rein over her head—I guess that's what I'm supposed to do—then I sit down on the ground. She continues to pull at grass as I feel the velvet of her nose with the back of my hand. The sun warms my back. It's going to be another hot day.

Rodney canters, slows, turns the pony with a smooth swoop. Its sides are heaving when he comes to a stop.

"Give them a rest, then we'll go on down to the lake," says Joe Nagel.

"Wish I could gallop like that," I say, looking up with a squint at Rodney.

He dismounts, crouches down beside me. Tipping his head back, he gulps from a canteen. "I'll teach you to ride one day," he says, wiping his mouth with a sleeve.

The reference to the future is comforting.

He offers me the water and I sip the half-mouthful that's left. "Here— thanks."

Rodney puts an arm round me, rests his hand on my shoulder, and I clasp hold of his fingers.

I feel safe.

Sunday, July 11

Gaynor took Betsy off with her to visit her boyfriend, a Huw Williams, who lives in Browen Bay.

Rodney asked if I would mind if he played a Sunday round of golf with his friend Todd Grimley. Won't be long, he said. His mother, I can call her Nancy, said she'd look after me.

His parents are a bit—strange. So is Aunt Glenda. Uncle Bertie's okay, I suppose.

I sit with my back straight and wait for Nancy and Aunt Glenda to serve tea in the living room, where the sofa is an orange moquette and the carpet is a scramble of Axminster.

I don't know how anyone could nod off in a room so luminous, but Uncle Bertie Bishop has managed to do just that. His head flops to one side, his mouth is a little O, his snore a soft rumble.

There's an elephant of a dresser to my left, in mahogany, and across from it, there's a glass cabinet full of brandy and jars of Dutch tobacco. And nearby, in a haze of smoke, sits my future father-in-law, Rodney Fanshaw Senior. He hasn't uttered one word yet.

Should I start the conversation?

But wait—I hear a snort as he shifts position in his armchair.

He takes a long drag from his cigar. "Last week, I played a quick nine holes with young Rodney." His announcement is made to the ceiling, then he pauses, leans forward. And farts.

"Anyway, I reminded my son that a man needs all the recreation he can get. Am I right? Eh? What?"

"Yes, I'm damned well right," he says, answering his own question.

He's an unusual-looking man. Prominent upper teeth rest on a moist lower lip, and his nose is perfectly hooked. A Mad Hatter if ever I saw one.

I nibble at the skin inside my mouth and study my sandals. Nancy and Aunt Glenda are taking an awful long time brewing that tea.

Desmond the dachshund jogs in, to mount Uncle Bertie's left leg.

"What the blazes?"

Well, that woke him up.

The more Uncle Bertie tries to break loose, the more enthusiastic the dog becomes, and the grip tightens.

And oh, dear God, my jaws ache, and I need to laugh so much. I take three slow breaths. *"Give him a kick!"* My advice is delivered through gritted teeth.

Uncle Bertie jabs with his free foot and the resulting dog-shriek finally attracts Rodney Senior's attention.

"Darling sausage! Whatever's the matter?" His voice is a simpering falsetto. "Looking for Mummy? Where's Nancy? Where's Auntie Glenda?"

In the kitchen, you old fart.

"I'll bet they're in the kitchen." He screws a finger into his nostril, twiddles, and flicks. "Where women should be, eh?"

This is hilarious.

Disgusting, but bloody hilarious. Oh God, wait till I tell Moira and Ingrid.

Auntie Glenda struts into the living room. "Hen-ry, Bertie, Bertie," she clucks. "Hot tea. Come on, Katie, sit up."

Clawing at a scatter of newspapers on the coffee table, she creates a space for the teapot, then sits next to me. "Hello, dear. It's lovely having young Rodney's *fiancée* with us. I heard the good news."

"Thank you. I'm glad to be here."

Nancy arrives. A tray is set down, holding cups, saucers, and a clutter of fondant cakes.

"These are Rodney Senior's favorites," she tells me.

Nancy takes two careful steps backward. She pauses, squats, and lands squarely on the leather ottoman, causing it to exhale with a hiss from its seams. Sitting with her legs well apart, her skirt drapes across her knees like a hammock.

An awful lot is on view. No one could miss the dimpled flesh bulging from support stockings. I wonder if they still do "it," her and Rodney Senior. A man needs all the recreation he can get, after all.

Stop it, Kate.

"Home-baked cakes!" bellows Rodney Senior. "Well done, Nancy. I married her for her baking, you know." Crumbs spit like loose sawdust from his mouth. "Married a good-un, didn't I?"

"More tea?" squawks Glenda. My cup is snatched before I have a chance to reply, and I'm poured another. She cocks her head to one side. "Katie's a pretty little thing, isn't she, Nancy?"

No answer.

"Waiting on the shelf before you met my son, weren't you, Kate?" smirks Rodney Senior. Rising from the armchair, he grunts his way to the corner of the living room. "Anybody mind if I watch the TV? No? Good." The television shows a picture, but emits no sound. "Hey, Nancy, the box is on the blink again."

Nancy whispers with Auntie Glenda, too engrossed to comment, so Rodney Senior tut-tuts his way back to his corner.

The minutes tick by.

Uncle Bertie dozes off again, and the hiss of secret conversation and his whistling snores lull me into a comfortable trance.

But then—

BANG! Rodney Senior smacks the television and it jolts to life. There's a boom, a blare, a blast. Women screech, sirens whine. Desmond yaps. Uncle Bertie sits bolt upright, and his eyelids bat.

"My favorite program!" blurts Rodney Senior. "*The Sweeney*. Look—the stupid sods just rammed their patrol car into a wall. What a cock-up!"

There's a rattle at the door and Rodney walks in. "Hello, Kate. I'm back," he beams.

Yes, he is. I put my plate on the coffee table and stand, reaching up to press a kiss on his cheek.

"I'd better drive you home to Dorton," he says. "Get you home before dark."

Nancy beckons at me elaborately, indicating the need to whisper in my ear. She has the same odor as her living room. Mildew, faint whiffs of dog pee and tobacco.

"Now don't forget next Saturday, will you?"

I raise an eyebrow.

"It's Father's birthday," she hisses. "I'm having a little buffet. Nothing too elaborate. You know, the usual thing, just a few friends and family."

"Can I help?" I ask.

She picks up the tray loaded with empty teacups and smeared plates. "Well, you're a Home Economics teacher. You could make the cake if you'd like, dear."

I look at the expression on Rodney's face, one of anticipation, and so I say, "I'd love to."

The television continues to thunder and blast. I say my good-byes, but Rodney Senior doesn't hear me, still mesmerized by *The Sweeney*. So I try a loud, "I'm leaving now."

"What a cock-up! What a bloody cock-up!" he exclaims.

Out in the hall, I collapse, double up laughing. "Oh, my God, your family," I say to Rod, my eyes blurred with tears. "They're all mad—but oh, *so* great!"

I can't quite work out the puzzled look on Rodney's face before he grabs hold of me and rams a kiss hard on my lips.

CHAPTER 34

◆

Sunday, October 24
33 Cherry Blossom Road, Dorton

"Oh, a winter wedding will be grand," says Biddy. "You did well getting Rodney Fanshaw to propose, Kate. Now stand still so I can see where I left off."

I grab hold of the back of the chair to keep balance while my mother pins the hem. She'd kept the gown for my wedding to Jack stored away. For sure, Kate, she said, didn't she know there'd be a next time, and why waste a good length of satin?

Rodney's a decent sort, she says, a man born to money, what with his inherited business and all. A financial advisor, no less. Streets ahead of that other fellow. Whatever was I thinking back then, would I please tell her? Now turn around.

Closing my eyes, I grit my teeth, trying not to smile.

Just wait till she meets Rodney Senior and Nancy.

"Great," says Biddy. "All I have to do now is sew seed pearls onto the sleeves. Get down off the chair."

She lifts the gown over my head and when I see daylight again, her eyes are riveted to my chest. I know what she's looking for. Swollen breasts. I push my arms into my sweater. Biddy won't find contraceptive pills in my handbag this time. Oh, no.

Not yet, I told Rodney.

Fair enough, he said.

Oh, I've learned my lesson well.

"Mum, why don't we have the bridesmaids in red velvet? Wouldn't that be Christmassy?"

"If you buy the fabric. I'll make Josie's," she offers, "you make the dresses for Gaynor and Betsy."

"Mum, I'm having Moira and Ingrid, and that's it."

Here we go again.

"And I wasn't a bridesmaid at Josie's wedding," I add, "so why should I—"

"Look at all I'm doing for you, Kate. I'd like Josie to be a bridesmaid. She's my godchild, after all." Biddy sorts through a box of buttons. "And you ought to ask the Fanshaw girls."

I sigh. But I suppose she's right.

"All right, Mum. Let's ask them to come to Dorton for measurements."

Because it's best Biddy never sets foot in the Fanshaw house, for as long as I can avoid it.

"Here," she says, "thread this needle for me. It's so fine I can't see the eye. Ah, five bridesmaids, we'll be the talk of the town."

I take the needle and look sideways at my mother. Not keen on my friends, but willing to compromise if it means creating an impression.

"What are you laughing at?" she asks.

CHAPTER 35

Friday, December 17
33 Cherry Blossom Road, Dorton

Smoothing away the kinks in the velvet of Betsy's dress, I hang it in my wardrobe along with the others. It took an extra yard of fabric to accommodate her girth.

Tomorrow morning, I'll take time smudging brown shadow on my eyes, painting red on my lips, sweeping a blush on my cheeks. I'll comb my hair straight till it shines. I'll slip into silk, pull on stockings, and step into shoes the color of buttermilk. Biddy will zip the gown, clip on the headdress, adjust the veil, then hand me the roses.

For tomorrow is my wedding day.

Five bridesmaids. Five ushers in morning suits wearing top hats and tails. One hundred and sixty-five guests, and a banquet at the Elms Hotel. A three-tier cake, formal and cream to match the bride's gown. A full mass at the Immaculate Conception complete with mixed choir.

Kate, when is Gaynor getting married, Biddy wanted to know. Next June? Ha! See if the Fanshaws can match *this* wedding. Am I pleased? It will take her and Daddy years to pay off the bank loan. Am I grateful?

Cakes, pastries, cold cuts, and pies from the Bread Shop are on lavish display for the houseguests. Those booked in hotels, please pop by. See the living room stacked high with your wedding gifts. Wrapped toasters, mixers, china, linen, steel pans, and canteens of silverware.

I have a gold band in a box.

A diamond ring on my finger.

A deposit paid, a contract signed, for a house.

Too late for second thoughts now.

Biddy's laugh rings out. She's in her element downstairs entertaining the guests in her new trouser suit. A green dress in worsted wool hangs under a red coat for the Big Day. A matching hat sits on her dressing table. A little black dress waits at the Elms Hotel for after the banquet, with new dancing shoes.

One of the musicians will play a few tunes during the reception. This morning, the hotel staff pushed his organ between the legs of the trestle tables, so everything's ready. Don't be dirty-minded, Kate, said Biddy. I know exactly what she means.

It feels like her own wedding, she's so excited. Daddy and her couldn't afford anything like this, two witnesses is all they had, no cake. A rented room was their home, no house, no honeymoon in Paris. I did well getting Rodney Fanshaw to propose. She wished she'd been so lucky.

There's a soft knock on my door.

"Oona!"

"Well, here's the girl herself, give me a big hug and kiss."

"Oona, you must be worn out after traveling all day." Her cheek is cool—it's freezing outside.

"Ah, yes, but nothing a wee drink wouldn't cure." She holds my hands and takes a step back. "But, Katie, it's you who's looking tired."

Tears sting my eyes.

"Whatever is it, Katie?"

"I don't know."

Oona's eyebrows knot together. She shakes off her coat and throws it onto a chair. "I'm off to get you a stiff drink. I'll be two seconds."

She comes back with a bottle of Bushmills and two glasses full of ice, and pushes the door shut with her bottom. "There's great merriment going on downstairs. What a crowd!"

"Is Rodney Senior, my future father-in-law, down there?"

"There's an auld man with a pair of teeth at right angles to his nose. Would that be him?"

I nod and grin, and Oona beams. "Ah! I got a smile out of you. And then there's a woman with a face the size of a bucket."

"Oh God! That's Nancy."

Oona puffs out her cheeks and crosses her eyes, and laughter bubbles out of me.

She pours the whiskey. "Jesus, Mary, and Joseph, and that Betsy is built like a tree-trunk."

"Ow, stop." I fall onto the bed and roll over on my back. Stitch seizes hold of my side and the more I laugh, the sharper it stabs. "God, I'm in pain, Oona."

She kicks off her shoes. "You should see your mam's face watching them—it's a picture. Here's your drink, move over."

Oona stretches out beside me, puts an arm behind her head and reaches for her glass. "Sla'inte. Now. What's wrong?" She crosses her plump legs.

"Cheers." The whiskey burns nicely, numbs my tongue. "I don't know," I say with a hiccup. "Truly."

"Ah, it could be nerves. What's your fella like?"

"Sort of solid, you know, reliable."

"A strong man?"

"Um, no. His job requires brains, not brawn."

Oona closes her eyes.

I sip my drink and my thoughts drift. Our new house is a complete wreck. Plaster crumbles off walls, windows are smashed, and there's no heat. Cracks in ceilings, leaking pipes. An old lady died there and the house lay empty for two years afterward. It was a bargain, and I can't wait to tackle it. Rodney isn't into renovating, he says, but he loves the place. He'll conduct business in the room at the back of the house when he's not in the office. I can push his desk over there. The golf clubs could stand in the corner. He reckons I'll soon have it shipshape. He'll keep a locked cupboard against the wall on the right, where he'll store his Masonic regalia.

And sure, what harm if he's a Mason, said Biddy. Don't that sort have plenty of money?

There's a wonderland at the back of 75 Copper Lane. Apple, plum, and damson trees with mistletoe, a sunken garden, creeping thyme, all manner of plants lying in secret ready to burst into spring.

"Your mam told Barney the Fanshaws are near millionaires," says Oona.

"Well, that's all that matters to Biddy," I say. "Pour me another drink."

"What matters to you, Kate, the size of his pocket or his pouch?"

I splutter on my Bushmills.

There's a tap-tap on the bedroom door, and Dad pokes his head in. "Hello, you two. Katie, I came up to let you know Mamgu and Griff phoned from the hotel. They want you to know they arrived safely."

"Thanks, Dad."

His face is pink and his grin wide. So he's had a few drinks, too. "Well, I'd better go back downstairs," he says. "Must help your mum."

I sit up and swing one leg to the floor.

"No, Kate, you stay with Oona," he says, showing me the palm of his hand. "It's your big day tomorrow, get some rest."

It's funny really. Dad doesn't mind me getting married this time. After meeting Rodney, he seemed content, sort of relaxed.

I lie back on the pillow.

Tomorrow is my wedding day. Tomorrow is my wedding *night*.

Rodney said his father called him to the bedroom last week, thought a man-to-man talk was in order. Showed him a pot of Vaseline, took a condom from a packet, and used Rodney's thumb to demonstrate. Well done, son, he said, with a wink and a nudge and a slap on the back.

My fiancé's expression when I hooted with laughter is best described as, um—bemused? No. More like perplexed. He's very fond of his batty father, and I shouldn't laugh. Must take more care.

I bought a beautiful black negligee with fronds of tan lace.

And our honeymoon is in *Paris*, no less.

Everything will be fine.

Turning to look through the window, I see snow float, as soft as powder I take a deep breath, and ask Oona if she was this apprehensive before *her* wedding day.

But she can't answer, because she's fast asleep.

CHAPTER 36

◆

Sunday, December 19
Copthorne Plaza Hotel, Horley, Surrey

Rodney pushes smoked haddock into his mouth. "Eat up, Kate. We have to catch the shuttle to Gatwick Airport in thirty minutes."

"Do we really have to be there four hours before the plane leaves?"

"Better safe than sorry, my little virgin bride."

Kate, be careful, said Biddy, or you'll lose him. Now don't go telling Rodney you lived in sin with Jack Thorpe.

Let's wait till we're in Paris, said Rodney, we ought to get a good night's sleep first.

I chew on my last spoonful of Rice Krispies.

"Ready? Then come on, Mrs. Fanshaw. We'd better get our act together *toot sweet.*"

Rodney rubs his hands in a napkin, rolls it into a ball, and tosses it onto my dish. "Goal!" he says.

After swallowing my coffee, I push the sleeves of my dress to my elbows, hoping I look like a *Parisienne,* and totter after him in my new black heels. "Do you like my new dress?" I ask as we climb the stairs.

"Very practical, but not sure about the shoes. Your feet may get swollen on the plane. Always happens to me. Must be something to do with the altitude."

Back in our room, he dons his cricket sweater. "Oh, Rod, you're wearing that?"

"It's comfortable."

"Okay." I kiss his chin. "Wasn't our wedding wonderful?"

Biddy was still dancing when we left.

Gatwick Airport

At the airport duty-free, I fuss around looking for a gift for Anthony Baster-field, and that really is his name. He's an accountant living in Paris, an old school friend of Rodney's. He's moving into his girlfriend's house while we honeymoon in his *appartement*.

"Tony is so generous, we must buy him something."

"If you think so."

I hold up a bottle of Johnnie Walker Red and a special reserve Cock-burn's port. "What do you think?"

"Whoa, go easy."

Before we head for the departure lounge, I arm myself with a couple of magazines. I've never been on a plane before in my life, and I'm shivering with anticipation. "Wait for me, Rod. Slow down." I grab hold of his arm and try to keep up with his marching steps.

In the departure lounge, I watch the planes as they lift their noses, then soar into the sky. Aer Lingus, Pan Am, Air France, Iberia. The roar of en-gines adds to my excitement.

And our seat numbers are called, and we step into the capsule, much smaller than I imagined, and I nod at each welcoming smile. Meet the cap-tain, say the stewardesses. Please have a pleasant journey—thank you—welcome aboard British Airways.

I fasten my seat belt. A whine follows a grumble, and there's a terrific gathering of speed along the flat, and a clunk, then a vertical pull. Up, up, up until my ears pop. And like magic, we're cruising above a duvet of clouds.

"Isn't this amazing?" I ask Rodney.

He looks out of the window before saying, "Oh, yes," and dipping his head back into a Harold Robbins novel.

Paris

Outside Charles de Gaulle Airport, a queue snakes along the pavement, and we tag onto the end of it for a taxi. No snow in Paris, but slanting needles of rain, and I never thought to pack an umbrella. My coat soon becomes a waterlogged sack.

"Rod, why don't we hire a car?" I ask, blinking rain from my eyes, licking it from my nose

"Too expensive, Kate."

It's not until twenty minutes later that's it's our turn to climb into a cab.

And after handing over a bundle of notes in Rue des Abbesses, Rod says, "Sodding hell, Kate, I think we'll stick to buses and the métro."

The taxi driver waves his fist before swerving away. "Did you remember to tip?" I ask.

"Not bloody likely."

We stand on a swirled pattern of cobblestones. I slide my shoe over a couple of them, then look across at a vast, flat building. Windows half-covered with iron grilles lie in perfect and balanced order. Down-pipes and gutters divide the building into narrow sections.

Rodney points to a middle section and says, "That's Tony's. He said it was buff-colored." He hoists his travel bag over a shoulder, picks up the box of duty-free, and says, "Let's go."

I hold on to the handle of my suitcase and ride it along on one foot. It's the only way I'll get it across the square, it's so damned heavy. Why the hell did I pack so much? Oh well, wait till Rodney sees me wearing the lingerie I've kept in wraps for too long—and the shoes. He'll love it all.

The lilt of French music and song drifts from a bar to my left, and it thrills and overwhelms me. Oh, God, we're in Paris! This is just so fantastic. Who cares about the rain dripping down my neck?

"*Bonjour.*" A woman with hair scraped into a chignon greets us at the door. She dries her hands on a tea towel, then tucks it into the belt of her apron. This must be *la concierge* Tony mentioned.

"*Bonjour,*" I say. "Anthony Basterfield?"

"*Pas moi,*" she says, smiling, showing a gold tooth. "*Je m'appelle Madame Bouton. Vous-êtes les Fanshaws?*"

"Yes, the Fanshaws," says Rodney, nodding wildly.

"*Un moment.*" Madame disappears and returns to dangle a bunch of keys under Rodney's nose. "Come," she says.

We're led to another door and we enter a tile-floored lobby. "Come," repeats Madame.

Her feet slip-slap up the wooden steps, and I clunk-clunk behind with my case. After four flights of stairs, I have to sit. "Beautiful stairs," I tell Madame Bouton, buying time to catch my breath. "So old and quaint."

Madame wags a finger at Rodney. "But, monsieur, it is the man who must carry *les baggages.*"

Rodney takes my case and hands me the duty-free. "This place needs a lift. Which floor, Mrs. Button?" he asks, skipping past Madame and disappearing out of sight.

She shrugs, then yells, "THE TOP!"

For the next two flights, she mumbles and mutters. When we catch up with Rodney, she says, "*Monsieur, de quoi est mort votre dernier esclave?*"

Mort—dead? *Esclave*—slave? Who knows what she said, but I'm enjoying every bit of it. This is France!

Rodney stops taking his pulse to take the keys from Madame. "Not bad," he announces. "Sixty-five beats per minute. I'm pretty fit, even though I say so myself."

Madame Bouton looks at me and pinches my cheek. "*Il a les chevilles qui enflent, eh?*" And she wobbles off, singing, "*A bientôt.*"

I breathe in a waft of garlic and onions. Someone's cooking and I'm starving.

"Rod, let's get out of our damp clothes and go eat! God, can you believe it? We're in Paris! Will we try snails? We're right next to Monmartre. Let's see the Eiffel Tower, the Louvre, everything—I can't wait!"

He carries my case into Tony's apartment, then drops his bag on the floor. "Nor can I," he says.

I put the duty-free on a counter top. "Just look at this place, Rod. Isn't it fabulous?" The kitchen, living, and bedroom run into each other. Totally *chic.* Dark floors are polished and gold curtains hang in abundance from brass poles. Gigantic posters in wild abstract hang on canary-yellow walls.

I spin around in circles and look up at a navy ceiling. "Let's see if there's wine in the fridge, Rod."

"Rod?"

He's standing by the bed with his zipper undone.

He grins.

"I said I couldn't wait."

He takes me by the shoulders, clamps his lips onto mine, and walks me to the bed. Sit down, he says. Another kiss presses, pushing my head back, and once more I'm looking at a navy ceiling. Wow, someone has stuck little gold stars up there. I try to speak, but my mouth is full of Rodney's tongue. When I'm released, my dress is shoved up to my thighs. "Rod—wait," I take a breath before his mouth silences me again. My knickers are worked down my legs, and then—

And then he's hard inside me. I jerk my head to one side. Why is it *hurting*? "Ow, ow, ow, ow."

And ow.

And it's over.

No Vaseline, thank God, but no condom, either.

"Ahh," sighs Rodney. And he stands up, and leaves.

"Rod, I thought you were going to use—um—things."

"I'm sorry," he says, soaping his hands with a thorough intensity at the sink. "I'll get some tomorrow. Let's see what the Frogs use."

"Would you like a drop of disinfectant?" I ask, smiling. I step to the bathroom with my silk knickers draped over one shoe. "Wow, there's a bidet in here."

With brass taps. Gosh.

"Highly unlikely you'll get preggers your first time," shouts Rodney.

The bidet's amazing. I want one of these.

Fluffy yellow towels. Gorgeous.

"Where shall we go to eat?" I shout back.

◆

After the cauliflower soup, when I'm savoring *foie gras* and sipping sweet wine at the *Pot au Feu* bistro in Monmartre, I think: *Everything will be fine.* I'm dry in my long skirt, new striped top, and suede boots, warm as Melba toast, drinking up Paris, the language, the aromas.

Life is looking up.

I watch Rodney sucking at the aspic on his fork. I take his free hand, examine his fingernails, and look into his face. "Hello, husband," I say.

A smile twitches on his face before a passing waiter catches his eye. He pulls away to hold up an index finger. "Yes, over here, please. Mercy bon."

"Encore un minute, monsieur."

"What shall we order next, wifey? What's on the menu?"

"Rod, the menu's so wonderful, I don't know where to start!"

MENU

Crème de chouxfleur aux girolles.
Salade de pommes de terre.
Sole poêlée, beurre noisette ou perdreau roti.
Fromage fermier.
Figues roties à la crème d'amande.

I have this fantastic idea.

"Rod, why don't I forget teaching, and think about catering? I mean, I don't have a new job yet, so how about I open a restaurant, or a bistro? I know that's impossible now, but I could start off with a small business, you know, a gourmet sandwich service for offices or something, to build up cash, but, Rod, you're a financial advisor, what do you think?" I take his hand again. "You could take care of the accounts and stuff."

The waiter arrives.

"*Stuff*? Dear Kate, I can tell you don't have one business cell in your little body. I'd rather hoped we'd make a son. You can't run a restaurant *and* rear a child." He looks up at the waiter to ask, "What's *perdreau roti*?"

Friday, June 10
75 Copper Lane, Oakley Green

"**God Kate, you're huge,** you poor thing." Moira circles her arms around my girth.

"I'm sorry I didn't call back till last week, Moi. I've had so much to do. Come in. Was driving along the M6 horrendous?"

"Not bad. Took three hours, that's all."

I reach for her case and she slaps my hand. "Are you kidding? I'll carry this. Lead the way."

Using the rail to hoist myself up each step, I list the progress made since her first visit to 75 Copper Lane. The heat is in, I say. New plumbing, new wiring. I removed yards of wallpaper from walls, burned paint off woodwork, dug out wet rot, repaired windows. Installed curtain poles, made curtains. The kitchen is a new color.

I stop for oxygen.

I've spliced, filled, glazed, stripped, scraped, plastered, peeled, varnished, tiled, scrubbed, and polished . . .

"You're nuts Katie, doing all this when you're preggers."

"Didn't quite plan on getting pregnant on my honeymoon, Moi," I say, easing myself onto the edge of the spare bed. "Do you like the taupe walls? I made this striped cover to match."

She rewards me with one of her animated nods.

Although, I think to myself, *a deep apricot with this pine furniture might have looked warmer.* For Moira's visit, I bunched peony roses together and set them in a green jug. She walks over to the nightstand to cup her hand under one of the blooms.

They're peachy-pink and round and plump. Just like me.

"Oh, and the garden, Moi. I dug, raked, lifted, shifted, planted, and pruned . . ."

Moira lays her case on the carpet and walks over to the window. "Beautiful." She shrugs off her cardigan and tells me to move over so she can join me on the bed. "Oh, look at your fat little toes in those slippers," she says.

When I try my best to look down at them, Moira's mouth spreads into a grin and we burst out laughing.

"I can't get my swollen feet into anything else. Oh God, Moi, it hasn't been fun. Rod can't help much with the house, what with the business and the cricket and the hockey and golf at the weekends. Oh, and the Masonic Lodge. You see, Moi, Rod says it's important to be a member of teams, clubs, associations, and such. It's how one retains clients and gains new ones. Amazing how many people he meets."

"Guess so."

"Biddy and Dad are wonderful. They've helped me knock down walls, level floors, hang wall units."

"But how are *things* with Biddy? You know, how are you getting on with her these days?"

"She's loving every minute. She helps choose colors, tiles, fabric, carpet. I'd have aubergine and citrus green everywhere if it wasn't for Biddy. I've never been good with colors, she tells me."

Moira pokes a finger into the fat where my rib cage used to be. "You allow her to dictate."

"Not really. She does have a good eye, honestly. But hell, her and Dad have worked so hard. Dad divided a room and made me a laundry, and Biddy stayed up the whole night fixing drywall. Doing all this for me has been a real treat for them, they said."

Moira shakes her head. "Oh dear, so now you feel obliged to put up with whatever shit comes your way." She jumps to her feet before I can respond. "Oh, God, Katie, wait till you see what I bought for little Rodney."

I blow a raspberry. "We'll see about calling my baby Rodney. Anyway, it might be a little Lucy."

She pulls a bag from her case and says, "Lead me to the nursery. You know Rod will have you beheaded if you produce a girl, don't you?"

The baby's room is as fresh as a lemon. No nursery friezes, no prints of teddy bears or bouncing lambs. *Remember now, Kate, babies do grow up, said Biddy. Let's choose a nice paint. Pale yellow. And neutral curtains. Forget Laura Ashley and her fancy moons, stars, and seashells.*

"Look, Moi," I say, opening drawers and holding up miniature striped sweaters and leggings. "Mamgu made them. And I made this for the Moses basket, and this for the crib." I shake out two covers appliquéd with row upon row of yellow ducks and wavy rivers.

"Well, you look over here," says Moira. "It's from Ingrid and me."

An exquisite christening gown flows from Moira's fingers.

"Silk?" I breathe.

She nods, and her eyes shine.

"It's—bloody gorgeous." Taking it from her, I trace my finger over the pleated bodice and whisper my thanks. "Tell Ingrid I absolutely love it, okay? Damn, you're the best friends on this earth, I swear."

Moira points to my bitten nails. "No polish?" She pulls the elastic band from my hair. "Oh, Kate, and your hair is so long, it reaches your arse."

Will she ever change? I hope not.

She looks into my eyes. "Are you happy, Katie?"

I think so.

"I can't wait to hold this baby," I say, running my hand over its form.

"Only three months to go," she says, punching me on the arm.

◆

"Here, Moi. Toss the salad."

I put a fish pie into the oven to reheat. "I'll open a bottle of wine for you," I say. "Shall we eat on the patio? It's still warm outside."

Moira's hair is cropped just short of her jawline. Her blouse is the same washed blue as her jeans and she stands tall in her trainers. She looks terrific, and seems so happy. Perhaps I can guess why. "When will you and Gus tie the knot?" I ask.

"Next spring." Moira's elbows are still. She lays down the forks and turns to lean against the kitchen unit. "Katie, looks like the publishers expect Gus to move to America for twelve months, to St. Louis. After we're married, of course."

"That's tremendous, Moi."

We settle a deal. Ingrid and me will be bridesmaids. I clink my shot of pure orange juice with her glass of chardonnay, and we make a second deal. She and Ingrid will be godmothers.

And then a door shudders open, and the now familiar thud of a dropped briefcase follows, then a slam, and a jingle of keys.

"Hello, Moira. Helping Kate, are we?" Rodney bounds in to give my shoulders a quick rub, before peering into the glass door of the oven. "Might sample a morsel before I set off," he says. "What is it? Meat? Fish? Cheese?"

Moira extends a hand. "Hello, Rod, how are you?"

"Could be worse. I'll be back in a sec."

He spins and strides back to the hallway.

"Where's he going?" asks Moira.

"Gosh, I don't know."

Rapid footsteps tell us he's scaling the stairs. Within minutes, he appears again with a sports bag under his arm. "Did you wash my kit? Can't seem to locate my shorts."

"In the dryer. Where are you going?" I take out the steaming fish pie and set it on a chopping board. Cheese bubbles on top, crisp and brown at the edges.

"Didn't you check the calendar, Kate? I'm playing squash tonight. Seven-fifteen at the Sebastian Crowe Leisure Centre, with Doug." Rodney delves a spoon into the pie and next thing, he's flapping his fingers at an open mouth. "Crikey. Bloody hell. Talk about hot. See you later, then. Must dash. Have fun. I'll be back in an hour or so."

I gather plates and salt and pepper and Moira unlocks the patio doors.

Rodney shouts from the hall. "Do leave some dinner for me, won't you ladies? Don't go eating it all!"

A turquoise sky melts to orange where it meets the poplar trees. The only harsh line is a silver streak left by a jet. "I'll fetch a candle," I say.

"And music?" calls Moira. I open the kitchen window and turn up the radio.

When the evening slips into night, Diana Ross sings "Love Hangover," and the conversation turns to Jack.

"Did you tell Rod about—"

"The miscarriage? Hell no."

Fluttering kicks remind me I'm pregnant again, and soon life will be—complete.

I dig at my thoughts, but they're too deep and I can't lift them to the surface. They're best left buried anyway.

"I'll get the ice cream," says Moira.

"Make banana splits?"

"Yeah—now that would be good."

While Moira's in the kitchen, I wonder what I'm looking for exactly. What more could I ever want? Biddy constantly reminds me of my good fortune. Just take a look at the size of my house. I drive my own car and my wardrobe is full of clothes. I eat fancy food in elaborate restaurants. I'll never have to go out to work. Rodney Fanshaw gives me far more than my father ever provided.

"Here we are." Moira sets down two sundae glasses. "Chopped walnuts, chocolate chips, sliced banana, and butterscotch sauce."

"Oh, dear God!"

But heaven.

Moira slips a mouthful onto her tongue and closes her eyes. "Orgasmic." Then she smirks. "What's it like with Rod?"

"You first," I say, laughing. "What's it like with Gus?"

Was that the front door I heard?

"Tender and thrilling," she says. "His touch makes me weak at the knees."

"Still out here, girls?" Rodney asks.

He's back already.

"Wah!" Moira shrieks. "You made me jump out of my skin, Rod."

"How was the game?" I ask. "Did you win? What was the score?"

Questions I ask most evenings, and every weekend.

Of course Rodney won. A swift 4–1, in fact. He sets the fish pie on the table, sits, eats with the serving spoon, stacking cold potato into his mouth. I want to say, please don't do that. But I don't say a word, because I'm a bloody mouse.

And I look at the moon, and think, *What's it like with Rod?* Well, the weight of him, the heat, and the suffocation is too much. It's a relief when he rolls off.

"Wow, it's getting a bit chilly, Moi," I say. "Shall we go inside?"

THE TALE OF A HOUSE MOUSE

Poor little house mouse. You
dip and soak and rinse and
rub, you wax and wipe
and dust and scrub.
You mix and make
and boil and bake,
you toil each day
without a
break.
You
shine
and
sweep
and
scour
and
mop,
you
cut
and
slice
and
mash
and
chop.
You
work
ALL
day,
until
you

drop.

CHAPTER 38

◆

Thursday, September 8
Priory Hospital, Oakley Green
11:42 a.m.

Nurse Meredith has my wrist grasped between finger and thumb, timing my pulse. "Induction at three, Mrs. Fanshaw?"

"Yes."

"Can I call you Kate?"

"Yes."

I'm four days overdue, the size of a bloated whale, and I feel lousy. She can call me whatever comes to mind. I don't care.

She pulls the curtains around my hospital bed and beams at me. "We have a little job to do this morning," she says, snapping on gloves. "Can we lift our bottom?"

We can, just about. A plastic sheet is slipped underneath.

"Now let's lift our nightie. Good. Open your legs, poppet."

I hear the rasp of a razor on skin, and feel fingers pushing my flesh this way and that. I've been pushed, pulled, poked, and pressed ever since I was admitted three days ago. I'm past humiliation, I'm on the conveyor belt, third in line for induction. I stare out of the window at a blank sky. Nothing of interest out there, so I watch the hands of a wall clock.

Twelve minutes click by.

"There we are, Kate. All fresh and clean."

I'm a plucked chicken ready for processing.

The nurse doesn't leave. She fiddles with a length of tubing and a kidney dish.

"I don't need an enema," I say, fighting to get my night dress over my stomach.

"Let's turn on our side. A quick squirt, then we can nip off to the bathroom, and we'll feel so much better."

"No, thank you. I'm fine." I pull blankets up to my chin.

"Let's not be silly, Kate."

That's exactly what Biddy said when I learned my parents had booked a holiday in Scotland. *Let's not be silly, Kate, no need to pull a face.* Yes, of course she knows the baby is about to arrive. What do I mean, I need her? I'm twenty-six years old and I have a husband. About time Rodney stopped living like a bachelor. She would like to catch a bit of fresh air and scenery before October. Would I mind?

Nurse Meredith leaves my bedside with her enema, promising to come back later.

I puzzle as to whether I'm being selfish wanting to share the birth of my firstborn with my mother—when the curtain flicks—and in she walks.

Am I dreaming?

"Mum!"

She kisses my forehead and rolls back the blanket. "Let me plump these pillows. Daddy will be here in a minute, he's parking the car."

Using my heels, I push myself into a sitting position. "They're inducing me this afternoon, did Rod tell you?"

"They are?" Concern washes over her face, but soon drains away. "I'm glad you're already in hospital. The only information your husband gave me was the number of the ward and the floor level."

Dad's face creases with pleasure when he sees me. "How's my Kate?" He presses his cheek to mine, then hands me a box of chocolates and a bunch of grapes.

"Thanks, Dad."

"I'll fetch you a chair, Tom," says my mother, her voice nipped and precise.

"Okay, Biddy. Well, Kate, I thought we'd pay a visit before we leave tomorrow." His face drops. "Your mum's not too happy. She hasn't finished packing the caravan yet."

Oh.

They're still going.

"Tom? Would you ever think of helping me carry these chairs?"

I stuff three grapes into my mouth. As I chew, tears course down my cheeks. Damn. I rub at them fiercely with the bedsheet.

Don't be self-centered, Kate.

I swallow, pips and all, and force a smile as Biddy slides the curtains along the rails.

Sharon, my pregnant companion opposite, waves.

"So, before we reach Scotland, I daresay we'll be grandparents. Do I look old enough?"

Biddy smoothes her skirt down before she sits.

"No," say Dad and me in unison.

"Now, Kate, be brave, and may God watch over you and keep you safe." She pushes hair from my eyes. "I know you'll be fine. We ought to go in about thirty minutes or so, Tom."

2:38 p.m.

"So, we started ourselves, did we, without any help?" says Nurse Meredith. "Oh, your Grandmother Mamgu called, Kate. She was all flustered, thinking you'd be on your own today, talking about trains, would she arrive on time. I told her not to worry, hubby plans to be here. My word, we're already two centimeters dilated, believe it or not."

I believe it. An iron fist is working its way through my lower back. "When will I have the epidural?" I ask.

"Oh, bless your heart, Dr. Bates moved to Australia."

"There's no other anesthetist?"

"Not one who specializes in epidurals. You'll be all right, chick. You're not the first woman to give birth. We have all sorts of pain-killing goodies. When contractions are twenty minutes apart, we'll scoot you down to the labor ward."

"They're coming every twenty minutes already," I say. "I've had five, I'm sure of it."

"Impossible."

And she leaves me.

Where's Rodney?

A man in a brown uniform wheels in a phone. "Contractions are coming every twenty minutes," I tell him. "Honestly."

"That's the porter, love," says the woman in the next bed.

"You have a call, Mrs. Fanshaw," he says, backing away.

"Hello?" says a familiar voice.

"Aunt Shauna?"

"Yes, sweetheart. I'll be with you in a couple of hours. They told me you'd started."

I bite my lip.

"Katie, are you all right?"

"Yes, yes."

"Now hang on a while, do you hear?"

"I'll try."

Dear Aunt Shauna. I dial Rodney's office number. No answer. I try home. No good. He must be on his way.

"How you doin', love?" asks Sharon from the bed opposite.

"Bearing up."

"As long as you don't bear down yet, love, you'll do just fine. Ha, ha."

Ha, ha.

3:55 p.m.

Nurse Meredith spears a syringe into my thigh. "We've had a shot of Pethidine, to ease the cramps," she says. "Let's take you downstairs."

6:20 p.m.

Aunt Shauna holds iced water to my lips.

"Thanks for being here," I say.

Her round face softens and her eyes smile. Her hair is peppered with silver—she's always been very pretty. "My poor Kate," she says. "I had no intention of being anywhere else. Biddy needs shooting, and I told her so."

Which means Aunt Shauna will get the cold shoulder for months, possibly years.

"What made my mother like this?" I ask.

"Very little, my darling. The same sister I've known for years. So like your Irish grandmother. Reap what you can."

I clench my teeth waiting for a wave of pain to ease. "Pass me the Entonox," I gasp, squeezing Aunt Shauna's hand.

"You're taking too much, Katie. You'll make yourself sick."

"Pass me the fucking gas."

I look at her above the rubber mask. *Oh God!* What did I just say? As I float to the ceiling, I'm aware of Aunt Shauna reaching for a button on the wall. "Time to call the obstetrician," she whispers.

Footsteps.

"Kate must be nearly ready." My aunt's voice is a million miles away, but I know she's laughing. "My niece is swearing like an old soldier."

"Ah. Excellent."

I speak into the mask. "Anyone there? Where's Rod?"

"Doctor Raphael here, Kate. I'm taking over."

I feel a kiss on my head. "You're doing well, sweetheart," says Aunt Shauna. "Won't be long now. I'm going to get out of the doctor's way. I'll see if I can track Rodney down, then I'll phone Mamgu and Griff. How about that?"

Her voice fades as she drifts past a nurse and out through the double doors.

I take another gulp of gas and my scalp tingles.

Did I hear someone say, oh, hello, Mr. Fanshaw?

"Seven centimeters." The doctor's head pops up from between my legs. "I think you'll be ready for the delivery room in ten minutes or so."

Ten minutes, ten minutes . . .

In the cold room full of stainless steel and bright lights, I see Rodney's glasses sitting above a white mask, and he's dressed in hospital green, hat and all.

"Where the bugger were you?" I growl.

"Had a quick nine holes with Father, then Mother cooked me dinner. It's okay, she's looking after me well."

"*What?*"

"Shh, Kate. I'm here now. I guessed you'd have a long innings before any serious batting."

"Do you play at Plattsworth Golf Course?" asks Dr. Raphael.

"Yes, I do, as a matter of fact."

Oh God, stop this pain, please.

"Good game?"

"Wonderful," says Rodney. "I beat the old man hollow."

"Did you get caught in that bunker before the fifth hole?"

"Did I, by crikey. I went too close to the ball and bladed the shot. I should have tried slicing with an eight-iron."

A sound escapes my lips like the lowing of a cow in Cloondray.

"DON'T PUSH," yells the doctor. "We don't want to rip, do we?"

Rip? Oh dear God. I slip into Never-Never Land where blades flash, needles jab, knives cut, and golf clubs slice.

I swim back.

"Are we all right, Kate?" asks Dr. Raphael. "We've had an episiotomy, a little snip down below. Won't be long now, dear. The pediatrician's standing by."

"Doctor Stubbs here, Mrs. Fanshaw."

I answer with a long grunt. Damn, I'm a pig now.

"Another good push please, there's a good girl, bear down. And here's the head."

The head? The head? The head! I push again and a mass slithers out. I hear a gurgle and a bleat, and the doctor holds it up.

It's a blue baby boy.

"Would the father like to hold him?" asks Dr. Raphael, handing my baby to the nurse to wrap.

I stretch out my arms. "He's mine."

I cradle my son, who's now pink, with skin like velvet. His button mouth twists when one of my tears plops onto his face. His hair is a swirl of beige-brown.

"Hello there, little chap," says Rodney.

The pediatrician smiles. "I'll have to check him over soon. Do you have a name, Mr. Fanshaw?"

"We do indeed. He shall be called Rodney."

"No. Charles," I whisper, kissing the little face that smells of me. "My Charlie."

Rodney pats my matted hair. "We'll see," he says.

PART THREE

◆

THE EIGHTIES

CHAPTER 39

◆

1981

Saturday, September 19
Sansouchies, Main Street, Oakley Green

Shane places an envelope full of brown locks onto the palm of my hand and closes my fingers over it. "I'm sorry, Kate," he says. "Charlie's curls just had to go."

My hairdresser takes hold of the chair and spins it around.

"*Wheeeeeee,*" says Charlie. "Again."

"If I make you dizzy," says Shane, "your mother may spank me."

Charlie blinks under his new shining bowl of a haircut. I bend down to kiss just under the bridge of his nose, that comfy little dip where my lips fit perfectly. His arms clamp around my neck, and with sugar-breath he whispers in my ear. "Can I have fruit pastilles now?"

"Okay." I pull off the white cape and he jumps down. "But first, we must pay Shane for doing such a great job."

"Why?" asks Charlie.

I laugh at my four-year-old, who fills his days with whys, wheres, whos, and whens. "Come on, scamp," I say, grabbing his hand.

Shane takes notes from me with delicate fingers, then folds his arms. "Dearest Kate, did you try a home perm? Your poor hair wants to die. Let me give it the will to live."

I shake my head. "It'll grow out."

"Just a little trim?"

"It's easy this length, a quick brush, a couple of elastic bands, and I'm done."

Charlie pulls at my skirt then shoves his hands into the pockets of his OshKosh B'Gosh jeans. Stripes encircle his frame in shades of blue. Mamgu spends hours picking old sweaters apart to make her Charlie *bach* little garments. I smile at my son's face and ache with love.

Shane snaps his fingers. "Kate sweetie," he says, "your middle parting is killing me, and tying your hair in two bunches is so—"

"Practical."

"Trashy."

"Mummy—*sweets*. You promised."

Shane waves his hand on a loose wrist to dismiss me. "You neglect yourself, Katikins."

And he flounces off.

We leave Sansouchies to step out into a warm day. A mellow day.

"Are the trees dying with cancer?" asks Charlie as he hops along the pavement.

"No, they're dropping their leaves. It helps keep them strong to survive the winter."

Charlie crouches down and reaches for a stalk. He peeps past the fan of horse-chestnut leaves and his eyes lock onto mine. "Will Griff survive the winter, Mummy?"

Oh dear God, I want him to live forever, Charlie.

"The doctors are trying their best, sweetheart." A lump constricts my throat. I swallow hard and put on a bright face. "Shall we drive to Wales next week and take him something special to eat?"

"Yeah! A piece of my birthday cake."

"There should be three slices left in the freezer. Come on, Charlie, let's buy your fruit pastilles."

"Was I good?" he asks. "Did I sit still? Why does Shane wear ladies' blouses? Daddy doesn't."

No, Daddy doesn't wear a lady's blouse, but he does like to imagine he's a sergeant major.

We'll send Charles to Sandhurst when he graduates, said Rodney one morning. Over my dead body, I replied. So, Kate, you're prepared to deny a father the opportunity to be proud of his son? Listen here, the British Army offers world-class leadership training. Rodney himself applied to

Sandhurst, but didn't qualify. And that was a huge disappointment, Kate, one he's never been able to live down.

Hence the fetish, the fantasies in the bedroom?

I asked Rodney why he didn't make Sandhurst. What happened exactly?

Well, Kate, he replied, spectacle correction must be no greater than minus seven diopters or plus eight in any meridian, and—

And his lenses are pretty thick.

"Oh, look, Charlie," I say, "here we are already, at Candy Corner."

The sight of silver and gold wrappers fills me with longing, so I pick up a giant bar of Cadbury's along with the fruit pastilles.

"Charlie, I just want to pop into Oakley Music Store. Let's see if they have anything new."

And there, we sort through a box of old LPs, and find an album called *Sing-Along Oldies*. What the heck, I think, why not? Something different.

"We'll have this, too," I say, showing Charlie a cover displaying a bright red bus: *All Day Long Fun for Tots*.

"Come on, Charlie, let's pay, then we'll search for the car and go home, shall we?"

Let's go to the home I've filled with handmade quilts, curtains, and loose covers. To rooms full of stripped pine and wicker baskets. To a kitchen full of chutneys, jams, and bread. To a garden full of vegetables, shrubs, and flowerbeds. To the nest I've built twig by twig for you, Charlie.

We eventually find the Volvo on the third floor of the car park. I'm always forgetting where I left it. After securing Charlie in the backseat, I squeeze behind the steering wheel, then break four squares of chocolate to eat while I drive. As sweetness melts on my tongue, I think, *what the hell? So I'm fat. Who cares?* My body swelled with gestation, it stretched, it ripped, it was cut and sewn up. There's no saving it now.

I start the car.

75 Copper Lane, Oakley Green

"Hello—Mum?"

"I thought you might have lifted the phone *some* time today," says Biddy. Did you forget you have parents?"

Damn, here we go.

"Why are you sighing?" she asks.

"I'm not sighing." I pant a bit for effect. "I'm out of breath."

"Why? What are you doing?"

My toes curl inside my shoes. "I ran to answer the phone."

"Where were you?"

"Oakley Green."

"I see. Tom! I didn't tell you to put that there. No—*no,* I said underneath, not on top. Hello?"

"Still here."

"Kate, do you realize your father and I haven't seen your face for five weeks? *Five* weeks. Tom, will you pick that up? Don't-put-it-back-on-the-work-surface, it needs washing. Hello?"

"Hello."

"Are you listening?"

"Yes!"

"You're sighing."

I close my eyes. Retaliate now and she'll maintain a stony silence for days, weeks.

"You can't be bothered to speak to your mammy, can you?" she asks.

Now, at this stage, I have to be careful. She's waiting for my answer and will listen with studied intensity to my very breath, voice intonation, and choice of words. If she detects guilt, then she has me.

God, she's impossible.

I change the subject. "Charlie and me were at the Fanshaws' last Saturday for a little get-together."

"Oh yes?"

"A buffet. Nothing too elaborate. You know, the usual thing, just a few friends and family," I say, imitating Nancy.

Silence.

I try again: "God, Mum, was it hil-ar-ious. Let me tell you what happened. Desmond the dachshund messed the floor and . . ."

"Uncle Bertie slipped in the pooh," shouts Charlie.

"Are your own parents allowed to see their grandson occasionally?"

"Mum, you know I try and avoid my in-laws like they have the plague."

"You're sighing."

Agghh.

"Kate, come for Sunday dinner, you, Rodney, and Charlie. I'll put a beef joint in the oven."

I slap my hand to my forehead. What can I do with her?

"Thanks, Mum, that would be great."

"No good asking you to join us at Mass, I know you rarely go to church these days, so Daddy and I will go to an early service."

"Okay."

"Could you get here by eleven? I'll make an apple pie. Wash your hair and put on a clean dress. Your father will buy the wine."

I am the child again.

"Mum, listen, Rod has already planned his Sunday, so he won't be with us. He's playing hockey at Surminster."

I say my good-byes and see-you-soons, and return the phone-kisses.

Charlie lies flat on his back on the floor next to Dinah the cat. "Did you ask Biddy if Abbott and Costello are okay?" he says.

"We'll look in Granny and Granddad's pond tomorrow, and see how they're getting on, shall we? Hey, just look at the time—I'd better start thinking about dinner. Come here, give me a hug."

Charlie jumps up. I reach for him and bury my face in his hair.

My baby smells of Imperial Leather soap.

"Do all goldfish grow too big for their tanks?" he asks.

Charlie is so tall. Well past my waist. One day, he'll be a teenager, next thing, a man, then he'll grow too big for this house.

Then my child will be gone.

I kiss Charlie's head. I have him a good few years yet. "We could buy some little fantails from the pet shop next week," I tell him.

"Or a snake." He looks up and laughs at my horrified face.

CHAPTER 40

◆

I lift my latest LP. *Sing-Along Oldies,* from my shopping bag, and laugh. Whatever possessed me to buy this? Switching on the record player, I wait for the needle to drop, then I go back to making bread.

> *"It's delightful to be married.*
> *To be, to be, to be, to be, to be married . . ."*

Oh yeah? I slap dough onto the chopping board and push at it with my knuckles until it's smooth and pliable. Until it's ready to rest in a bowl, to breathe, to puff to double its size.

"Mine's ready," says Charlie, handing me a gray lump.

"This will make a nice bread roll for Daddy," I say. "Now go and watch TV, or do you want to play with Lego?"

Charlie skips out of the kitchen, shouting, "TV, TV."

"Wash your hands before you go to the living room, okay?"

> *"There is nothing half so jolly as*
> *A jolly married life . . ."*

Singing along, I pour myself a big glass of Rhône Valley red.

Hacking at a large onion—damn, it's potent—I sob profusely. I toss the chunks into sizzling oil along with blocks of carrot and smashed garlic. My heart isn't in this. Rodney shovels his food, hardly tastes it, so there's no need to be too particular.

We've been married for five years now. Do I know Rodney? I mean, *really* know him?

I mull over his father's theory. *A man needs all the recreation he can get. Eh? What?*

Well, my husband gets plenty, for sure. He gets to play with his balls every weekend, from morning till night.

"Golf, hockey, squash, cricket, billiards. Rod plays with a whole variety of balls," I tell the wall.

Shit, I'm talking to myself. I need another drink.

I gulp wine and laugh. Adding a lump of mince to the pan, I attack it with a wooden spoon, teasing it out, encouraging it to mix with a can of tomatoes, a handful of herbs.

What a loyal spectator I used to be at cricket matches. For hours on end, I'd watch Rodney rub the ball against his groin with frenzied pleasure, shining it on one side to make it pitch with a curve and a spin. Bernoulli's Principle, doncher know. I endured the ins and outs and overs of the game for a couple of years. Dragged Charlie along, too, before Rodney said, "Wouldn't you rather stay at home?"

And there I was, thinking he wanted my company.

I stir my sauce until it changes from pink to beige to brown, then slosh in some wine. I must get Rodney to buy more of this Rhône Valley. The plum tones are *verrrry* addictive. Now for pasta. I fill a pan with water and put it on the stove.

> "A gang of good fellows are we, are we
> With never a worry you see, you see
> We laugh and joke, we sing and smoke—"

As I wait for a racing boil, I ask the wall if it thinks it strange that Rodney enjoys communal showers. Creates a rapport within the team, he says. That and eating meat pies and drinking at the bar until eleven at night.

Soap, sup, sip. Then he comes home for Saturday sex.

I plunge a fistful of spaghetti into the saucepan.

> "We love one another we do, we do
> With brotherly love and it's true, it's true—"

His snatching every spare minute to play with balls is one thing. But then with tied wrists, a bare breast, trouser legs rolled up to his knees, with a prick of blade against skin—*touché,* he was initiated a brother of yet another Masonic Lodge.

I hardly see him.

Of course, I resent all this. Who wouldn't?

I grumbled forever one night before he eventually turned from the TV to ask, "What exactly *do* you want?"

My answer of "a husband" was met with a blank stare.

"You're bored, Kate, you don't have enough to do, that's your problem," he said. "I suggest you take up a sport. Golf would be an excellent choice."

He didn't get it.

Well, I didn't learn how to tee off, I learned not to care a bugger instead. With Rodney so occupied, at least I'm free to create my own little world. I can play house, concentrate on loving Charlie, drink good wine, play loud music.

I can sing my heart out, sing about fine romances with never any kisses.

I lift the bread dough from the bowl and drop it back onto the chopping board. I punch away its puffiness before shaping it into a fat ball to rise again.

I make plans. Before next spring, I'll take Charlie to visit Ingrid in Provence again, stay in that gorgeous house she afforded in the middle of lavender fields. What a dream job she has, working for the *Merci France* magazine.

And one day, we could fly to St. Louis and stay with Moira.

Charlie would love that.

Damn, I missed her when she moved. Still, Gus would have been crazy to turn down the offer of a *permanent* job in the States. Well, Katie, said Moira, now she has a choice. Shall she stay at home and have babies or work at a place called *Walgreens*?

Pity I lost touch with Angie. The last I'd heard, she and Josh moved to Chelsea.

I tip the *al dente* pasta into a colander, then empty the last of the Rhône Valley into my glass. "Cheers," I say, "to my life. This is as good as it gets. I haven't got a chance, this is a fine romance."

"Who are you talking to, Mummy?" asks Charlie, grinning up at me.

"The wall."

I pinch his nose. "Are you looking forward to going to Dorton tomorrow?"

"S'pose so," he says. "I like Granddad." He holds a finger to his ear. "Listen! Daddy's home."

The front door shudders open, followed by a slam and a jingle of keys. He's early.

"Hello, son. Hello, Mummy!" He wears shorts and a blue hockey shirt. "Dinner smells good. What a bloody racket! What are you listening to?"

"*Sing-Along Oldies,*" I say.

"Good Lord!" Rodney switches off the record player and the music slows to a growl.

"*Pack up your troubles in your old kit bag and smile . . . smail . . . smoil . . .*"

"Came to collect little Jamie's coat," says Rodney. "He left it behind after Charlie's party."

"Rod," I say, "the spaghetti bolognese is ready. We could eat together."

"But, Kate," he says, "I need to pop back to the club to give Jamie's father this coat. Won't be long."

He's going back to the club and he won't be long? I won't see him before midnight.

I put my loaves and Charlie's bread roll into the oven.

When the front door shudders open again, followed by the slam and the jingle of keys, I tell Charlie to set the table for two, there's a good boy.

CHAPTER 41

◆

Sunday, September 20

I open one eye and pat the other side of the bed.

No Rodney.

Yes, and it is one-thirty in the morning, the alarm clock assures me.

Where is he? I smack my lips together. The roof of my mouth is blotting paper and I need water. Must go to the bathroom.

And there, I find a naked figure slouching and spread-legged. Rodney has fallen asleep on the bidet again. I slip past him to fill a tumbler at the sink. "Rod," I whisper, "wake up."

He doesn't move.

It's Saturday. He likes sex on Saturdays. If I leave him there, I won't have to—

I creep past, but an arm shoots out and a hand clutches at my night dress. Rod smiles, even though his eyes are still shut. "Where do you think you're going?" he asks.

◆

In bed, my husband performs sexual intercourse. I study the ceiling and pat his back as he reaches orgasm.

"Say thank you to Sergeant Major," he gasps.

◆

CHAPTER 42

Morning already? Coming to my senses slowly. I can't believe I've woken up with yet another headache.

Believe it, booms my head.

I crave coffee.

"Morning, Eva! Is Mike there?" Rodney cradles the receiver between neck and shoulder as he hops around the floor, trying to pull on red socks. "Hey, Mikey, are your knees well oiled, old chap? Feel like shoving a ball around with a stick today?"

Sounds like he's one man short for the hockey team.

Wonder what time he'll be leaving.

"Ten-thirty push-off. Blue shirt. Home at Oakley Green Clubhouse. Playing Tinchley. Cheers, Mike."

On cue, the clock pings. One, two, three—eight, nine, and—ten. He'll be leaving in mere minutes.

Rodney peers down at me. Neat teeth grin under his Sergeant Major moustache. I see he's waxed the thing.

"The team's waiting. I'm late. Must dash." He slaps on his tweed cap with a thwack.

"You look funny, Daddy," says Charlie from the doorway. He runs in holding poor Dinah under the armpits and tosses her onto our bed.

Rodney's nylon tracksuit sports a geometry of lime, pink, and acid yellow, and he wears a pair of black dress shoes.

"This is how sportsmen dress at the weekend, Charles. New haircut, eh? Very smart indeed. Looking more like your dad every day."

"When are we leaving?" asks my son.

I tell Rodney we plan to drive to Dorton for Sunday dinner. "Jolly good," he says. "Crikey, I'm late."

Charlie puts one leg under the cover and looks at me. "Okay," I say, "a quick cuddle, sweetheart, then we must hurry."

Wow, I slept late this morning.

◆

The Volvo grips the road as I wind around bends, dip into valleys, and climb hills. Here's Brickshaw at last. "Look at the colors of autumn," I tell Charlie as we whiz past a texture of trees and hedges.

"Red and yellow and brown," he says.

"Crimson, mustard, and bronze," I sing.

"Toffee, chocolate, and peanut butter," laughs Charlie.

Approaching the motorway now, I tell him to look out for the ninth exit. Just before Sitbury, a sign displaying a knife, fork, and a petrol pump looms up. I'm tempted to stop for more coffee, even motorway coffee, but think it wise not to keep Biddy waiting.

Seventh, eighth, ninth exit. Brickshaw Village next, then Daleport.

And at last we're driving along the narrow roads toward Dorton, to Bryre Hill, to the roast beef and apple pie.

33 Cherry Blossom Road, Dorton

And there they are, waiting for us in the driveway. Biddy walks to the car door with arms outstretched. I hop out to hug her and she tugs me closer. Looking over her shoulder, I smile. Dad's face lights up—I see his hair has a touch more silver as he bends to swoop Charlie into his arms.

"Now give me a kiss, Charles," says Biddy, pointing to her cheek. "Well, aren't you the little Fanshaw? I don't see much Cadogan or Geraghty in him, Kate."

"Here," I say. "A cottage loaf for you. I made a batch yesterday."

She tucks the bread under her arm and says it will come in useful.

Charlie walks hand-in-hand with Dad. "I want to see Abbott and Costello," he says.

"*Please,* Granddad," prompts Biddy.

"Wait till you see how they've grown," Dad says with a laugh. "They're like orange torpedoes."

"What are torpedoes?"

"Kate, will we follow them?" asks Biddy. "I want you to see the garden."

Dad finally got his promotion, and Biddy sold the Bread Shop, so she spends most of her days gardening. Every twig is pruned, shrubs are mulched, delicate shoots lie beneath cloches in rows.

"It's perfect, Mum."

Her green eyes are on me. My skin, my posture, and my clothes are scrutinized as we walk. She pushes her glasses down onto her short nose for a closer look at my hair and runs strands of it through her fingers.

"What brand of dye are you using?"

"None." I stroke my hair, trying to flatten it.

"Your hairdresser doesn't know what he's doing. Just look at it."

"Shane didn't do this, I tried a home perm."

"It's pure moss, so it is. And I see a few streaks of gray already."

I wait for the sweet to follow the sour.

"You should take more care, Kate. Pamper yourself." She holds her head to one side. "Beautiful skirt and cardigan, where did you get that little outfit?"

"I've had the cardigan a good while. The skirt is from Marks and Spencer's."

"How much?"

"Twenty-two seventy-five."

"You've gained a few pounds. You'll be out of the skirt soon. Would you think of letting your mammy have it?"

"I have a whole box full of clothes for you in the trunk, Mum."

"I appreciate it. Tom, go and get those tulip bulbs I promised Kate. They're behind the shed in a little sack. Tom, behind *the shed*, not inside the greenhouse." Biddy's head swerves back to me. "Thirty-one and wearing such high heels? You'll end up crippled, Kate." Attention is then focused on Charlie. "Don't lean over the pond. You'll fall in and ruin the lining." Followed by, "Tom, will you come on? Dinner will be burned to a crisp."

She smiles and kisses me on the forehead. I need every second of my mother's sporadic approval. Her method of affection is best described as a controlling passion. This fifty-seven-year-old woman hurts, insults, brings tears to my eyes, but after four years with Rodney, I'm in desperate need of any attention, no matter how stifling.

Try and concentrate on Biddy's good points, said Oona. Cling to those odd loving times.

I owe Oona a letter.

◆

Tender beef, carrots, peas, buttery mashed, and crisply roasted potatoes. Sunday dinner is delicious.

"It's the Fanshaws' anniversary in a couple of months," I remind my parents as I cut Charlie's meat into bite-sized pieces. "It's their ruby wedding anniversary. Gaynor and Betsy are organizing a party."

"Daddy and I won't be going."

"Why?" asks Charlie.

"Your granddad has to stay here and clean the gutters."

Clean the gutters?

Biddy leans over to whisper in my ear. "Sure, and isn't it a gutter your in-laws live in? Their house stinks."

Yes, it whiffs somewhat. And I know the very thought of socializing with Old Fart Fanshaw horrifies my father.

"How's Rodney?" asks Biddy.

"Fine."

We eat in silence.

And my mind dips back to last night.

Sex.

I don't encourage, I avoid. I can't enjoy, I cringe. I lie awake as he snores. I shrink away from every brush of foot or unconscious sweep of fingers.

"Katie." Dad searches my face. "Anything the matter?"

"No." I take a sip of wine, search for something to say. "I was thinking the wine was a bit sweet."

Oh, well done, Kate, now you're in trouble.

"What's wrong with it?" Biddy grabs the poor bottle by its neck. "It cost a handful of money. I do know the difference between good and bad wine, you know."

"The bottle is a very pretty blue."

Shit, that was lame.

"Sky blue, sea blue," pipes Charlie, "*Blue Peter* blue!"

Perhaps I should see a doctor. Is there something wrong with me?

Say thank you, Sergeant Major!

I watch peas drop from my fork, one by one, back into the gravy. "I think I'm full now," I say, pushing the plate to one side and dragging my face into a smile.

"Kate, tell your own mother and father what's wrong," says Biddy.

"Later," I say, cocking my head toward my son. "Yum, wasn't dinner great?"

Charlie nods and licks his lips. "Granddad, I'm going to school next spring," he says, wide-eyed.

"What a big boy you are." Dad puts an arm around Charlie's shoulders. "Doesn't he look like Katie when she was this age?"

Biddy cuts into the apple pie. "Not really," she says. "Hold out your dish, Kate."

The pastry crumbles under my spoon, and when I take a mouthful, sweet custard blends with the tang of fruit. Mamgu makes pies like this with the bilberries they find among the heather and gorse bushes.

"Dad, how's Griff?"

"Not too good, Katie. He'd like to see you."

"We're going to Llandafan on Friday." Charlie holds up his fingers to count. "One, two, three, four days to go."

"I should learn to drive," says Biddy. "What do you think, Tom? Traveling wherever I please. Wouldn't that be grand?" She folds her arms, sits back in her seat, and crosses her legs. "Ah, life is great. No more getting up at six in the morning to work. I'm a lady of leisure now, Kate, just like you." She looks sidelong at Dad. "And about time."

"About time? What does that mean?" he asks.

"What does it mean? I've worked for the last thirty-three years, Tom. I was ready to drop with exhaustion, but what choice did I have?"

"What are you insinuating?"

"Someone had to pay the mortgage."

"In the winter," says Charlie, "Daddy works on a hockey field, and in the summer, Daddy works on a cricket pitch. Can I have more pie?"

Biddy cuts another slice. "Kate, do you know how lucky you are, married to a man with an established business?"

Uh-oh.

I jump up and head for the kitchen. "I'll make the coffee," I call, aware of Biddy's brisk footsteps behind me.

I spoon instant coffee into three cups then reach for a glass for Charlie's orange juice. Biddy scrapes leftovers into the kitchen bin, her movements stiffly efficient. Dad scuffles towards the sink, grabs a saucepan, and scours furiously.

"Mummy." Charlie leans against the doorframe. "I'm going upstairs to fetch my dot-to-dot books. Will you help me do some?"

"I'll help," says Dad. "Bring them down, and we'll work on the kitchen table."

"Shall I help load the dishwasher?" I ask Biddy, trying to lift the mood. I drop one artificial sweetener each into my parents' cups. Sugar for me.

"No, thank you. I can manage," she says, deftly slotting plates.

"Dinner was wonderful, Mum." I dissolve the coffee and sweeteners with boiling water and when she straightens up, I nudge at her with my elbow. "Why don't you and Dad keep me company at the anniversary party? God, please—help me out! They're crazy!"

Biddy laughs and pulls me to her. "All right. We'll go. They'll expect a little gift, I'm sure."

"Something ruby, something red."

"Letterbox red, soldier red," says Charlie marching in with his books and pencils.

Biddy squeezes Dad's arm, and it's over. I pour milk into the cups and stir.

"Here's your orange juice, Charlie." I pick up my cup and saucer and ask Biddy if she'd like to sit with me in the living room.

She lights a cigarette. "Sure."

Coffee—horrible. Conversation, not bad. We gossip about the Fanshaws, and flip through magazines. Things are definitely getting better.

Dad appears, only to be told to go back to the kitchen to fetch more coffee and a packet of chocolate biscuits.

"Katie, will you come close while I tell you something?" Biddy lowers her voice. "Did you know that some couples go down 'there' on each other? And I mean *between the legs*. God Almighty! Now can you just picture that? Who would want to be that close to a man's *taypot*?"

Dad's slippered shuffles announce his return and I don't have time to answer, but the way I feel these days, I'd like to live three hundred miles away from Rodney's taypot.

Dad puts the coffee and a plate of biscuits on the ottoman.

"Charlie, sit on the floor like a good boy," says Biddy. "Tom, go back and get a cloth, sure haven't you just spilled coffee into the saucers?"

Dad leaps to his feet.

"You'll stay the night, won't you, Kate?" asks Biddy.

I'd better. I'm overdosed on syrupy alcohol.

"Shall we?" I ask Charlie.

"Yay!" he shouts, munching on biscuits.

"Okay, I'll go and phone your dad."

❖

I dial our number.

"Hello?"

"Kate? You'll never guess! Todd and Penny turned up at the clubhouse."

"Oh, I'm sorry I missed them."

"We're off for a meal at the Horse and Jockey. The three of us managed to fit in eighteen holes this afternoon. Superb game of golf."

"Great, great. Rod, we've decided to stay the night at Dorton."

"Fine with me."

Dad rattles a box, arches his eyebrows, and I nod and smile. "Listen, Rod, must go, I'm off to play Scrabble."

"Kate, before you go—" His voice slips into a whisper. "I enjoyed last night. You certainly made Sergeant Major stand to attention."

"Dad's calling me, Rod."

"Fair enough. Say hello to the old boy—and Biddy, of course. Oh, Kate?"

"Got to go, Rod."

I hear a snigger. "I'm charging you with AWOL. In which case, a reprimand is in order, don't you think?"

Absence Without Leave.

"Bye, Rod."

❖

After tucking Charlie into my old bed, I make my way in Biddy's nylon night-dress to the bathroom. As I fill the sink with warm water, there's a rap on the door.

"It's Mammy, let me in."

She pulls down her knickers and sits on the toilet.

Lathering my cheeks with soap, I say, "I'm thinking of making an appointment with my doctor to see if he'll refer me to a consultant."

"Jesus, Kate, did you find a lump? You fed that child for too long. He was eighteen months when you stopped. Ridiculous."

"No, no, nothing like that. Although"—I splash my face, then feel for the towel—"*something* is physically wrong with me, I'm sure of it."

"What?"

"I hate sex with Rodney." I peep from behind the towel to catch her reaction.

"Ah, there's nothing wrong with you. What kind of woman enjoys sex?" She tugs at toilet paper. " 'Tis nothing but a grubby necessity. Why don't you try giving in just once a month?" She reaches between her legs to wipe. "Could you manage that?" Standing to flush, she adds, "Kate, look at all you have. Play your cards right, and you'll get to *keep* it all."

"I've learned how to avoid," I say. "I have it down to a fine art."

"Then he's a very patient man, and you're lucky. Pity your father isn't the same."

"I keep my sexy lingerie wrapped in tissue."

"Kate! Why would you want to dress like a tart? There's never any need for that kind of thing."

❖

Lying on the spare bed, I listen to the whistling breath of my sleeping son, and I think about 75 Copper Lane, and the nest I built twig by twig for him. The home I filled with handmade quilts, curtains, and loose covers. Rooms I filled with stripped pine and wicker baskets. A garden full of vegetables, shrubs, and flowerbeds.

A kitchen full of chutneys, jams, and bread. I hear Biddy telling me I'm lucky, so lucky to have a kitchen like this. And to be honest, what could be more sunny than bright yellow cabinets? Shelves of turquoise canisters, rows of blue-striped salt and pepper pots. I even have a pink aluminium flour sifter. *Très* fifties.

Warm colors to enjoy in a gray marriage.

I roll onto my side. Oh, life's not that bad. I have my cooking, which I adore. What could be better than whisking, baking, kneading, tasting?

With senses fulfilled, it's easy to forget my world beyond the mixing bowl. Which reminds me.

I must bake that cake I offered to make for the Fanshaws' ruby wedding anniversary soon. It needs time to mature.

I drift into sleep and I'm spinning with a swirl of sugar frosting. Shall we take Griff something special to eat? A piece of my birthday cake will make him strong, says Charlie.

There it is, I say, pointing. Can you see it? But when I grab Charlie's cake, it crumbles into dry sand and sifts though my fingers. I look into the clouds to see if there's another one, but they've all gone.

You can make a new one, Mummy, whispers Charlie. Don't cry.

CHAPTER 43

◆

Thursday, September 24
75 Copper Lane, Oakley Green

"Oh, Kate bach, Griff isn't with us anymore."

"But—but Mamgu, no, I—"

Leaning against the wall, I sink to the kitchen floor, and I sit there, trying to block the light from my eyes with one hand.

God, please no.

Rodney zigs to the counter, zags to the table, asking, where are his keys? Where did he leave his bloody wallet? Do I know? Then he looks at me, and wants to know what on earth I'm doing. I cover the receiver. I can barely push the words from my mouth. *Griff has died.*

Tears fill my eyes. Come now, says Rodney, it's best my grandmother doesn't hear me crying, I'll only upset her more. He's sorry, truly sorry, and he wishes he could stay, but he's late for a meeting. Big client and all that. He'll be back early tonight, around seven. Okay? Good girl. We all knew it would happen soon. Griff had a good life.

I listen to my grandmother weeping softly. It's all right, Mamgu, I say. I'm here. Shh. It's all right, I keep saying.

"I brought him hot milk with a spoonful of honey this morning. 'It's strange,' he said, 'but I feel no pain today.' And we talked about you and Charlie coming to visit. He told me to stop fussing with the cushions. I was trying to make him comfortable in the old rocking chair. 'Make sure you fill the coalscuttle tomorrow,' he said, 'ready for a nice big fire at the weekend. Charlie loves a fire.' He stared at the flames, Katie. I'd just put a light to a nice piece of coal with a fat log on top. He smiled and shook his head and said, 'Mildreth, listen. Tell Katie to keep climbing those spiral steps until she finds the right door.' 'What are you talking about, Griff,' I said, 'you old fool.' He closed his eyes, told me to shut up and give him a kiss, and his head lay to one side, and I thought he was asleep, but—"

I lift my face to the ceiling to ask God why Griff had to go so soon. Why were we not granted one last weekend with him?

"He's gone, Katie."

"He was like a dad to me, Mamgu."

"It's all right, Katie. Shh. It's all right."

CHAPTER 44

◆

In Memoriam

May memories comfort you
Kate and Charlie, please know how much you are loved,
and how much your loss is felt by us

Gus, Moira,
Sasha & Sophie

May God heal you in this time of sorrow.

Blessed are they that mourn: for they shall be comforted.
MATTHEW 5:4

So very sorry, Kate.
Our love and thoughts are with you.

Oona and Barney

In Sympathy

My heart goes out to you.
Katie, so sorry about Griff.
Wishing I could be by your side at this time

With much love,
Ingrid

CHAPTER 45

◆

Wednesday, November 18
75 Copper Lane, Oakley Green

Autumn is over. I look out of the kitchen window at a mist hovering over the lawn.

I might as well go to bed.

Rodney watches a game show with vacant intensity. *"Blankety-blank, blankety-blank,"* trills the signature tune as the last contestant hops onto the set.

"What time will you be home tonight, Rod?" I ask, lolling against the wall, waiting for him to finish chewing on a mouthful of macaroni and cheese.

"Tenish."

"Where are you going?"

"Lodge of Instruction at the Masonic Hall. By the way, Betsy called me at work." He runs his tongue along the prongs of his fork. "She said not to forget Mother and Father's ruby wedding anniversary on Saturday. Ho, ho, ho—did you hear what Terry Wogan just said? 'That answer alone deserves a *Blankety-blank* checkbook.' Ha!"

"I haven't forgotten the party. I made two cakes last week, one big, one small. I plan to decorate and put them together on Friday."

"My sisters are going to all sorts of trouble, you know, inviting Mother's bridesmaids, planning a lavish buffet. They'll expect you to make something to help out."

I baked two cakes.

"How about a fancy cake?" asks Rod. "You're good at those, and they'd appreciate the effort."

"*Blankety-blank, blankety-blank,*" sings the TV. The game show is over, and Rodney must dash. And crikey, he's late, just look at the time.

Blankety-blank.

Friday, November 27

"What do you think of the cakes, Charlie?"

"They look like two tables."

I tap his fingers as he reaches to touch. "Good, because that's how they should look."

Fondant tablecloths hang in folds over bands of ruby ribbon. I punched holes for the lace edging, then embroidered with fine lines of royal icing. It truly looks like broderie anglaise.

Chef's Tip

Fondant icing is perfect for celebration cakes.
With a little patience, it can be fashioned to any form,
and with the addition of a little food coloring,
it can satisfy any creative calling.

I step back to admire my efforts. If this doesn't dazzle the Fanshaws, what will? Perhaps they'll allow me to step out of the audience and join them on stage, *i.e.,* recognize me as a member of the family. It's been a battle, but I keep trying.

"Mummy, have you finished now? What are these for?"

I take the four little pillars from Charlie's fists. "When the icing is dry, I'll put one cake on top of the other. It will be a two-tier cake."

And then I'll add the final touch. A tiny bunch of ruby-red rose buds.

Won't that gain a spot of recognition from the Fanshaws? A sweeping brush of admiration?

Griff would have liked my cake. *There's pretty,* he would have said.

And I see him now, limping along Llandafan Station in his flat cap and tweed jacket as I jump from the train. "Welcome, *cariad.*" I hear his false teeth click as he kisses me on the cheek, and I hug his bones, his stick-thin frame.

Tell Katie to keep climbing those spiral steps until she finds the right door.

What did he mean?

"Mummy, you look sad." Charlie tugs at my sleeve.

"I'm thinking about Griff."

When I see Charlie's bottom lip jut, I hold his face in my hands. "Granny and Granddad will be here soon. Will you help me tidy up?"

And I have *got* to clean the bathrooms—they're awful.

"Can I play football instead?" Charlie does a few jumps backward to escape, then turns and runs. "Okay," I shout. "Take Dinah outside with you— and put on a warm coat."

Now. I must get to work like a crazy thing.

❖

"Oh, your poor hair," says Biddy. "What kind of bra are you wearing? You need more support." She preens her newly coifed locks. She has the blackest hair, not even a whisper of gray.

Unlike her daughter.

We exchange hugs.

When Dad puts Charlie down, he walks toward me with pursed lips. I turn my face for a kiss.

Biddy rubs Charlie on the head and when she straightens up, she asks, "What's that odor?"

I tell her to choose between a list of cleaning products, or is it the cottage pie she smells browning in the oven?

"Did you put garlic in it? Your father doesn't like garlic."

"Smells great to me," says Dad.

"Tom, take our cases to the attic bedroom. Shall I make a cup of tea? Kate, you haven't told me I've lost weight yet."

"Wow, you've lost weight."

"You didn't notice as soon as you set eyes on me? I've lost five pounds."

"And it shows, really." I tug my sweater over my bottom and thighs. I should change out of these leggings and slippers.

Biddy picks a bowl out of the sink and her face screws up. "The base of this is covered with grease."

I nudge her out of the way and hold the bowl under hot water. "Take off your coat, Mum. I'll make the tea."

Or God knows what she'll find next. While the kettle boils, I check to see if the cottage pie is ready, and it is—crisp and brown and perfect.

"Is the gravy too thick?" asks Biddy, rolling up her sleeves. "Shall I peel the vegetables?"

"The vegetables are already done. The gravy is best made thick to begin with, it gets thinner in the baking."

"I know how to make cottage pie, no need to tell me."

Huh?

Biddy opens my yellow cupboard doors and drawers. "Where is the sugar kept these days? Where are the spoons?"

Feeling uneasy watching her study every tin, packet, bottle, and carton, I say, "I'll see to everything, you sit at the kitchen table. Relax, put your feet up."

As I'm putting the cozy on the teapot, I hear my father and Charlie laughing together on the stairs. "Come on you two, dinner's nearly ready," I say.

Biddy gazes out the window. "Your garden's looking grand, Kate."

"Really?"

"You've done a good job. Shall we have a walk out there after dinner?"

I revel in her praise. "I worked hard this week. Because we've had no frost recently, I managed to open up a new flowerbed and I plan to put woodland plants under those old trees in the spring. Bluebells, ferns, foxgloves—Mum, bring your tea with you. Come and see the cake I made for the Fanshaws."

"Kate, I have an idea. Why don't I stay a few days? Daddy could leave me here until next weekend. Would you like that?"

"I would love it."

I really would.

"Your cake is beautiful," she says. We stand in the pantry, arm in arm. Me in my old slippers, Biddy in her patent flats. She looks at me, her eyes enormous behind new owl-glasses. "My daughter is a clever girl," she says.

Yes.

For continued approval and admiration, I know I must pander to her. But—that's okay. It's worth it.

And what harm?

CHAPTER 46

◈

Saturday, November 28
198 Merton Avenue, Plattsworth

Gaynor answers the door wearing pink pleats cascading over a pregnant body. "Good Lord, Kate, what do you have there?" She waves a champagne glass at the cardboard box I'm carrying.

"It's the anniversary cake," I reply, wishing she'd move to one side, because it's bloody heavy.

"Good Lord, Kate," she says again, rolling her eyes to heaven. "You'd better come in. Hello, Charlie—oh, and *hello*, Mr. and Mrs. Cadogan, thank you so much for coming!"

My parents exchange nice-to-see-yous and how-are-yous and Biddy asks where she should leave the gift. In the living room, along with the others, replies Gaynor. Oh, a set of ruby-rimmed cocktail glasses? How lovely. How fabulous. Her husband is around somewhere, she thinks. He'll take their coats. Huw? Huw? Oh, there he is. Do mingle and join in the fun, Mr. and Mrs. Cadogan. Mother and Father will be so pleased to see them.

I raise my eyebrows and smile. "Where shall I put the cake?"

"Oh dear. Did it cost much?"

"I made it, Gaynor."

"Oh, Lord."

Timothy, Betsy's three-year-old, stands solidly in front of Charlie. "I'm Spider-Man, so watch it," he says.

"You two boys play together nicely now. This way, Kate."

I'm led to the kitchen. And I stop dead.

What the shit?

On the counter sits a white-iced slab. The words "Happy Anniversary, Mother & Father, from Rodney, Gaynor & Betsy" swirl across it in gay and red abandon.

I look at Gaynor.

She smiles widely. "Superb, isn't it? Betsy ordered it specially."

"But I said I'd make the cake."

"You did?"

"I told Rodney, too."

"Oh, *men*. I ask you, eh? Well, just pop it there for now, next to the bread bin."

Timothy stomps in and tugs at my dress. "What you doin' here?" he asks me.

Gaynor carries the white cake to the kitchen door. "You know what we could do, Kate? Serve yours as a lovely dessert. Why don't you cut it up into neat little slices and set it on a nice big plate? Fabulous."

You haven't even looked at it yet, you airhead.

"You know where to put your coat," she shouts. "Help yourself to drinkies. Timothy, darling, do stop screaming, you'll give Auntie a migraine. That's better. Yes, this *is* a great, big, huge, white cake. Oh, bless you! What a loud sneeze. You'd like to blow out the candles? Oh, but there aren't any." Gaynor calls for her sister. "Betsy? Please, dear, do see to Timothy's nose." She shrugs. "Oh dear, she can't hear me. Ah well. By the way, love your outfit, Kate. It's um—nice and cheerful."

She leaves, and I look down at my cheerful frock. I suppose the flowers are a bit wild, but it's very comfortable. And loose. And Timothy is sitting on the floor looking right up it as he sucks at a lump of bread.

"Did you find that bread in Desmond's dog bowl?" I ask him.

"Not telling you."

Biddy walks in.

"Jesus, Mary, and Joseph," she whispers, "will you just look at the filth in here?"

Even the sweet smell of fondant icing cannot mask the odour of rancid cheese, mildew, and mouse.

"Well, you know what they say, Kate," she adds. "Where there's muck, there's money."

I tell Biddy about the cake. "Oh God, the hours I spent, Mum, I'm not kidding, and it's full of dried fruit, walnuts, raisins, and brandy. And I bought roses, and lace-edged the icing, and bought pillars, and I went to so much trouble, and—and do you know what?"

"They already have a cake. I saw it."

"Yes. An inscribed tombstone. What does Gaynor think I have sitting in this box? A Swiss roll? Serve it as dessert, Kate, she says, cut it into neat little slices, set it on a nice big plate."

Timothy opens a cupboard door and then proceeds to have a thunderous time with saucepan lids. *"Ohhhhh—the gran ole Duke of York!"* he yells.

Biddy cups her hand to my ear. "Swap the cakes. I'll keep a look-out."

"He had ten thousan' men—"

Yes! I grin and I give her the thumbs-up.

"An' when they were up, they were up." BANG! *"—An' when they were down, they were down—"* CRASH!

"Jesus, Mary, and Joseph," mutters Biddy.

❖

In the dining room, an oversized sheet covers the serving table, and it hangs conveniently low at the front. Low enough, in fact, to hide a big white cake if it was shoved underneath.

I assemble my creation in its place, and when I step back, I have to catch a scream before it leaps from my mouth. "Timmy!"

He's a solid little boy—a walking ball with hunched shoulders and clenched fists. I watch his fat bottom wriggle as he squirms under the table.

"Vroom, vroom. I keep my cars under here, I do." His face beams from under the hem of the tablecloth as he hurls each car across the brown linoleum. "Why is Nanny and Grandpa's cake sitting in my garage? Why?"

Timothy crawls back out, clutching a battered Tonka truck.

"Let's pick your cars up together," I say. "Shall we find a new place for them?"

Hurry up, you little tyke. Let's get out of here before Betsy and Gaynor catch me.

"Nah!" he replies with a mucousy snort.

"You poor little thing, you do have a bad cold. Take my hand. Let's go and find Charlie."

Timothy takes aim and I'm too late to skip aside before he smashes the Tonka truck into my leg. The pain is sharp and it hurts like absolute bloody hell.

Fuck.

I grab the Tonka, put it on top of the dresser, and make my way to the living room. God, do I need a drink.

Timothy lunges past me. "You look horble, you do."

When he reaches his mother, Betsy swings him onto her lap and bounces him up and down with such force that the child's eyes swim in his head. "*Oh, the Grand Old Duke of York*," she sings. "*Hup-hup.*"

"At-ish-hoo!"

"Do stop sneezing, Tim-Tim," she says.

Speak roughly to your little boy, and beat him when he sneezes. He only does it to annoy, because he knows it teases. Where are the bloody drinks?

Rodney's back from the game, here at the party, and wearing a suit, too. "Hi, Rod. Would you get me a drink, please?"

"Hello there. Hang on a second." He takes three strides toward a bald man and pounds him on the back. "Dave? Yes it is! Dave Bloody Thorngate, well I never. How are you doing, old boy?"

"Rodders! Well, I never, has it been, what, seven years since we fraternized on the cricket field? Good to see you!"

Well, that's that then.

Feeling a gentle pressure on my arm, I expect to see my dad, but it's Uncle Bertie. He hands me a large measure of Scotch, whiskey, brandy? Whatever it is, it will do.

"Cheers, Bertie."

"Bottoms up," he replies, and sways off to an armchair in a quiet corner.

The amber liquid smells smoky, tastes malty. I hold my glass up to Nancy and Rodney Senior and mime them a toast, and receive quick nods of acknowledgment.

I survey the scene.

Cuthbert Downey, an ex-army type, is talking down at Dad, who has Charlie on his knee. Gaynor entertains the guests with enthralling conversation, and she throws her head back, laughing hugely. Betsy is still bouncing Timothy senseless. A woman built like a horse grabs Biddy's hand. How do you do, she neighs, she's Thelma, one of Nancy's bridesmaids, haw-haw.

Nice to meet you, Biddy, has she seen the cake yet? It's magnificent. Who made it?

Biddy sends me a sly wink.

The doorbell rings and more guests pile in. Would you help please, Kate? Yes, of course, Gaynor, I say. Would you fetch the quiche and a few other things? Yes, Betsy, just point the way.

"ARE WE ALL HERE?" booms Rodney from the living room. The rumble of conversation in 198 Merton Avenue drops to a mumble, to a mutter, to a few scattered coughs.

"Silence, please. Silence, silence. Ladies and gentlemen, would you please proceed to the dining room and assemble there? Thank you so very much."

I slink to the back of the room and motion Charlie to stand in front of me.

Rodney Senior, Nancy, Rodney Junior, and his sisters line up in front of my cake. I lean to one side, but Gaynor catches my eye. The look spits venom. She beckons to her husband Huw to join her, darts a second vicious glance at me, then smiles and calls Betsy's husband, too. And little Timmy, how could she forget him? Oh, he's such a good little boy.

And there they stand complete: The Fanshaw Family.

And here I remain with my son, still a member of the audience in the cheap seats.

Rodney tinks a fork on the side of his glass to settle the crowd, to hush their aren't-they-a-lovely-family oohs and ahs.

Gaynor produces a little speech and a tear or two. And now, ladies and gentlemen, she would like to read a poem she composed her very self, before she hands the spotlight over to Rodney Junior and then Betsy.

"Ahem.

A lot has happened over forty years
Plenty of laughter, a few little tears.
May the love that keeps the Fanshaws together
Go on forever and ever and ever."

"For Thine is the kingdom, and the power, and the glory, Amen," I whisper in Biddy's ear.

"Happy wedding anniversary, Mother, Father."

As Gaynor and her parents embrace, a loud *"Vroom, vroom"* is heard.

"Vroom-vroom." Timothy's face grins from under the hem of the table-cloth. "I've got a race track," he shouts, pushing the white cake from under the table for all to see.

Oh, holy shit.

A network of tire-tracks has turned *Happy Anniversary, Mother & Father, from Rodney, Gaynor & Betsy* into a scrambled mess.

"Splush, vroom, crash!" yells Timothy, as he creates ditches and ravines.

"Charlie, do you need the bathroom?" I hiss.

"No."

"Yes, you do. Come with me."

Biddy follows, and on the stairs, I turn to give her a horrified look.

And her face collapses, and the next thing, I'm weak, I'm useless, I can barely climb the last three steps. "Oh God, oh God," I splutter when we reach the landing.

I push Charlie into the bathroom and close the door.

"Oh, Kate," says Biddy, holding her stomach. "How do you put up with this family? You poor creature. How did Rodney survive?"

We shake with silent laughter, just like Moi and me used to do at Shawhurst High School.

But how long will this last?

CHAPTER 47

◆

14th December 1988

Oona!

Where do I start? St. Louis is really a FANTASTIC place, despite the freezing temperatures. We went to the top of the Arch today—a dizzying height of 630 feet! So far, we've visited the zoo, the planetarium, and the science center. Gus took Charlie to watch the St. Louis Blues play ice hockey yesterday. Moira and the girls are well, and look just great. Wish I had more space on this postcard to tell you EVERYTHING. We're having great fun! I'll give you a call when we get back to England, promise.   Love, Kate and Charlie X X X

TO:

OONA GERAGHTY,

LONGSHAFT FARM,

CLOONDRAY,

NR. BLAKESTOWN

EIRE

CHAPTER 48

Saturday, December 17
75 Copper Lane, Oakley Green

"So, when will you two visit us again?" Moira's voice is a gentle drawl. "The girls sure do miss Charlie already."

I smile, listening to my friend's changed accent—it didn't take her long. I picture her seven-year-old twins the day we met them at Lambert Airport, and God, had they grown since we last saw them. Long legs, brown faces, hair as white as snow, dressed in green dungarees and lemon sweaters. When Charlie pulled a face at them, they laughed showing pink gums without even a peep of new front teeth yet.

"Sasha and Sophie are gorgeous, Moi."

"And Charlie is a yummy cutie pie, good enough to eat."

There's a pause.

"Listen, Katie, you're all right, aren't you?"

"Katie?"

"I'll be okay."

Mamgu clatters saucepans in the kitchen. I fetched her from Llandafan yesterday to spend a few days with us. She's frying sausages and mashing potatoes for Charlie. She mimes a "sorry," and I shake my head to let her know not to worry.

And Moira mustn't worry either, everything *will* be okay. I'm used to Rodney, really, used to taking my mind somewhere else until it's over. I hunch over the phone so Mamgu doesn't hear me. "It could be far worse, Moi. He's not a wife-beater, nor does he have affairs." I offer a little laugh to stop her fretting. "As far as I know!"

I couldn't tell her *everything*. It's too—comical. Bizarre, I suppose. Well, I think it is.

Some women might not.

"Katie, why couldn't you tell me what goes on in the bedroom? How weird is it? Look, we're talking on the phone, not face to face. Would it be easier to tell me now?"

"Oh, it's not that bad, I mean, oh hell, Moi." I lower my voice. "It's a bit difficult to talk right now. You're a sweetheart worrying about me, but I'm used to my life and the way things are."

I hear a sigh. "Okay," she says. "By the way, my folks said August would be a good time for Gus, me, and the girls to visit them in Cardiff."

"That's wonderful! And really, Moi, I'm fine. Remember, I have Charlie."

"He's about to start grammar school, Katie. Years whiz by, you know that. You can't keep him forever."

I run my hand over the wall I ragged and stenciled. "I have the house."

"Uh-huh."

"I'd better go, Moi. Thank you a million times for inviting us to St. Louis. God, and as I kept telling you, your new home is fabulous."

Open plan and vast, polished floors, gigantic fridges, huge beds, high ceilings—and a *swimming pool*.

"Gus and I enjoyed your visit. Come on over any time, do you hear? Now go and tart yourself up for the dance."

"I will."

"Kate?"

"Yes?"

"You looked great with only one chin."

"Shut up."

"Shut up yourself."

I laugh as I run upstairs to fetch Charlie. I *do* look better with only one chin. The diet was worth the agony before we flew to the States. There was absolutely no way I would have let Moira see me in a swimsuit otherwise.

❖

And I fit into the frock! It rustles as I lift the skirt to smooth on barely black stockings. I sort through my jewelry for a clustered necklace and a chunky bracelet. I need something a bit trashy in contrast to set this dress off.

Standing in front of the mirror, I brush the hair that's so long it reaches my arse, and twist it into a topknot. Yes, I know, I know, I tell myself, thirty-eight *is* too old for hair this long. I should go for the chop, let Shane of San-souchies have his wicked way.

As I step downstairs in my black taffeta, I hear the sound of rapping knuckles on glass, and when I round the corner, I see Rodney at the hall window, waving at a black cab outside.

"Haw, haw, Todd Grimley, you silly old bastard." I'm awarded a fleeting glance before he asks, "Ready? Good. Taxi's waiting. Todd and Penny are sharing the fare."

"How do I look?"

"You look bloody cold in that outfit," he says, twanging one of my shoulder straps. "I'll go parley with Todd while you fetch an overcoat. Chop-chop, get a move on, now."

Rodney bristles with excitement, for this evening, *ta-dah,* it's the Masonic Ladies' Night Ball at the Tropical Gardens in Moreditch.

"Mamgu? Charlie? We're leaving now." I push my arms into my coat.

I hear odd noises outside, strange sounds—whistles, whoops, and puffs. When I peek out of the window, I see Rodney in the light of the security lamp shuffling in circles, pretending to be a locomotive. He can be such a twit at times.

I run to the kitchen to smack kisses on each of my son's cheeks. "Mamgu's going to teach me how to play bridge and poker," says Charlie, shuffling cards.

"Gambling, eh?" I laugh.

"Mum? Mamgu says her neighbor's tabby had six kittens."

"And?"

I know what's coming next.

"Wouldn't it be great to have another cat? I miss Dinah tons since she died."

I do too, my tan cat, my little companion.

"We'll talk about it later, sweetheart."

Charlie tips his head to one side and raises an eyebrow. *"Please?"*

"Oh . . ." The long blast of a horn summons me to the taxi. "All right!"

"Thanks, Mum. You're the best!"

"I'll see you both tomorrow morning, then," I say, hugging Mamgu. "We won't be back till the early hours."

"You look a picture, Katie *bach*."

Charlie grins at me. "So we can bring a kitten back from Llandafan?"

The taxi horn *pip-pip-pips*. Oh, for God's sake, hang on, Rodney.

"Yes, Charlie. Now, I have to *go*!"

"I'm going to call it Velcro, Mum."

❖

"At last! Here's Katers!" says Todd. "Woo-ee, plant your tidy bottom right here, next to me, that's it, sweetie."

He has the smallest head and the tiniest of black-currant eyes, and one peg of a tooth is larger than the other at the front, yet it all seems to fit together okay. I settle between him and Penny in the back of the taxi, and bid my greetings.

"Well, are we ready?" asks Rodney. He sits on the little extra seat opposite. "How are you these days, Todders?"

"Feeling utterly delicious, now I'm next to your wife, dear boy," he says emitting a low growl.

Take your hand off my thigh, sweetie.

"This is one ample thigh under my hot little hand, Rodders!"

I turn to Penny, who grimaces into a little mirror, checking her teeth. She wears a mass of pastel flounces. The handbag on her lap is white, her shoes are white, her gloves are white. "How are things, Penny?" I ask.

"Fine," she answers, and looks out of the window.

She has always been a bit of a snooty cow.

And so.

I have no choice but to listen to Rodders and Todders exchange blow-by-blow accounts of birdies and bunkers. From the taxi scramble of radio signals, I snatch the time. Six-thirty-five p.m.

❖

We arrive at the Botanical Gardens on the stroke of seven. "Well done, Mr. Taxi Man," says Rodney, holding his hand out for Todd's portion of the fare.

God, it's cold. We follow a flutter of women in sequins and silk, a waddle of men in dinner suits. I listen to delighted squeals, mumbled greetings, and catch a secret handshake or two as we make our way to the lobby.

I stand behind Penny at the cloakroom.

"Next, please?"

I hand over my coat, take my ticket, turn, and—

Penny disappears into the crowd.

Rodney and Todd are busy hailing fellow brothers, so I head for the bathroom.

As soon as I open the door, I hear the loud ring of my mother-in-law's laugh. "Haw-haw, haw-haw."

Yep, that's her. Amid a brood of ladies, I see her jostling for a free space, trying to claim a mirror. A woman in a slink of yellow georgette clips her bag shut and I jump at the chance to take her place. I beckon to Nancy to join me.

"Hello, Kate." She tugs at her wig. "Arrived on time I see, haw-haw."

Auntie Glenda stands two bodies to the left of me, plucking her eyebrows into surprised arches. "Kate, dear, you look lovely, doesn't she, Nancy?"

"Yes. Shall we join Rodney Senior and Bertie?"

Pursing her lips to a point, Auntie Glenda touches my cheek with a quick peck. Then she and Nancy leave with arms linked, busy in conversation.

I check my lipstick and blusher and pin up a few strands of loose hair. Staring hard at my reflection in the mirror, I determine to enjoy the night.

A drink might help.

As soon as I step outside, Rodney grabs my elbow and marches me to the entrance hall. I trot to keep up with him. "We have to be announced," he says, pushing me into position next to a fat man holding a staff.

With his nose in the air, Rodney clicks his heels and stands erect.

"Brother Rodney James Henry Fanshaw and Mrs. Kate Marie Fanshaw."

I kiss the red face of His Worshipful Master Bertram Bosworth and the powdered face of his lady. Rodney swings me round and flash! Another photograph to shove to the back of a drawer.

We move on to the reception hall with its gold painted walls and endless carpet. All swirls, whirls, and filigree.

"Sherry, madam?" asks a waitress.

I take two glasses, one in each hand. Four sips, and they're empty.

"Simon!" splutters Rodney. And off he bounds across the room, leaving me stranded.

"Sweet or dry?"

I exchange my empty glasses for a third dry and focus on the crowd that stands around the bar area. Is there at least *one* familiar face or body I can attach myself to? I don't recognize any of them. Folding my arms, I study the ceiling. Tapping one foot, I try to appear occupied in deep thought.

Bang! A gavel is slammed. Oh God, it must be a summons of some sort. Yes, the brothers and gentlemen are to take their ladies to table.

Where the hell is Rodney?

There's a gentle tip-tap on my shoulder.

Todd Grimley.

I don't bother to ask where Penny is. I'm just relieved to see someone I know. I take his proffered arm and we head for the dining hall. A blaze of scarlet balloons and poinsettias greet us, a complication of crimson bows and baubles meet us. Red, red, red, red.

My father-in-law stands behind the head table scratching his groin. Next to him is Auntie Glenda. Her head pivots, her eyes dart, and Uncle Bertie—well, Uncle Bertie was nodding off in his chair before his wife delivered him a smart slap on the back of his head. Nancy continues to tug at both her wig and at the rivulets of satin that have gathered under her breasts.

I thank Todd for leading me to our table, and his black-currant eyes twinkle.

Rodney's place setting is to my left, Todd's to my right. "Hello, Rod. Where did you get to?" I ask.

Thumping gavels echo throughout, so I miss my answer. *Slam, bang, slam.* The thunderous chatter in the Dining Hall tones down to whispers, to silence. The Grand Master Bertram Bosworth and Mrs. Eunice Bosworth are to be ceremoniously welcomed to top table. The rhythmic clapping begins at slow tempo and speeds up to reach a crescendo of applause.

The honored couple settle in their wooden thrones and nod to all past masters and their ladies. *Bang, slam, bang.* The master calls on the chaplain to say grace. "For what we are about to receive, may the Lord make us truly thankful and ever mindful of the needs of others."

Amen, amen, amen.

Todd whispers in my ear. "You know what *my* needs are, don't you? You *naughty* little thing."

There's a scraping of chairs and the chatter resumes. Todd holds Penny's chair for her to sit, then mine.

Oh boy, it's going to be one long night. Oh boy, here comes the wine. The waiter has two bottles swaddled in white cloth. "Red or white, madam?"

I decide on the chardonnay to go with the soup set before me. I pick up my spoon and fish around, chasing a floating crouton.

Rodney slaps me on the back. "Meet the wife!" I'm introduced to Maurice and Fred, new members of the lodge, and their wives, Amy and Nicole. Maurice wobbles a sloppy jowl and repeats my name. Amy nods once. Florid Fred, his face as red as the blazing balloons, shakes my hand, and Nicole smiles broadly.

Rodney will now ignore them. That's what he does.

Soup bowls are cleared. "Goujons?" inquires the waitress.

"Yes, goujons, thank you!" Three battered fingers are served on my plate.

"Chardonnay?" asks the waiter.

"Yes, thank you!" My empty glass is refilled.

Todd traces the clasp of my suspender belt with his fingers. "Grrrrrrrr," he growls softly.

Rodney rubs his hands together. Why does he keep doing that? "Kate, throw over the menu, let's see what the main course is. What a fantastic spread!"

Bang, slam, bang.

"A toast to the queen and the craft."

Everyone stands. There's a flurry of napkins, a clink of glasses, a mumbling wave of response. "The queen and the craft, the queen, the craft, the craft—"

My head swims.

Bang, slam, bloody bang. "His Worshipful Master would like to take wine with all the ladies present."

"Ladies, ladies, ladies."

The main course is cubes of steak in gravy. Rodney reaches across my neck to take the carrots and peas from Penny.

Todd rubs a socked foot up and down my ankle.

Rodney summons the waitress. "More roast spuds, please, miss. I'm a growing boy!"

Todd closes one tiny eye and winks at me. "More chardonnay?" He snaps fingers for the wine waiter.

I slope to my left. "Hey, Rod," I whisper, "Todd keeps stroking my thigh."

"Over-sexed bastard," he says too loudly and with great mirth. "He'll go for anything in a skirt, old Todders will."

And then comes dessert.

More toasts, more prayers, more songs, and many more *slams* and blasted *bangs* later, I realize I've drunk too much. Here, at home, wherever I am, I drink too much. Oh, what the shit, and don't those red balloons, bows, and poinsettias look bloody gorgeous?

And it's time for the Ladies' Song, and warm Masonic hearts will meet us, and hands of fellowship will greet us. I look around at women crying, giggling, yawning, and I wonder what is really going on inside their heads. I know I feel completely detached, just floating along, doing the right thing. Standing when I should, sitting when I should, smiling when I should.

"A liqueur for madam?"

"Ouzo, please."

Ouzo, because I'm an oozie-woozie-floozie. When it arrives, I feel my eyes crossing as I watch the flickering blue haze in the liqueur glass. I puff away the flame and take a liquorice sip.

The brothers stand.

With hands on hearts, they sing in chorus, but why doesn't Rodney look at me?

And the men may smoke. A few of the ladies at our table make a move to visit the bathrooms. Rodney moves to the empty seat opposite Penny to discuss golf clubs and score cards.

And Todd moves in on me.

And finally, ladies and gentlemen, a cheese board is served with coffee, and Todd feeds me black grapes, and Rod and Penny take absolutely no notice.

And boy, they must have come from the same pod, they're so alike.

Music bounces in the background.

"Rod," I hiss, "Todd has asked me to dance."

"You swanky devil, Todders! See you two later. Penny and me are still knee-deep in pars and strokes!"

So we walk to the dance floor, where Auntie Glenda has a tight grip on a bunch of satin around Nancy's waist as they dance a rapid fox-trot together.

The music trips to an end. "And now, ladies and gentlemen, please take your partners for the waltz. *And* one-two-three, one-two-three."

Giggling because everything is oh, so funny, I watch as couples swirl and swish by. I truly cannot dance one step of the waltz.

Todd mushes his lips against the tips of my fingers. "Come on."

"I can't."

"Hush, and hold on to me. No, closer. I'll lead."

"I can't waltz!"

"Closer!"

What the heck. Nuzzling my face into the curve of his neck, I wrap my arms around Todd's shoulders.

"That's the girl."

I melt into the languorous beat. No resistance, no repulsion, bodies pressing, Todd pushing, feelings stirring, head swimming, a sleeping desire slowly rising. I look into his black-currant eyes. The alcohol molds his features into acceptable, agreeable, amiable, likeable.

"Feel what you are doing to me, Katers."

I feel, very obviously, what I am doing to him. My response is unexpected and confusing. No resistance, no repulsion, I'm dancing, one-two-three, one-two-three, I mean to tease, to tempt, to flirt, one-two-three, one-two-three.

Todd circles his hands over my hips.

It's never like this with Rod.

And the music ends, and harsh beams of light play over the crowd. Quickly dropping my arms to my sides, I take a step backward.

Clang, crash! A tinny smash of cymbals announces the next dance. "And now, gentlemen, ladies, please form a circle for—*the Birdie Song!*"

Rodney gallops toward us, flapping his elbows. He loves this dance.

But I slope off to the bathroom, because I need to think. I might even cadge a cigarette from some friendly lady. I'll take a walk through the Tropical Gardens all by myself, and I'll talk to the mynah bird I know they keep in a cage there.

Cover the butter.

Hide your sexuality.

Sex is just a grubby necessity, what kind of woman likes sex?

When Todd phones, and I know he will, I shall put the receiver down.

PART FOUR

◆

THE NINETIES

CHAPTER 49

◆

1995

Monday, April 10
75 Copper Lane, Oakley Green

"**Mum? I'll get the post,**" shouts Charlie. "There's a pink envelope, it looks like a card, and hey—there's a parcel, and it smells like chocolate! Great stamps. I'll leave everything in the kitchen, okay? See you later, then. I'm off to Baz's house."

KATIE
Your friendship is:
Eggs-citing, eggs-cellent, eggs-traordinary,
and eggs-tra-special to me!
HAPPY EASTER!
Oodles of love, Moira

Un lapin en chocolat avec un panier rempli d'oeufs pour toi!
Joyeux Pâques!
Ingrid & Thierry

Thursday, April 13

1995. I can't believe I've been married for almost nineteen years now. I can't believe I stayed, but I did. I can't believe I'm forty-three, but I am.

I can't believe I've managed to avoid sex for so long, but I have. It's one of the reasons I managed to stay. And I'm thankful Rodney left matters as they were. He never raised the subject, was too occupied, didn't seem to care—

Until this morning.

As he sat on the bidet, he shouted, "Kate, on the subject of marital relations—"

Oh.

Shit.

"Rod, don't shout. Charlie will hear," I said, throwing on clothes. "We'll talk over breakfast."

Of course, the *main* reason I stayed was for Charlie.

◆

It's like this, Rod, I said, placing a bowl of cornflakes in front of him. I'm a night owl and you're an early bird, that's the snag. We keep different hours. These things happen, but it doesn't matter, a lot of marriages are like this, and people still get along, I've read about it in magazines.

Which ones?

She and *Cosmopolitan.*

Blow *She* and *Cosmopolitan,* he says, according to the national average, we should be doing it two point three times a week. So why don't we spend the Easter weekend together in Crickmouth Bay and have some fun, eh? Let's get our marriage back together.

"Oh, I don't know, Rod. Will Betsy and Gaynor be there, too, with their broods?"

They haven't spoken to me since the Anniversary Cake Saga of 1981.

"I believe not, but Father and Mother plan to be there."

Oh.

"At eighteen, Charlie is old enough to hold the fort," says Rodney.

"Charlie wouldn't want to come, anyway," I remind him.

Why is Rodney suddenly concerned about our marriage?

He seems happy enough. Loves his lifestyle. Sports gear regularly cleaned and pressed, *a man needs his recreation, son,* dinner on the table and wine left to breathe, no matter when he returns from wherever he's been, be it the checkered floor of the Masonic Temple, the pitch on a field, in a bunker, or on the flat. A warm house to return to, with light, television, papered walls, scrubbed floors, and white sheets.

When Charlie leaves home, is Rodney frightened I may go, too?

Friday, April 14

I'd better start packing.

I smooth my sweaters over dresses, skirts, and trousers. Skimming my hand over a silk camisole, I wonder, if I wore this, would sex turn into love-making?

Rodney barges in, rubbing his hands. "All ready?" His eyes dart to the bed. "You haven't packed your mackintosh or Wellington boots. Think of April showers, Kate. Why the lacy stuff? You'll most likely need warm pajamas. And bed socks. Where do you think we're going, South Africa?"

Well, I guess the silk and satin are for dreams, nothing else.

"Don't forget how chilled you get in bed," he says. "Did you remember my swimming gear?"

No, I forgot, but I did remember to pack the lotions and potions Rodney needs to aid, prevent, ease, and loosen. He tosses in his swimming trunks, and then pulls two stuffed plastic bags from his wardrobe. ARMY SURPLUS, they say.

"What's in those?"

"Nothing."

I catch the twist of a smile on his lips before he snaps his case shut, grabs the handle, and aims for the stairs.

I call Charlie, who promised the party will be a small one while we're away. He saunters in and slouches against the wall, studying his shoes. I resist telling him to tie his laces. He's too old for that now.

"Twelve people only, promise me."

Charlie answers with that crooked smile I love so much.

"Can I trust you?" I wrap my arms around his waist, run fingers down his lean back. When did he grow so tall? Pushing him away, I flick his brown hair from his forehead.

"Tell the old man to drive carefully," he says.

"Charlie, don't forget to feed Velcro. There's an open can of cat food in the fridge to use first. I've already fed Goldie, Fred, and Mabel, just one small pinch of fish flakes a day, okay?"

"Yep."

I add pajamas and several pairs of bed socks to my holiday ensemble.

Asking Charlie to carry my luggage to the car, I run down to my kitchen to put the picnic sandwiches together, ready for the beach tomorrow.

CHAPTER 50

◆

Saturday, April 15
Crickmouth Bay, Farmouth

CATHY'S COZY CAFÉ

Delicious Breakfast
(For Two)
Egg, Bacon, Sausage & Fried Bread
Plus a Pot of Tea £8.50

I set down my knife and fork and look around. The place is empty. We must be the first customers of the day.

"God, I'm tired," I say, stifling a yawn.

"Your idea to get up so bloody early," says Rodney, mopping egg yolk from his plate with bread.

Then he taps at his pocket watch and frowns.

Time. Rodney is obsessed with every hour and minute of it.

Sex. I'm still distressed by the very notion of it, which is why I crept out of bed, got dressed—swiftly—and planned breakfast at Cathy's Cozy Café before he woke up this morning.

He beams, exclaims, "Easter Sunday tomorrow!" and reaches for one of the pamphlets strewn across a neighboring table.

"I suggest we attend the morning service at All Saints Chapel," he says. "Let me see here. What about ten o'clock?"

"But you never go to church. Our wedding was the last time."

"Thought it would make a nice change."

"No golf?"

"Left the clubs behind."

Gosh. He is making an effort, but—

I don't go to Mass anymore. Biddy's labeled me a lapsed Catholic, and it's breaking her heart, she said. But what's the use, I asked. Rodney plays crick-ethockeygolforsquash the whole of Sunday morning, isn't going to church supposed to be a family affair? Then take Charlie, she suggested. Well, Mum, I replied, no can do, because he claims to be an atheist.

After an exasperated sigh, she changed the subject. Why doesn't she spend another few days with me at Copper Lane? Would I like that? We'll paint the living room a nice beige. She hates my mustard walls, they're the color of a loose cow-pat.

Relieved that the ever-looming topic of religion was dropped, I said okay, let's decorate.

Great! Let her go and fetch the swatches from her handbag. Do I have paintbrushes? Mum, I said, I have thirty paintbrushes, and rollers, a drill, a sander, and a circular saw, remember? I'm the handyman, the decorator, the laborer, the gardener. Oh, Kate, she said, what a sharp tongue, she has a good mind to tell me to paint the damn walls myself, now.

"Kate?"

"Yes, Rod?"

"Well?"

"Okay, we'll go to the chapel," I say, because he's trying, after all, and so should I.

"More tea?" asks Cathy as she plods in, cradling a teapot to her bosom. "So nice to see you both, after all these years."

I smile. "Wonderful breakfast, Cathy. The eggs were perfect!"

"Well, I'll tell you why they're so good, dear." She pours us a second cup of tea. "Last autumn, I bought myself a few hens. Oh, and a speckled roos-ter. He's such a fine gentleman. Churchill, his name is. Did you hear him crowing his head off this morning? The coop is right next to your in-laws' backyard."

I shake my head. All I'd heard this morning was the frantic shrieking of gulls.

"I'll tell you what." Cathy sets the teapot on our table. "There's a batch of eggs due to hatch by tomorrow. Would you like to see the chicks?"

"She'll be too busy," says Rodney

"How sweet!" I say, "And tomorrow morning would be the perfect time to see them!"

Chicks on Easter Sunday. New life. A new beginning? You never know.

◆

What a compact little resort Crickmouth Bay is, where river mingles with sea. I love its familiar smell of salt and seaweed. There's a purple haze of hills behind the cliffs, where we went pony trekking all those years ago, before we married.

I'll teach you to ride one day.

But he never did.

Damn, where *is* Rodney? I laid everything out on the bed ready, so what's keeping him?

"Kate," he shouted from the bathroom last night, "I think I'll wear a rubber cap as well as inserting earplugs. You know, for double protection."

"Rod," I said, when he came into the bedroom, "you're wearing a lady's bathing hat, and it's covered with daisies."

"It's Mother's. Just checking to see if it would fit."

"Oh, God, you can't wear that."

"Why not? It will prevent ear infections."

"I think your father catches those nasty infections from the mackerel guts the fishermen empty from the pier."

"Nonsense."

"Try diving from a different launching pad."

"Unnecessary."

I saunter down to the wall that separates the beach from the car park, thinking, *So let him jump off the pier, what the fuck, he knows best—when—* there he is, waiting.

"Oh, was I supposed to meet you here?" I ask.

It takes me a while to realize my mouth is open.

"Oh, Rod, what *are* you wearing?"

"Did you pack the flasks?"

I glance around at staring eyes. Couples nudging, kids giggling, men smirking. Rodney resembles a pupa, so cocooned is he inside a thick lump of a toweling robe. Soon, his body will emerge and we will see the transformation from larval stage.

Rodney, you idiot. A pink robe and a flowered bathing hat?

"What are you smiling at?" he asks. "Did you bring sandwiches?"

I swing the raffia bag in front of him, to indicate I've remembered everything.

"You have my goggles?" Rodney snaps them on. "Earplugs?" He twists them in. "Thermometer?" He hands me his robe and he's ready for takeoff. Goggled, plugged, and capped.

"Oh wait, Rod. Those trunks are far too big for him." They bag down to his knees and the waistband reaches his nipples.

I raise my eyebrows.

"I wear these all the time at the Sebastian Crowe Leisure Centre."

He flips his hand at me, his irritation evident. "Just give me the thermometer, would you?"

Avoiding the slick algae and the scragged remains of jellyfish, Rodney zigzags down the ramp to take the sea's temperature. "Forty-eight-point-five degrees Fahrenheit! Bloody freezing, eh?" he shouts.

But that's exactly how he likes it.

"Remind me to jot it down in Father's record book," he adds.

He returns the thermometer to the raffia bag, and onto the pier he goes. Teetering on the edge, he takes his pulse before diving into the waves.

A child screams with delight. Gulls cry, begging for bread. The beach is already busy with families claiming their patches of sand. Striped deck chairs are scattered at all angles, surrounded by bags and buckets and spades and kids. The tide's coming in, so Rodney is bang on schedule, steadily breast-stroking his way toward the sand spit. He plans to beat Father's record, Kate. He reckons he could make it there and back in ten minutes flat. Easily.

The call of the beach is too much for me to resist. I slip off my sandals and flip my legs over the wall. Limping over pebbles, I set the raffia bag down, pad onto firmer sand, and wade into the frothy scum of spent waves.

I lift my skirt and venture further, and I tip my head back to accept the early rays of a morning sun.

◈

"Good God, woman, get out of the bloody water!" yells Rodney. "At least wear suitable clothing."

I make my way back to the shore, then spread the picnic blanket over a table of sand, and I sit, knees drawn up, to look at the man I'm married to.

"Where's the towel?" he asks, dripping from body and nose.

I tell him.

"Did it in nine minutes flat, Kate. What do you think of that? Wait till I tell Father I've beaten his 1991 record."

"But he's seventy-eight, Rod," I say, reaching for the flasks. "Here, take this."

I hand him a steaming cup of coffee. Italian roast.

"Smells like cat piss," he says.

After dressing, Rodney sits to read the newspaper.

And the sun grows hot.

I lay back to watch cloud-puffs drift across the sky, and as I drift with them, I fall into a delicious half-sleep.

No warmth, no softness in my dream. The stone is cold under my feet as I climb the spiral stairway. I find doors I've never seen before, but they're the wrong color. *Tell Katie to keep climbing those spiral steps until she finds the right door.* Searching for a red one, I stumble, then a yellow one, I fight for breath. Is there a green one? No, but there is a mirror. Biddy's face fills it, a young face framed with black curls. She's soft in a sweater with embroidered rosebuds.

I know I'm dipping further now, deeper, plummeting into real sleep, because all outside noises are fading. I'm a child, caressing my mother's cheek with splayed fingers. Let me tie the bow in your hair, she says. Come to Mammy. Her smile spreads to expose the gap between her two front teeth, and her features shift, transform, and now she's Rodney, with a moustache and square glasses. Sand fills my mouth, I can't shout out, can't speak.

And down, down, I fall, back through the tunnel, into a pit where it's dark and gray and claustrophobic, full of handmade quilts, stripped pine, and wicker baskets.

"Stay!"

I wake up. A baby laughs. Gulls screech. Waves sigh.

"What?" asks Rodney. "I'm not going anywhere."

He's not going anywhere. For once, he's not going anywhere.

"Rod, you must stop going out, leaving me behind in the house all the time, and don't bloody tell me to take up golf, because that isn't the answer, okay?"

"What on earth's wrong with you?"

I rub my eyes. "How long have I been asleep?"

"Over an hour."

I've woken up angry, bloody angry. The pit I fell into was my house, and it felt like a prison. I couldn't shout, couldn't scream, and isn't this just like my life? Leaping up, I brush sand from my legs, beat the creases from my skirt, and when the sole of my foot lands on Rodney's goggles, I kick them into his lap.

"Hey, hey, calm down, old girl. The sun's got to you, hasn't it? I knew you should have worn a hat," he says. "And now where are you going?"

"Nowhere special," I say, fighting with my sandals. "Do you mind?"

"Fair enough."

◆

When I reach the dunes, I sink down onto a drift of sand, where it's private, where I'm hidden, where I can think some more. I look out at the horizon.

I sang in my chains like the sea.

Griff's favorite poet wrote that. Dylan Thomas.

I never forget I'm a mother, but I often forget I'm married. Here I am in Crickmouth Bay, alone with Rodney, without Charlie, for the first time in years, and it feels wrong. Unfamiliar.

Subconsciously, did I marry Rodney because finally Biddy approved? God, am I really that sad?

Always searching for the mother in Biddy, I've tolerated, endured, complied, adapted. Depended on the isolated sparks of love.

I'm pathetic, and there's no other word for it.

How do you put up with the Fanshaws, Kate? You poor creature, said Biddy.

And we shook with silent laughter, and I hoped this moment would last.

But it didn't.

Biddy could never compensate for Rodney's indifference, so why did I keep trying?

My toes find something sharp. A bleached twig. Grabbing it, I snap it into pieces, then sigh.

What am I supposed to do now?

I mean, what's done is done, and here I am, still very married to Rodney Fanshaw.

And so—

What else is there to do but try and make a go of it?

CHAPTER 51

◆

It's a chilly night, but exhilarating and salty-fresh. I ought to do more walking. Something new to try when I get back to Copper Lane.

As Max the West Highland and I walked along the shore, I thought, right, Rodney Fanshaw, I'll give you one more chance, but you're on trial from now on. Frightened of me leaving, are you? Then you'd better change. I'll lay down a few ultimatums. You're not my jail keeper, you with your jingling keys and slammed doors.

I let Max into Cliff House, then stoop down to stroke his ears. After unclipping the leash, I follow him up the stairs. This dog's a lot friendlier than old Desmond (may he rest in peace in dog-heaven).

Max heads for Rodney Senior and Nancy's room. I head for the bathroom.

The toilet paper has NOW WASH YOUR HANDS printed on each hard sheet. I spread it on the seat before I sit down, wary of the skid marks I've just seen inside the bowl.

Kate, you know what they say, said Biddy. Where there's muck, there's money.

When I open the bathroom door, I find Rodney Senior standing outside carrying a bucket full of pee. He's wearing nothing but an undershirt. "Ah, good. You've finished," he says. "I have to empty this. It's rather full."

His teeth glint in the dim hallway, and I concentrate on those to keep my eyes averted from what dangles elsewhere.

So the bucket's a chamber pot.

Ye Gods.

In our allotted bedroom at the back of the house, I find Rodney sitting up in bed peering into my hand mirror, twisting the ends of his moustache.

"How are you feeling, old girl? Got a spot of sunstroke, Mother thinks, bounding off to the sand dunes all by yourself."

"Fine. Great. But Rod—"

"Uh-huh?"

"Stop calling me 'old girl.' "

"Fair enough."

I walk over to the window to draw the curtains. Why do the Fanshaws always leave them open? Must be in the genes. Peeping down into the yard next door, I see that Cathy's hens have gone to roost. All I hear is the odd cackle.

I undress, pull on pajamas and bed socks, and slip into bed. I reach for a magazine, and Rodney reaches for the clock.

"I'll set it for, let's see, seven-thirty. That will give us plenty of time to eat breakfast before church."

Ah yes, church.

He leaps up to stride over to the closet. "Where are you going?" I ask.

"To get these." He holds up the two ARMY SURPLUS bags, then promptly drops them to the floor. With nose in air, he salutes.

"I'm not getting into this, Rod."

He marches in circles. Arms straight, knees high, left, right, stark naked, about turn.

"Rod, STOP."

I giggled when this first started. A bit of horseplay, I thought. Harmless clowning, that's all it is. But he wouldn't stop, couldn't stop, which is when I learned how to avoid.

He pulls a jacket from one of the bags. Navy, gold buttons, yellow stripes. Then a peaked hat. I sink under blankets that smell of sour milk.

"Come on, Kate. Salute Sergeant Major."

He stands resplendent in a uniform minus trousers, and I burst out laughing.

"You are to address me in the correct manner." His eyebrows knit and he wags a finger. "Otherwise, you shall be court-martialed."

"Cut it out, Rod. It does nothing for me. You look idiotic."

This is crazy, ludicrous, absurd. I'm not going back to this.

"One, two, three. One, two, three." He stands to attention by the bed, and my face is on a level with his erect bayonet.

"You're a fool, Rod."

"What did you say?"

"You're insane."

"Discipline is required."

He lunges at me, and I beat at his chest with my fists. *"Go to hell."*

I'm thrown onto my stomach and his knee pins me down and I howl into the pillow. "Get off me, you stupid bugger! *Get off me!"*

"Haw, haw, haw, that's the spirit."

Oh dear God, help me. I'm *encouraging* him?

I flop into submission. I want it over. Tears of rage sting my eyes.

"One, two, three. One, two, three. ONE, TWO. Yes!" He shudders. "And a—THREE."

No, no, no, no.

There's a knock on the door.

"Everything all right in there?" asks Nancy.

"Everything's fine, thank you, Mother," shouts Rodney. He lowers his voice. "Just having fun, aren't we Kate?"

No, we're bloody not.

"Okay, dear, see you in the morning," sings Nancy. "Must have been Cathy's chickens I heard."

I'm still on my stomach when I hear the rustle of plastic bags. "I'm off to wash my hands," says Rodney. "I'll be back in two ticks of the clock."

"You'll never do that again," I hiss. "I won't ever let you near me, do you hear?"

He didn't hear.

"THAT'S IT!" I yell.

But he's already gone.

◆

Easter Sunday, April 16
Crickmouth Bay, Farmouth

I look up from the bed, and all I can see are Rodney's flared nostrils. He's dressed, and he isn't happy. Not one bit.

"Now listen here," he says, wagging a finger. "All this nonsense about a migraine and you'd rather see bloody chicks because it's Easter than go to church. Are you out of your mind, Kate?"

He's the driveling idiot, not me.

He shoves his arms into a jacket, slaps on a hat, then hurls a bunch of keys onto the bed.

"Take the Range Rover," he snaps. "I'll walk. You'll catch the end of the service if you hurry."

I'm not going.

"Yes, Sergeant Major, sir," I mumble.

"What?"

"I'll get dressed."

Rodney folds his arms.

"And I'll take the car," I say.

Because I will.

Rodney's expression smoothes to one of satisfaction. "Good girl." He checks his pocket watch. "As soon as we get back, I'll have a morning swim while you prepare a little picnic. And afterward, how about we go for a brisk walk? We'll take Max if you like."

I listen to his descending footsteps. "Morning, Mother. Breakfast? Oh, all right, but just a quick bite of toast and a cup of tea."

I dress quickly and wait fifteen minutes before creeping out to peer through a blur of net at the hall window. And there he is, standing to attention on the pavement. He does an about turn, then marches off in the direction of All Saints Chapel.

I patter down the stairs, scoot past the dining room, and skip out into a bright morning.

The door of Cathy's Cozy Café pings as I open it. "Morning!"

"Goodness, whatever is it, dear?"

"Show me the Easter chicks, Cathy! Did they hatch?"

"Bang on time," she says. "Follow me."

◆

The henhouse fills the whole of the backyard, and inside one of the nesting boxes, there they are. Squirms of chirping fluff. Very yellow, very soft. Cathy sits one of the tiny birds on the palm of my hand and I stroke its downy head with a finger. "A new life, Cathy."

"We could all do with a new life, love."

I tip the chick back into its box, gently, then put my arm around Cathy's shoulders. "Happy Easter!" And I laugh, feeling mischievous, disobedient.

I just *had* to see the newly hatched chicks—first.

We could all do with a new life, love.

"Oh Lord, Cathy, I'd better go."

"Go where?" she asks.

◆

At five minutes past eleven, I pull out of the car park and drive along the road that leads to All Saints, and when I see the chapel doors open, I accelerate, and I keep my foot down until the melee of bells and choir and organ fade.

And I keep on driving.

CHAPTER 53

◆

After covering about a hundred miles, I approach Moorely Village. Pollen-powdered catkins hang from branches, daffodils nod in the breeze, and lambs bounce in fields.

I pull up by a gate.

Because, oh God, what am I supposed to do now? Back at Cliff House, the word "escape" screamed inside my head. It nagged, it urged, it pushed, it persisted.

But now what? Where the hell am I going?

I start the car again. I'll look for a pub for lunch, and I'll phone Rodney. What I shall say, I don't know exactly.

But I need time to plan. How will I do this?

◆

"Excuse me, do you have a pay phone?"

The barmaid nods at the darkest corner in the pub.

Here goes.

"Hello, Nancy. Could I speak to Rod please?"

"The car! Do you have the car? It's a company car, you know."

"I'd like to speak with my husband."

"Rodney?" she shouts, followed by a muffled, "It's *her.*"

"Kate, what the blazes—?"

"An emergency, Rod. It was so strange, but *something* told me to call Charlie on the way to the chapel, it just hit me—*BANG!* Just like that. Well, turns out we may have a burst pipe."

Come on, Kate. Think, think.

"So, anyway, turn off the water, Charlie, I said, and I'll drive right back to Oakley Green this very minute."

Silence.

"That's what I said."

Keep going.

"I told him not to panic."

Silence.

"Damn, what was I thinking, Rod? I should have scribbled a note for you before I left. Sorry."

You're doing well, Kate.

"Rod?"

"Sounds like it was a jolly good job you phoned Charles."

Yes!

"Rod, you could travel back with your parents, yes? I'm halfway home now."

"Well, don't worry about me. I'll borrow a few irons from the clubhouse. Hold on. Hey, Father? Fancy a quick nine holes today? Yes? Champion! All right, fair enough, Kate. I'll see you tonight."

I put down the receiver.

Right, Kate. Time to get your act together.

◆

CHAPTER 54

75 Copper Lane, Oakley Green

Entering the vault of trees that border Copper Lane, I pull onto the driveway. As soon as I climb out of the Range Rover, my neighbour Pam canters across the road and accosts me with:

"Bad news for you, I'm afraid, Kate. We had to call the police."

What the hell happened?

"Shit, what happened?"

"A bit noisy in the wee hours. High spirits, that's all. You're a brave soul, letting Charlie have a party."

Party. Oh damn, yes, the party.

"Shall I go in with you?" asks Pam.

How bad can it be?

I decline the offer, but thank her anyway.

"Toodle-pip, then," she says.

◆

I open the door to 75 Copper Lane. After swinging my luggage onto the tiled floor of the hall, I step in, skid, and land hard on my rear. As I sit in cat vomit, Velcro greets me, waving his string of a tail.

"Bad cat!"

I haul myself up, toss my jacket in the direction of the washing machine, and head for the kitchen in search of mop and bucket.

And I freeze.

I stand for a while with my eyes closed until I feel ready to look again.

Shards, chunks and splinters of glass form a neat pile in one corner. Congealed egg yolk streaks down walls. Curtains hang by one hook from rails. The dishwasher yawns open with a load of beer cans and foil cartons. In the sink, cigarette stubs and globs of pizza float in beige water.

And a stagnant pool puddles by the back door.

Someone has *peed* in my kitchen.

To hell with the sunflower-yellow cabinets I sanded and painted, the shelves I sawed and measured for the turquoise canisters. To hell with all the blue-striped salt and pepper pots I've collected for nearly nineteen years. Nineteen years! To hell with the floor I stripped and polished until my knees throbbed. Someone has *peed* in my kitchen.

I run upstairs and bang on my son's door with clenched fists.

"Follow me." Is all I can say.

And he does, he saunters downstairs with a coffee mug in his hand.

I stand in the middle of the mess and look at my son, and when I read the cool indifference in his face, tears sting my eyes.

Leaning against the wall I'd sponged in four different colours, he shrugs. "Chill out Mum," he says. "It was just a party. You know—gatecrashers and all. No big deal."

Charlie doesn't care? And now I'm drowning in a spin of fury and confusion. He doesn't bloody care! Smashing plates to the floor, and why the hell not, please let me join in the fun too, I watch them explode into little pieces. Six, seven, eight, nine shattering plates. And when I'm done, when I see Charlie gazing through the window, tapping his foot to a tune in his head, I slump onto a chair and cover my face with my hands.

What has happened to my little boy? I feel his downy head under my chin, smell his familiar baby-scent of talcum powder and milk. I hear his first words, his chuckling laugh, see again the liquid of his brown eyes. I ache with love for him, but reality punches me hard in the stomach. As much as I want to hold him, and search his face for the love I can't see right now, I resist.

I snap a paper towel from the roll to blot my face. *Now bend down, Kate, open the doors under the sink and throw the paper towel away.* I give myself orders, needing to function. Above the bins a limp condom hangs over a copper pipe like a dead slug.

I'd hardly noticed Charlie's transition from child to... to the age when...

Charlie peers under the sink. "It's not mine."

"Get rid of it."

I send him to his room. I don't want his help. I need the time to think. To plan.

❖

As I tidy, disinfect, scrub and bleach, I drink three double shots of Rodney's Scotch, one for each hour, and somehow manage to put a meal together afterwards.

Charlie eats, then leaves.

Sleep, eat, leave. That's the pattern now, I've come to realise. I can no longer cling to the reason I've stayed so long. My son is no longer a child. I've filled this home with handmade quilts, chutneys, stripped pine and wicker baskets. I've built this nest twig by twig for Charlie, but he no longer needs it. Or cares for it. I wasn't sure if he cared for *me* any more.

When the cotton wool leaves my mouth and the knot at the back of my neck unravels after too much single malt, I come to the conclusion it's time to taste the musty oak in a glass of Shiraz.

Or two.

I put on opera, Gounod's Faust, and I turn it up good and loud, really loud, to help me think.

As Mephistopheles snarls, and Marguerite wails, I set wine, a slice of bread and a wedge of cheese on the table and sit down to think some more. Then in comes Rodney.

"You're back," I say. "How was the golf?"

"Good."

He slams his house keys onto the pine table I wax every day and walks over to the microwave. "This my dinner?" He peers at the plate inside, then jabs at the buttons to warm his meal.

He snaps off my music, switches on the TV and the history of Wolves Football Club replaces Faust.

I watch him eat as he stares ahead at the screen and twirls strings of pasta around his fork. The starchy ball won't fit into his mouth, so he gobbles at it.

His hair sticks up in tufts and I try to find it endearing.

I try to love the sound of his voice. "Kick the ball into the bloody net, you great fairy," he growls, waving a fist.

I try to yearn for the touch of those thin lips that bristle with a moustache the texture of coconut husk.

"Rod, look at me for a second." I search for emotion in those milky eyes. "Charlie's party got out of hand."

"Oh dear."

His eyes float back to the TV.

"Rod, they drank beer and more besides, and for some reason, they stacked the cans in the dishwasher and dropped an empty bottle of Vodka into the fish tank."

"GOAL! And about sodding time!"

"At least, I think it was empty. Goldie seems none the worse, but Fred is swimming in spirals and Mabel is floating belly-up. A couple of our lamp-shades are cracked, the brandy goblets are in pieces, and should we cut Charlie's allowance to pay for replacements?"

"The referee's blowing the whistle. Would you bloody believe it?"

"Isn't the game you're watching three years old? I'm afraid I smashed nine plates. Someone peed in the kitchen and you won't believe what else I found. Five broken canisters, four exploded light bulbs—"

"They should sack that wanker."

"—along with three French hens, two turtle doves and a condom in a pear tree."

I think I'm very drunk, but lucid enough to vow that from this day on, I shall never, ever, sleep with Rodney Fanshaw again.

"Rod," I said, "I feel a bit sick—I'll sleep on the sofa tonight."

◆

I make a bed with a quilt and pillow. When Velcro settles on my tummy, I close my eyes and drift onto the deck of a ship that bobs and dips, and when it lurches, I slip into rolling waves. Water gurgles in my ears, but within minutes I shoot to the surface and drink the air inside the kitchen of 75 Copper Lane.

I climb a spiral stairway, because I see a tiny door at the very top. I stumble up the steps, fighting for breath because the atmosphere is heavier than lead. There's a table next to the door, with a key lying on it. But when I reach out, it vanishes. Searching for somewhere to escape, I see a hole full of light, but the soil crumbles when I try to scramble out, and I fall down, down, and dirt fills my mouth and I can't shout out. I hear the hollow drip of water and down, down, I go.

CHAPTER 55

◆

Monday, April 17

Wallpaper, dado panels, and borders did nothing to improve the corridor-look of the hallway. Rodney stands at the far end of it now, watching me hover by the entrance to the attic room. He tips his head to one side as I mumble about the trouble I've had sleeping recently, and oh, gosh, Rod, ha-ha, your snoring is getting worse. Maybe a few nights by myself and . . .

"We must talk," says Rodney.

After all these years, we must talk.

I follow his naked body, noticing a new hump on his back, a larger rib cage, a carpet of hair. I haven't *looked* for years. I've noticed, not studied, I've glanced, not examined. I've cast my eyes away from the floating penis when I find him submerged in bath and book. I've diverted my gaze from his bent backside.

Rodney climbs onto the king-sized bed, settles in the middle, and sits up against pillows.

He points to the cane chair by the window, so I suppose that's where I'm to sit.

I will do this. I will tell him.

"I'm sorry, Rod. I just don't like sex."

Although hugely relieved I've said something at last, I didn't say it right. There's nothing wrong with me, it's *him*.

His knees make a tent of the quilt, and he stares at the ceiling.

"What I mean is, I don't want to do it with you ever again. Have you any notion why? All this Sergeant Major stuff, it's just plain creepy, Rod."

He moves his lips around like he's chewing something.

"Also, Rod, I hardly see you, I don't know who you are anymore, you've become a stranger."

"Rubbish."

One word, is that all I'm worth? Frustration and anger spike though me, wanting to get out. I jump up and pace the floor. "Is that all you're capable of saying?" I want to drag words out of his skull. "Did you hear what I said? I never want you to touch me again, do you hear?" My voice is a siren. "For God's sake, say something! What the hell is wrong with you? Do you know what I look like? I'm a woman! What's my favorite color? What do I do all day? Where do I go? My whole damned life revolves around you, Rod!"

I use the heels of my hands to press the throb away from my temples. "Speak, damn you!"

I open my eyes to see him scratching the end of his nose.

"You've never enjoyed the act much, have you, Kate?"

"The act, Rod? The *act?*"

"The sexual act."

"FUCK you, Rod!"

"Did you say . . . did you say . . ." Biddy could hardly talk.

"Did you say *fuck?*" asks Rod.

"Did you say fuck?" asked my dad.

"Yes, you're bloody right I did."

He narrows his eyes, then smiles. "It takes two to tango, my dear. I did suggest we try varying positions, but you wouldn't hear of it."

"Do you love me, Rod?"

"That goes without saying. Now, for pity's sake, pull yourself together, Kate. Are you going through the change, perhaps?"

"I want a divorce."

"Ha!" Rodney reaches for the alarm clock. "I have an early appointment at nine. Get into bed, and stop being silly."

"Todd Grimley's a lawyer," I say quietly. "Tell him your wife's leaving you."

He reaches for the pull cord. "Fair enough," he says.

I hear a shuffle of pillows and the bed creaks.

Then all is quiet.

Is that it?

Is it done?

This easily?

Meaning, I should have done this years ago?

"Good-bye, Rod."

CHAPTER 56

◆

Tuesday, May 23

A new day already?

Velcro kneads at my pajamas with sharp claws. Face down, I'm stuffed inside the quilt with the cat. Clammy, sticky, overbearing, too much, I turn over to kick off the cover, then grab hold of the clock. Fluorescent figures tell me it's eight in the morning.

I count how long I've slept by myself in the attic, how long it's been since I stopped cooking for Rod, washing his socks, his underpants, his cricket whites. Thirty-six days. We've barely exchanged five words in a row.

My head hammers, and the incessant trilling of the doorbell doesn't help. I slip out of bed, wrap myself in a dressing gown, and shuffle downstairs.

It's Pete the postman. He hands me a fan of envelopes and in the middle, there it is, creamy and white. "Need a signature for that one, luv," he says, handing me a pen.

"Thanks, Pete."

I close the door and open the envelope. A ripple of nausea flutters in my throat, for under a crested letterhead, Rodney is informed in courier typeface that Mrs. Kate Marie Fanshaw wishes to formalize aspects of the separation.

I see the word "divorce" is sidestepped, but dear God, I did it. I actually went and did it. I'll phone Biddy and Dad later.

At first, I was surprised how easily my parents accepted the news. Oh,

Kate, said Dad. No, I can't live like that. Not natural. Why didn't I tell them sooner?

And then:

Imagine this, Kate, said Biddy. A new house and a little garden of your own. Move back to Dorton, it'll be grand.

It was then I realized why they were smiling. No, Mum, I replied, not Dorton. Not sure where yet, but I need a completely new start.

"London" flashed in my head, but I kept quiet at the time.

Dad said he's just happy to be getting his daughter back. Biddy asked am I *sure* Rodney did those strange things in the bedroom? She can't imagine it. He seemed such a nice man. Still, I'll get plenty of money out of him. Don't be silly, Kate, don't start fretting over Charlie, he's a big boy now, he'll understand.

When the time's right, said Dad, I must gather my precious belongings. Pack them in boxes, and they'll hide them in their garden shed.

I walk to Rodney's office, the room where there's an oak desk I scraped with a triangle of glass to remove the varnish. I leave the letter from Bellini and Co. on its French polished surface.

I open the purple envelope on the way back to the kitchen—it's from Ingrid. She knows about the divorce, which is why it's addressed to just Charlie and me. I phoned Moira in St. Louis and Ingrid in Provence and sobbed with relief when they both sympathized, and please, they said, lean on them, they understand, they'll help me through all this.

A sprig of lavender floats to the floor.

Kate and Charlie,

We have the joy of inviting you to be present at our marriage,
which will take place on Saturday, the Twenty-fourth of June,
Nineteen Hundred and Ninety-Five,
at three o'clock in the afternoon,
at Saint Germain Church.

Reception afterward at:
5 Place de la Joliette,

Montaurelle,
Aix-en-Provence.

RSVP

Thierry & Ingrid
Bisous! X X

Above the sinking sadness I feel for myself, my heart races for Ingo. At forty-four, she's marrying the French beau she's lived with for five years.

My years of marriage spread muddy-brown behind me—although I did have Charlie, my most precious asset. I smile. I'm over the party disaster now. He said sorry, a little too late, but at least his apologies were profuse. I think he saw a new me.

My spirits rise, only to dip again. These days, Charlie spends most of his time wrapped around an exquisite creature he found at college.

Daphne her name is.

Stuffing the wedding invitation into my dressing gown pocket, I heave a sigh and head to the kitchen for coffee. And there I gaze at the sunflower-yellow cabinets I sanded and painted, at the shelves I sawed and measured for the turquoise canisters. I count the blue-striped salt and pepper pots. I slide my foot over the floor I stripped and polished until my knees throbbed.

And yes, I'm even ready to leave the house.

I prepared friends and anyone else who cared to listen before I found my lawyer, Sukey Smith of Bellini and Co. I think this is what you have to do, set people straight and offer explanations, because I've heard it's the one who initiates a divorce who always gets the pointed finger. The blame. You're not supposed to care what people think, but you do.

Rodney's a bastard, I told Pam who lives across the road, and she shook her head and said, but he's a decent fellow, Kate. I told my hairdresser Shane that for years, like a fool, I've shared a house with a stranger. I told the open-mouthed newsagent that I have no intention of settling Rodney's delivery bill. I just couldn't stop myself. I told the man who comes to read the gas meter I won't be living at 75 Copper Lane for much longer, because unfortunately, my husband and I are separating. I told anyone who made eye contact that I was planning on moving to

London. Yes, London, to that lonely city, but it couldn't possibly be worse than the life I lead now.

I waited in the college grounds to take Charlie home. Another mother, once an acquaintance, became an ally when I spilled a few details. Intimate, blow-by-blow amplification followed. She's halfway through her own divorce, and now she's a new friend. Her name's Maggie.

I haven't told Charlie yet. If I keep putting it off, someone else will tell him, and that would be terrible.

I'll try talking with Rodney first. We should tell Charlie together, because that's what the books suggest. The self-help literature is piled on the night-stand next to my bed in the attic. Highlighting phrases has become an addiction, and I fall asleep exhausted after I've spent hours searching for revelation, for an explanation, for clarity.

CHAPTER 57

◆

Wednesday, May 24

"What the hell are you wearing, Dad?"

"You can see it's a tracksuit, Charles."

"Cool."

Rodney strides into a floor lamp. "Who put this sodding thing here?" he asks.

I push past him, I need to get back to the attic, but he grabs hold of the hem of my cardigan.

"I found a pretty letter on my desk last night. Been very busy, haven't we?" His voice is a rasp, hot in my ear.

"Mum!" shouts Charlie, "I'll be back later, I'm off to buy a couple of CDs." Slam. He's gone.

For once, Rodney looks at me. Really looks at me. I feel his eyes comb my body up, over, then too slowly down. "Let go of me," I say, pulling my cardigan from his grasp.

"Oh, you think I want you, do you? Are you out of your tiny mind?"

His mobile sings, and I snatch at the opportunity to gallop up the stairs.

"Yes, Todders, I do need to speak with you," I hear.

Dear God, he really *is* going to appoint Todd Grimley as his lawyer. Old black-currant eyes.

I'm breathing fast by the time I reach the attic. I flip the lock and press my face against the door, listening, waiting for Rodney to go. I've never seen him like this. Never read such livid passion, such simmering rage. Well, fuck him! Who does he think he is?

I lie on the bed. I'll wait another fifteen minutes, then he'll be gone. I reach for Mamgu's photograph and hold it against my chest, and I close my eyes, imagine I'm clinging to her. She was ninety-nine when she slipped away last year. Missed the queen's telegram by a few months. I was with her when she lay her knitting down on her lap, when she sighed away her last breath.

I reach for the little china cat she gave me, hold it in my fist. *You collect Goss china,* cariad, *she said. Here, look what I found at the Boy Scouts Sale. You can call her Dinah.*

There's a crest on the cat's back, showing an anchor, a sword, and a rose, and underneath, it says, BEWDLEY.

I watched my grandmother's body slide into a hatch to the hum of organ music at the crematorium. Biddy hadn't spoken to Mamgu for ten years, but she still cried, pressed a hankie to her cheek, because that's what you do at funerals.

Biddy hasn't spoken to Aunt Shauna for seventeen years—not since Charlie was born.

◈

There's the faintest jingle of keys, then a thud. Has Rodney gone?

When I'm sure the coast is clear, I slip back downstairs, calling for Velcro to join me in the garden.

For I plan to lift and pot a few shrubs.

CHAPTER 58

◆

I agreed to go the gym with my neighbor Pam, God help me.

I wait by my car—no—I wait by the *company* car. See that Passat sitting in the drive? Not yours, said Rodney this morning as he fetched his own cereal.

"It's not possible to seek a divorce based on irreconcilable differences," explained Sukey Smith of Bellini and Co. "The law demands something different." Her upper lip was a thin line, the lower, a cushion. "English law insists that either the marriage has broken down irretrievably, or one of the parties has behaved in such an unreasonable manner that the other finds it intolerable to live with him. Or her."

Sukey wore a navy suit over a crisp white blouse. "Now, Kate," she said, "tell me the truth. Did you find a new man?"

"No."

"Then keep it that way. Live like a nun until decree absolute."

"YOO-HOO!" Pam bounces me back to Copper Lane. She jogs toward me, resplendent in orange Lycra.

I'm in black. The swimsuit I have rolled inside a white towel is charcoal gray.

Live like a nun.

"Let's go!" sings Pam.

Sebastian Crowe Leisure Centre, Oakley Green

The gym smells of bleach, sweat, and feet, and it's full of pedaling, pumping, grunting men. Pam introduces me to the apparatus with a sweep of her arm. "Choose your torture," she says.

I climb onto a metal praying mantis. "Where do I put my legs?" I ask.

"Not up there, save that position for your gynecologist," quips Pam. Oh, she's so funny. "Don't forget to breathe correctly," she adds.

I strap myself in and shoot her a helpless look.

She mouths a *Go on!* and skips off to tackle a running machine.

I'm left to fight with springs and levers and rubber. One-two-three, one-two-three, breathe correctly, Kate, knees high, pull, push. Rodney marches inside my head, one-two-three, one-two-three, arms straight, stark naked, about turn, one-two-three—

A curl of laughter sticks in my throat and I can't swallow it, nor can I move. I see Rodney as a buffoon, a raving clown. Suddenly, everything is hilarious—not tragic—just bloody funny.

But I can't stay here, not in this gym.

Must get out.

I'm constricted, trapped, and harnessed.

Padded, belted, girdled, strapped.

Jumping off the praying mantis, I swoop up my towel, my swimsuit, and bag. I pass Pam, gabble a quick I'll-meet-you-in-the-pool, okay?

And I flee.

I promise myself I'll swim four lengths, maybe six.

Plunging into the warmth of blue chlorine, I zip like a dart underwater. When I'm bursting for air, I arch, reach up for the pool's edge and grab hold of a foot instead. I let go, and my smile of apology freezes when I see one big toe is missing a toenail.

Because it's Rodney's foot.

His body looms. "What the devil are you doing here?" His voice echoes.

"I'm swimming," I reply.

Come on, Kate, try again.

I jut out my chin. "Why? Am I not allowed?"

Then Todd appears. "My, my, it's Kate," he says, offering me his hand.

I graze my knee as he pulls me out and he bends down to catch a trickle of blood with his finger.

"Must dash, Todders," says Rodney. "I'll be in touch."

Did they have their meeting in the sauna? Is that where they discussed ancillary relief and the division of assets?

This is the way the English law looks at it, said Sukey Smith. The divorce is the main issue and resolving the financial issues is "ancillary" to that.

Rather a misleading way of putting it, she must admit, because in practice the main dispute in any divorce is likely to be over the question of money, and that is very often the case when there are significant assets in dispute.

Todd, still sitting on his haunches, licks my blood from his finger then looks up with his black-currant eyes and winks.

"You kept putting the phone down on me, Kate." He stands up and pats me on the cheek. "You shouldn't have done that."

Bewilderment and anger band together in my head, and I turn to dive back into the pool.

I'll swim six lengths.

Maybe eight.

But after this, I'll never come to the Sebastian Crowe Leisure Centre again.

◆

"Come across for coffee," says Pam on the way back to Copper Lane.

And as I drink, and take tiny bites from triangular sandwiches, I tell her more than she probably wants to know, every embroidered detail, and she says no more, please, because, think about it, Kate—*Rodney* is her friend and neighbor, too. She shows me the flat of her hand like a policeman does when he stops traffic. Enough, she says, would I like more coffee? Another cucumber sandwich?

This is something else that happens. Many friendships deepen, others are confirmed shallow. You seek out new friends.

Maggie is a new friend, the one I stand next to when I wait for Charlie to appear at the college gates. It's easy to pick out those who are going through the same ordeal. You can sense it, almost smell it.

❖

Saturday, June 10
75 Copper Lane, Oakley Green

Do I really want Charlie with me at Ingrid's wedding? He'll come if I want, but, Mum—Baz, Matt, Daphne, Louise, and it sounds like Kev might be interested, too—anyway, they were thinking of borrowing a couple of tents that weekend to camp in Newquay. Yeah, he's finished his college essays. Yep, every one of them. Honest to God he has.

Charlie lies widthways across my bed in the attic, his legs dangle, his head hangs. I pull my arm from under the blankets and reach for his hair. It drops through my fingers, silk-soft and heavy. It used to be brown. Now it's the color of wheat fields.

Daphne made my son blond in my kitchen, using my bowls and my pastry brush. She filled my domain with her presence and the smell of ammonia as she dabbed my son's scalp with hair dye.

I lean against the pillows and pick up the mug of coffee Charlie left on the nightstand. My eyes are still gritty with sleep, because he woke me at six this morning. Our intimate talks have become a habit since I told him about the divorce. Rodney told me to relate the good news myself, then face the bloody consequences.

And I expected rejection and blame, not acceptance. Charlie wasn't surprised. He hardly knows his father either, but he's used to the old man and the way he is. But, hell, being married to a wanker like that, how did I manage to put up with it so long?

My son offered protection and understood. And I was so grateful, I cried into his sweater. Overwhelmed with relief to learn he still cared for me, words tripped from my mouth. Secrets were pulled from black holes, and true feelings flowed. Details, justification, apologies.

"It's pissing outside," says Charlie. He leaves the bed to look out of the window, and tells me the clouds are gray, the sky is dark, and, Mum, he doesn't want to move to London with me. He wants to move down south and live with Baz and Matt. Maybe even try for Southampton University.

"Will you be okay, Mum?"

Let him go, Kate.

"Come here," is all I can whisper.

I hold the reason I've stayed so long, rock him like a baby. "Fetch me some toast," I say, gulping away tears and pain.

Crossing my hands over my own body when he's gone, I slot my fingers between my ribs.

I'm thin again.

The smell of toast and the drift of music reach the attic. Charlie's playing his CDs too loud. Oh hell, what am I talking about? Too loud? Not loud enough, because I need to hang on to the words I hear. An incessant rap, a rhyming beat that claims it's a mother who teaches you everything.

As much as she could, anyway.

CHAPTER 60

◆

Saturday, June 17
Sansouchies, Main Street, Oakley Green

Shane chews on gum as he mixes product in little pots. That's what he calls his powders, solutions, and sprays—product.

"Going anywhere nice tonight?" he asks, slapping on gelatinous coppers, terracottas, and burnt earths, with a mere whisper of honey, and I'll love the end result, Kate darling.

"I'm going to a wedding in France. Are you sure this will look okay?"

"Darling, *anything* would look better than what you walked in with."

"Ouch."

My hair's falling out, Shane, can't you see? I'm stressed to the eyeballs.

"You have to suffer to be beautiful, sweetie."

"Did it hurt, having your nose pierced?"

"Not as much as some other delicate place else. All right, nearly done. And this should help straighten out the frizz, too. We'll pop you under a dryer, and then, Katie, let me cut."

Let you cut.

"Katie, love, if I may suggest?"

"Yes?"

"Your nails. Dolores, come and do Mrs. Fanshaw's nails." He pats me on the shoulder. "On me, my sweet. Free gift."

I'm wheeled to a dryer, and as Shane disappears through a pink plastic curtain, he shouts, "*Bold Burgundy* polish, Dolores. And, Kate, try *navy* at home. I kid you not."

And later, after Shane is done with massaging my scalp, after he's finished satin-smoothing, stroking, probing, tugging, cutting, I'm left with a mahogany bob that reaches a square jawline I didn't know I possessed.

"Drop dead sexy," he says.

"Where do I go for a tattoo?"

I wouldn't dare.

But it felt good asking.

◆

CHAPTER 61

Tuesday, June 20
Aix-en-Provence, France

"We're both starting a new chapter in our lives," says Ingrid, squeezing my hand as we speed along the AutoRoute.

A little later, I glance at her profile as we bounce over the dusty road toward Montaurelle, at the sweep of her hair, at the new roundness of her body. Everything is softer now.

"I'm so happy for you!" I say.

"Life *can* begin after forty, Katers—it's never too late."

Her car, an old Ami 8, groans as she turns into Place de la Joliette. We step out into a warm blanket of an evening, noisy with the trill of crickets. "God, Ingo, I love Provence," I say.

"So move here." She creaks open the trunk and swings each case and bag to the ground. "You've brought enough luggage. Still the same old Kate, I see."

"Shut up," I say, grinning.

"Shut up yourself. Come on, you must be starving. I'll take this one, you carry those."

A scent, a blend of garlic, wood smoke, and Gauloises fills my senses when a door opens.

Thierry whoops a welcome, *"Salut, ma choupette!"* before his beard tickles as he kisses my cheeks.

I laugh. "Congratulations, Thierry!"

"Enfin, hein? It is about time I make her an honest woman." He reaches

for Ingrid, nuzzles into her neck, and then he grabs my cases. "Erik," he shouts, "*viens,* I need you here."

Who's Erik?

A man appears, a man whose hair falls in a crescent as he fires up a cigarette with a chrome Zippo. He doesn't wear a shirt, just a sweater, tight and ribbed and stretched. Jeans, no socks. Leather sandals.

"Kate, I don't think you've met Erik Tober," says Ingrid.

His eyes are dun-brown, his stare intense behind round, tortoiseshell glasses.

He pockets his lighter and our hands slide together. "Pleased to meet you, Kate. I've heard a lot about you." His lips wrap each word, his voice is little more than a whisper, and he's English.

Thierry kicks open a door to reveal a wooden staircase. *"Dépêche-toi, Erik. Je veux que tu fasses la salade."*

Erik slips the cigarette into the corner of his mouth, sweeps up the remaining luggage, and when his footsteps fade, I turn to Ingrid. He's a friend of Thierry's, she tells me. *Son copain.* An estate agent. Lives in L'Auberson, a few kilometers away.

"Oh."

Why does Ingrid smile? I follow her into the kitchen to find crooked drawers and mismatched cupboards nestling between ancient beams. Bowls sit shiny on buffed surfaces, jars are stuffed with handfuls of flowers and twigs.

"What do your mum and dad think of the new villa, Ingo?" I ask. "It's just beautiful."

She laughs. "They love it, but they think we ought to keep a few chickens and goats."

She picks up a tea towel to take the "rabbit casserole, is that okay?" from the oven. When she lifts the lid, I see a bubble of rich gravy, pearl onions, and prunes.

"Smells wonderful, Ingo."

She slices a baguette and asks, "How are you coping, Kate, love? What are your plans?"

"Plans?"

"What will you do?"

"Teach. Move to London."

A depressing fog shrouds my future and I don't want to think about it. I want to enjoy what's happening now.

Thierry's song, "Boom-boom-boom, padam," announces he and Erik are back downstairs.

Feeling hot and grimy after the flight, I ask if there's time for me to take a quick bath.

"Of course," says Ingrid. "Your bedroom is the one two doors along on the right."

When I reach the staircase, Erik waves from the lounge, calls my name. I tug at my hair. Did Shane cut it too short? Are my chinos crumpled at the back? An involuntary smile twitches on my lips, but Erik's is slow and re- laxed. Deliberate. He offers to fetch a drink, suggests a wine he knows I'll love, a Bandol red.

He's a head and a half taller than me when he stands. Come, he says, I brought three bottles with me, they're over there, in that rack.

"Padam—padam—padam—," sings Thierry in the background.

The wine is velvet on my tongue.

The spice is intense, says Erik, the plum tones are deep, and would I like to sit next to him on the sofa?

I say, thanks, but I must go upstairs, I really need to change. I'll take the wine with me.

And I'll wash my hair, I tell myself. I'll be quick. I'll make my eyes dark with shadow, step into my brown dress, wear the belt that lies on my stom- ach in a V.

Thierry peeps into the lounge and laughs. "Erik, go! You promised to make your famous salad! Je te l'ai demandé six fois déjà!"

I grin all the way to the bathroom. How much I've missed! Forty-three, and I'll soon be single again!

❖

The water is silk, and I slip down into it, let it close my eyes and fill my ears. I'm in Provence, miles away from Rodney and affidavits and court orders. When I resurface, I run soap textured with specks of lavender over my arms and breasts.

I'm liberated, unfettered. I reach for my wine, let it slip down my throat. I'm free.

I'm in Provence!

Wednesday, June 21

Ingrid opens the window to let a breeze flutter in. "Get up!" she sings. "We're going to the market." She sits on the bed and sets a tray between us. The bowls of milky coffee and warm *pain au chocolat* smell like heaven.

Propping myself up against a mound of pillows, I say, "Hey, you shouldn't be spoiling me like this! You're the bride. Shall I buy you lunch today?"

"You're on."

She smirks.

"Erik called, he has a recipe book you might like."

"Oh?" I trace my finger along the stitched channels of the duvet. "So when are we leaving for the market?"

"In half an hour. Wear shorts—it promises to be a blister of a day."

I avoid her gaze, concentrate instead on a square of sky captured by the window frame. "I'd like to buy a blue dress," I tell her. "For your wedding." And then I give in. "Okay, so he's pretty good-looking, and Ingo, you monkey, did you arrange for Erik to be here *just* to make salad last night?"

"I knew he'd like you, Kate. He's forty-seven, and well divorced."

"Well divorced?"

"Thoroughly, absolutely."

"But I'm only half-done, so give me some time, okay?"

"Get up," she replies.

◆

What Ingrid didn't tell me was that to get to the market, we'd skin our shins on bikes, steer through honking geese, and rattle through dust and grit.

That laughter would be shaken out of me.

We whizz down slopes through fields ribbed with lavender, gulp perfumed air, and pass orchards scattered with olive trees before we finally reach Montaurelle, to wobble over cobblestones.

We weave through buildings held together with aged stucco, bump the bikes down steps, and as we round a corner, the market leaps at us—a riot of noise and color.

I find the blue dress straight away, a crinkled cheesecloth with short sleeves. "There, Ingrid, doesn't this just shout *Provence*?"

"It's made in India," she says, pointing at the label.

But I buy it anyway. There's lacing at the back to tug in the waist, and it's the deepest shade of periwinkle.

We fill brown paper bags with apples, potatoes, and carrots. I stand cobweb-laced bottles of wine in the basket at the front of my bike. Dry white, for the bouillabaisse I'll make for supper tonight. "Okay, Ingo. You'll have to help me choose the fish. You know what my French is like."

"*Qu'est-ce que vous désirez?*" The vendor wears a head scarf around a face creased by the sun.

I nudge Ingrid. "Go on, tell her!"

"*Qu'est-ce que vous recommandez pour la bouillabaisse?*"

"You're so smart, Ingo."

The vendor throws trimmings, fish heads, and fillets onto the scales. "*Trois palourdes, un peu de perche rouge, de la dorade, trois morceaux de turbot . . .*"

"You'd soon pick it up," says Ingrid, "if you moved here."

"I couldn't live in France. Biddy would flip her lid."

"*Merci, madame, vous êtes très gentille.*"

"Hell, Kate, when will you grow up?" Ingrid's response is a sharp slap in the face. "Seriously, Moira and me have been wondering. You're a bloody pain at times, to put it bluntly."

She shoves the fish next to the wine, looks at me, and sighs. "I'm sorry. But all your life, you've pandered to your mother. Can't you do anything without her approval?"

As I march along in front, the bike pedal hacks into my ankle. "Sod this heap of iron!" I say, shaking the handlebars.

"Kate, don't be stupid, slow down."

Pander to Biddy, do I? Seek her approval? They've always said that. *You're frightened of her, Katie.*

I look at the circular tablecloths swirling over tables, hanging from poles, vibrant with dots, stripes, and trellises. I clomp to the next stall to see a display of corkscrews, with or without arms, with flat, metal, or ceramic heads.

Elaborate garlic presses, wonderful spoons. Sacks of grain, lentils, corn, and flour, rough with husk.

The next stall is piled high with waxlike peppers, eggplants, and silver cabbages, and as I gaze at them, I think hard. The day I woke up from a dream on the beach at Crickmouth Bay was the day I woke up to my life. So what am I going to do about it? The divorce is one thing, but what else? What next?

When Ingrid catches up with me, I try a weak smile. Her eyes soften. I whisper a sorry, she and Moira are so right, and I'm too old to sulk.

The wheels whirr and tick as we push our bikes along in silence.

We pass bread crocks, huge bowls, tall pitchers. Earthenware sprigged with daisies, plates bold with purple blooms, glazed pottery from Luberon.

A clear picture forms in my head. I see my cannisters and salt and pepper pots lined up on stone shelves. A whitewashed room. Dough rising. Fruit steeping in liquor for pies. Preserves in clear jars. I'd cover the tables with circular cloths, serve coffee, or English teas with breakfast. Spread my quilts on the beds. I'd need help, of course.

I grab a bunch of yellow mimosa from the next stall. *"Combien, s'il vous plaît?"*—I know how to say that.

"Here, Ingrid." I press the flowers into her hand. Their fragrance is sickly-sweet.

"Kate?"

I know she's questioning the look on my face. Taking a deep breath, I say, "All right, Ingrid. I'll do it. I'll move to France."

She takes hold of my neck and we're touching foreheads, and I'm laughing, even though I shake inside, because I don't know how the hell I'm going to pull all this together.

"Let's do lunch," says Ingrid. "There's something I'd like you to see."

We prop our bikes against a wall next to *Le Petit Paris*, then step through the café's door.

Cakes, like smooth discs, lie on a marble slab. I see pink icing decorated with rosemary and a scatter of lavender. Red currants and splinters of chocolate on one, toasted peaches with slivers of vanilla pod on another.

"That one," says Ingrid, pointing, "is coffee with walnuts. I had a slice last week."

"I could make cakes like this, Ingo," I breathe.

"I know," she says.

CHAPTER 62

◆

Saturday, June 24

We walk in procession from the church and gather for more photographs in the sun-baked yard of Ingrid and Thierry's villa.

A breeze swirls a drift of confetti into the air and puffs out Ingrid's dress, a sleeveless haze of peach georgette. Moira's twin daughters are in peppermint gauze with white sashes.

I'm already giddy with champagne, floating in a pastel world of sugar almonds.

I stand in my new dress with an arm around Moira's shoulders for the photographer. Then Erik joins us. We three are the bride and groom's best friends.

Erik came to 5 Place de la Joliette every day to share warm evenings and wine. We made soup and risotto while Ingrid and Thierry made wedding plans. Erik is Jewish, born in Winchester. He has one child, Zoé, who's twenty-two now. She lives near Paris with her mother.

The divorce was many years ago, he said.

Accents rise and fall. Ingrid's dad tries to talk with Thierry's *maman*, rounding his words for her like she's an imbecile. "Perfect day for a wedding. Beautiful day. Sun. Blue sky." She nods her elegant head and replies in French, and when the response is a bewildered smile, Erik turns to me and laughs. "Kate, *est-ce que tu parles français?*"

His arm still holds my waist.

Moira rests a hand on my shoulder, tells me to be sure I sit at the same table as her, she's off to search for her camera.

"I can hardly speak any French," I tell Erik. "I'm useless."

"Then we'll have to change that." One of his eyes ever-so-gently casts to the right. A stripe of grey runs through the softest hair I've ever seen on a man. "Listen," he says. "Are you seriously thinking of moving to Provence? Do you want me to help you look for a house in Montaurelle? I have a few listed."

"I'd like somewhere in the village. Cheap. I could do it up myself." I look away, suddenly embarrassed. "I want to run a guesthouse, sell cakes—things like that."

I turn to face him again, to see if he's laughing.

He dips his face under the brim of my hat. *Vouloir c'est pouvoir.* There's a place not yet on the market you might like to see." Then he reaches for a drink and raises his glass. "A toast to the bride and groom!" he shouts. The guests, a kaleidoscope of shifting color, stop in their tracks. The laughter, the shrieks, the chatter—all conversation halts. We're left with a background of clattering plates as the caterers spread out the wedding breakfast.

And everyone cheers for Ingrid and Thierry.

Monsieur et Madame Granville!

◆

The celebrations tumble into the evening. Mosquitoes fidget around the tiny lights that swing from tree to tree. Bowls of *cassoulet* are passed around with thick slices of bread. Jugs of red wine are set on the tables. An accordion is played, a woman, short and dark, sings like Edith Piaf.

"Postpone your flight back to Birmingham Airport," says Erik. "I'd like you to see a house *au coeur de la ville.*"

"Where?"

"In the heart of Montaurelle, near the market square."

I tell him I'll phone Charlie to let him know I'll be a few days late.

I'll send Biddy and Dad a postcard.

CHAPTER 63

Tuesday, June 27
6 rue Fabienne, L'Auberson, Provence

I climb into Erik's car, then push back the sleeve of my cardigan to read my watch. "They'll be in Paris now, " I tell him. "Thierry said he's taking Ingrid to the opera tonight. It's a surprise. Do you like opera? I wish I knew more about it. I like *Carmen.* Have you listened to Gounod's *Faust*? In one part, the violin has to reach an impossible note. Do you like jazz? I'm not too keen on country . . ."

I'm nervous, gabbling like an excited teenager. And what does he do? He just smiles. I sit on my hands when I realize I'm waving them about. We're going to see that property in Montaurelle, and I can't wait. After I've seen Erik's house, that is. He'll show me what can be done with properties in this area, Kate. So much potential.

He turns sharply with a skid, pulls at the brake, and my head is tossed when we come to an abrupt halt. "*Et voilà,*" he says, pointing a finger.

So this is his house, sprawling against a face of rock. Beige stone crumbles under a spread of vine, green shutters hang from rusted hinges. Haphazard shrubs, but mostly weeds, dry in the sun. It's beautiful.

Erik grins. "The exterior needs a bit of work, doesn't it?"

"I love the window boxes."

"Come on," he says.

So this is Erik's home. This is him. A flagstone floor, cool as slate. Shall I flip off my sandals? I want to walk barefoot. Later, maybe. The walls are rough, their texture made clean with cream paint. The table in the hallway has dark legs and a blond, shiny surface. Chairs are mismatched, and a single lampshade hangs low. Everything's tidy, everything's neat. The oil paintings are enormous, splashed with fields and trees and stripes of lavender.

"Erik, did you paint these?"

"Yes."

So this is him.

"They're amazing."

He shrugs. "Let me show you the rest of the house."

I leave my sandals behind and pad after him. And I see his neck is brown, and his shoulders are wide.

"There are three bedrooms on the upper level of the house." He takes my hand, and when we reach the landing, he says, "*Alors, madame,* here we have an old stone house, a house full of character."

"I'll buy it," I say.

"It's at the very top of L'Auberson village, among several other houses below the castle." He pulls me to a window. "It looks out onto a yard shaded by chestnut trees, and beyond onto a vine-covered plain." He pauses. "Why are you leaving your husband, Kate?"

His eyes lock onto mine as he waits for an answer.

Rodney's cold, I say. Detached. Aloof. Arrogant, and, oh God, does Erik really want to know more?

Yes, he says quietly, he does.

"I'm trying to work out why I stayed with him so long," I say, "and it's difficult to come up with clear answers. It became comfortable, almost."

When the sex stopped.

I swallow.

"But then . . ."

"Yes?"

"Oh, he's just a bit weird."

Why must we talk about this?

I drop Erik's hand.

"I'm sorry, Kate. It's none of my business, is it?"

"I don't mind."

I really don't, but this isn't the time to be talking about Rodney. "So show me the rest of the house," I say, smiling.

"Next is the bathroom. Follow me. It's fully tiled, with tub, sink, and a small armoire for towels. There are three bedrooms. As you see, they are well appointed."

The beds are tightly made, the sheets crisp.

"My God, Erik, you are so tidy!"

"Ha! You think *I* keep the place like this?"

He has a girlfriend? *Damn and blast.*

"Madame Jaccard from the village cleans for me."

I grin like a fool and start running downstairs. "And now, I'd love to see your kitchen."

A spindly cactus is the first thing I see, pointing up to a pink ceiling. Ochre walls, bleached cupboards, and a quarry-tiled floor. Wow.

"The kitchen is entirely restored and rebuilt," says Erik, standing in the doorway. "Walls are plastered, floors are leveled, electric is installed, and the plumbing is new and complete."

"You are the typical estate agent," I tell him.

"Aren't I just."

He heads for the fridge, then piles the table with cheeses, rice, mushrooms, and wine. And when he proudly sets down a jar of truffles, he tells me he'll make the best risotto I've ever tasted. He pushes his horn-rimmed glasses over the little bump on his nose. "After we've seen your new guesthouse," he adds. "Your future *chambres d'hôtes.*"

When I push my feet into my sandals, Erik bends to fasten the buckles.

"Let's go," he says, dropping keys into his pocket.

9 rue Sainte-Marthe, Montaurelle, Provence

Erik parks his Peugeot. We walk down a few steps, then into an alley that can be no more than four people wide. The houses, all joined, are like vast castle walls. Cables crisscross above, from roof to roof.

"*Mon agence immobilière te propose une propriété de caractère.* It's the last one," says Erik. "The tallest. Can you see that wrought-iron lamp? We're almost there."

Striped canopies shade the large windows on the ground floor, pale blue shutters lie flat against others. Little pots of geraniums, badly in need of water, form a neat line along the *trottoir,* the narrow pavement.

"We'll open everything up," says Erik. "My friends, a gay couple, used to run a little *crêperie* here. They bought an old farm building about six months ago, it came complete with a vineyard—their new venture. Still needs a fair amount of renovation, but they were able to move in a couple of weeks ago."

My heart sinks. "So nine rue Sainte-Marthe will be sold soon?"

I have no money to buy anything yet.

"Claude and Bruno are in no great hurry. They thought they'd better see to the attic rooms before they put the house on the market."

An oak door with iron hinges sits inside a stone archway. It's buffed to a dull sheen, and polish fills a collection of woodworm holes around the handle.

"Translate how much they'd want into pounds for me again, Erik."

"About a hundred and twenty-five thousand." Erik fits the key in the lock, and we step into darkness. "I'm sure they'd accept a lot less if you'd take it as-is."

"Oh! Is this the kitchen?"

Erik opens the window, then the shutters. The late sun streams in, spot-lighting an industrial stove, a row of gas taps, two super-sized ovens. There's a deep butler's sink with a gingham skirt. Cupboards are spacious, dug into the stone walls, glazed, bordered by ancient pine. A large table. Would they want this? Does it come with the house? Whatever's left behind would be mine, says Erik. Cast iron pans! What about these? He nods. Go and look at the room across from here, he says.

"One, two, three, four—eight tables, Erik!"

Chairs are stacked against the walls, their blue paint peeling and chipped.

Upstairs, there are five bedrooms with sloping planked floors. The rooms are small, but big enough for double beds, and I'd fit wash basins. How old is this place? And I gasp when Erik says late eighteenth century.

"So what do you think?" he asks.

"Let me see the attic rooms."

Oh, do they need work. But—

"This is where I could sleep," I say. "And Charlie, when he visits."

Plaster hangs from walls, and roof rafters are exposed. But hell, I just love attic bedrooms.

There's more, says Erik. *Quatre caves voûtées dont une avec un four à pain.*
"What?"
"Four vaulted cellars, one with a baker's oven."
"You're kidding!"
"And a courtyard at the back. Opens onto the market square."

◆

In Montaurelle, villagers huddle, deep in conversation. Voices are soft, transparent, as the evening slips into a purple night. We pass a fountain, the water is a dribble, no sprays, no splashes. Such peace and calm.

When I hear gentle *tok-tok* sounds, I look around, wondering where the noise is coming from.

Erik points. "They're playing *pétanque.*"

The boulevard is a dappled mixture of streetlight and shadow. Men with stomachs bursting against trouser braces toss metal balls at other metal balls, but mostly at a small wooden one. Sometimes the metal ball ricochets against a board barrier with a soft *thwack.*

"The wooden ball is called the *cochonnet,*" says Erik.

"Oh."

"It means, 'little pig.' "

I catch a twinkle of laughter in his eye.

"Shall we make our way back to the car?" he asks.

As we walk, I ask how long he's been buying and selling properties in France.

Fifteen years.

I ask for his mother's name. Jeanette. Father's? Harold. When did they pass away, Erik? Within months of each other, four years ago. Will I meet his daughter?

Testing, wondering.

Yes, of course.

What's Zoé's stepfather like? Oh, him. A Gérard Depardieu sort of bloke, a mountain of a man with a nose shaped like a penis.

Erik adores the way I laugh.

"So, dinner before I drive you back to Place de la Joliette?"

I feel in my pocket to make sure Ingrid and Thierry's key is still there, then say, "I'd love that."

♦

And back at his home in L'Auberson, he says, "By the way, Katie, I do like jazz."

I'm asked what I'd like to hear, but I tell him to choose, and more of Erik is revealed when "So What" flows like a smooth, then rippling river.

"We'll drink pastis," he says, filling a small pitcher with water in the kitchen. "Fetch the glasses. They're above the sink."

The tall, narrow ones, he says. I'm to pour in two fingers of pastis. Here, this one, *La Fée Verte*. Just one ice cube each, yes, they are too big for the glasses, but they must hover like boulders above the green liquor as he trickles water over them.

Like magic, the drinks turn cloudy, phosphorescent. And the taste is of liquorice, anise, and herbs.

◆

CHAPTER 64

Friday, September 29
75 Copper Lane, Oakley Green

Three months since Provence. The divorce drags, and although Claude and Bruno are busy converting their vineyard outhouses into rentals now, I'm still worried I'll lose 9 rue Sainte-Marthe. Why does everything take so long? I asked Sukey Smith.

Mr. Fanshaw won't disclose his income or send copies of the firm's accounts, she said.

She'll arrange a court order.

I listen for the jingle of keys, the shudder, and then the slam of the front door.

BANG!

Good. Rodney has left for work.

My heart flutters. I'm to gather a few precious belongings together, pile them into the Passat, and then meet Dad and Biddy in Dunleigh.

"Why Dunleigh?" I asked Biddy last night.

"I thought we'd spend the day there, Kate. It's a lovely little town. We could have a picnic."

My eyes dart left then right. What do I want my parents to hide in their garden shed? Where should I start?

In my kitchen.

My best saucepans, steamers, cake tins. My knives. Chopping boards. The cannisters and salt and pepper pots. The dinnerware? Cutlery? No. I saw Rodney carrying the canteen of silverware to his car last week.

Believe me, you'll fight for the last wooden spoon, said my new friend Maggie.

I run to the living room and scan all surfaces. The buffet. I sling a pair of leather horses I bought in Paris into a box. The mantelpiece. I'll take the candlesticks. I throw a drawer full of photographs into a second box. There are many of Charlie, and Rodney can't have those.

Records, CDs . . .

I run upstairs and bundle six of the quilts I patched together into bags. A few treasured books. Holy shit. It's ten-thirty, and Dunleigh is fifty miles away. I'm late.

Always late. Biddy doesn't know how I get by half the time. And how on earth will I manage putting together a list of expenses for Bellini and Co.? I don't have a clue, do I? Biddy will draw up the list of expenses for me. Leave it all to her. Let's screw Rodney.

No, Mum, I'll manage, I replied.

As I pack the Passat with what feels like stolen loot, I look over at Pam's house, and the quick flick of a curtain catches my eye. That's another thing, said Maggie. Neighbors love a divorce, a scandal. You'll be watched. Every move noted. Every word recorded.

Sod you, Pam.

I slide into the car and look down at my jeans. I didn't have time to change, and no, Biddy won't tell me why I should wear a nice dress today, I'm to wait and see. It's a surprise.

My mobile phone purrs.

"I just wanted to hear your voice."

"Erik."

My face melts into a smile.

I lift one shoulder to hold the phone to my ear, then turn the wheel to swing out of the drive. Erik calls me three times a week. We talk while I hide under a cave of blankets in the attic, when I'm waiting in a queue at checkout, when Rodney barges past me in the hall looking for his cricket pads, when I must say, hello Maggie, or Ingrid, or Moira, thanks for calling! Good to hear from you.

"I'm meeting my parents," I tell Erik. "For a picnic."

Then a click tells me he's gone. The phone's battery has died, and I grapple with flexes to recharge the damn thing, but it'll take a while. Ah well.

I put my foot down. I'm thirty minutes late already. I open a window to feel the rush of wind in my hair. The sky is brushed with clouds, but the sun is warm, and I wonder what the weather in Provence is like today.

❖

"Green tea, Earl Grey, oolong, or herbal?" asks the waitress as soon as we settle at a table near a window.

"Three cups of plain, strong tea, please," says Biddy. "Tom, would you like a scone? Yes, he would. I'll have a slice of Victoria sponge. How about you, Kate?"

"Just tea, thanks."

I can't believe I wasn't reprimanded for being so late.

Dad's eyes twinkle behind new glasses that are too black and heavy. His face is pale, his hair white. Poor Dad. "We have something to tell you," he says.

Biddy takes a bundle of papers from an envelope and places them in front of me.

61 Low Meadow Road, Dunleigh, reads the first one. With gas-fired central heating, at £195,000, the accommodation comprises: entrance hall, kitchen, large living room, bathroom, three bedrooms, garage and utility.

"Keep looking," says Biddy.

I put the papers on my lap so the waitress can set out the teacups and plates.

39 Pipers Way, oil-fired central heating, double glazing, direct access to secure parking. Hall, living room, kitchen/dining room, three bedrooms with closets. Two bathrooms, small gardens to front and rear. £202,500.

"Whoa. Property is expensive in Dunleigh, isn't it?"

"Kate," says Dad, putting his hand on mine, "our house in Dorton is for sale—the garden's too big for us. We're getting old, you know."

"Hey, you, stop this old stuff!"

"Sign's up already," adds Biddy.

"You're thinking of moving here?"

"Yes, but to a little bungalow," says Dad. "We'll help you buy the larger home."

"We could live in the same street," says Biddy. "Help you rear Charlie."

"Charlie's going to Southampton University, Mum. He's past rearing. He was nineteen this month, remember?"

And letting go is worse than having a tooth wrenched, but I must still do it.

I gaze out of the window at the sleepy town of Dunleigh. Passing traffic is the odd tractor, a cattle truck, and a bus.

Followed by a hearse.

I look back at my parents, from one face to the other. Dad's fingers tap. Biddy's clenched fists rest on the table in front of her Victoria sponge.

"Well, what do you think?" she asks.

I try to keep my voice gentle, but firm. "Mum, I told you what my plans were when I came back from Ingrid's wedding. I'm moving to France."

"You're still obsessed with that notion?"

"Yes."

Dad sucks in his bottom lip and dimples pepper his chin. His voice is a croak. "Wouldn't you like to live here?"

"Near your own parents?" asks Biddy. "You could take in a few students, teach them privately."

"We're getting old," says Dad.

The tea pains my throat as I swallow it down hard, and suddenly, 9 rue Sainte-Marthe seems a million miles away.

"Isn't that a little Catholic church?" Biddy peers through the window and makes a sign of the cross. "Now isn't that grand? Right here in the High Street."

"Mum, my plans to move to France are definite."

Biddy keeps one eye on Dad, and I'm not entirely sure, but was that a sly wink? Nevertheless, she says, Daddy and her are still keen on moving to Dunleigh. "So why don't we keep the appointment already made with Mr. Belcher, the estate agent?"

◆

And so we trail after Mr. Belcher, admiring pleasant views, useful pantries, and compact kitchens. Dad will fix this, Biddy will see to that. She has a wardrobe to fit over there.

"What brings you to Dunleigh, Mrs. Fanshaw?"

"She's thinking of moving here," smiles Biddy.

I shake my head, and mime a no, but I'm ignored. I told you to wear a decent dress, she hisses.

"Let's find a nice spot for our picnic," says Dad, a whole two hours later. "After that, we'll load your boxes into the Audi."

When the job is done, I slip my mobile phone into my bag.

We find a field full of clover. A brown stream pushes through, lazy and slow. I spread a tablecloth on the ground, vibrant with dots, stripes, and trellises.

"Do you like it, Mum? I bought it in the market at Montaurelle."

"A bit gaudy, Kate, but nice enough."

I help lay sandwiches on plastic plates. My parents sit on canvas chairs and I settle on a cushion of grass, and when Dad says he's so happy, Katie, that we're a family again, my mobile phone rings.

"Hello?"

I jump up, and with my head bowed, I aim for the stream. "Erik!"

He tells me about another property I might like, due on the market in a month's time, just in case I lose 9 rue Sainte-Marthe.

I look back at my parents, who look smaller, older, and very alone in the middle of the field.

And my emotions play tug of war.

CHAPTER 65

◆

Tuesday, October 3
75 Copper Lane, Oakley Green

"Charlie! Supper's nearly ready."

I drop the can opener when a jagged lid bites. A berry of blood bursts on my finger—*sod it*. Now I have to search for a plaster. I can't poach the eggs, fry the potatoes, or heat the baked beans fast enough. I must get out of this kitchen before I hear the jingle of keys.

More often than not, it is the husband who leaves the matrimonial home, whether as a result of choice or following an injunction, said Sukey Smith.

But Rodney chose to stay.

He still refuses to lock the bathroom door. I must continue to swerve away from the sight of his penis floating in bath water, do an about-turn when I discover him sponging his privates on the bidet, retrack my steps as he pulls up his underpants in the hallway. He doesn't care. It's his house, he says. Why am I looking anyway? Am I still interested, dear?

I set up a room next to the laundry, where I used to keep baskets of washing and the ironing board. I pushed an old desk into a corner and wired up a spare phone. As long as I take care to use it when Rodney's out, it's okay. There's a little TV and an armchair. Curling up on a floor cushion, I drink wine and listen to music. The key to that room and the attic hang from a chain around my neck. These are the rooms I hide in, where I dream of lavender fields, count my days, and wait for the divorce to end.

"Charlie! Hurry up!" I wrap a plaster around my finger. The cut is deep.

My son slopes into the kitchen.

"My God, Charlie, what have you done?"

Three lines are shaved through his left eyebrow. "Neat, huh?"

I kiss the corner of his lop-sided grin and call him an idiot. "Here's your supper. Are you going out tonight?"

Of course he is.

"Yeah. Going to hang out with Baz, maybe see Daphne. Can I eat this in the living room?"

I say yes as I chew on a sandwich, because I'm not bothered about sauce on sofas or crumbs on carpets anymore. Dust can pile, grease can congeal, weeds can climb. I don't care.

When the front door slams and keys jingle, I still have pans to scrub.

Rodney struts in. "Excuse me," he says, spilling a grocery bag onto the counter.

I turn to leave, but he stops me with a, "Wait a minute."

"What?"

"I thought you'd like to hear what Todd Grimley said today." After selecting a packet of chicken joints, he leans against the counter and smirks. "He thinks you're a tart, dear. Your constant flirting has been futile. He's not interested, and never will be."

"Me flirt? Ha! He's a lecherous sod, and you know it. I don't know how Penny puts up with him."

"He can't believe you asked Sukey Smith to represent you," Rodney continues, turning his back to tear at cellophane. He digs his nails into a piece of raw chicken to rip off its skin, then drops it into a pan, covers it with water, and sets it over a gas flame.

Rodney creeps toward me, and his half-shut eyes are an inch from mine when he smiles. "Your brain is the size of a pea, Kate. You'll be penniless. In fact, I shall make sure of it. I'll run your lawyer's fees up to the heavens. She charges beaucoup bucks."

"Get away from me."

"Please, sir, get away, get away." Rodney raises himself on tip-toes, flaps his hands, and dances in circles. "Such a little girl, aren't we?"

When I grab a bottle of wine from the rack, he flinches. Oh Lord, did he think I was about to crack it over his head? As I struggle with the corkscrew, I start laughing. What a goon. What an oaf! I fill a tumbler, the nearest thing. Switching on the radio, I turn it up loud, exceptionally loud, to annoy him.

You don't scare me, Rodney Fanshaw.

As Billy Joel sings about setting himself up for the kill, Charlie walks in. He jives to the music, then hands me his empty plate. See you later, Mum, he says, kissing me good-bye.

He waves to his father, and he's gone.

I stand by the dishwasher. Why should I leave? I don't have to. Rodney pokes at the boiling chicken with a spoon, and damn, if I don't feel a pin-prick of compassion. Should I help him out? But good God, why? Out of habit?

"It could have been so different, Rod."

He sneers.

Fighting against sympathy and guilt, words and thoughts tumble together. *Was it my fault everything went horribly wrong?* "I tried, Rod, really I did."

I'm drinking my wine like pop.

"Tried?" He hacks out a laugh.

Emptying more wine into the tumbler, I take another swig. I shoot him a list, hit him with bullet points: I was compliant, subservient, I pandered to his self-centered lifestyle. I detail the sacrifices I made, express the sheer exhaustion experienced over the years. Yes, *exhaustion,* sod him, it was sheer hard labor working on this house, and there was never any recognition. And I was fucking lonely, Rod, didn't he get it?

"Utter drivel," he says, tipping a packet of instant mashed potato into a bowl.

I sway out through the doorway in search of a dictionary.

driv-el *To slobber; drool. To talk stupidly or childishly. Stupid or senseless talk.*

"How dare you! How bloody dare you!" I run back in the kitchen to spit insults. "You fool! You wasted nineteen years of my life!"

But inside, I'm thinking, no, it was me who wasted my own life. Imagining Rodney would be my refuge, then living in a domestic dream-world, pretending everything was all right.

"I don't have to listen to this," he says. "Why don't you just get out of the house, for fuck's sake? Leave me and Charlie in peace? Now, if you don't mind, I'd like to eat my meal."

I follow him to the table, slopping wine. "Fucking Sergeant Major!

Clown! Sex with you was a joke! What happened in Crickmouth Bay was nothing short of rape—"

For the first time in years, Rodney looks into my eyes. His stare tunnels. Drills. "Like I always say, it takes two to tango," he says. "You enjoyed every minute." He wraps his tongue around a forkful of potato and smiles.

It's then I realize I'm screaming at a brick wall.

My feet float above the floor as I make my way to the living room. I sprinkle fish food into the tank and wonder how I'll transport Goldie, Mabel, and Fred to France, because I'm leaving bloody England, yes I am. Amidst the swirl in my head, I try to think logically, but all I truly want is to drink myself into oblivion. I fall to my knees to open the cupboard for another bottle of wine. I catch my finger on the hinge—the fresh blood is bright under the plaster, but the throb is distant.

In my head, I map out the way to the room next to the laundry, and when I'm safe inside, I pull the chain from around my neck and lock the door. Setting the wine and glass on the floor, I lie flat out next to them.

Closing my eyes, I'm sucked into a tunnel of swirling light, and I slip, slide, tumble into churning waves, and my mouth fills with sour seawater before I'm sick on the floor cushion.

❖

And much later, when I come to, my pounding head reminds me that making oneself blotto isn't the way to deal with things.

CHAPTER 66

◆

Sunday, October 15
33 Cherry Blossom Road, Dorton

A week has passed, and rain continues to hurl itself against windows. The FOR SALE sign in my parents' front yard sways in a gush of wind. They have a buyer already, they say, isn't that wonderful?

Everybody is leaving or moving.

Everything is changing.

Charlie passed his driving test, so he and Matt buzzed off to Southampton for the weekend. I feel the dent in my finger, where my rings used to be. I sold them to buy an old car for my son's birthday. I had no right to do so, said Rodney. He'll inform Todd Grimley.

The boys have a list of flats to look at, and they can't wait. They'll crash out on a friend's floor, so don't worry, okay, Mum?

Divorce may make teenagers feel hurried to achieve independence, said one of the brochures piled on my nightstand.

"He'll be more worried about his own welfare than yours," said Sukey Smith, handing me an invoice for £7,657.

Biddy's voice breaks my thoughts.

"Give over, Tom. I'm trying to put a meal together."

"I'll get out of your sight, Biddy, would that suit you?"

"Katie?" Dad joins me at the dining room window. "What are you thinking about?"

"The divorce," I say. "Rodney won't disclose his income or send copies of the firm's accounts, so Bellini and Company are billing me for the effort it takes to persuade him."

"Don't you worry." Dad kneads my shoulder. "We'll help you out, help find you a home."

Gazing through the window, I watch the storm bend trees into submission. "No, Dad," I whisper. "I'm moving to France." Before I have a chance to say more, I hear the *clip-clop* of Biddy's mules.

"Here's a little check for your birthday, Kate." Her features are set, her walk stiff.

"Thanks, Mum." I open the card. "Lord, to think I'm forty-four now!" *Not a child.*

"Sorry it's so late," she says, "but we haven't seen you for so long. Put it into your bank account. You'll need it."

Yes I will, I think to myself, to pay for the many calls I make to France. Did Ingrid go to the market today? Is my house okay? Erik, it's not for sale, yet, is it?

And calls to America. I wish Moira could see 9 rue Sainte-Marthe, she'd just love it! I thought the living room would look fantastic in terracotta. And navy chairs would look superb with the polished tables—what did she think?

"Here's your Fry's chocolate with peppermint cream," says Dad, taking the bar from a drawer and grinning.

I hug him. "Hey, you used to buy this for me every Friday."

"Well, I feel I have my daughter back."

"Dad, I really do have my heart set on that guesthouse."

"Kate, do you still live in Wonderland?" asks Biddy. "Sure, how will you run a business in a foreign country, not able to speak one word of French? The potatoes are done," she says. "Tom, didn't I ask you to set the dining room table?"

"How are we expected to visit you in France, Kate, as we get older?" asks Dad. "We won't be able to travel."

"I'll visit you."

"Oh?" Biddy's eyes flash. "And where will you get the money for plane and boat fares? From your *guesthouse*? It's chilly in here. Tom, didn't I ask you to light the fire? Well, great, now we have no choice but to eat in the kitchen."

"It's cozy in the kitchen," says Dad. "Come on, Kate, it'll be just like the old days, won't it?"

"Cozy? *Cozy?*" asks Biddy, her face red from the heat of the oven. "We should be eating in a dining room on a Sunday, not in the kitchen. Dragged up, you were, Tom, not reared. Fed with salt fish and broad beans, so what would you know?"

"That's enough, Biddy."

"Shall I carve the beef?" I ask.

"I'll do it," says Dad.

"You'll do it, Tom? When was the last time you took a knife to a joint of meat?"

He stomps out.

I set three plates on the table. "What's going on?" I ask.

Biddy saws one slice of meat. "It started with your father saying he's sick of me watching every move he makes." Then a second slice. "That in my eyes, he can't do anything right." And a third. "He called me a bitch, Kate." She waves the knife at me. "So—now what do you think of your father? Believe me, he's changed. You wouldn't know him."

Dad appears in the doorway. "I heard every word you said, Biddy." His chest rises and falls with each breath, his fists are clenched, his eyes pop. "Would you like to know why I called your mother a bitch, Katie?"

"No."

I really wouldn't.

"Because she called me a Welsh bastard. I'm a piece of filth compared to Mrs. High and Mighty over there."

As Biddy thumps the masher down onto the potatoes, there's a crack of thunder, a spike of lightning.

"Who the hell do you think you are, Biddy?" Dad circles the floor, drags his fingers through his hair. "Answer me!"

I've seen him simmer, but never boil with such rage.

Biddy talks from the corner of her mouth. "Did you know your father could roar like a bull, Kate?"

"You Irish—*witch*," says Dad.

Biddy turns around, takes brisk steps toward him, and spits fair into his ear.

Dad's lips churn. Biddy's about to get a mouthful.

"*STOP!*"

Good God. I'm yelling.

"Cut it out, the pair of you!"

Biddy's mouth pinches. "Give me Sukey Smith's phone number, please, Kate," she says. "I'm leaving your father."

I fetch my handbag, not for the phone number, but for the photo taken of Moira, me, and Erik at Ingrid's wedding. I sink down onto a chair and slap it on the table. "I'm moving to France as soon as the divorce is final. I met a man who lives in L'Auberson, the little village near Montaurelle. His name is Erik Tober. He's forty-seven. He has a twenty-two-year-old daughter called Zoé. He's helping me find a property, and I really like him. There."

The rain drums, the wind howls, the thunder rolls.

Biddy picks up the photo.

"Dinner's getting cold," I say. "Shall I start serving?"

A few words are exchanged. Polite words. Open the wine please, Tom. Which bottle, Biddy? The blue one, the one with the nun on the label. Fruit and cheese for dessert, Kate. Would I mind putting a few crackers on a plate? Tom, please get the butter from the fridge.

Thank you.

Well, at least they're treating each other like human beings again.

We eat a lukewarm meal in silence.

Then we slice apples, divide a bunch of grapes, cut cheddar cheese.

"Lovely sharp cheese, isn't it, Tom?"

"Very tasty." He stands up. "Excuse me." He takes a packet of cigarettes from the counter. He offers one to Biddy before sitting down again.

She flicks a lighter, then leans across the table for him to pull at the flame.

"Cover the butter, please, Tom."

A wisp of smoke escapes Dad's nostrils, curls into his eyes.

My mobile phone rings.

"Who's that?" Biddy clicks her fingernails on the Formica.

"Erik, can I call you back later?" I ask.

Dad makes a halfhearted move to stack plates. Biddy tells him to sit down.

"Well, this is a nice surprise, isn't it, Tom?"

My mother's face tells me nothing. It's solid stone.

"It's too soon, Katie," says Dad. "You're not even divorced yet. It was him who called in Dunleigh, wasn't it?" he asks. "When we were having our picnic. That's why you got up and walked away, so we wouldn't hear."

I count the worry lines on his forehead, one, two, and three, so I shake my head to dismiss his question, because it isn't really his business, is it? Not sure. Don't think so. Dear God, why does he do this? I'm not sixteen. I ask if I can please have another cracker.

Biddy inhales deeply. "Kate, you're a liar."

"A liar?"

"You didn't mention a man was the reason for your divorce."

"He isn't. Wasn't. I told you why I'm leaving Rodney. I hadn't even met Erik when I filed for divorce."

"And I don't believe Rodney did any of those things in the bedroom."

What?

"What?" My voice is a strangulated squeak.

Dad tap-taps his cigarette over the ashtray and avoids my eyes.

What's happening here? Minutes ago, he was the challenging aggressor, the raging bull.

Dad, please say something.

But he's watching her, reading her, using her like a weapon, a snare. Confusion stabs my heart.

"She'll be the death of us, Tom. Pass me another cigarette." Biddy looks at the photo again. "This Erik's one eye is crooked."

Okay. This is ridiculous. Respect for parents is one thing, but hell, none of this is right.

Unacceptable.

I snatch the photo from her fingers.

"He has an unusual nose," she says. "Let me see that pretty picture again."

Dad nods at me, meaning go on, show her, do as she says.

The thunder is an explosion, a deafening crack. "I'm getting out of here," I say.

"He's Jewish, isn't he? Hah! I knew it, see Tom? That's why she won't let me have another look."

And she has my fist, and she's trying to pry open my fingers, and her nails dig, and she's saying through clenched teeth: "You will let me see this photo. I am your mother. Don't, don't, you're hurting me. I have arthritis—Tom, tell her."

He looks sidelong at Biddy. "What are you trying to hide?" he asks.

I jump up, the chair topples over, and I snatch my hand away. And I'm running, and my damned jeans are falling down because I've lost so much weight, and they won't let me scale the stairs two at a time. Biddy is in hot pursuit and Dad yells, "Do as your mother says, Kate! Do you hear?"

I'm in the bathroom, and I catch a glimpse of Biddy's face in the mirror before I slam the door shut. Her eyes were angry, her mouth laughed—

"Open this door *now*."

Bang, bang, bang.

I shove the photo inside my jeans.

BANG. Biddy's voice deepens. "Open. This. Door. Now."

I take a deep breath. This has to end. It's so sodding *stupid,* and I need to see a psychiatrist. It's my fault I've allowed this woman to control my thoughts, my decisions, my whole bloody life.

I let her in.

She's breathing hard, like she's out of breath. She grabs my wrist, tunnels her fingers up my sleeve. She lifts up my sweater and I snatch it from her grasp. I can't push her away, she's a shrunken version of what she used to be.

"Oh dear God—*Mum?*"

Here's the mammy who used to smile with dimples until I grew up, who wore the softest sweater with embroidered rosebuds. The one who sang, *Go to sleep, my darling, close those big, brown eyes,* when she rocked me to sleep.

I want to release all the confusion and hurt I've bottled up for too many years. My head spins. I want words, I need words, but they won't come. My mouth opens and shuts. It feels like the dreams I've had when I scream, but no sound comes out.

Then Dad arrives, and the three of us are stuck in a tiny bathroom, and I'm slipping down that claustrophobic tunnel, going down, down.

"FUCK! I'm forty-four years old, you *CRAZY WOMAN!*" I shout.

Dad stares at me. "Did you say *fuck?*"

Biddy's hand rises.

And my eyes snap shut as I feel the sharp burn of a slap across my face.

"Get out," says Dad.

Putting my hand into my jeans pocket, I pull out the bar of Fry's dark chocolate, the one filled with peppermint cream. And it's soft now, and the peppermint oozes from the split wrapper.

I throw the damned thing at my father's feet.

◆

And as I drive back to Copper Lane, something occurs to me. If I remove myself from their lives, they'll resolve their own differences, won't they? Be at peace?

And then, feeling miserable, mentally abused, I slam my hand hard against the steering wheel until it stings.

So angry, so tormented, wanting to scream.

CHAPTER 67

◆

Thursday, October 19
75 Copper Lane, Oakley Green

Ten-thirty. Reaching over the desk to close the blinds, I shut out the night. Chewing at my nails, I add up my predicted living expenses, then move on to listing the contents of 75 Copper Lane.

I finish my glass of wine. Just one.

I'm tired. So damn tired.

I move the radio to my desk and turn it on.

"*Ave Maria, gratia plena.*" The soloist's voice is a melodic ascent. "*Maria, gratia plena, Maria, gratia plena.*" A descending spiral.

The phone rings and my hand hovers. *Don't pick up the receiver, Kate.* Instinct, something, tells me it's Biddy. She's given up trying to get me to answer the mobile.

"*Ave, ave Dominus, Dominus tecum . . .*"

The phone won't stop. It is her, I know it, pressing redial, demanding, insisting. This is crazy. I'll stand up to her. *I will.*

"Hello?"

Biddy's sigh is labored, drawn out. "You're a cruel little madam, aren't you?"

"Mum."

"Yes, it's your own *mother.*" I hear the shaking, muted weep usually reserved for Dad. "Tom, I'm all right, don't worry, *please.* You wouldn't think of calling, would you, Kate? Oh, no, not you. Not Kate Fanshaw. We could be lying dead, for all you care. Dear Lord in Heaven, the sheer grief you're putting us through is sinful."

"*Benedicta tu in mulieribus, et benedictus . . .*"

"You stupid, foolish girl," she says. "You meet a man, and in five minutes, you lose your head. Not once in your life have you had an ounce of sense." Dad rants in the background, "You're making a big mistake."

I close my eyes. God help me. I've ignored their calls two, three times a day since that Sunday I fled from 33 Cherry Blossom Road.

"*Et benedictus fructus ventris . . .*"

"That Erik Tober's after your money," Biddy hisses. "You know what Jews are like."

"*What?*"

"Your grandmother was right, God rest her soul. She said the only decent Jew that ever existed was crucified."

"*Ventris tuae, Jesus. Ave Maria.*"

"Mum, you've said enough. That's disgusting."

"Tom, your daughter thinks I'm disgusting. What do you think of that?"

"*Ave Maria, Mater Dei, ora pro nobis peccatoribus, ora, ora pro nobis . . .*"

There's a pause, then Biddy starts again. "Well, would you believe it, Tom? Kate listens to Our Lady's prayer, and there she is, wallowing in sin."

Biddy's going out of her mind.

"*Nunc et in hora mortis, in hora mortis nostrae . . .*"

Then I'm hit by a wave of sympathy, a stab of love. She's demented, she has to be. "Mum," I say gently, "I think you might be ill."

"I'll show you how ill I am. If you move all the way to France, Kate, your name will be wiped off our will. Do you understand?"

In France, I'd be too far away for my mother to oversee my life.

"*Ave M-a-r-i-a.*" The soloist's voice melts, fades away, and there's a click on the line.

A click? No, it can't be Rodney. Surely not. It's Thursday, he goes to the Masonic Lodge on Thursdays. He never returns to Copper Lane till the early hours.

Is that my mother's breath I hear?

"Mum, you know I don't want your money," I say. "You know I don't think like that."

Click.

Another click?

"Let me speak to Dad."

"He doesn't want to speak to you."

"Put Dad on the phone, Mum."

There's a shuffle, a crackle.

"What do you want?" he asks.

"Dad, I can't wait to start a new life in France." My voice is a harsh whisper, like I'm sharing a secret. "It'll all work out, you'll see."

"How could I ever like a man who's taking my daughter away?" he asks.

What the hell?

"Erik isn't taking me anywhere, Dad, but didn't Rodney do just that?"

I close my eyes. Oh God. Now I see it. Even though we were married, Rodney was never a threat. The rare times we were together, my father saw no intimacy, no intensity, which meant he still had me. But Erik is an unknown.

"You're obsessed with that Erik," says Dad. "It's all wrong, Kate. He has some strange hold on you, I can tell. It's not natural."

Biddy is back. "If you move to France," she snarls, "I wouldn't even bother to visit your grave to—to spit on it, should you die."

"For Christ's sake, are you crazy?" I ask.

"Are you drunk, Kate?"

I hurl a scream for both of them to hear. *"Can't you be happy for me?!"*

"She's going out of her mind, Tom. Listen."

Reaching for the phone base, I swipe it off the desk, then fling the receiver after it.

There's a hollow rap. "It's Charlie, Mum. Let me in."

Breathing slowly, I wait for my neck muscles to relax.

He rattles the doorknob.

I grab the toppled phone and put it back together.

"Come on, Mum. Open up."

I unlock the door. Charlie picks up two mugs of tea from the top of the washing machine. "I was about to kick my way in," he announces.

"Oh, Charlie!"

He sets the tea on my desk, and turns to hold me. Pressing my head against his chest, he says, "It's okay."

I bury my nose in his shirt and cling to him.

"Who's Erik?" he asks.

So my son heard everything. "A man I met at Ingrid's wedding," I tell him.

"Is he French?"

"No."

A Gregorian chant now floods my hideout.

"Your taste in music sucks," says Charlie.

I manage a smile. I reach for the tea, wrapping my hands around the mug to warm them. Charlie drops onto the floor cushion. "Spill," he says.

Well, I've only just met Erik, I say, and I do more than like him, but it's early days yet. And I answer most of the other questions my son asks, as many as I can. He already knows about the guesthouse, I told him about that as soon as I got back from Ingrid's wedding. He hopes I manage to get it.

He runs a hand through his hair, twists the stud in his ear.

"Charlie, when did you get your ear pierced?"

"Yesterday, after Daphne got her navel done."

Everything's changing.

"Charlie?" I search his face. "Stand up and give me another hug."

"Mum, Biddy's driving you crazy." His eyes grow as big as lamps. "I can't stand the woman—shit, she's never liked me."

"Oh, I think she does . . ." But I stop. Why should I protect her? Shaking my head, I say, "I've often wondered if she's capable of loving anyone, Charlie."

"Are you okay?"

"I'd better see a doctor. And I might spend a few days with Maggie."

"Mum, I'm playing football for the college on Saturday."

My hand rushes to my mouth.

"Yes, Dad will be there, so you don't have to come if you don't want to. We'll get slaughtered anyway. We've never beaten Gremwall Tech." He pauses. "Why don't you try and sleep?" he asks.

I reach up to rub his shoulder. "Okay, let's get out of here."

I remember to lock the door.

"Night, Charlie. I love you. You won't believe how much."

Charlie climbs the stairs. "Love you, too, Mum."

The TV is on in the living room, showing a film with subtitles. When I walk in to switch it off, there's Rodney, lying flat out on the sofa, but wide awake.

When did he get back?

"Hold on, Kate, don't go . . . ," he says.

"What is it?"

"Who's Erik?" he asks, his eyebrows shooting above his glasses. "Hmmm?"

I heard a click on the line. No—it couldn't have been Rodney. Surely not.

Shit, shit, holy shit.

"My, my, got rather distraught, didn't we, dear?" His face slops into a smirk. "To put it mildly."

When he leaps up, I twist on my feet and head for the hall, and his hand is a claw, tearing at my sweater. I scrabble on all fours up the stairs, and my heart hammers until I reach Charlie's door—and there I stop, and wait.

"Come any closer," I say, "and I'll scream blue murder."

"Yes, you're very good at that."

I fold my arms and narrow my eyes. *Stay where you are, you bastard.*

"I took notes, Kate. Detailed notes." He looks at Charlie's door and lowers his voice. "I listened to every word. What a simple creature you are. Did you not think I could hear?"

He takes a step forward, and I stand my ground.

He sneers. "Don't worry, I'm not stupid. I won't touch you. There's no way I'll get thrown out of this house. Every brick of it belongs to me, you know." His eyes flick over my body. "I can't imagine how you found someone else, but the fact that you committed adultery will weigh against you nicely."

"You're a bloody buffoon, Rodney. Go boil your head."

"Instead, I think I'll send a fax or two to Todd Grimley." He pulls his pocket watch from his waistcoat.

"I'll send it now. Then he'll have the whole weekend to peruse. Good night, dear."

CHAPTER 68

◆

Friday, October 20

I squint at the alarm clock when the phone rings. Eight-thirty.

"Hello?"

"Hello, Kate. Sukey Smith here."

I hear a shuffle of papers.

"Well, first of all, congratulations! You've put together some superb spreadsheets. We'll have this divorce wrapped up and put away very soon."

Thank God.

"Now, Kate, on a personal note. Are you still there?"

I yawn. I didn't sleep too well last night. "Morning, Sukey. Yes, I'm here."

"Got a call half an hour ago from Todd Grimley. Well, to *précis*, he told me you'd found another man."

"That's not exactly how I'd put it."

"Kate. What was my original advice?"

Live like a nun until decree absolute.

What is it about me that makes people think they can monitor and supervise my private life? Now I have complete strangers butting their noses in. Most of this has got to be my own fault. Damn, I've been so—*weak*. Lying back on my pillows, I wait and study the curtains I made for the slanted windows, where I matched each seam, lined up every stripe, the yellow with the blue.

"Kate, Kate, Kate. Forget the man. Be independent for once in your life."

"Do we have a court date yet, Sukey? This has been dragging on for months."

"You're making a big mistake. When did you meet this Erik?"

"Sukey, that's my business. I have the particulars of a property I plan to purchase in France, plus a breakdown of renovation costs. The building will provide a home and income. The trouble is, if matters aren't tied up within the next few weeks, I'll lose it. Can we set up an appointment?"

Silence.

Then there's a clipped, "Would Monday the twenty-third at ten suit you?"

"Perfect."

The nerve!

As soon as I press the end button, there's another call.

A Dorton phone number. It's Biddy again. Or Dad.

Nine o'clock. And they try again at ten minutes past, twenty past, half-past, and at ten. I bury the mobile phone under the mattress.

It's high time I was showered and dressed.

◆

Feeling refreshed, I pull on thick tights, a black polo, a red skirt, and as I make determined steps downstairs, because I'm strong, I'll show everyone, the bloody hell I will, I hear:

"Oh, yes, Biddy, I know, I know."

I stop, motionless. *Rodney is still here.*

"Says she met him in France, did she? Well, well. Believe me, I was perfectly happy. I was stunned when she asked for a divorce. A business? Well, wonders will never cease. Ha! Our Kate plans to run a guesthouse? Good Lord."

Our Kate? I swallow and wait for more.

"I have no intention of losing contact with you, Biddy. Not after all these years. What do I think? Oh, Kate's behavior is *appalling.*"

My mouth is dry, my head swims.

"See you on Saturday, then. Bye, Biddy. Call anytime, do, please."

See you on Saturday?

And the bastard walks past me, smiles, and thrusts his nose in the air.

The front door shudders open, followed by a slam and a jingle of keys.

Mum? Dear God. *Mum?* My stomach churns, my heart sinks. So what she seeks now is nothing short of revenge. Rodney will offer all the support she needs. Who else, who better, than an ex-husband to join forces with? He'll justify her bitterness.

I sink down onto the last step, hold onto the handrail. A scatter of red dots dance when I close my eyes. *Dad? Mum?* Shit, why are you doing this? How could you stoop so low?

I howl like an abandoned child. I sob, cry out, question the air, until my neck throbs, my stomach hurts, until I'm reduced to shaking silently, groaning, with my face in my hands.

And when I'm done, I dial my doctor's home number, tell her I need help, agree to meet her at the surgery in thirty minutes.

I twist at the taps in the bathroom until water gushes, swirls like a whirlpool in the basin. I soap my face and rinse, and to make it a ritual, I rinse seven times more.

Because I will cry no more for my parents.

Maythorne Surgery, Oakley Green

Let the world go to hell. Let Pam go to hell, who ignored me when I waved. Let all the neighbors who huddle with arms folded go to hell. What a scandal. Shh. Here she comes. Hello, Kate, how are you? Poor Charlie. Tell them more.

"Kate Fanshaw? The doctor is ready to see you now. Room five."

Dr. Talwar takes her phone off the hook. Take as long as you like, Kate, she says.

My doctor is a beautiful Indian, plump and large-bosomed. Without embarrassment, I describe Rodney's sexual preferences. And my God, she *laughs*. I tell her about his arrogance. His detachment.

She nods. She understands. "Gracious! Why did you put up with this for so long, Kate?"

"Because I was some sort of martyr," I reply, ashamed at having to admit this.

She urges, cajoles, demands, until finally, the child inside me talks. The child who was never allowed to express real anger, fear, or sadness.

Then I disclose every detail, open every wound, relate every curse that slipped from my mother's lips when I was a teenager.

I remember every violation, from both recent years and those long past.

"Go on," says Dr. Talwar. "You mustn't stop."

"My mother scrutinized my appearance and social life," I say. "Forbade me to question or disagree. She never cared to notice when she hurt me."

I express the devastation I felt this morning, upon discovering Biddy had called Rodney.

"Outrageous," says Dr. Talwar, "ludicrous, unbelievable. And what kind of man is your father? Has he no balls?"

I lift my head to look at her kohl-lined eyes, and when I see them dancing, my face loosens into a smile. "But look at me," I say. "I'm exposing how weak and pathetic I am, too."

The doctor rests her elbows on the desk and clasps her hands. "Kate," she says, "for a period of time, you must separate from your parents, both emotionally and physically. If you choose to sever your relationship permanently, then that's fine. You have permission."

I'm allowed?

Relief washes over me, but then: "Suppose they fall sick? I wouldn't be able to help. They could die, and—"

"Kate, this is their choice. They made the decision, committed the final act to alienate and dismiss you. And dear, unfortunately, we all get sick. We all die. Death has no respect for age."

So it's time to stop trying, time to simply—give up?

"Here's a plan of action," says Dr. Talwar. "Could you move in with a friend?"

"Yes, Maggie has already suggested it."

"Remember to change your mobile phone number." She scribbles on a pad. "Take this prescription to the pharmacist—take one a day. These will help, Kate, but . . ."

"Yes?"

"It's time for *you* now."

I squeeze her hands with mine.

"How's Charlie coping?" she asks.

"He's been great," I tell her.

"Of course he has," she says, smiling.

My eyelids are swollen, spongy, half-shut. My face is raw, my hair matted, but I leave that surgery floating on a cloud.

183 Sycamore Road, Oakley Green

Maggie stands on her path, sleeves rolled up. "Let me help you, Katie."

"Are you sure this is okay, Mags?"

She presses her cheek on mine. "Of course." Her voice is a dramatic, concerned gush. Throwing a bin-bag full of my clothes over her shoulder, she says, "Come on, love."

Maggie's body is lean, her legs thin in Levi 501s. I step into the calm sanctuary of her home that smells of sweet almonds and camomile.

"Sit down," she says, plumping up cushions. She squats on the floor, tilts her face to one side. "It was easier for me, Kate. I had the support of my family. But you do have friends who love you, okay?"

"Thanks so much, Maggie."

"So, what now?" she asks.

"Sukey left a message on my landline before I disconnected it. I have a court date at last. November the twentieth."

"And?"

"Oh, we're to split the assets, you know, the house contents, but Rodney refuses to accept my list. To hell with everything, he said, what does he care, let the court sell the whole fucking lot."

I play with the hem of my sweater. "I'll never get *anything* sorted at this rate, Maggie. Rodney's off to Holland any day now. He's planned a hockey tour."

"Oh, love. Why don't you have a bath?" she asks. "Light candles, relax, and afterwards, we'll order a take-away, and play music. Or—shall we get a video?"

And it's when I'm wallowing in warm, scented water that it hits me.

My idea, my plan.

CHAPTER 69

◆

Sunday, October 22

"**Mum, you won't believe this,**" says Charlie. "Biddy and Granddad watched me play football yesterday. What fuckers!"

"*Charlie!*"

Maggie throws me a puzzled look, so I cover the mouthpiece—*I'll tell you later*—

"Well, they are, Mum. This is the first time they've watched me do anything. They had a picnic with Dad at the side of the field."

"Good God, Charlie."

"They've got to know I'd tell you."

I'm too numb to feel pain, too weary to react. "Ah well, Charlie, Biddy does love her picnics."

In fact—it's almost comical.

"Mum, you sound spaced out. Are you all right?"

I'm a robot, going through the motions of arranging furniture removal, finalizing affidavits, packing suitcases, booking flights. And I'm taking Prozac. No wonder.

"I told Biddy to get lost," says Charlie. "She said I was a brat, no better than my mother."

All I can focus on is the future.

"Charlie, I'm leaving for France on the thirtieth. Will you come, too?"

"To live? Mum, why are you springing this on me?"

"You don't want to?"

"I can't, Mum—I mean—no, I don't want to. God, and Dad has been trying to get me interested in Sandhurst, and the army's not my scene, either. No way. Me and Matt have that flat lined up. I told you ages ago. You seemed okay then."

Let him go.

"We're moving to Southampton early in December. *I told you,* Mum," he repeats. "I twisted Dad's arm to pay the rent."

As much as I want to cling, I resist.

"I'm sorry, Mum."

"Maggie said you can come here after college next week," I say brightly. "Whenever you like."

"I'll do that."

"Have supper with us?"

"Can I bring Daphne?"

"Yes, of course. Charlie, will you come to France at Christmas?"

"Yeah, that'd be great."

I tell him about my idea, my plan, that I'll collect my share of the furniture from 75 Copper Lane the week after next, when his father's in Holland.

Whatever, he replies.

CHAPTER 70

◆

Tuesday, November 7
75 Copper Lane, Oakley Green

A tower of a truck fills the drive of 75 Copper Lane. FASTMOVE INTER-
NATIONAL.

"Oh God, Maggie—just look at it!"

We pull up on the road behind Charlie's car, and I'm gripped by a mixture of excitement and dread. Already, curtains twitch, neighbors ogle.
Charlie blows his horn and Daphne comes trotting out of our house.

Daphne?

I'd hardly noticed Charlie's transition from child to . . . to the age
when . . .

"Bye, Noah," Maggie says to her son.

"Bye, Mum. Bye, Kate." Noah climbs from the backseat. Charlie's driving
him to college this morning.

The engine roars, tires screech.

And they're gone.

"Right," says Maggie.

So we meet Bert, Bob, and Mike, who will pack my share of household
effects and transport them to storage units. "Bonjooer," says Mike. "I believe
you're moving to France, Mrs. Fanshaw."

"Would you boys like a cup of tea and some buttered toast?" asks Maggie.
I smile. Maggie always offers buttered toast.

Looking back at the truck, at the open cavity waiting to swallow my furniture, I think, *It's really happening.*

I'm leaving Rodney.

I'm leaving!

Maggie aims for the kitchen and I head for the living room, where I find a neat stack of boxes. I lift a flap—and there are my saucepans and leather horses. So, my parents returned the loot from their garden shed.

That's it then.

Keep busy, Kate, I tell myself. *You have to get everything piled into that truck before Rodney comes back from Holland.* I tear tape from the roll Bert gave me and start sealing things up. When I come to the third box, the flat one, I bury my hands in the pile of photos. I never did put these in albums, but I will, in Provence. I sit on the floor, stack all those of Rodney in my lap, then spin each one though the air and watch them scatter. *Fucking Sergeant Major.*

There's a clump of black-and-white photos at the bottom. One of Biddy reclining on a grass bank, face as round as a moon, a red-lipped smile, coy eyes. Feet in peep-toed shoes, ankles crossed. Her pleated skirt spreads over a soft mound. She's pregnant, with me. Did she caress her stomach, experience flutters, feel my kicks? Did she love the baby growing fingers and toes inside her?

I swipe away the tears.

And here's a photo of Dad, with hair that's Brylcreem shiny, combed flat, like one of those film stars in old movies. He wears slacks, and his waist is bound tight with a leather belt. His hands are in his pockets, and he grins, showing even teeth.

Oh, Dad.

Maggie arrives to set tea and toast on the coffee table. She's dressed in dungarees, ready for work.

"Thank you, Mags. You can't imagine how much I appreciate this."

"Oh, don't you look sweet?" She swoops for a photo of me as a child, a bridesmaid in an angora bonnet and bolero. My dress is a net meringue, and I clutch daisies in my fist, and there's another of me in a crinkled swimsuit, stabbing at sand with a spade. Biddy sits next to me, in shorts, with her legs drawn up, a cigarette dangling from her fingers.

There's a sandcastle in the background, patted smooth and decorated with seashells.

Did Dad make that?

I hold my forehead and sigh.

"Come on, Kate," says Mags, resting her hand on my shoulder.

Bob and Mike stride in, both bandy-legged, both wearing woolly hats. "Here, Mrs. Fanshaw," says Bob. "Stick these labels on everything you want shifted."

I look at Maggie. "Shall we get started?" I gulp some tea, take a deep breath, and lean over to slap a sticker on the sofa. There. Rodney can keep that armchair.

We climb on chairs to reach shelves, twist out screws, wrench out nails. Our legs bend under the weight of oak planks. I'll use these for my guest-house, I say, *mes chambres et tables d'hôtes*. Yes, tables as well as beds, because I'll serve dinner for my guests as well as breakfast, Maggie.

What about the washing machine, the dryer, the freezer, Mrs. Fanshaw? No, they won't work in France, nor will the power tools, Bert, but I'll take my hammer and saws. Oh, and all the garden tools.

We tie mounds of cushions together with rope, take only the brightest, sunniest curtains. I give Maggie one of my quilts, a Star of Bethlehem in copper and rusts. She'll treasure it, Katie.

I look around for something else I want Maggie to have.

Velcro. He's too old to move to a strange place, please have him, Mags, I ask, kissing the fur on his head. Hand him over, she says, cradling the cat in her arms. He'll be her little companion.

Charlie's keeping the goldfish, taking them to Southampton in a bucket.

I pass the chunkiest glassware to Mike to pad with newspaper, but leave the crystal and the silver goblets. Bread crocks, ceramic bowls—I'll need those.

After lunch, I run upstairs to the bedroom I once shared with Rodney. Rifling through his drawers, I search for his swimming tackle.

I stuff the rubber cap with socks until it's smooth and as round as a skull. There. That's the head. Goggles make good eye-sockets above a row of earplug teeth. I lay Rodney's robe flat on the bed, cross its sleeves over its heart, and tuck the swimming trunks inside. I prop the thermometer upright, so it rises stiffly from the crotch.

And I leave a scribbled note: *At ease, Sergeant Major.*

From Charlie's room, I grab boxed games, call to Mike to help me carry down a wooden train track, a fleet of toy cars. I mean, I'll have grandchildren one day, won't I?

I lift a huge container of Lego, remembering to drop a couple of bricks into Rodney's slippers as I pass by.

It's when Mike, Bert, and Bob are struggling out with the last cupboards and chests that I realize the house echoes.

"Because it's virtually empty, now," I tell Mags.

Arm in arm, we stand in the doorway, watching our three musketeers close the truck, and we wave them good-bye.

Mauve and peach bands of color ribbon across the sky. Night is on its way.

We did it.

We made it.

"Rodney will want to kill me."

"You left him well over half, Katie."

"Yeah, plus the lawn mower, power tools, and the vacuum cleaner."

We shake in a silent fit of giggles, and God it hurts, and then Maggie goes and lets out a loud splutter. "Wait till Rodney sees the effigy you left upstairs!"

We can't stop laughing, because suddenly, everything is so very, bloody funny.

The phone rings. "Mum?" says Charlie. "I'm at Maggie's house, and Noah and me are starving."

"Okay, we won't be long now."

We close the door to the house, and plan on fish and chips for supper.

It's when we pull into Maggie's drive that it dawns on me that I forgot to say good-bye to 75 Copper Lane.

But I think that's a good sign.

CHAPTER 71

◆

Friday, November 7
183 Sycamore Road, Oakley Green

Dropping the newspaper, I search for my mobile phone, to find it wedged between the cushion and the arm of Maggie's sofa.

"Kate?"

"Morning, Sukey."

"Just had a call from Todd Grimley. Rodney was none too happy about you removing household effects without prior consultation."

"Too bad."

"But get this," she continues. "Grimley says you may keep what you've already taken, but he expects you to transfer all your legal estate and beneficial interest in 75 Copper Lane to his client."

I built this home, this nest, twig by twig, for Charlie. Nineteen years, nineteen years of my life.

"No!"

"Listen, Kate," she says. "Shall we try a round table meeting?"

"Which is?"

"A mediation session."

"No!"

"We could avoid court altogether."

No.

Is this woman really a *lawyer*?

"Kate? Are you still there?"

I inhale deeply. "No mediation session, Sukey. Absolutely not."

Silence.

"Should we appoint a barrister for the court hearing?"

"Yes."

"He's expensive."

"Fine."

I'll show that bastard Rodney, I'll show him what I can do.

CHAPTER 72

❖

Monday, November 20

The building is a brick and terracotta fantasy. A gothic fantasy. JUSTICE GIVETH EVERYONE HIS OWN, it states, above a carved St. George and a slaughtered dragon.

A pulse whooshes in my ears as I push my way through the revolving doors. I'm as nervous as hell. But there he is, there's Percival Wilcox, my appointed barrister. He's a big man, said Sukey Smith, bald and bulky. You won't miss him. Quite a character.

"Mr. Wilcox?"

"Ah, and this must be Kate." His skin is opaque, his palm clammy. "Please call me Percy," he says. "Shall we take the lift?"

My hand slips from his. Percy is the man I'm to depend on today.

The lift comes to a shuddering halt, the doors glide open, and, "Good morning, James," says Percy. "Stay there."

The youth in a waistcoat steps back, waits, presses buttons, and, yes, sir, he does have the files with him.

Percy snuggles the papers under his armpit, then reaches to rub James's nose with his thumb. "I see we have a little smudge."

The barrister turns to me. "Sukey is waiting on floor three," he says.

Ping.

"Ah, and here we are."

And there she is.

She stands against a pea-green wall. "Ready, Kate?"

I pull a face and shake my head.

"Is Todd Grimley here yet?" asks Percy.

Sukey shrugs.

"James, see if you can find Mr. Fanshaw's lawyer." The barrister's eyes follow the youth as he sets off in the opposite direction. "Lovely boy, lovely boy." Then, "Shall we proceed to the main hall?"

I fiddle with the blouse Maggie insisted I borrow. The collar is a piecrust, hot and stiff against my neck. Look smart, be confident, show that bastard Rodney what you're made of, she said, and here's a black jacket.

God help me.

We approach a sweep of stairs, a curling handrail. Why are there so many corridors in this place? We pass a stained glass window showing a nymph entwined with a snake, next to a wench, blindfolded and naked. What do they symbolize? Good and evil? Ignorance and truth? Percy and Sukey?

"In we go," says my barrister.

Into a vast area crowded with sitting, slouching, distressed human beings. A toddler rolls on her back over the linoleum floor, chanting a bored lah-lah-lah. A woman with white-bleached hair chews on gum, slots a feeding bottle into her baby's mouth to stifle its cry. Men sit with arms folded, mouths set. A pensioner weeps, dabs her eyes with a ball of lace. Eyes look up, left, right, focus on doors, check watches.

"There's Mr. Fanshaw," says Sukey, nodding over at the far corner.

With hands in pockets, Rodney paces. One, two, three, turn. One, two, three, turn.

"We'll stay here," says Percy.

I sit on a bench, sandwiched between my lawyer and barrister.

"It will be Judge William Garrett," says Percy.

Sukey crosses her legs. "Uh-oh," she says.

"Peng versus Peng," announces a speaker. A tiny Chinese man scuttles past James.

"Ah, James." Percy smiles. "Did you find the missing lawyer?"

"Mr. Grimley's still in courtroom number three, sir, with another client."

Percy dismisses the youth, laughs, and smacks his hands together. "Judge Garrett hates to be kept waiting."

"Fanshaw versus Fanshaw," crackles the speaker. "Courtroom number eight."

Sukey jumps up. "I'll deal with it," she sings, walking toward a robed woman behind a desk.

❖

The hearing was to be sixty minutes long. It was to begin at eleven-thirty. It's almost twelve when Todd Grimley shoots out of courtroom number three. His black-currant eyes search the hall, land on me, flick over to Rodney.

"Let's go," says Percy.

We push through a maze of benches, step over feet and legs to reach our allotted room.

At the head of a monumental table, Judge Garrett peers over half-moon glasses. He nods as we each grant him a good afternoon. His forehead is a crisscross of wrinkles, his eyebrows a wiry tangle, his mouth a mean slash. He points at three chairs to his left, then his fingers perform a steady tap-tap, on the tape deck in front of him.

Todd Grimley's bowed figure appears, and he offers his most humble apologies.

"Good afternoon, Your Honor!" Rodney bellows. He sits. He grins. He rubs his hands together.

He called me at Maggie's house this morning before I left. Am I ready? Am I prepared? As a businessman, he's used to the courtroom, m'dear, but I may find it rather unnerving. Now do remember to address the judge in the correct manner, haw-haw.

Did he like the arrangement I left on the bed? I asked.

You're such a child, Kate, he replied.

Judge Garrett's nostrils flare. "Mr. Grimley, you NEVER keep a judge waiting. Am I now expected to wrap this case up in twenty minutes? *Twenty minutes?*"

Todd Grimley's head drops, and he writes furiously, busily, on a large pad. When I glance at Rodney, he swings his nose in the air.

Silence.

The judge gathers the papers before him and arranges them in two neat piles. "I note the household effects have been divided successfully."

"My client doesn't think it was a fair division, Your Honor," whines Todd Grimley.

"Are you pregnant, Mrs. Fanshaw?" asks Judge Garrett.

My eyes pop. "No, Your Honor."

"Charles is the only child of the marriage, and now aged nineteen?"

"Yes, Your Honor," says Percy.

Then Todd Grimley stands. "May I show you these notes, sir?" He struts around the table. "You'll find dates, facts, and evidence that will clearly indicate that *she*"—he tips his head in my direction—"committed adultery prior to decree absolute."

Percy presses his knee against mine and drops a pen to the floor. Our faces meet below the level of the table. "Relax," he whispers. "Everything's ticking along nicely."

I've already discussed the Erik situation with Percy on the phone. He knows the score.

When I resurface, I see Judge Garrett shuffling through the notes. He grunts. "Who is Erik Tober?" he asks.

Percy's turn. "Mr. Tober is an estate agent in Provence, sir."

"The man she intends to marry, Your Honor," adds Rodney.

"Oh dear, Mr. Fanshaw," says Percy. "Give a lady some time. How do we know?"

I cringe. I'm tired of having my private life invaded, picked at, examined. *Judged.* When will it ever end?

Judge Garrett takes off his glasses and rubs his eyes. He then folds Todd Grimley's notes in half, runs his nail along the crease, and hands them to Percy. "Let Mrs. Fanshaw do whatever she may please with these," he says.

He folds his arms. "The divorce itself, Mr. Grimley, Mr. Fanshaw, is simply the process by which a marriage is brought to an end, which means either party is then free to remarry or dance a jig on Mount Snowdon, if they so wish."

The judge picks up a small microphone and proceeds to record the date, the time, the parties involved, the case number. And his decision. "Seventy-five Copper Lane is to be sold, and proceeds are to be divided equally."

"My client will need a car, Your Honor," says Percy, my rock, my ally. "The Passat is a company car."

A Fanshaw car.

Judge Garrett rubs his chin, grunts through the papers again. "Plus an additional lump sum of—"

More than I expected.

There's a snuffle, a puff, a shift, a scrape of a chair.

"Mr. Fanshaw, would you *please* allow me to continue?"

Rodney diverts his attention to me. I'm held, shackled by his stare. His eyes narrow, his mouth curls, but I can't decipher the words that spit silently from his mouth.

"Mr. Fanshaw is to provide—" Judge Garrett looks at Percy and lifts one wiry eyebrow. Percy states the monthly sum, the judge runs a finger down several columns of figures, then nods.

Did I really need a barrister? Yes, I did. Seems like Percy multiplied my sorry figures, my timid suggestions, by *three*.

"And the Respondent, Mr. Fanshaw, is to pay the Petitioner, Mrs. Fanshaw, periodical payments, which are to commence on the first of December, 1995, during their joint lives, until the Petitioner shall remarry or further order."

Sukey gives me a sharp nudge.

Oh God, is it over now? Is that it?

I see a whitewashed kitchen, a table in oak. Dough rising. Fruit steeping in liquor for pies. Preserves in clear jars. Tables covered with circular cloths, beds draped with my quilts, and rooms painted. One blue, one ochre, others deep pink or sage green. Tables in the courtyard, too. Palm and bay trees in pots, rosemary in borders, and creeping thyme will fill every crack in the paved floor.

Wine in the vaulted cellars! And maybe, just maybe, Claude and Bruno will teach me how to use that baker's oven.

I read the brochure "Divorce, What Is It?" as I wait for Percy and Sukey to wrap everything up. They won't be long, they said.

In rare cases, there is such a thing as a delighted divorce court victor, when the other spouse will feel defeated and humiliated.

The great hall is emptying now of bodies, of faces elated, devastated, relieved, and angry.

Rodney leans against a pillar by the exit, not too far from me. With arms behind his back, he studies the ceiling.

There's a tap on my shoulder. "All over. All done and dusted," says Percy.

I shake his damp hand and smile at Sukey. She was pretty useless, but, oh, who cares now?

"Thank you both, so very much."

And as we trail past Rodney, he announces, by crikey, Todd, just look at the time! The hockey team is waiting for their captain!

Humiliated? If he is, he won't show it. Not Rodders.

Then he'd better get his skates on, old boy, advises Todd.

C H A P T E R   7 3

◆

Thursday, November 30
Birmingham Airport

I hug Maggie, who weeps. We could fill a pond with our tears, I say.
Then it's high time we stopped, she replies, we've done too much of it.
But when I promise our friendship will grow, *dear God*—then I start
crying.

I cling to Charlie, who says don't look now, Noah, but there's a really hot
babe behind the British Airways counter.

I run my fingers down my son's lean back. When did he grow so tall?
Pushing him away, I flick his hair from his forehead.

It's still the color of wheat fields.

See you at Christmas?

Cool. He'll get to meet this Erik Tober.

I roll my eyes.

◆

The plane slopes upward, pushing its nose through clouds, and I think of
the parents I'm leaving behind. The parents I lost.

They only have each other now.

And me? Well, I mustn't wallow in grief. I must pass through the anger
and blame, learn to trust again on my way to somewhere else.

◆

To fields ribbed with lavender, to orchards scattered with olive trees.

EPILOGUE

◆

Christmas Eve
9 rue Sainte-Marthe, Montaurelle, Aix-en-Provence

I knew I shouldn't have pinned Mamgu's Willow Pattern plate above the door so soon, but I wanted everything to look perfect. The paint was still tacky, but oh, yes, yes, the blue and white was such a beautiful contrast against the ochre walls.

Ingrid agreed. This shade's warm, luscious, tons better than white paint in a kitchen so large, she said.

I leaned against the table and, with brute force, inched it to the middle of the floor.

I needed seven chairs that night, but eight for Christmas Day, an extra place for Charlie. I was to meet him at Marseilles Airport, and I couldn't wait to see him.

I'd already sanded and painted fifteen chairs. Twenty-one more to go. I planned on having the dining room and three of the bedrooms, at least, finished before next Easter. Oh Lord, then there were jams and chutneys to make, and cakes to bake and decorate for the market, to build up the cash. Would this place ever be ready? I looked with fondness at the slanting beams, the crooked doorways. Closing my eyes, I absorbed the sheer age of the place.

It was all mine.

A pot roast bubbled gently in one of the ovens, and on the range, Christmas puddings steamed. Oona sent those as a housewarming gift, along with a dressed goose, and God willing, Katie, she and Barney would spend the next Christmas in France, and what's the betting my guesthouse would be simply grand by then?

The kitchen was toast-warm. I patted at the perspiration on my forehead with a tea towel, dying to shed my wool tunic.

Seven o'clock. Time to brave the cold bathroom, then search through the trunk for my brown dress. The very same one I wore the first evening I spent at Ingrid's house, at 5 Place de la Joliette.

The water flowed rusty, like weak tea, into the bath, but oh, it did wonders for my hair. I splashed on Paloma Picasso, *the signature fragrance that pulses with passion and intensity.* Grinning at my reflection, I then burst out laughing. Damn, I felt happy. Deliriously so.

I buckled the black belt around my waist, the one that lay on my stomach in a V.

Then, sorting though my new CDs, I picked out *Seasonal and Downright Medieval.*

"It should be remembered that many early carols have dance origins," said the blurb on the back. *" 'Pat-A-Pan' being a good example of this."*

> *Guillaume prends ton tambourin*
> *Toi, prends ta flûte, Robin;*
> *Au son de ces instruments*

Medieval instruments flowed, chimed, tapped. Reedy, hollow sounds, and a haunting repetition of drums and tambourine. Music and voice followed me from room to room. I checked the lounge that led to the courtyard, to see if the fire was burning well. It was. I added two more logs, still damp with snow, and they sang and sizzled as flames leapt. I punched at the cushions on the overstuffed sofas, brushed off the cat hairs.

> *Turelurelu, patapatapan*
> *Au son de ces instruments*
> *Je dirai Noël gaîment*

In the far corner there stood my Christmas tree—tall, elegant, sparkling with white light.

"Marmalade? Lady, Lady? *Minou, minou, minou . . .*"

In she came, little orange paws patting on the stone flags. Scooping her up into my arms, I asked if she liked her new home. I'd found her only a week before, a tiny, sorry mess, abandoned in rue Sainte-Marthe.

L'homme et Dieu sont plus d'accord
Que la flûte et le tambour;
Au son de ces instruments

I danced with Lady. With bare feet, I twirled like an idiot, climbed steps, touched walls, reached for cobwebs, until she meowed, begging to be let loose, poor thing.

Turelurelu, patapatapan
Au son de ces instruments
Chantons, dansons, sautons en!

It was then a loud rap echoed, voices chattered, and feet stamped the snow. And as I skipped down the stairs—

Ingrid: "Open up! It's bloody freezing out here!"

Moira: "C'mon, honey, get to the door, quick as you can."

Sacha: "Jeez, Sophie, quit treading on my foot, okay?"

Thierry: "*Turelurelu, patapatapan, Joyeux Noël, la-la-la-lah.*"

Gus: "Ah! Here she comes. Man, can you smell that roast?"

Me: "Come in, come in! Welcome! Throw your coats on the bed upstairs. Leave shoes to dry by the fire if you want. Wow, you all have red noses!"

Chantons, dansons, sautons en!

And I hugged them all, one by one. The dessert, Ingo? Put it in the fridge. Yum. Oh God, Moi, the punch smells heavenly. Yes, Gus, in the lounge, and you'll find a ladle on the sideboard, a silver one. Lord, Sasha, Sophie, you two look *gorgeous,* what fantastic earrings! Yes, please, Thierry, go ahead and light the candles.

And Erik, well, he just stood there in the stone archway, waiting, smiling. He carried something huge, square, tied with string. I was to follow him to the dining room, where tables were still stacked and walls half-finished.

He switched a few of the ceiling lights on, propped the flat parcel against a bench, and told me to go ahead, tear off the brown paper.

I pulled at the string, and the scent of fresh linseed oil grew more pungent as I tore off each layer.

"An oil painting, Erik?"

"Yes, Kate, for you," he said.

Colors flashed, cobalt, vermilion, against subtle sages, grays, and worn creams. When I looked closer, I saw pitting, layering on the walls, paint peeling off the door. Cracks, raw wood, rusted hinges. The door was open, just a peep, and a brass handle was there, waiting.

"It's my front door," said Erik.

"It's beautiful," I replied.

"Thought it would look good in here."

His hair fell in a crescent as he fired up a Gauloise with a chrome Zippo. He shrugged off his coat, and lay it on the bench. He wasn't wearing a shirt, just a sweater, tight and ribbed and stretched.

I took the cigarette from the corner of his mouth, dropped it to the stone floor, and he extinguished it with the toe of his shoe.

There are many ways of saying thank you.

◈

Griff smiled, shook his head and said, Mildreth, listen. Tell Katie to keep climbing those spiral steps until she finds the right door.

What are you talking about, Griff, she said, you old fool?

Acknowledgments

Many thanks to my agent, Zoë Pagnamenta, my editor, Laurie Chittenden, and their assistants, Emily Sklar and Erika Kahn.

Barbara Vieru, my language consultant.

Love to my critique partner, Karen Abbott, and my reader, Maggie Dana.

Special thanks to my darling Trollops, for your constant support and loyalty. More thanks to members of the famous Posse for your valued friendship and enthusiasm! And for your interest and encouragement, dear members of the Cave, my thanks go to you, too!

About the Author

Carrie Kabak is a former children's book illustrator. Born and raised in the United Kingdom, she now lives in Kansas City, Missouri, with her husband. They share five sons, a Labrador, and a tabby cat. *Cover the Butter* is her first novel.

Raising Hope
Katie Willard

There couldn't have been two more different girls in the town of Ridley Falls. Ruth Teller, raised by a hardworking single mother, barely scraped through high school before she settled into a minimum-wage job. Sara Lynn Hoffman, doted upon by her well-to-do parents, graduated top of her class before conquering college and law school. Their paths shouldn't have crossed again, but life doesn't always work out they way you expect. Together, they are raising a girl called Hope, who came into their lives as an infant and changed everything.

Set in the summer of Hope's twelfth year and moving back and forth in time, this heart-warming novel is the story of an unlikely family. It's the story of Hope, on the edge of growing up and yearning to find out everything she can about her birth parents. It's also the story of Ruth and Sara Lynn – the girls they once were and women they've become. Finally, it's the story of Aimee, Sara Lynn's mother, and Mary, Ruth's mother, both of whom raised their daughters for better and for worse.

Raising Hope is a luminous debut novel about mothers, daughters and the power of family love.

'Raising Hope does just that. A sweet, optimistic debut.' Claire Cook, author of Must Love Dogs

The Orange Blossom Special
Betsy Carter

Recently widowed, Tess and her teenage daughter, Dinah, move to a small town in Florida, following in the tracks of the Orange Blossom Special, the first passenger train to connect New York to Miami. At first, Tess struggles to make ends meet, and Dinah's depression shows no signs of abating. However, both women are certain that the late Jerry is still very much present, and through their interpretation of 'signs' only they can see, Tess is guided to a new job, and Dinah makes some unlikely yet sustaining friendships.

But, as the forces of a changing world fling them into a larger universe, the residents of this insular town find the innocence of the 1950s giving way to the turbulence of the 1960s. Tess, Dinah and their new neighbours are all tested – and transformed – by changes in their midst. Strangers become friends, friends become lovers, and the relationships formed during these tumultuous times surprise everyone involved...

Praise for **The Orange Blossom Special:**
'[A] warm, wise book.' *Elle*
'A high energy debut novel.' *O: The Oprah Magazine*
'The Orange Blossom Special marks the promising fiction debut of Betsy Carter...insightful and compassionate.' *Harper's Bazaar*

Maybe a Miracle
Brian Strause

Maybe a Miracle opens on the night of Monroe Anderson's senior prom. He is uncomfortably dressed, dying for a smoke, and worried about his sexual prospects for the evening. Then he sees his 11 year-old sister, Annika, lying face-down in the family swimming pool. He breathes life back into her body, but her mind remains in a deep and mysterious coma. From this moment on, Monroe's life will be different. As family and friends rally round, hoping and praying that Annika will wake up, strange things start to happen around her...

Whilst Monroe doesn't believe in miracles – let alone think his little sister can perform them - it seems others are more easily convinced. As stories of Annika's healing powers spread, Monroe can only stand by and watch as his mother, her church and the media attempt to elevate his sweet, annoying and wonderfully ordinary sister to virtual sainthood....

'Incisive...laugh-out-loud funny...provocative and unique' *People*

'Strause's debut is as tender as a slow dance, as sassy as a rap song, and an utter joy.' Jacquelyn Mitchard